The Twin Ascendant

Book Two of the Song of the Burning Heart

Ben Spencer

Cover Design by JV Arts

Map by Joshua Hawkins

ISBN-13: 9781971995014 (Hardcover)

ISBN-13: 9781971995007 (Paperback)

ISBN-13: 9781971995021 (Ebook)

KNOCK-KNEE BOOKS

About the Author

Ben Spencer lives in Concord, NC, with his wife and daughter. Please sign up for his newsletter at benspencer.substack.com or visit his website at benspencerwrites.com. Ben's novelette, *Last Performance at the Three Dragons Inn*, is available for free to newsletter subscribers.

ALSO BY BEN SPENCER

The Song of the Burning Heart

Book One: *The Prophecy of the Yubriy Tree*
Book Two: *The Twin Ascendant*

Novelette: *Last Performance at the Three Dragons Inn*
Short Story: *Falling from a Golden Sky*

Many Savage Moons

The Deer King (Novellas)

The Deer King
The Sundering
Last of the Baronites

For Charlotte

Ragar Or
Cape of the Dying Suns
Wayskin Ocean
To Clycsia

DRAMATIS PERSONAE

It's been nearly two years since the publication of *The Prophecy of the Yubriy Tree*. For those in need of a refresher, I offer the following capsule reviews of the major players for your reading pleasure.

Johanna Salk—The daughter of the powerful Lord Daguss Salk. Johanna spent her young adult years struggling to overcome her designation as the "lesser twin." Shut out of family politics, Johanna angered her father by smuggling poison to the condemned Axton Boil, the rebellious prince of the Blackstar Isles, who used the poison to try and assassinate Easton Dayborn, the king's second son. In the ensuing fallout, Johanna was commanded by her father to "bond" Easton Dayborn. Determined to control her own destiny, Johanna convinced Easton to abscond with her, with the ultimate plan of leaving the brash young prince once she was away. A dragon sighting and a confrontation with a powerful woods witch, however, changed Johanna's feelings toward Easton. The young couple bonded in a private ceremony deep in the woods.

Now deeply in love, Johanna is grappling with the realization wrought by defeating the woods witch: she is a jeyedoshi, capable of a powerful magic that she scarce understands and doesn't know how to control.

Silas O' the Songs—A down-on-his-luck musician, Silas entered a competition at the Golden Pear in the hopes of catching the attention of the Swans, the king's performing arts company. The night turned to horror when a group of men wearing the avian insignia of the eastern houses burned the tavern to the ground. Rescued by Wyn Dunkin—a rat-faced fiddler with a penchant for mischief—Silas and his new friend escaped to safety.

Together with Wyn, Silas traveled to the Yubriy Tree, where he discovered an overlooked prophecy leaf. Inspired by the message on the leaf, Silas wrote a song that he was certain would bring him the notoriety he had long craved. Silas and Wyn then traveled north, ultimately performing an altered version of the song for the Dayborn king and queen. Shocked to discover that the king and queen were awaiting the arrival of a prophesied lutist, Silas struggled to reconcile the song he had performed with the leaf's true message.

Increasingly aware that he has entered a political tempest, Silas worries what will happen if the realm's elite discover that he is in possession of a Yubriy leaf. Meanwhile, the true version of the song tempts Silas's lips, begging to be played.

Gregor Thorn—The king's supposed bastard half brother, the Sagekind, and a rumored jeyedoshi. With the Blackstar Rebellion ended, Gregor feared that the powerful lords of Ragar Or—chiefly Lord Daguss Salk and Lord Dante Heron—were secretly conspiring to topple King Micah. As the evidence mounted, Gregor hatched a plan to bring the king's enemies to heel. King Micah, heedless of the dangers, pushed north, eager to capitalize on an opportunity to bring Kalandragote, a minor kingdom, into the fold.

A rift between Gregor and the king drove Gregor to the brink of despair, where he ingested sea fingers, a mortally dangerous marine fungi. Upon recovering, Gregor discovered that he could see the skulls of certain people behind the fleshy veneers of their skin. Troubled that the visions were omens of impending death, Gregor worked desperately to expose a treasonous plot against the Dayborns. Capitalizing on the arrival of the prophesied lutist, Gregor was able to weaken the strength of Lord Daguss Salk by implicating Betrard, a priest of the Twins, in the plot. Buoyed by the victory, Gregor began the journey north to Kalandragote, hopeful that disaster had been averted.

The Yubriy Tree—The famed prophecy tree of Ragar Or. Every year, at the moment of abscission, prophecies manifest on the Yubriy Tree's leaves. Usually, the king directs servants—a collection of holy men and women from the realm's two major religions—to collect the leaves. But this year, one of the leaves was stolen and one disappeared into the forest unseen.

Wulfess Salk—The sister of Johanna Salk. Renowned for her beauty and confidence. Wulfess agreed to bond Cato Ollspaer, the savage son of the Kalandragotan king, in order to strengthen her father's standing among the Ontish people. Though close to her sister, their ties were fractured when Wulfess was named the Twin Ascendant by Lord Daguss.

Traveling north with her father, she works to advance the family's interests as the realm's power players advance on Kalandragote.

Easton Dayborn—The second son of King Micah Dayborn. Known for his wildness and wanderlust. Feeling indebted to Johanna Salk for saving his life, Easton agreed to help her escape Coffyn Castle.

Now deeply in love with Johanna, Easton hopes to reach the capital of Union and shore up his father's support.

Micah Dayborn—The headstrong king of Ragar Or. The realm's longstanding fractures between the Struvan and Ontish people resurfaced during Micah's reign.

Having subdued the Blackstar Rebellion, Micah hopes to reinvigorate his reign by bringing the minor kingdom of Kalandragote to heel. But the lords he must rely upon to accomplish the task—chiefly Lord Daguss Salk and Lord Dante Heron—may be working behind his back to bring about his downfall.

Wyn Dunkin—The ragged-haired, rodent-faced fiddler. Suspected by some to be a woodkin, a supernatural servant of the Yubriy Tree. Wyn saved Silas O' the Songs' life at the Golden Pear and accompanied him to Dunning Harbor.

Impish and enigmatic, Wyn lives life with an ever-ready quip on his tongue and a dagger hidden up his sleeve. His unpredictable nature makes him impossible to pin down, as evidenced by his theft of a Yubriy leaf and subsequent disappearance from Dunning Harbor.

Ajax Dayborn—The firstborn son of King Micah Dayborn and crown prince of Ragar Or. Bonded to Greta Worrint, a common woman.

Convinced by Gregor Thorn that a plot against the king was in motion, Ajax started south with a small portion of his father's men and half of Dante Heron's army in tow.

Greta Worrint—The common bond of Ajax Dayborn. Seen by many as unsuited for a life in court due to her lowborn status. Greta won the admiration of Gregor Thorn during the perilous journey north.

Determined to defend the Dayborns, Greta is quickly coming to understand the scope of the numerous threats facing the family.

Anjay Dayborn—The queen of Ragar Or. Strong-willed and fiercely independent. Originally from Clyesia, which makes her an outsider at court.

Anjay believed that the arrival of Silas O' the Songs, the prophesied lutist, ensured the safety of the family as it traveled north.

Madrig—Also known as Madrig the Mute. Cousin to Lord Daguss Salk. Big-hearted and bloody strong. Bonded to Jacy, a warrior woman from Tonhit.

Upon meeting Silas O' the Songs and Wyn Dunkin near the Yubriy Tree, Madrig became enamored with their musical gifts. Along with Jacy, Madrig defended Silas against various dangers and helped him make the journey to Dunning Harbor.

Madrig strives to see beyond the power politics of the moment in the hopes of doing what is in the best interest of Ragar Or.

Jacy—Plain-faced, wiry-limbed, nicknamed "the Bear Dancer." A stellar fighter. Bonded to Madrig.

Dante Heron—A young and powerful lord from the east. Thin-lipped and arrogant. Forever dressed in white.

During the Blackstar Rebellion, Lord Dante spearheaded the mustering of a large army from the east, ostensibly for the purposes of aiding the king. Suspected by Gregor Thorn of plotting against King Micah. Dante's strength was potentially undercut when the king ordered Prince Ajax to return south with half of Lord Dante's forces.

Unbeknownst to those traveling with the king, men bearing the avian-themed insignia of the eastern houses have been wreaking havoc down south in the king's absence.

Philemon Yurk—The bow-shouldered, disgraced son of Lord Delton Yurk. Blessed with a penchant for making money. After being disowned by his father, Philemon worked his way into the favor of young Lord Dante Heron.

Philemon was present at the Golden Pear shortly before it was attacked by men from the east. Silas O' the Songs suspects that Philemon both poisoned him and had a hand in arranging the attack.

Daguss Salk —The powerful Lord of High Osgood. The Salk family once ruled Ragar Or, before a civil war made possible the ascension of the Dayborn dynasty.

With the help of other powerful Ontish families, Lord Daguss crushed the Blackstar Rebellion before King Micah Dayborn could lead his forces north. He then helped negotiate a deal to bring the minor kingdom of Kalandragote into the fold. Rumored to want the throne for himself, Daguss seemed to prove his loyalty to the king by killing the Ontish firebrand Reginald Burntree.

Cato Ollspaer—The son and heir of King Horos Ollspaer of Kalandragote. Known for being a savage fighter. Rumored to have participated in the twin-death rite as a boy.

Cato traveled south with Lord Daguss after helping end the Blackstar Rebellion. Now pledged to bond Wulfess Salk, Cato's true loyalties and motives remain uncertain.

Deglan Whisk—A young knight, pledged to defend the Dayborns. Loyal to Gregor Thorn.

Deglan suffered a wound attempting to stop an assassination attempt against Ajax Dayborn by an innkeeper from the Blackstar Isles. Upon recovering, he hurried to Gregor Thorn's side in the hopes that he might be of continued service to the Dayborn cause.

These are the major players and should put returning readers on solid footing heading into Book Two. For a full list of all characters (both major and minor) that appear in *The Prophecy of the Yubriy Tree* and *The Twin Ascendant*, please see the character guide in the back of the book.

And so, without further ado, our tale begins in Kalandragote, where Horos Ollspaer is preparing for the arrival of the king of Ragar Or and his traveling court.

Prologue

Why did you bring the diviner here?

The answer came to King Horos immediately.

To better take your mind off the woodkin in the dungeon.

King Horos could see why he had once chosen to believe in the diviner. Her hair alone, the mane like a storm of flame, was its own form of persuasion. Combine that with the unapologetic way she went about her work—at the present moment, for example, she was combing through the entrails of a fox not ten feet from the Winterworn Chair, having spilled its guts without waiting for so much as a go-ahead from him—Horos had to admire that about her, he really did. She *committed* to the part. But beyond her hypnotic beauty, beyond her no-nonsense mien, beyond her convincing Werring-may-care indifference to his reaction to her readings, Horos could see her for what she really was: a charlatan, rolling around on the throne room floor, playing in blood and guts.

"Enough," he said.

She pretended not to hear him.

"Enough!" he thundered.

"I see the path forward, my king. I can tell you what you need to do." She looked up at him with her hands covered in gore, remaining in character.

But, unlike her, his wasn't a part to play. Horos Ollspaer was the king of Kalandragote. His words had real meaning. "Take her away. Hang her."

Horos watched as the diviner tried to still the tremor of fear that threatened to overcome her body. He watched as she tried to pin him—him, the king!—with her pale-green eyes, before delivering the revelation that she hoped would save her. "You are Daguss reborn, my king. Cut away the Struvan sickness. The king that comes north is Corosian-cursed. Kill him."

"Burn her," he said, his voice level and calm. Horos cast his gaze on the three others present in the throne room, his most trusted advisers. Bernsward, the gorgostrine. Gothred, the commander of the Ascendant Few. And Wren, his older sister. They stared back at him against the backdrop of the throne room's thirty-seven turrets, miniature towers carved in relief against the throne room walls. Bernsward, sweating. Gothred, grimacing. Wren, floating above it all. "She is playing a game with me, and I will not suffer it! Tie her to tinder, set her aflame, and let her ashes snow down up on the city. Gothred! Do you hear me?"

Gothred gave an uncertain look at the diviner—who had seemingly been in the king's favor mere seconds ago—and then returned his gaze to Horos. The commander of the Ascendant Few hid his thoughts, as always, behind the dirty beard on his face. "Yes, my king."

The next few moments were ugly. There was slipping and thrashing in fox blood and guts, screaming, cursing, bargaining, begging. Gothred, at different points, took hold of the diviner by her arms, her legs, and her hair in his efforts to wrest her from the throne room. King Horos quietly watched the diviner go, settling over the power of his spoken word like a great bird to roost. He paid no mind to her curses, for he was not afraid of what she had to say. Her curses were false. Empty threats.

Unlike the ones made by the woman in the dungeon.

When at last the diviner's screams could be heard no more, Horos addressed his sister. There was a lash to his voice when he spoke to her, for all the usual reasons.

"And what advice would you offer, sister of mine? Or is it your intention to judge me with your silence?!"

Wren looked down on him from the tower of her birth order, obscured within the soft recesses of an indigo cloak. Embroidered frostflowers filled up the cloak's right side, the stitching a light blue accented with threads of soft yellow. "I do have advice to offer you, Horos. Only be sure you want to hear it first."

He appreciated the sting of Wren's chastisement. She was a person apart in Kalandragote, entwined with the time before he became king, all those many years ago. Horos didn't like Wren, and she certainly didn't like him, but their connection existed in a space that transcended petty concerns like personal affection.

"I would hear what you have to say," he said, calmer now.

"A game of sennequi is played, not solved."

Horos snorted, then laughed, a caustic half cackle. Even Wren's best bits of advice came coupled with a barb. "A game of sennequi is played, not solved" was a Struvan aphorism, meaning, more or less, that there was no point in getting too far ahead of oneself. The fact that she had delivered her wisdom with a Struvan sliver was vintage Wren, her way of letting

Horos know that she wasn't afraid of him. No one else would have dared invoke Struvan culture in the Kalandragote kingdom.

"You mean to say that the game is still being played."

"Is it not?"

It was true enough. It was rumored that Dante Heron was in favor of an Ontish/Struvan schism, but what were promises from a bird? Horos felt more confident in his understanding with Daguss Salk, but that was only because they were both Ontish. Even then, Horos didn't know Daguss. Not really. There were those in the Kalandragote camp who liked to say that Daguss Salk's blood was Redd through and through, but it was hard for Horos not to be blinded by Daguss's surname. As a Kalandragote monarch, Horos knew well the many Salk monarchs that had marched north in the hopes of conquering his home.

That's all any of them want, in the end. The frostflower prize. And if you don't dictate what happens next, that's what history will remember you for. Surrendering Kalandragote to the false lie of Union.

But Horos had no intention of that. The Blackstar Rebellion had made it clear that the world was changing, that Kalandragote could no longer stand apart. But when the deal for the new world was struck, it would be on Horos's terms.

Even if the terms were bloody.

"You are right, Sister. The game is still afoot. There is no point in deciding upon a move until I'm surrounded by the players." In truth, Horos still had a difficult time believing that the Dayborn king was coming to *him.* For years, Horos had been hearing reports of the Dayborn dynasty's decline, but nothing had convinced him more than Micah Dayborn's overeagerness to pluck the frostflower. *Once he is in the web, I will decide. Once the Dayborn king is here, in Kalandragote…*

Horos's gaze swung to the gorgostrine. Bernsward. The beak-nosed holy man wilted under his glare. Unlike the gorgostrine that preceded Bernsward, the current priest of the Twins was a weak man, dogmatic in all aspects of the faith of the Twins except those that didn't suit Horos, at which point Bernsward invariably acquiesced.

Horos studied Bernsward by the light of the brazier fire. The gorgostrine was dressed in the nattiest gray robe Horos had ever seen on a priest of the faith of the Twins. Horos despised the priest for his petty vanities, but they were also a large part of why he kept him in the position. Horos had long ago decided that he preferred the company of a weak-minded priest over a strong one.

"What about you, Bernsward? What advice would you give your king on the eve of Micah Dayborn's arrival in Kalandragote?" Horos advanced on the gorgostrine as he spoke, drawing ever closer until his breath was hot on Bernsward's face. Bernsward's expression turned statuesque as he tried to hold up under the weight of the king's closeness. "Careful, Bernsward," Horos warned. "As you've seen, I'm in no mood to suffer fools tonight."

Bernsward stared straight ahead, deciding it best to stick with silence. *Smart decision,* Horos thought. He had half made up his mind to slap the gorgostrine the instant he opened his mouth. Bernsward's silence, on the other hand, disarmed him.

"Out," Horos ordered after it was clear that Bernsward would not take the bait. "The both of you. Out."

The priest and Horos's sister departed the throne room. Bernsward on winged feet, Wren with studied deliberation. Alone now, Horos moved to the Winterworn Chair. He sunk his bones into the kurmenhi wood, sliding down until his eyes were positioned over the fortification of his generous belly. The moontar mead from dinner sloshed in his gut, evil and thick.

His mood was growing foul, and he was determined to let it fester.

After a time, he could hear the woodkin's words rising from the dungeon. He always heard her if he was quiet long enough. "**The Twin Ascendant will take your crown**." Delivered in that lilting voice of hers, an incongruous sound coming from the grotesque mangle of her mouth. He sometimes heard her in his nightmares. "**The Twin Ascendant will take your crown**." Horos bit his lip. He would not argue with her. He would not. He would march into the dungeons and draw a blade across her throat before he would argue with her. Or so he told himself.

"*I* am the Twin Ascendant," he said aloud, breaking the promise. It was a mistake, he knew, the start of a rebuttal he had sworn not to make, but before he could stop himself, he was arguing in full.

"Who but a true Twin Ascendant would kill not one, but two *heki plasuk* on the day of their twin-death rite? Who but a true Twin Ascendant would conspire to murder their brother the king?" His voice wavered, tripping on an unexpected snag of emotion. Horos powered through and spoke the most damning proof of his truth aloud. "Who but a true Twin Ascendant would order that his two sons fight to the death, even though they were not twins? Who?" He rose from the Winterworn Chair, in challenge to the ghosts now filing into the throne room. "Who, I ask of you?! WHO?!"

The ghosts did not respond. Instead, they spread out around the room and turned their pale gazes on the Kalandragote king. Horos knew them all. The blurred body in the far corner was the first *heki plasuk* that Horos had fought on the day of his twin-death rite—the first man that Horos had ever killed. Standing in front of the blurred body and in better focus was Kwelkis, the only *heki plasuk* to emerge victorious that day, the man Horos had broken tradition to demand to fight. They had danced a dangerous dance, Kwelkis and he, a dance that nigh cost Horos his life. But the risk had been worth it. When the victory was won, Horos was a Twin Ascendant esteemed above all others. Without that acclaim, the kingdom would have never accepted the steps he took to win the crown.

Horos turned to the ghost standing in the slash of starlight streaming in from the towering western windows. Tesken Ollspaer. The Ten-Day King. Horos's older brother. Tesken, his face like a chiseled jag, made no sound, only stared back. "Don't look at me like that. You damn well know that you would have killed me, had Wren and I not killed you," Horos said. Tesken, as always, did not reply. Horos sneered at him. "It matters not what you think. Your death *made* me. I *am* the true Twin Ascendant precisely because you no longer exist. I am the true Twin Ascendant precisely because I had the fortitude to kill *you.*"

Strength surged through Horos. There were plenty of so-called Twin Ascendants in Kalandragote, noblemen who had survived the modern mockery that was the twin-death rite, but there were *none* who exemplified the ideal like Horos. Feeding off this strength, Horos turned and faced the final ghost: the fruit of his loins, the lesser twin to Cato's Twin Ascendant.

The son he had sired for slaughter.

Onav.

Horos stared at Onav Ollspaer without remorse. "Hear me, boy. There is a price one pays for being a true Twin Ascendant. Know that I would have paid that price a thousand times over." He forced himself to keep his gaze fixed on Onav, but the boy's expression unnerved him. An amalgam of distance and darkness, it reminded Horos of the stoic way Onav had faced his death that day. Horos shook his fist at the boy, treating him like the enemy that he was. "So be gone now, boy. You and all the rest. All you *lesser* creatures. You did not have the strength to live, so do not dare to reproach me in your deaths. The Twin Ascendant demands it."

His words worked like magic, causing the ghosts to dissipate into the ether. Horos watched them go in triumph. *Victory. The true Twin Ascendant fears nothing. Not even ghosts.* With the spirits departed, Horos moved into the beam of starlight where his brother had stood. He looked up at the snow glistening against the towering panes of glass. A moment later he noticed that smoke was rising to meet the snow, twisting and turning like sorcerer's hands working an incantation.

Horos moved closer to the windows. From there he could see flames dancing in the courtyard, in the center of the Circle of Stones. The diviner was tied to a stake in the center of the flames, her mouth agape in agony. Around her, a small party was gathered. Horos watched with pleasure. He grew quiet, hoping that if he listened hard enough, he might hear the diviner scream.

But he did not. Instead, the voice started up again.

"**The Twin Ascendant will take your crown**."

Beads of sweat formed on Horos's brow. "I am the Twin Ascendant," he said in response. But the refrain did not stop. Instead, it swelled, exceeding all sense of proportion, buggering Horos's brain.

The voice is making me mad, he thought. But madness did not frighten Horos. How could it? He had lived his entire life on the precipice of madness. The way a true Twin Ascendant should.

"Fine," he said at last, when the voice refused to stop. He reached for the baselard on his belt, his weapon of choice. It was a fine blade of mounted silver, one he had used many times. He nodded once, as if confirming a decision with himself, and then he took to his feet.

To the dungeons.

The dungeon beneath the Old Tower was closer to a grave than a prison, buried so far underground that to visit it was to imagine that the world above did not exist. In the center of the first floor of cells, a subterranean shaft was cored into the ground, revealing a spiral staircase that plummeted like a bad thought into the Kalandragote abyss. Horos made the descent quietly, listening for the woodkin's voice, but, to his surprise, he could no longer hear it.

Sfen, the dungeon master, tried to explain the silence. "Singing? She might sing, aye, but if so, Sfen hasn't heard her. But do not doubt it, she is in there and alive, sire. Promise. Sfen visits three times a day to check. But she's terrible quiet, she is. She'll go weeks, months even, without saying a word. But she's in there. By the light of her wicked eyes, you'll see."

Horos's madness had cooled considerably. It was the singing taunt that had fired his fury, and now that he could no longer hear it, he wasn't half as eager to rush into the woodkin's cell and end her life. *Maybe it's all in my mind,* he thought. But he didn't believe that. Not really. Woodkin were a resourceful lot when the matter at hand was mind games, and Horos could think of no more worthy target for a woodkin's warfare than the king of Kalandragote.

They reached the bottom of the stairs. Sfen's torchlight revealed nothing at first, only cool stone and deeper stores of silence. But then the probing torchlight fell upon black iron bars. Horos watched with a keen interest as the dungeon master waved the torchlight back and forth, uncovering the secrets of the cell. For a spine-chilling moment it seemed that the light had come up empty. But then there she was: sitting in the center-back of the cell on meager haunches, staring at Horos with piercing eyes.

"There she is!" Sfen announced, triumphant. "You see her, sire? Evil eyes. Always finding me before I find her! But she cannot escape."

Horos stared into the woodkin's eyes. Out of nowhere, he remembered the name that she had shared when they first detained her. *Anis. Like the mad daughter of Daguss Salk, the first king of Ragar Or. The one who tried to tame the dragon.* He was so entranced that for a moment he didn't notice the woodkin's sneaking rotten-toothed smile, opening like a snare around his unsuspecting attention. Horos startled when he suddenly saw it, and the woodkin laughed, a wheezy blast of triumph.

"Hand me the torch and keys, then leave," Horos ordered Sfen. The dungeon master, who had had the good sense not to react when the king flinched, handed over both straightaway. Sfen then turned for the stairs before turning back, deciding at the last second that there was something he wanted to say.

"Careful, sire. Woodkin are wily. If you mean to—"

"Leave," Horos ordered again. The dungeon master did as he was told.

Horos planted the torch in a sconce on the wall near the cell. He thought perhaps the woodkin would move to one of the cell's darker corners, but she stayed in the same spot, her eyes the only mobile thing about her. Horos took a minute to study her. He remembered from the time of her arrest that she was a slight thing, and that had been before her ordeal in the dungeon. Now she was little more than skeleton chaff. *She'll be dead soon, regardless of what I do,* he thought.

"Do you know…do you remember…who I am?"

"Aye," she answered. Her voice sounded like dust and dried leaves, but as she continued talking, more color came into it. "You are the king of the frostflowers." She laughed, as if being the king of Kalandragote was some sort of joke.

Horos kept his composure. "That's right. I am the king. But I am more than that, aren't I? I am the reason you are jailed here. I am the reason you will never again see the light of day. I, King Horos Ollspaer of Kalandragote, am the Twin Ascendant."

Horos expected more laughter, or an irreverent rejoinder, but instead Anis the woodkin simply narrowed her eyes and turned up her lips in a nasty grin. When it was clear that words weren't forthcoming, Horos continued.

"You do remember why you are here, don't you? The message that you were spreading in the Kalandragote streets?"

Still no response.

"I certainly haven't forgotten it," Horos continued. "I still hear it, in fact. You sing your message to me from this very dungeon, don't you? These bars are no impediment to your purpose. So long as you live, you will find a way to work your Corosian curse into my ear. Won't you?"

She sat unmoving and unspeaking, like a tree stump. Eyes like sprigs of green.

Horos worked the key into the lock. He entered the cell expecting to be overwhelmed by the usual degradative smells associated with the long-interred, but instead he was hit by an earthy aroma, like rotting wood. Ignoring this, he walked toward the woman. *Anis. The woodkin.* A memory returned to him of the day they had locked her away. She was in manacles, and Bernsward had laid his hands on her, revealing her true nature with the glyphs. Horos had watched with wonder at the transformation. Before him had been no woman, but rather a tree masquerading as flesh.

Over a year later, here she remained. The myth of the woodkin made manifest. What even was she? There were gorgostrine who preached that woodkin were the descendants of the Firewalker: they believed that the line degenerated into woodkin over the centuries. Others said the origin went back further than that, to Werring's supposed rape of Beoliotius. And yet others in the faith—including Friyik, the gorgostrine who had preceded Bernsward—claimed that woodkin came from the flowering of the accursed Yubriy Tree: in the spring its pollen spread far and fast into the waiting arms of woods witches, who used Corosian-cursed magic to make little tree men and tree women from the seed. The sole purpose of these wretched creatures was to wreak havoc on Daguss's line, the sons and daughters of the Twin Ascendant.

Horos bent down to the cold stone floor. He took hold of the hem of the woodkin's coarse brown dress, rubbing it twixt his fingers. It frayed in Horos's hands, creating a hole. Beneath the woodkin's dress were her legs, or rather, the wasted remains of them. *If I were to rub the skin, I might make a hole there as well.* He looked up at the woodkin. She was all eyes, green orbs floating above a nothing-nose and the twisted hole that was her mangled mouth.

"Say it to me once more, woodkin. Remind me why I've kept you here in my dungeon."

The woodkin worked her disturbing mouth, but she did not speak. She watched Horos instead, amusement playing at the corners of her sandpaper lips. Horos was tempted to reach up and take her by the throat, force the words out, but it seemed possible that she might disintegrate at his touch, like a pillar of salt.

"Your life is forfeit this night," he said. "But before I kill you, know this. I am the Twin Ascendant. Not Micah Dayborn. Not Daguss Salk. Not Dante Heron. No one will take my crown. No one—"

"None of those."

Had she spoken? He grabbed her by the shoulders, repulsed by the wasted flesh beneath. It was like grabbing hold of hollow wood. "What did you say?"

She looked at him again, but it was as if her face was collapsing in. She opened her mouth and Horos thought he saw a fibrous mush. The words that escaped were an echo of an echo, the sound of a tree falling in the forest. "None, none, none. But along comes the soon-to-be bonded."

Horos's head spun. "Soon-to-be bonded?" His mind solved the puzzle immediately. "Are you speaking of Cato? My son?" He shook Anis the woodkin hard by her shoulders.

She gave a broken, sickly laugh in response. In the dark of the dungeon, Horos wasn't exactly certain what he was seeing, but the woodkin seemed to be disintegrating before his very eyes. The aroma of rotting wood grew overwhelming. Horos reached for the baselard on his belt, and without thinking he plunged it deep into the woodkin's chest. "I am the Twin

Ascendant! No one else!" he shouted as the blade moved in what felt like pulp. He twisted and turned the steel, searching for the woodkin's death.

It was some time before he realized that his eyes were closed. He didn't remember shutting them. When he opened them, the woodkin was dead. The baselard was plunged deep into her chest, but Horos neither saw nor felt the blood. He extricated the blade and the woodkin slipped to the floor. Dead in all the usual ways. He looked at her in the flickering torchlight, trying to see her magic, but instead he only saw the dead body. He stared and stared, waiting for a final revelation.

At last, he saw the woodkin changing. Into the corpse of Cato. His son.

"I am the Twin Ascendant," he said to the vision. "No one else."

Johanna Salk

Johanna hadn't touched the new-growth hair on her head in days. In fact, she had scarcely thought about it—being the object of Easton Dayborn's worshipful attentions had somewhat diminished her capacity for self-consciousness. But when the tuneful girl drawing water from the well turned to look at her, Johanna's hand instinctively moved to cover the already-hidden jeyedoshi whorl.

"That's a beautiful song you're singing, child," Easton said to the girl, drawing her attention to him.

"Thank you. Sir. Lord." The girl eyed Easton carefully while stealing surreptitious glances at Johanna, who was sitting high atop Bitterboy. The girl looked like she desperately wanted to comment on Johanna's strange hairstyle but was doing her best to refrain. "Are you a bonded pair?" the girl asked after a moment. It seemed from the look on her freckle-spotted face that she had opted for asking the question she was second-most curious about, better discretion having foiled the first.

"We are indeed," Easton answered. It was the first time he had confirmed their bonding to an outside party. Johanna loved the solidity of the statement, the present and future fixture of the words.

The girl smiled, pleased to have her instincts confirmed.

"Might you point us to the inn, dear?" Johanna asked. Johanna would not have traded her time together on the road with Easton for anything, but a good night's rest in a decent bed was the best imaginable way it could come to an end. *Though no doubt I'm kidding myself about the rest,* she thought. So far, Johanna's bonding to Easton Dayborn had been nothing like her first bonding to Nicholas Raleigh, and that included the joyous abandon of their couplings. It had been a relief—not to mention a revelation—to discover how different *everything* could be when you were with someone that you *wanted* to be with.

The girl weighed Johanna's request on the scales of her munificence and found it sufficient. "It's next to the temple. There's a green tree painted on the door. That's why it's called the Green Tree Inn. My aunty works there. Keep on the main road, and your horses will lead you right to it. Simple as singing." The girl, who was in the last stages of childhood, made an impromptu skipping movement, as if to emphasize her youth. "Your horse is beautiful," she said to Johanna when she had finished skipping, fixing Johanna with her friendliest smile.

"Thank you. I call him Bitterboy."

The girl giggled. "I'll sing for Bitterboy as you ride past. And I'll sing for you. And your newly bonded."

"That's sweet of you."

The girl, eager to start, began a new song in time to Bitterboy's proud clip-clopping. Johanna rewarded the girl with a gracious smile as she rode past. But the smile faded when she recognized the tune.

"Whyever would she sing that?" Johanna asked Easton once they were past the well. The gates to Hornwell were open, and they rode in unobserved.

"Sing what?"

""The Stone on the Hill.'"

Easton chuckled. "Was that what she was singing? I didn't even notice." He gave the matter a moment's thought. "She is young and probably only knows a handful of songs. In all likelihood it was the first one that popped in her mind."

That makes sense, Johanna thought. She remembered being young and hearing "The Stone on the Hill" for the first time, the tragic sorrow she had felt upon grasping the meaning of the lyrics. "Young love perishes more often than not," her mother had explained to her matter-of-factly when Johanna asked about the song. What worried Johanna most as a child was how she wanted to hate the song but couldn't; she was too spellbound by its terrible beauty. *It's only a song,* Johanna told herself now. *Not a curse.* All the same, she hoped that she would forget the girl's singing of it soon.

Hornwell was a wealthy little town located on the Borne River, far enough south to have a Struvan sensibility. Most of the homes were made of timber, but Johanna noted that a few were made of timber and brick. What townsfolk that were in the streets made stink-eyes at Johanna's hair, but, noting the quality of her horse, kept their thoughts to themselves. *I need a hooded cloak,* Johanna thought. It was a thought she had had multiple times since escaping Shayla the woods witch, but, now that she was once again among people, the necessity was more pressing.

Near to the heart of the town, they came upon the Stavusian temple. The design was striking. From her previous experiences with the Stavusian faith, Johanna knew that the temples were designed to maximize the glory of natural light. This meant that large sections of their exterior were covered in glass. This particular temple had somehow procured the services of one of the masters of the form—facing the street, a dazzlingly intricate masterwork of gold and crystal glass blended together before rising to meet a majestic, stained-glass hawk at the apex of a pointed segmental arch. Unlike the stained-glass windows lining the sides of the temple, the hawk design faced the outside, which meant that an extraordinary amount of energy and effort must have been expended to keep the glasswork clean.

"Careful. If a Hawk's-Eye catches you staring rapt at the glasswork, he'll try and make you a Winged Woman."

Johanna turned to find Easton wearing that shit-eating grin of his. She gave him one right back. "Maybe. But if he sees me looking at you, he will realize just how ridiculous the notion of making me a Winged Woman is."

Easton laughed. Then they exchanged a look—*the* look, Johanna thought of it—that usually sent the two of them clambering down from horseback, tearing at each other's clothes, and melting into each other's arms. It was only being back in civilization that stopped them from following through, though, in the intensity of the moment, Johanna wondered for a suspended second if they weren't going to abandon all decency and dismount. But a second later Easton gave a different, less certain laugh, and the madness passed.

"There it is. The Green Tree Inn." Easton brought the gray-dappled palfrey, whom he had taken to calling Cloudy, alongside Bitterboy. Cloudy eagerly picked up speed, sensing the end of the road.

The Green Tree Inn had white-washed walls and a run of timber-paned windows that looked like curious rectangular eyes. Johanna and Easton dismounted near the last of the eyes, beside the stables. Two grooms presented themselves forthwith, chaps disciplined enough not to stare at

Johanna's hair. Bitterboy, sensing the grooms' professionalism, went with them without protest, eager for a bit of pampering. Cloudy followed suit.

Once inside the inn, they were quickly sorted out by a bosomy middle-aged woman who, after taking stock of them, elected to err on the side of hospitality. *The singing girl's aunt,* Johanna supposed. When Johanna produced a brogan's-head, the woman grew positively chummy. "Milady, you've come to the right place. The Green Tree Inn has every luxury you might want, including a heated stone washtub." She eyed Johanna carefully, studying her hair, considering her next words. "And, if I might be so bold, I know of a handful of women in town who might be of assistance with your…um…hair. Wigmakers, stylists, the like. They work a mean magic. I only await your word."

The woman made good sense. But Johanna's heart hardened at the idea. "I don't need help with my hair. What I need is a hooded cloak. And a bath. I do want the bath."

Johanna knew that she sounded unreasonable. The innkeeper, to her credit, continued, as if keeping a half-shorn hairstyle was a sensible decision. "Of course. A hooded cloak. We will see to it. Mariva," she said, snapping her fingers at a young woman nearby, "show our lady to the bath. Sir, I will show you to your room. Afterward, you can bathe too, if you like. Later, once you're settled, the both of you will return downstairs for supper. There's lemon trout and a Qorlish sweetgrass stew and a blackberry goat cheese pie."

The description of the meal made Johanna's mouth water. They had eaten well enough on the road, but most of their food had been unadorned game, caught and promptly cooked. To eat a variety of food again would be a delight.

The bathwater was just short of scalding. Johanna luxuriated in it, feeling the heat working its healing powers all the way to her bones. It was strange being away from Easton; they had not been out of each other's sight since their near-death experience with the woods witch. Johanna tried to focus her thoughts as she relaxed in the tub, hoping to remember who she was outside of being in love. There were matters of the mind that she had too long neglected, not the least of which were the twin facts of her jeyedoshi powers and forever-flower longevity. *Though we are bonded, Easton will never be like me. Only I can bear the burden of this jeyedoshi fate.* It was a stark reality, she knew, but one she needed to accept.

Before Johanna was finished with her bath, Mariva returned and laid out a hooded cloak. The cloak was a beige nearly identical in color to the heraldry of her house. Putting it on made Johanna feel uneasy; she felt like a snake trying to disguise itself in shed skin.

Dressed, she fished the sennequi piece that she had pocketed in Coffyn Castle out of her heavy coat. *The small girl. The Red Queen. The dragonfeeder.* She stared at in quiet contemplation and found that it wasn't difficult to bridge the divide between the sennequi piece and the woman that she had killed. *Shayla. The woods witch.* She had played the miracle of Shayla the woods witch's death over in her mind a million times, but, try as she might, Johanna could not connect to the person she had been in that moment, the wind-wielding jeyedoshi.

Or perhaps the greater truth was that she didn't want to. Reaching for her jeyedoshi powers made Johanna feel as if she wanted to vomit. There had been a moment when she was under the woods witch's tutelage that she had tapped into the essence of her jeyedoshi self, but now that the woods witch was dead, Johanna could not separate her jeyedoshi side from the example Shayla had set. She stared hard at the sennequi piece. *I am not you. Do you hear me? I would sooner die than become what you were.*

She felt better. Cleansed. She considered leaving the sennequi piece on the edge of the stone washtub as an offering for her whispered prayer. But in the end, she returned it to the pocket of the heavy coat, which she gathered up with her as she left the room.

The meal was a marvel. They ate it in a reverent silence, relishing every bite. The sweetgrass stew especially was a wonder of complex flavors. Johanna had eaten sweetgrass stew before, but never like this: every spoonful was a subtle dance of sweetness and spice. Thankfully, the blackberry goat cheese pie was compelling enough to elevate the remainder of the meal above being a sad reminder that they were no longer eating the stew.

They said little to each other throughout. Johanna supposed this was due to the meal's deliciousness, or at least she did until the last of the blackberry goat cheese pie was devoured and the conversation failed to quicken. *It's like we're seeing each other for the first time,* Johanna thought. She realized in a way that this was true: they hadn't seen each other primped and clean since Coffyn Castle, and that was back when they were antagonists, not bonded lovers. Realizing this, Johanna settled into the joy of simply studying Easton, while he, ascertaining the game, did the same. It turned into a contest, one that, when it was on the verge of crossing over into farce, Easton graciously conceded.

"That was certainly better than another night of eating spitted rabbit."

"I won't argue with you," Johanna responded, dabbing at pie residue with table linen. The common room had filled with a solid score of diners, most of whom were lost in sweetgrass stew bliss. Johanna noted, and not for the first time, that the Green Tree Inn was of a quality considerably above the standards of most of Ragar Or. There were even unlit meriwax candles on the tables, the expensive type that could only have made their way to Horwell through Wrain.

"I choose not to take your comment as a slight on my cooking skills," Easton said, feigning offense.

"Perhaps you're insulting me? I skinned and spitted at least half those rabbits, thank you very much," Johanna rejoindered, pointing her linen at him.

"Hmm," Easton said, narrowing his eyes as if reflecting on Johanna's cooking prowess. "That you did. Whose rabbits were the better, I wonder? Mine or yours?"

"Mine. You don't remember the wild seasonings I gathered? But I'm happy to settle the matter in the kitchens, if you're so inclined." Johanna had a talent for the culinary arts, one she seldom got to display. Growing up in High Osgood, she had had full run of the kitchens, but as the Lady of Thistleton, it had bothered her bonded Nicholas Raleigh when she engaged in 'menial labors.' *My second bonding will be different,* she told herself. *This time, I will do as I please.*

"A challenge? I accept. Once we're in Union, we'll make each other a meal. Whoever breaks down and begs the other for an encore feast first is the winner."

Johanna leaned forward, put her elbows on the table, and fixed Easton with a lascivious smile. "Are you challenging me to a contest to see who can set the other to begging first?"

"It seems that I am. Though now that I pause to reflect, I do recognize potential pitfalls that might arise along the way."

Johanna laughed. She then reached across the table and grabbed Easton by the collar of his blood-orange cloak, pulling him under her hood for a kiss. They gathered stares along the way, but she didn't mind, and neither did he. When the kiss ended, they parted lips but not eyes.

"Union?" she asked.

"If it pleases you. Yes. Union."

Johanna didn't immediately respond. Their first few days together had been spent chasing a dragon, but ever since the madness with the woods witch—and Johanna's failed and humbling encounter with the dragon—they had been slowly moving south, toward…domesticity. What surprised Johanna most of all was that Easton was the one leading the charge. If there was one thing she hadn't expected, it was that their bonding would turn a prince known for his wanderlust toward home. *It seems that for all he's inflamed my wildness, I've equally inflamed his sense of responsibility.*

"Union," she said at last, in a tone that suggested uncertainty rather than agreement. Did she want to go to Union? That truth was that she didn't know what she wanted outside of knowing that she wanted to do it with Easton. The true north of her soul was caught up in a turmoil. The dragon and the woods witch had left indelible marks on her soul, marks that she didn't know what to make of. The woods witch was dead and gone, but the dragon was still flying high above Ragar Or, waiting for Johanna to understand the question it had asked of her when it peered deep into her jeyedoshi soul.

Easton sensed her conflict. "We don't have to go to Union. I only know that I want the people in the capital to see the two of us together, bonded and in love. Dayborn and Salk. But once they've seen us, we can go on a sweetmarch proper, wherever you want. Clyesia, Cordova, the Cape of the Dying Suns. Teak, Qorl, Wrain. Or, if those places aren't adventuresome enough for you, we'll commandeer a skiff and head for Thralk-Braktur, see if we can meet up with some of the pirates my mother was always warning me about."

Johanna laughed again and reached for her cup of wine. It was Marrows wine, the kind produced in the vineyards north of Thistleton, southeast of here. The best in all the land. She downed a hearty swallow. "Let's do it. Let's go to Union. Let's show all of Ragar Or our love."

The blush of the wine was on both their faces when they noticed their fellow diners gravitating toward the windows. Some even stopped eating and walked outside for a better look. Curious as to what could be so compelling as to pull people's attention away from the sweetgrass stew, Johanna and Easton stood up and followed the others out the door of the Green Tree Inn.

A sunset ceremony was taking place at the temple. Winged Women, clad in the purest white, had lined up facing the western sky and were engaged in the chanting, rhythmic movements that adherents of the faith believed help settle the sun to sleep. Johanna knew from her time with the Raleighs that Stavus—in his celestial sun form—was loath to relinquish watch over his children at night. The chanting and the movements were the faithfuls' way of promising Stavus that they would honor his rest by resting as well. When the ceremony was over, the Winged Women would file back inside the temple and remain in repose until dawn.

"Imagine being a Winged Woman during the winter months," Johanna muttered, suppressing a shudder. "Long nights, those." She reflected for a moment on her father's threat to make her a Winged Woman if she didn't bond Easton. *What would you think if you saw me now, Father? Following your wishes and ironically the happier for it.*

When the Winged Women were finished, the Hawk's-Eye emerged from the temple carrying the Illuminated Scrolls. To Johanna's surprise, she recognized him: the Hawk's-Eye was Shupert Press, who had been the chief priest at the Stavusian Temple in Thistleton when Johanna was bonded to Nicholas Raleigh. Shupert had grown older, but he was still in possession of his signature feature: the bushiest pair of eyebrows in all of Ragar Or.

Shupert ambled toward the Winged Women. Young acolytes in front of and behind Shupert carried incense burners from which thin streams of smoke curled upward into his eyes. Shupert waved away the smoke wearing a good-natured smile. *He's just as I remember him,* Johanna thought. During Johanna's time in Thistleton, no one had been kinder to her. Her last memory of Shupert was of him consoling her while she wept on his shoulder on the day of Nicholas's burial.

Easton, seeing the Hawk's-Eye, scoffed. "The chief fool arrives. Fitting. A fool's ceremony must end with a fool, I suppose."

"He's no fool," Johanna responded. "He's a good man. I know him. He was the Hawk's-Eye at the temple in Thistleton when I was bonded to Nicholas Raleigh." Johanna wasn't a strong believer in either of Ragar Or's two principal faiths, but there was a distinct difference between believing in a religion and respecting those that did. Shupert had been kind to

Johanna at a time when she needed it most, and for that, she would always be grateful.

Easton replied with an agnostic *harrumph.* Regardless of the fact that he was the progeny of the Holy Son of the Air (the king's title as it pertained to his position in the Stavusian religion), Easton was no friend of the faith.

They watched the remainder of the ceremony in a prickly silence. Shupert, working his white-bearded jaw with a distinctive goatlike rhythm, read two passages from the Illuminated Scrolls. The first, the day's-fall passage—which was always read at sunset ceremonies—he recited from memory without glancing at the scrolls. For the second, Shupert squinted at the parchment in the day's dying light, being sure to get the words right. It was a peculiar selection, one Johanna didn't recall having heard before.

> "Where darkness falls
> We will find lost brothers and sisters
> Aching for the light.
> The prudent venture not into the darkness,
> But the winged bold
> The blessed few
> May yet risk the black
> And bring the lost into the light."

Finished reading, he rolled up the scrolls and addressed all who were gathered. "We live in a dangerous world, my children. And though I am grateful for the prudent among us, I also thank Stavus for the bold, those who venture into the dark to bring the lost back into the light. If Ragar Or is ever to be made whole, we must pray that the bold are successful in their endeavors." He then gestured with his right hand up and away from his body with all five fingers spread, the sign of a traditional Stavusian blessing. "Look to the hawk. To the sun. To the sky. Look to Stavus."

Thus ended the ceremony. Everyone took the Hawk's-Eye's cue and departed, with the ironic exception of the sun, which remained smeared on the hilly horizon. Pockets of pious babble filled the air. Johanna watched Shupert from the partially obscured confines of her cloak, trying to decide whether to approach him or not.

Her desire for a reunion won out.

The Hawk's-Eye didn't see Johanna until she was nearly upon him. Shupert startled, confused by the vision of the woman in the hooded cloak.

A pair of bats dove in the black-violet behind Shupert, angling for the same insect.

"My lady. How can I be of service to you?"

"Forgive me, Your Light. I know that my face is obscured, but do you recognize my voice?"

Shupert cycled through a variety of expressions before settling on shock. "Lady Johanna? Johanna Salk?"

"Yes, Your Light."

Shupert moved closer, angling his body as if trying to shield her from an invisible threat. Johanna thought at first that he was going to hug her, then realized that wasn't his intention. "My lady, what are you doing here? Your father is in the far north with the king, is he not?" The Hawk's-Eye dropped his voice, while the lines on his face bunched together in anxious folds.

"It's good to see you too," Johanna replied in a partly joshing, partly peeved tone. "If you must know, I am here of my own accord. Besides, I might ask you the same. Why are you here instead of in Thistleton with Lord Raleigh?"

"Lord Raleigh is…" Shupert bit his tongue. He looked more closely at Johanna. "Lady Johanna, what has happened to your hair?" The Hawk's-Eye tilted his head until it was nearly horizontal to the ground, and peered up into the hood. "Oh, that is barbarous work! Who assaulted you? My child, you must let me help you. Come with me into the temple, we can take refuge there until—" Shupert's gaze, struggling with the deepening dark, alit on something—or rather, someone—behind Johanna. "Who are you?" he whispered, his voice quiet and quaking. "Are you the person responsible?"

It was Easton, of course. How much he had heard of what Shupert said, Johanna didn't know. Easton's cheeky reply suggested that he had caught only the tail end. "The person responsible? Sounds like me." Johanna assumed that Easton was wearing his shit-eating smile, but the gloaming made it difficult to tell.

"You did this to her?!" Shupert looked for a second like he was going to strike Easton, but remembering his age, thought better of it. "Come quick," the Hawk's-Eye said to Johanna. "Take hold of my arm. We will away to the temple. He won't touch you, not here in this holy town, not with a servant of Stavus at your side."

The folly was getting out of hand. Some of the Green Tree Inn guests who had ventured outside to watch the sunset ceremony had stalled their leaving, trying to figure out why the Hawk's-Eye was in a huff. "Your Light. Please. This man has not laid a hand on me." Johanna knew what she meant, but even so, the bald falseness of the statement made her blush. Not that anyone could see in the burgeoning dark. Desperate to straighten matters out, she reached over and took Easton by the hand. "This is my newly bonded. The son of King Micah. Easton Dayborn."

Shupert was dumbstruck. He blinked a few times in rapid succession. When that didn't do the trick, he pushed his eyebrows back with his fingers, as if they were impeding his ability to see Easton for what he was. "Easton Dayborn," he said at last. He pried Easton's hand away from Johanna and took it in his own. Then he dropped to one knee. "It is an honor, Your Highness. An honor indeed."

Easton cut a quick glance at Johanna, as if to suggest that he had been right about the man being a fool. But his actual reply to the Hawk's-Eye was generous and kind. "Thank you, Your Light. Please, don't kneel on ceremony," he said, helping Shupert to his feet. "My newly bonded, whom I adore, speaks highly of you. And as my father the king has communicated to me many times, any friend of the Raleighs is a friend of ours."

Shupert gave an awkward, anxious little head bob. *Why is he so nervous?* Johanna wondered. She reasoned that it was connected to meeting royalty, but it still seemed excessive for a man who had experience with noble families.

The bystanders lingering on the periphery of the conversation had transformed into full-on gawkers. Having heard the words "prince" and "Dayborn," they were now pressing closer, eager to make a determination for themselves. Johanna experienced a sinking feeling in her stomach. It seemed the days of traveling anonymously through Ragar Or with her newly bonded were coming to an end.

"Yes. Friends of the Raleighs. The Dayborns are that, are they not?" Shupert said the words like he was asking the question of himself. The deepening darkness had all but wrapped its cloak around the Hawk's-Eye, making it impossible to read his face. Johanna sensed, however—as she had from the beginning—that something was amiss.

"Your Light. Is something…wrong?"

Shupert sighed and shook his head. He then stared at Johanna for a long moment, his visage cast in darkness, only to turn to Easton before replying, "Lord Wessel Raleigh is dead. He was traveling north with a sizable host when his belly burst."

Johanna envisioned Lord Wessel Raleigh in her mind's eye. Her erstwhile father-in-law. Dead. Like Nicholas, his one and only son. Johanna had never been especially close to Lord Wessel, but all the same, the news of his passing stung.

"This is sad news indeed," Easton said. A frown formed on his face. "But why was he traveling north with an army? The Blackstar Rebellion is no more. The Salks and the other Ontish houses saw to that."

Shupert pawed at the ground with sandaled feet. He switched gazes once more, turning to Johanna. "Forgive me, my child, for what I'm about to say." His eyes bounced back to Easton. "Lord Wessel Raleigh was traveling north with an army at the behest of the Sagekind. The king's bastard half brother had written Lord Raleigh to inform him that the king's life was in peril, and that he should come north straightaway." The Hawk's-Eye cast his gaze upon the ground. "Lady Wenavere Raleigh commands the army now. She is encamped just outside of Hornwell, less than a mile to the south. Her intention is to follow through on Lord Wessel's mission." Shupert's eyes flitted back to Johanna's. "She intends to ensure that King Micah Dayborn's life isn't made forfeit at the hands of Daguss Salk."

They returned to their room at the inn. Alone, together.

But in truth, they weren't alone. The world outside was at their door. A world consisting of a bad-news-bearing priest, an army-fronting former mother-in-law, and two fathers who, from the sound of it, were going about the business of plotting to kill one another.

"I don't know this priest, and I don't know your father. Not like you do. So, tell me: do you believe what the Hawk's-Eye said was true? Do you believe that your father would try and overthrow the Union throne?"

Easton's question was like a knife blading into Johanna's skin. "I don't know," she answered reflexively, eager to pull away from the pain. But there was no avoiding it. She had to speak the truth. "But I wouldn't be surprised if it were true. My father is an ambitious man. And a Salk, to boot. With the instability in the realm, I have no doubt that he's been busy positioning himself to take advantage. Does that include plotting to kill your father the king?" She looked away. "He didn't really keep me in the loop as to his plans. My sister the Twin Ascendant, yes. Me, no. So the only answer I can give you is 'maybe.'"

Easton sucked his teeth. Anger bloomed on his cheeks. His tongue readied something sharp, but all at once the fight went out of him. He sheathed the words away.

The floorboards shook beneath their feet. Downstairs, in the common room, the guests of the Green Tree Inn were dancing and singing. From the sound of it, the pious dispositions brought into being by the sunset ceremony had not carried over into the night. Peals of laughter filled the gaps between the music, laughter born aloft on the wings of Marrows wine.

Easton sat down on the bed beside Johanna. He brought his elbows to his knees and clasped his hands together. His expression was mournfully dark. "My father…" He trailed away, sighed, and took up the effort again. "I think it was about a year ago when I first realized that his kingship was failing. The raiders from Thralk-Braktur, the Blackstar Rebellion, the Ontish grumblings, the Struvan discontent…the problems were mounting, everyone could see it. My first instinct was to blame him. Being a king is like being in possession of a very particular type of magic: the magic to convince others that yours is the rightful authority. When a king can no longer sustain that, how does that person continue as king?"

Johanna shifted closer to Easton. When he glanced at her, she gave him *go on* eyes.

"But he's also my father, isn't he? And as the king, he's had to bear burdens that I can only imagine. Sometimes I see it in his eyes: he's jealous of me for being the second son, for having the freedoms that I do. But he's never begrudged me for them. Not once. So, who am I to judge him? He's done the best that he can, flawed though he may be."

Johanna didn't know how to respond. King Micah wasn't spoken of highly up north, but that was to be expected in the Ontish parts of Ragar Or. If she were asked to judge, she would agree that the king had recently made a mess of things, but that didn't mean she supported her father's purported coup.

Easton pinched his eyebrows together with his right thumb and index finger. "Ever since I was a boy, if Father preached anything to me and my brother, it was the importance of Union. *The Dayborns saved this kingdom at the end of the War of the Three Brothers,* Father would always say. *We saved Union. That's our charge. Keeping Ragar Or together.* And that's where I, for all my wildness and wanderlust, have to draw the line. I will defend Union against anyone who would try and tear it asunder. Even if that…includes your father."

Johanna gave a tiny, uncertain nod. She had grown up in High Osgood, where the rhetoric surrounding the Union of the Ontish and Struvan peoples was decidedly mixed; the general consensus was that it had been a decent idea when the Salks were on the throne, but with the Dayborns in charge, it was once again open for debate. As for her own father, she had never heard him speak a word, not one, on the subject. As a highborn family, the Salks had as much Struvan in their bloodline as Ontish, but Johanna instinctually understood that living in the north precluded them from speaking highly of Struvan nobility, the Dayborns especially. You could bond a Struvan, sure. But you couldn't confirm their right to rule in front of other Ontish.

"I'm not on my father's side," she said. A memory flashed like a bolt of jagged lightning in her mind: her father's words to her the day she fled Coffyn Castle. *If ever there comes a day when a consequential decision is yours to be made, I advise you to side with your family. Your true family. The Salks.* Her father had been planning even then to overthrow the king, hadn't he? *Of course. Why else do you think he said what he said?* But it also wasn't like her father to fail once he set his mind to something. Regardless, there were decisions to be made, in the Hornwell here and now. "I am on your side. *Our* side." She reached out and took Easton by the hand. "The Struvan *and* Ontish side. Union."

The ruckus in the Green Tree turned percussive. It was a moment before they realized that it wasn't the downstairs music, but someone knocking at the door.

Easton returned Johanna her hand. He walked over to the door and opened it a smidge.

The innkeeper stuck her snout inside. “My lady. My lord. A word, if you please?”

Easton looked to Johanna. She nodded her assent.

Once inside, the bosomy woman’s moon-wide eyes spoke volumes. It was clear that she had heard the rumor circulating around the Green Tree Inn, the one about the Salk daughter and Dayborn son on the grounds. “Not meaning to bother you, but we would be honored if you would join us downstairs. If you were to show your faces—”

“Who exactly do you think we are?” Johanna asked.

The woman shifted her eyes uncertainly between them, a hopeful smile still on her face. “The son of the Dayborn king, and a daughter of Lord Salk.” She lowered her voice, as if taking them into her confidence. “That’s what everyone is saying.”

“I’m sorry,” Johanna replied, making her voice kind. “We are merely a young, bonded pair, traveling through Hornwell on our sweetmarch.”

“Swear on Stavus?” the woman asked, suspicion in her voice. “There are those who heard you speaking with the Hawk’s-Eye—”

“Yes,” Johanna interrupted. “My bonded’s father is a wealthy trader who works the Wrainish circuit. He knows everyone in the Struvan cities—”

“Everyone,” Easton chimed in.

“—including His Light, Shupert Press. I worried when the others snooped on our conversation that there might be some misunderstanding, but I would have scarce imagined that we’d be mistaken for royalty.” Johanna gave a gentle laugh. “So you see, our presence downstairs would only entail disappointment, and explanation. And as we are paying customers in good standing, and desirous of a night alone together, I hope you'll be so kind as to bear the burden of both for us."

The woman fumbled over an apology. "Yes. Of course. I shouldn't have… I'm so sorry." Once the epitome of graceful hospitality, the innkeeper now stumbled over the hem of her long green-and-white dress. She gave Easton and Johanna an awkward smile and departed.

The innkeeper's footfalls moved quickly away. Johanna turned to Easton. "I did not want a decision made for us before we could make it for ourselves."

Easton brought a hand to his intemperate head of brown hair and messed it. "We'll leave. Tonight."

"Is that what you want?"

"Is that what *you* want?"

Silence reigned. Upstairs and down. *Why isn't the music resuming?* Johanna's faraway mind mused. Her tongue, however, stayed attuned to the present. "If we are going to reenter the real world, I want to do it on our own terms."

"Let's leave, then."

"Okay. Yes. We'll leave."

"And go where?" Easton's green eyes grew imploring. "I still think we should go to Union, Johanna. Lord Saylet is sitting regent in my father's absence. If something were to go awry in the north, I should be in the capital to defend the Dayborn claim. It's what Father would want me to do. I'm sure of it. If you were there with me, as my bonded…if the people saw us together, a Dayborn and a Salk…the message it would send would be unmistakable."

Johanna looked upon Easton with wonder. *Is this the same boy who stole into my room at Coffyn Castle?* If she had once thought him capricious, she no longer did. He was made of stronger, deeper stuff. The stuff of roots.

"I'm for it. Let's go to Union. Let's *be* for Union. Together." For a moment her mind drifted back to Coffyn Castle: she saw the image of her father peeling an apple while he explained what would happen to Johanna if she defied him. She forced the vision from her mind. "Come what may."

Easton grinned at her, a grin that softened into a loving smile. He returned to the bed, where together they fell back on the mattress and faced each other lying on their sides. There they nestled into the strange, still quiet of the inn, lips inches apart. They were about to kiss when the quiet was interrupted by steps on the stairs, multiple pairs, the sound loud enough to give them pause.

"Is the innkeeper returning, do you think?" Johanna asked.

Easton dismissed the idea with a devilish smirk. "If so, she'll knock. Until then…"

His lips had resumed their forward advance when the knock arrived. Except this time the knock wasn't a question but rather a declamation. No more had the knuckles finished assaulting wood than the door swung open. Easton and Johanna jumped up from the bed as two knights cleared the doorway for a woman dressed in a splendid red-and-white surcoat bearing the distinctive heraldry of the Raleighs: three red chevrons, pointing skyward, against a blank white field. She looked a force, the woman, eyes alight with intelligence, age-tempered red hair swinging in a battlefield braid.

She looked exactly the way Johanna remembered her.

"Lady Wenavere?" Johanna felt her cheeks burning red with embarrassment.

Wenavere Raleigh took in Johanna and her half-shaven head with the dispassion of a battlefield commander. "Hello, gooddaughter. The Hawk's-Eye said that I would find you here." Her gaze tracked to Easton. "My prince." There was a glint in her teeth as she spoke. "I'm glad that I found you. We have much to discuss."

Silas O' the Songs

The road to Kalandragote was long. Plenty of time for thought. Silas O' the Songs, sitting muleback, kept returning to the same one.

Loath to admit it though he was, he missed Wyn Dunkin.

Why? It was because the little man possessed what he lacked. A certain…verve. Punch. Panache. The fuck-it-all'ery to finagle his way into the court of kings and queens and not give two copper squibs how he was received. The silver tongue to smooth out any misunderstandings along the way. And, most importantly of all, the magic to disappear when the moment no longer suited his skill set.

Silas, on the other hand, lacked the aforementioned attributes. It wasn't that he was entirely without social talents—he had once impressed the Arcs enough to win a residency at Castle Greenwell, hadn't he?—but the tools at his disposal simply weren't sufficient for the moment at hand. He needed to be more like Wyn. And quickly, too. This traveling Dayborn court was a dangerous one, and Silas was only going to survive if his tongue stopped tying itself in knots and his balls ceased trying to tunnel back up inside his stomach.

What worried him most was his deteriorating relationships with the king and the queen. King Micah, for the most part, ignored him. Queen

Anjay, on the other hand, interrogated him daily, only to come away ever more displeased. She wanted revelation from him, but the revelation in Silas's possession was too confusing to give to her. He was certain that the truth would only make matters between himself and the Dayborns worse.

Then there was the matter of the Sagekind. That bony bastard somehow knew that Silas was holding out on him. Every day the Sagekind would find the time to listen to Silas play "The Queen's Burning Heart." And every day, when the playing was through, the Wraith in Red would stare at Silas with sinister *I see through you* eyes, then walk away in silence, a silence that promised he would continue to return until the day Silas played the *real* version of the song.

The man frightened the shit out of Silas. Why? Because Silas had seen with his own eyes that the jeyedoshi rumors surrounding Gregor Thorn were more than rumors. *That man will make mincemeat out of my insides the day he discovers that my song is a lie. What I need is Wyn with me to keep the Wraith in Red off balance.* Wyn had unsettled the Sagekind. Silas knew this for a fact: he had witnessed the Sagekind's unease around Wyn with his own eyes. Somehow the little rat-faced fiddler gave pause to an in-the-flesh jeyedoshi.

Probably had something to do with Wyn being a woodkin, Silas thought, remembering the surreal strangeness of seeing Wyn Dunkin transform into tree bark in the flesh.

Yes, probably something to do with that.

Silas shook his head. Breath steam poured from his nostrils in the cold northern air. *Enough obsessing about Wyn. Wyn is gone. And remember—you wished him away. The only one who can save you here is...you.*

The day's procession came to a halt. Silas checked the position of the sun in the cold blue sky.

Time for the midday meal.

Silas took a deep breath. His presence was required whenever the king and queen sat down to eat. Unconsciously, he began working his fingers, readying them to play.

In the near distance, the Dayborn pavilion was rising from the ground. Silas used the time to look behind him. The procession was still coming to a stop, like the rippling vertebrae of a monstrous creature willing itself to be still. The immensity of the line heartened him: whatever dark northern heart they were heading into, at least they were heading there with numbers. *Never mind the fact that those are Ontish standards flitting far in the back.*

He took his own advice and ignored the flags.

When a sufficient amount of time had passed, Silas dismounted from the mule and led the animal by its reins toward the royal pavilion. There he handed the mule off to a waiting groom, stepped inside the tent, and was handed his leather lute case for the first time that day. The rosewood lute Merjy the woods witch had given him lived a separate life during the traveling portion of the day: it spent time in a covered wagon with the Dayborn family's finest possessions. Silas didn't like letting the lute out of his sight, but Queen Anjay had insisted upon it when she saw Silas try to stuff the instrument into Brown Boss's saddlebags. *It feels wrong going all day without touching it*, he thought for the thousandth time. But the guilt was deeper than that. Wyn and Merjy the woods witch had chided him for losing his first lute, back at the Golden Pear. Letting the second one out of sight felt like a betrayal of the lessons he had learned during his time with Wyn.

Stop it! You didn't even like the annoying little cuss. He stole your song, remember?

A smaller voice rejoindered: *But he helped find you a new one too, didn't he? And a better one at that.*

Inside the tent, scores of servants abounded, working hard to turn the snow-packed circle into an abode fit for royalty. Pallets of wood overlain with sumptuous rugs served as a makeshift floor, braziers were set in the tent's center and respective corners, and handsome wooden chairs were placed throughout, transforming the space within minutes.

Silas paid the servants little mind. Instead, he set about removing his lute from its leather case. His heart rate slowed as he moved his hands over the wood. The instrument felt like home. No matter where he went in the world, so long as he had a lute in his hands, he belonged.

He turned, looking for the chair that the servants usually set out for him. As expected, it was already in place. How did Silas know the chair was his? Simple. The back of the chair was carved into the design of a seven-stringed lute. It had stunned Silas the first time he saw it—had the Dayborns been traveling with the chair in tow all over Ragar Or? Or had they commissioned it shortly after he first came into their service in Dunning Harbor? He wanted to ask but feared the question would make him seem provincial. Power, he was learning, was many things, but included in its definition was the ability to produce a chair carved with a lute design on demand.

The servants began filing out of the tent. Meat aromas wafted in through the flaps. The king's cooks, preparing the meal. Silas's mouth watered at the smell, but his fingers had many a mile to walk before he would eat. He set his mind to music.

He wasn't exactly sure what to play, but as was often the case, his fingers took the lead for him. Today, they were feeling pious. The song was a surprise even to him; Silas was halfway through the first verse before he realized that he was playing "On Wings of Light," the Stavusian temple song. As he played, he kept time to a different version in his head, one performed by a harpist of otherworldly talent. *Isbel Wicker. Isbel Wicker was her name. She played a song that put mine to shame.* He tried his best to perform a version worthy of hers. As the last of the notes rung out, his mind's eye replayed the image of flames dancing on the roof of the Golden Pear.

"I never took you for… Was that a temple song?"

Silas recovered from his spell to find a wiry wolf of a woman standing beside him. One of his few friends on this long journey north. Jacy. Or at least he hoped that they were still friends. It was difficult to know where he stood with her and the big mute Madrig after all that had taken place in Dunning Harbor.

"Something like that." He didn't mean to be rude, it was only…he hadn't played the song because it was a *temple* song. He had played it because…well, the emotions he was harboring from the trauma of the last few weeks had to come out somehow, didn't they?

"Silas O' the Songs playing a temple song. Are you devout?"

Silas relaxed his grip on the lute. Looking across the tent, he spotted neither king nor queen. *Ask her now, you coward.* "Devout enough, I suppose." He fixed his eyes on the warrior-woman. Tried not to shrink in her formidable presence. "What happened back in Dunning Harbor? Did Lord Salk send someone to kill me and Wyn after you told him about us? I know that you and Madrig are the king's protectors now—"

"You think that I know?" Jacy interrupted, sounding offended. "I wasn't overly fond of your little friend, but Madrig and I would never have told Lord Daguss about the two of you if we had had the slightest indication it would end with someone trying to kill you. What sense does that make? We risked our lives defending you back at the Yubriy Tree, remember? Madrig genuinely thought that Daguss meant to bring you safely to the king."

Silas nodded. "I assumed that's why the two of you swore yourselves to the king. Because Madrig no longer trusted his cousin."

Jacy's expression twisted with uncertainty. "Madrig doesn't know what to think. Neither do I. I doubt you want to hear this, but Lord Daguss might have been telling the truth. Betrard the gorgostrine might have been behind all of it."

Silas scoffed.

"Like I said, I didn't think you would want to hear it."

There was movement on the other side of the massive tent, near the back flap. In walked the king and a select retinue: Queen Anjay, the Sagekind, Dante Heron, and Daguss Salk. *Talk about keeping your enemies close,* Silas thought. The five power players sat together round an oakwood table. Seconds after they were seated, five servants returned to the tent carrying plates piled high with the afternoon's offerings: a carrot-and-onion medley, boar meat, and a hearty mushroom harvest, piled like tiny fallen trees on the corners of the plates. *Takes me back,* Silas thought, remembering the many mushroom meals Wyn had prepared for them during their journey north.

Jacy smacked him hard on the shoulder. "Play, you fool. The queen is staring daggers at you."

It was true. Silas dipped his chin in deference and took the lute back up. His scrambling mind settled on the first song that came to him: "The Queen's Burning Heart."

It felt like the wrong choice the instant he started playing it. There was nothing technically wrong with his playing, nor his singing, but the song selection was wrong all the same. He hoped against hope that he was the only one who felt that way, but when his eyes alit on the table, he saw King Micah shifting uncomfortably in his seat, as if every note was a torture. The king's discomfort soon changed over to a palpable anger, and Silas, distracted by the king, found himself unable to infuse the song with its customary vitality.

"Stop," King Micah suddenly growled, giving the oakwood table a sharp little slap. "Stop playing." The king's gaze trailed over, and, for the second time in less than two minutes, Silas found himself on the sharp end of a monarchal stare. Not knowing what to do, Silas sat there, lute in lap, looking dumb. He felt his face growing red, fueled not only by embarrassment but anger too. It was all he could do to stop himself from skewering the king with a stare of his own.

"Come here," the king said after what seemed like an interminable pause.

Come here? This was odd. Fright displaced fury. Silas nodded in response to the king's command. He rose unsteadily to his feet but didn't move.

"Come, I said. Let's get this over with."

Silas made his way over to the table. *What am I supposed to do? Where am I supposed to look?* He felt like a rabbit approaching a pride of lions. Were Wyn here, he would have no doubt deployed a witticism to balance the power dynamic, but Silas had no such defense. The only weapon at his disposal was his lute, which, he realized, he was still holding.

"He carries it with him like a child," Dante Heron scoffed, nodding at the lute. Silas, before he could process what he was doing, shot the eastern lord the angry look he had held in reserve for the king. The young lord, clad in white silk and a cloak of white satin, laughed in amazement. "My, my, my! I was right! Only an overprotective father would be so stupid as to glare at a lord!"

Silas blanched, then backtracked. "I'm sorry, my lord. Please forgive me. I…I…I'm protective of my lute, is all, you have to understand—"

"Stavus save us," the king interrupted, shaking his rather sizable head. "Shut it, Silas. I didn't call you over here to hear your apologies or suffer your glares. Truth is, if I had my druthers, I wouldn't suffer you at all. You've been nothing but a source of trouble since the day you came to us." Silas, confused by the assault, looked to Queen Anjay and the Sagekind, but they offered him no succor. "But I digress. Daguss," the king continued, looking down at the white-bearded nobleman sitting beside him, "say what you will."

Lord Daguss Salk rose from his seat like a planet ascending the nighttime firmament. He wore a moonbear coat over cloth of gray. Unlike Lord Dante, who wore his white with pristine grace, Daguss Salk's ensemble called to mind a rugged but stately wealth. His demeanor was the opposite of the king's: measured, intentional, and mild.

"Silas O' the Songs," Lord Daguss began, surprising Silas with the musical honorific, "I want to offer my sincere apologies for the attempt made on your life in Dunning Harbor. I swear to you that it was not my doing, despite the fact that Betrard was my man. As you know, Betrard lies dead now by my own sword. I pray his death and the deaths of those who tried to kill you has put your mind at ease. And I pray that you will accept my apology for these events, the same as our good king has."

The inflection of Lord Daguss's voice was sincere. His facial expression, however, suggested detachment. Regardless, Silas knew that when a man of Lord Daguss's stature apologized to you, there was nothing to do but accept.

"I—"

"Of course he accepts," King Micah butted in. Then the king raised a finger and wagged it admonishingly in Silas's face. "Lord Daguss was no more responsible for that attack than you were for your little friend's disappearance. Isn't that right?"

Why is the king chastising me? Silas once again looked to the table. This time the Sagekind met his gaze, but Silas could not interpret the too-subtle expression on the Wraith in Red's face. Juddering words convulsed off Silas's tongue. "Y-y-y…yes. Of course, of course!" He half turned to Lord Daguss. "I never once thought," he lied, "that a man of your honor, your integrity… I knew the instant you explained it that the gorgostrine, the priest of the Twins"—*now you're getting somewhere*—"Betrard, he was the one behind everything…and now it's as you said, my mind is at peace, at ease, I've never been happier"—*Stavus save me*—"I'm so fortunate to be here, in the service of my king."

By the time his rambling had ceased, Silas was staring at the ground, chin dipped in shame. He sensed, however, that his shame was shared. With a quick glance at the table, he saw that he was right, at least as far as the Dayborns were concerned. They had the good training not to show it in the same overt way, but in their pinked expression and cutaway eyes Silas understood that his shame was also theirs, even if he didn't understand why.

Masticating sounds broke the silence. The Heron, chewing on pig meat. The gravity in the tent shifted in the Heron's direction. "He sounds sincere, Your Grace," the Heron commented after swallowing. He gave a smile that only Silas could see, strings of boar meat glistening in his teeth. "I say you dismiss the man to play his lute."

King Micah expelled a great breath of air. He sat back down in his chair and looked at no one. "I would hear him play no more tonight. Be gone with you, Silas O' the Songs."

Silas turned toward the tent's front flap. *What just happened?* He cast bemused, beseeching glances as he went, but no one—not even Jacy—would meet his eyes. He collected the leather lute case along the way, then finished his walk of shame, back out into the peninsular cold.

Silas needed to get away, to clear his thoughts. But that wasn't going to happen if he stayed in the body of the great processional beast. All around him and to the south, midday fires sent smoke prayers to the heavens, thin fingers of beseeching gray. The sounds of men talking, laughing, and arguing filled the southern horizon. There were men out and about in Silas's section of the procession, too, but they were the knights paramount of the realm: your Braxton Walshings, your Larin Doves, your Jakastor Weylcoins. Men who went about their talking and eating with restraint. Men who paid no mind to musicians.

To the north, on as-yet-untrod land, two snow-strewn hillocks promised privacy. Silas started that way, spoiling the unblemished landscape with every footstep. As he walked, he remembered the lute in his hand: it was the first time in days that he hadn't surrendered his instrument upon leaving the company of the Dayborns. His heart, harried as it was, calmed a little at the realization.

He rounded the crest of the first hillock. Two hares scampered away at the sight of him, revealing sitting nooks, resting crannies. Silas chose one, found that it suited him. He stared north into the nothingness, allowed it to settle all around him. He breathed slowly in and out.

He positioned the lute and began to play.

Part of him knew that he should be trying to puzzle out what had gone wrong with the king, but the unexpected joy of playing solely for himself was too strong to deny. There was no king or queen present to critique his play, no Wyn Dunkin to interrupt him with nonsensical drivel, no Madrig or Jacy to impress. He played what he wanted: river ditties familiar only to the denizens of Ragknot, fragments of forgotten melodies, unloved songs that had fallen from the collective memory but were kept alive in the collective consciousnesses of knowing musicians.

For a time, his soul was satisfied. A murmuration of starlings visited, undulating overhead. They seemed Stavus-sent. The scenic tableau and his playing mollified the worry in his heart. *If I keep playing, I don't have to worry about what it all means…*

But then a strange thing happened. A pressure mounted, a pressure that asked a question of him, a pressure that needed, nay, *demanded,* that he play a specific tune. The pressure built and built until Silas's only two choices appeared to be to either stop playing entirely and confront the day's troubles or submit to the pressure's demands.

The decision was no decision at all.

He began playing the true version of "The Queen's Burning Heart."

Silas closed his eyes. The Yubriy leaf lyrics fell from his lips like fire. Singing the true version had a cleansing effect, like he was purging his soul. He felt like a bird taking flight. It was a short song, using only the words given by the Yubriy, and before he knew it, he was circling the song's end, approaching the name written at the bottom of the leaf. The one that he dared not speak. But today he belted it out, scorching the already song-singed air. Notes gathered around the name: luscious, weaving, working notes, notes that knew their underpinning purpose. They waited until the name was vocalized, and then they sped away like shooting stars, flying here and there until no sound remained but day-bright silence.

Silas opened his eyes. The world was as he had left it. Bright. Bold. Cold. The only difference was that he now felt clear-eyed and clear-headed, ready to assess what had happened and make a decision as to what to do next.

That was when he heard the voice.

"Who is Weston?"

The shock made Silas's system go haywire. He turned, searching for the source, while his heart relocated to his ears and blood thundered through his veins. He didn't have to look hard. Wulfess Salk was standing on the crest of the hillock in all her fulsome beauty. She was dressed in expansive black furs, and she wore a not-quite smile on her face, a smile that played with the very concept of what a smile could be, a smile that suggested that Wulfess might smile at you in a thousand different ways and you still wouldn't know the authentic smile at the center of her soul. She looked like beauty incarnate.

And what a terrible beauty it was.

"Who?" Silas asked, trying to buy time. He instantly knew that he had made an error: the smarter reaction would have been to express surprise at seeing her, but instead he had doubled attention on the one question he wanted to avoid.

"Weston," Wulfess answered, direct as an arrow. "The name at the end of the song. 'The Queen's Burning Heart,' isn't it? I must say, those lyrics are quite different from the ones I've heard you sing before."

He couldn't think straight. The secret of his song was out and needed to be explained away, but he *could not think,* not with the incapacitating wonder that was Wulfess Salk bearing down on him, demanding an answer. She moved in close without apology, stealing into his personal space. He stopped breathing when she stepped in close. She was close enough to kiss him. Not only that, the wicked look on her face suggested that she might.

"I demand an answer, Silas O' the Songs," she said, her breath hot on his face. "Who is Weston?"

Gregor Thorn

Young Deglan was the first to spot a frostflower. "Sagekind," the young knight said while looking west, his voice filled with wonder. Without looking, Gregor guessed what had captivated the young man. But when Gregor turned, he found to his surprise that the sight of the flower filled him with wonder, too, a wonder that temporarily assuaged his half-maddened mind.

This particular flower was a loner, a renegade droplet of blue cresting the snow-caked ground. Gregor had expected the unnaturalness of the blue to be off-putting, but instead the flower soothed him at first sight. Together with Deglan, he trotted over on his mount to get a closer look.

Up close, there was even more to admire. The snow was nearly six inches deep, but the flower had tunneled through using a tornadic strength, spiraling up and up with sharply closed petals until, once it was atop the snowbank, it unfurled its majestic glory. The blue of the flower was bold without crossing over to gaudy. A dot of gold in the middle. Entranced, Gregor reached down to rub the funnelform petals. The texture was mind-blowing. Touching the outside of the flower was like touching a changeable carapace; Gregor could feel the flower adjusting to the threat level posed by his touch, stiffening when the pressure firmed, softening when it gentled. The inside, on the other hand, felt like the smoothest vellum.

"They don't seem real," Deglan commented. "And to think that there are thousands surrounding Kalandragote—"

"Millions," Gregor corrected. "Or so they say."

Whatever they said, Gregor soon discovered that it was an understatement. The frostflowers multiplied by the mile from that point forward, transforming the landscape. Pinpricks of blue became patches, which shortly became islands. The sea of snow-white that they had previously been swimming in narrowed to the river of the road, which ran inexorably toward Kalandragote.

"The flowers have us hemmed in all sides," Deglan said as a joke.

Gregor could not find the humor in it.

As suffocating as the road felt, riding it was better than staring at skulls. Since leaving Dunning Harbor, Gregor had traveled at the front of the procession, doing everything in his power to minimize the time he was forced to spend looking at those marked by death. *We're all marked by death,* he told himself again and again, eager to believe that the sight of the skulls didn't mean what he thought it meant. Not that he could convince himself. At least the landscape filled with frostflowers was a distraction, so long as one didn't take too metaphorical a view of their encroachment.

By the time they reached the Brokebone Pass, the world was naught but snow, evergreen trees, and blue petals. The Moonfield Mountains, rising like walls to the east and to the west, narrowed the road even more, but at least they provided a break from the flower-filled tableau. To a degree. The flowers were still present but had moved to the Moonfield peaks, where in smaller numbers they spied on the invaders below. *But we're not invaders, are we? We're honored guests.*

The pass was as gentle as all the history books proclaimed, gliding toward Kalandragote, but it was easy to see why every southern incursion had ended in slaughter: any army that advanced through the pass was bound to clog, and it was then that the Kalandragotans pressed their advantage, using their superior understanding of the mountains to rain arrows and hellfire on the invaders below.

This time, however, there was no bottlenecking counterforce. No mountain-emerging archery men. Only the advance scouts, reporting back time and again: "The road to Kalandragote is clear."

They advanced up the Brokebone for days. A Stavusian sky overhead, gentle and blue, filled with so much hawksong that Gregor struggled to accept that they were entering the heart of the faith of the Twins. The mood up and down the procession was genial, buoyant. History was turning on its head. A new age was dawning.

The Kalandragote honor guard met them at the pass's end, a small and unimposing contingent of ten. The guard advanced at a moderate clip across the wide and welcoming valley. Frostflowers all around. Gregor—along with the king, the queen, Daguss Salk, Dante Heron, Wulfess Salk, and Cato Ollspaer—rode out to the front to greet them.

Gregor was greatly surprised when he saw that the person at the front of the honor guard was a woman.

"Your Highness. I am Wren Ollspaer, the sister of Horos Ollspaer. Welcome to Kalandragote."

Wren Ollspaer was a hard-looking woman. It was not inconceivable to think that she had been a wild beauty in her youth, but time and her surroundings had molded her into the severe creature before them. Gregor could usually get a feel for the essence of a person at the outset, but he could not see through to the center of Wren Ollspaer. She sat tall in the saddle, surrounded by nine knights, three of whom carried the Kalandragote heraldry: a sickle moon encircling a frostflower, on a field of white ringed with black.

"My lady, we are well met." Gregor watched as King Micah drew himself up into his kingly form. For all his flaws, the man had a presence, which counted for quite a bit in a king. *If only we were a few generations deeper into the Dayborns, his performance would be a fait accompli.* But instead, Micah Dayborn was surrounded by men and women who in their heart of hearts believed that they had as much right to a throne as he. *But if he can thread the Kalandragote needle and sew the entire kingdom together…thus are dynasties made.*

"Indeed." Wren gave an awkward little bow in the saddle. The other members of the contingent followed suit, looking ridiculous to the point of mockery.

King Micah, however, took it in stride. "Where is Lord Horos?" he boomed, surveying the landscape. Gregor appreciated the way his brother made sure to call Horos *Lord.* "I would welcome him into the kingdom of Ragar Or with a brotherly embrace."

"He awaits the honor of your presence in Winterworn Castle. A great feast is being prepared as we speak. It is tradition in Kalandragote to feed guests immediately upon their arrival." She turned away from the king for the first time and looked down the line. Something resembling a smile crossed her face when her eyes found Cato. "Nephew. Welcome home. All of Kalandragote is eager to celebrate your bonding ceremony."

"I am glad to be home, *hestrum,*" Cato replied, dipping his chin. Cato's usage of Old Ontish sent a chill up Gregor's spine. The context was innocuous enough—*hestrum* was Old Ontish for *aunt,* Gregor knew—but it was also bad form to speak Old Ontish in front of the king without his permission. Cato, seemingly oblivious to the offense, continued. "May I introduce to you my bonded-to-be. A true *Ontish* beauty. Wulfess Salk."

Had the Kalandragote heir emphasized the word "Ontish"? Gregor squirmed in the saddle. He had been around Cato for weeks and hadn't heard the young man say anything remotely tribal, but now they were two minutes returned to Kalandragote and Cato was showing his true colors. *Calm yourself.* Gregor stole a look at his brother, the king. Micah clearly wasn't bothered by Cato's word choice. *But he wouldn't be, would he? No, he and his skull have determined upon a course, and there isn't a warning sign in the world that could deter him.*

"It is an honor to meet you, Wulfess," Wren said.

"The pleasure is mine," Wulfess replied. The two women gave each other knowing looks and respectful nods.

The remainder of the introductions were made. Queen Anjay, Lord Daguss, Lord Dante. Wren Ollspaer expressed perfectly benign welcomes to each. *She has a sort of hard haughtiness to her,* Gregor thought. When it was time for his introduction, Gregor watched as the distance grew deeper in Wren's eyes, a sure sign, Gregor assumed, that she was working extra hard not to betray how she truly felt about the jeyedoshi in her midst. She tried to move past the greeting quickly, but Gregor brought his horse forward, ready, as always, to play the role that life demanded of him.

"Before we proceed to Winterworn Castle, my lady, I think it important that we clarify a few matters concerning the reception and safe passage of the king."

Wren Ollspaer considered Gregor anew. A split second of this, and she cast a cutting chin behind him. "If the procession at your rear can't guarantee safe passage, I'm not sure that I know what will."

Half of playing the diplomat, Gregor knew, was knowing when to pretend that the other person hadn't spoken. "As long as King Micah and Queen Anjay are inside the Kalandragote city gates, there will be no limit on the number of Dayborn men-of-arms allowed inside the city. Lord Horos will not object to or attempt to circumvent any security measures the king decides are necessary during his stay. This includes removing Kalandragote men-at-arms from Winterworn Castle as King Micah sees fit. Lord Horos will make a show of obeisance to King Micah immediately upon their meeting. On the day of his son's bonding ceremony, Lord Horos will pledge an oath of loyalty to the Union Throne in front of all who are gathered."

Wren Ollspaer smiled at the last. "That is why we are here, Sagekind, is it not?" She sharpened the edges of her grin and presented it fully to Gregor.

"Yes, it is," Gregor said flatly.

"Good. Then we are all in agreement," King Micah chimed in, edging his horse forward. Gregor's steed fell back to make room. "Now, if my lady would be so good as to lead us to Winterworn Castle, I am eager to meet Lord Horos."

They set off together across the valley floor. Gregor glanced behind him and saw, to his satisfaction, a multitude of double sun standards trailing in the royal wake. *Good,* he thought. The Dayborn faction didn't have the advantage of numbers compared to the whole of the column, but Gregor had arranged it so that they would be in the majority inside of the Kalandragote city walls. The Ontish lords that had traveled north for the bonding ceremony—Seydron Qorl, Grocian Mock, Darryn Coffyn, and Mactus Garstring—were also in the mix, but they only had a small number of armed men in their respective retinues. The Heron had been permitted to bring a slightly larger contingent into Kalandragote, but the majority of his martial strength would remain outside the city walls.

If it weren't for the skulls staring back at me, I would almost feel proud of my maneuverings. He thought again of the letter he had sent to Wessel Raleigh upon his departure from Dunning Harbor. A letter sent without his brother's knowledge or permission. *It's not enough that Ajax has gone south with half the Heron's men. We need an army advancing on the Brokebone whose loyalty isn't in question. Micah can hate me all he wants when he discovers what I've done. So long as I usher the family safely through the coming days and weeks, nothing else matters.*

Gregor tried, if not to relax, then to at least soak in the wonder of the tableau before him. Crossing the grand expanse of the famed snow-and-frostflower-covered valley made Gregor feel like he was traversing history's own pages. Since Gregor was a boy, he had studied the history of the defiant, Twin-Ascendant-obsessed kingdom, but never had he imagined that he would experience the surreal sensation of seeing Kalandragote in person. But here he was. And there…there was Wrepta Mountain, the dark jag of rising rock shaped like a serrated knife, butchering the sky. In his mind's eye, Gregor envisioned the dragon known as the Ice Ghost perched upon the ridge, which was where the dragon had purportedly lived during the mysterious interim of time after the War of the Three Brothers.

Beneath Wrepta Mountain, Winterworn Castle brooded, its gray stone muddling into the surrounding white. The anomaly to Winterworn's stone was the infamous Bloodbone Tower: even from a distance Gregor could see the thread of dark-red brick running up the tower's side like an ugly scar. *King Greffen's father lived there. Roop Ollspaer.* Gregor's thoughts trailed for a moment over the small book with the blue boards that he had taken from the Sea Swoon, now resting inside of the saddlebag at his heel.

The gate guarding Kalandragote ran raggedly from the base of Wrepta Mountain to the base of a less-impressive peak to the east. *Mt. Jorndo,* Gregor remembered, recalling his studies. The center of the gate was open, and inside, Gregor could see the sprawling meshwork of mostly black-timber abodes that made up the city. Kalandragote's black architecture, taken together alongside the snow-and-frostflower-covered ground, was an alien, unsettling sight. *This is an unnatural place,* Gregor thought. *The blue of the frostflowers offset against the black of the buildings looks like a spreading bruise.* The affront of it made him queasy.

But there was no choice other than to go forward. Soon they were through the gates, and here the character of the place came more fully into focus. Hundreds, if not thousands, of hard-boiled faces had gathered to watch the spectacle of their new king pass them by, faces lined with the rigors of living in a harsh environ, faces that gave little indication as to the underlying mood of the population. They stared with an unabashed shamelessness that Gregor struggled to interpret. He felt within the crucible of their gaze that an important test was being administered, but whether or not King Micah was passing it, he did not know.

Inspiration struck him. He turned in the saddle and looked behind him, and there spotted Silas O' the Songs, riding on his mule fifteen yards back.

Gregor was reticent to leave the king's side at such a dangerous time, but intuition told him that the reward would be worth the risk. He directed his horse to the side of the procession, slowed its gait, and waited for Silas to pull alongside.

The lutist wore a faint look of alarm to see the Sagekind. *He is no valiant,* Gregor thought. Though perhaps Gregor was being ungenerous. Silas had endured enough ordeals—including his attempted murder at the Sea Swoon and, more recently, King Micah's lashing tongue—to demonstrate that he wasn't altogether white-livered. All the same, the lutist struck Gregor as a man caught in a constant state of indecision, which didn't inspire confidence.

He is a manifestation of the Yubriy Tree's unknowable ambitions. A tool. Use him for what he is.

"You are coming with me to the front of the procession," Gregor announced, taking Silas's mule by the reins.

The mule took being manhandled in stride. Silas did not. "Whatever for?"

"These people need to know who their king is. You will announce him as we ride by. It will be a good use of your singer's voice. You do know the king's full title, do you not?"

Silas furrowed his brow, looking like a disconcerted child. When he answered, it was with surprising force. "King Micah of House Dayborn, the first of his name, Holy Son of the Air, the Twin Ascendant, and the Rightful Ruler of Ragar Or."

They were drawing stares from other members of the procession. Wulfess Salk's gaze was especially intense. "Emphasize the Twin Ascendant part. Understood?"

Silas nodded, but there was a recalcitrant gleam in his eye. "I was ill-treated by the king in front of Lords Salk and Heron the other day."

"What of it?" Gregor snapped. He immediately regretted how he sounded. "He used you as a tool to help with a delicate political situation. Get over it, and get used to it." He lowered his voice. "If it's any consolation, he oft does the same with me."

"You? But you're the king's…the king's…"

Gregor watched Silas struggle to find the right word with bitter amusement. "I am the king's instrument, the same as you," Gregor said at last, rescuing the flailing lutist. "Only my work is darker. Now hurry, we will have passed half of Kalandragote by if you don't start soon."

Seconds later, Silas was ringing out the king's title. He did his duty passingly well. The denizens of Kalandragote bent their ears to better hear Silas's declamation. Kalandragote was the only city in Ragar Or where Old Ontish remained the chief language, but Struvan was common enough that most understood what was being said. Afterward, the Kalandragotans sized King Micah up, as if comparing the veracity of the lutist's words against the proof of what they saw. Gregor could not deduce their feelings on the matter, but at least it was some consolation that the case had been made.

The truth is, I don't have a good enough understanding of what the citizens of this place think. I need to know how they feel about Horos Ollspaer's decision to join the kingdom of Ragar Or. I need to better understand what happened here during the Blackstar Rebellion. All the information the Dayborns knew about Kalandragote's decision to join Ragar Or had first passed through the filter of Daguss Salk. Daguss's translation, fortunately, had been confirmed by others—the blockade around Kalandragote during the Blackstar Rebellion had caused considerable hardship among a population that had for years been becoming less self-reliant—but now that Gregor was here, he needed someone in his own camp to confirm the details for him.

Young Deglan. It would have to be the young knight. Gregor trusted no one else in the Dayborn camp half as much. He only hated that he would once again be exposing the young man to danger. Gregor turned to the stalwart knight sitting high in his saddle. *The older he grows, the more I think of him as young. The guiltier I feel about sending him into danger, the more inclined I am to do so.* At least he saw no skull beneath the young man's impassive, flesh-full face. A dark thought burned bright against the skyscape of Gregor's sea-fingers-addled mind. *If you send him to his death, at least that will allow you to put your assumptions about the skulls to rest.*

Deglan took Gregor's order in stride. "I will go now, if you think it best."

"I do." Gregor pressed a pouch of silver Salks into the knight's hands. If he was to get anywhere with the populace, bribery would have to play a part. *Although he is as like to get another knife in the belly as he is answers.* Gregor pushed the thought from his mind. "Learn what you can. Return to the castle by nightfall."

Deglan gave a resolute nod. Then he dug his heels into the horse's side and disappeared into the city.

As the procession drew closer to Winterworn Castle, the Kalandragotans fell away. By the time the vanguard of the procession progressed within the perimeter of the castle's shadow, there was no one left for Silas to announce the king's title to. Up ahead were the castle gates, but still no sign of Horos. *I should have insisted that Horos make his first show of obeisance outside the castle gates, in front of his people.* But it was too late—they were already passing through. On the other side of the stone aperture,

Gregor took stock of the guard accompanying the king, the many skulls that had sworn to give their lives for their Dayborn sovereign. And there they were, in varying degrees of skeletal transparency: Braxton Walshing, Larin Dove, and Percy Moon rode directly behind the king, while, off to the right, Jakastor Weylcoin rode next to Dante Heron, ostensibly ready to intervene on either the king's or Lord Heron's behalf if called upon.

The other two sworn defenders of the king—Madrig and Jacy—rode a little distance back. Despite the heartfelt nature of the big mute's pledge to protect King Micah, Gregor had been wary of letting the bonded pair close to the king, for the obvious reasons. That aside, Gregor had detected nothing false in their bearings, and was beginning to think there was a chance that the two lovers' motives were genuine, and not tied to the feared machinations of one Lord Daguss. Glancing at the stone above, Gregor couldn't help but give a little laugh. *If we have friends here, or enemies, I'm sure I'll know soon enough.*

There was still no sign of Lord Horos in the outer yard. One hundred soldiers—over half of whom were Dayborn men—were now inside the castle gates. All handed their horses over to Kalandragote groomsmen. Everything was unfolding just as Gregor had planned. *A preponderance of suns inside the castle gates, and a preponderance of birds out.* To Gregor's relief, Lord Dante hadn't argued when Gregor explained what he had in mind. Nor had Daguss Salk. *Everyone was in a right mood for acquiescence after the fallout at Dunning Harbor.* If there was scheming at hand, Gregor wasn't privy to it. He caught sight of Seydron Qorl, who gave him a deathly stare, but Gregor ignored it. He tried to take a moment and appreciate the reality of what was taking place: for the first time in history, southern soldiers had breached the gates of Kalandragote and Winterworn Castle.

Wren Ollspaer led them into the great hall. The hall itself was a great improvement over Saltbend—unlike the smoke-choked hall at Dunning Harbor, here the ceilings were as tall as mountains, providing ample space for the smoke from three great hearth fires to dissipate. Sounds, sights, and smells barraged the senses: the savory smells of a dozen Ontish dishes competed with the sounds of a pretty music troupe and the startling sight of an enormous moonbear moving in step to the music in the middle of the hall. Gregor realized on a slight delay with everyone else that the bear was chained to a stake. It made him glad that he had left the two greyhounds, Black and Tan, with the train's gamekeeper; otherwise, there might have been an incident. Still, the bear was a startling sight. It caused a few of the men to nearly jump out of their skin.

Good-natured laughter echoed round the hall. There was a raised platform near the front, and that was where Wren Ollspaer led the royal contingent. The remainder of the party took up their places on the low benches. It was then that Gregor saw him, sitting up on the dais: the erstwhile king, Horos Ollspaer, undergoing his metamorphosis to lord. Horos looked like a molting thing: his gray-black beard was ragged and uneven, and his face was full of pits and ridges, the skin thin against the sight of a horrible skull. He wore an expression that suggested permanent disgruntlement. Or at least he did until he noticed that he'd been spotted: all at once the old king's face flushed with color as he moved to a standing position while screwing on a semblance of a smile.

Gregor walked a few steps behind King Micah. Stepping up onto the dais, Wren intercepted Horos and whispered a few quick words in his ear.

But the interaction ended quickly, for in the next moment the two kings were face-to-face. For a strange second Horos's hard black eyes flashed across the hall. But in the next his hand was reaching for the king's. Horos took Micah's hand in his own and began the seemingly arduous process of dropping to one knee.

"Your Highness, I—"

The moonbear roared, loud enough to shake the stones of the castle. All eyes turned. Even King Micah's. But not Gregor's. He kept his eyes on Horos, who, pressing ahead, finished the half-spoken sentence. "—welcome you to Kalandragote, and Winterworn Castle." Then Horos was up on his feet again, his knee scarcely having grazed the ground.

Was I the only witness to Horos's genuflection? It certainly seemed that way. Nervous laughter bandied about over the common refrain of "nearly pissed my breeches," but already the moonbear had resumed its dance, the roar a strange and sudden blip. *The timing of the roar was a coincidence,* Gregor supposed as he worked his way to his seat, which ended up being four down from the king; Lord Daguss, Lord Dante, and Queen Anjay were in-between.

Gregor was still trying to get his head around what had taken place when the servants began bringing food to the table. The first dish was that famed Ontish delicacy, roasted heartbirds. The birds were presented on a wooden skewer, their tiny black wings tucked over the bloodred breastplate of their chest. One glance was all Gregor needed to know that today would not be the day that he broke his lifelong custom of not eating songbirds. *I suppose that's one advantage to being the Wraith in Red: it's difficult to give additional offense.*

Lord Dante Heron, sitting beside Gregor, crunched the creatures' bones with a refined gusto. Gregor used the opportunity to study the moonbear. He had half hoped (and half feared) to see his first moonbear in the wild, but now that he was in the presence of a tame version, he was glad that he'd missed out on the feral. Whatever spell the beast was under seemed to be a weak one, for in its slavering, two-step dance it wasn't difficult to imagine the creature breaking from its trance and commencing a massacre. From all outward appearances, the beast was in good health: a sizable portion of the animal's pelt was still thick and lush, and the coloring was as silver-white as moon-streaked snow.

Out on the benches, men quaffed their mead. The energy in the hall had an uneven quality, seeming as like to go right as it was to go wrong. All the while the bear continued to dance, stepping back and forth, back and forth. The music troupe, led by a rotund, self-assured, black-goateed lutist, stood up and started playing "She Loves Cream, He Loves Pie," which kicked up a roar from the Struvans in the hall. Some of the men left the benches and started to dance, edging precariously close to the bear. The lutist took to the floor to offer encouragement. It wasn't long until he was the closest to the moonbear of all.

"That string-plucker is twice as brave as yours is," Lord Dante leaned over and remarked to Gregor. "Or twice as intoxicated."

Gregor did not respond, though his eyes went searching for Silas O' the Songs. He spotted the songsmith sitting on a back bench, looking forlorn without his instrument. *We have been too careless with this man's spirit. I had best make amends.*

Gregor continued to study Silas. He thought at first that the reason for his transfixion was that he could not see Silas's skull. But the longer he looked, the more convinced he grew that it was something else. Silas was sitting so far in the back of the hall that he was recessed in shadows, like a man strung between this dimension and the realm of dreams. And then it seemed that Gregor was slipping into a dreamspace, that meditative place, as all around Silas O' the Songs large orange leaves began to fall, dull, lifeless things, except for one brilliant exception that twirled and danced and swooped and fell into the very center of Silas, suffusing him with a blindingly bright light—

"Yot kuho! Yot kuho! Fiv pla sfuka yot kuho!"

The sudden chant brought Gregor back into the present. He translated the words from Old Ontish.

"A kiss! A kiss! Give the moon a kiss!"

The cry was taken up by the Kalandragotans. "She Loves Cream, He Loves Pie" had ended, but the lutist was still playing, a riff seemingly intended for the ears of the denizens of the peninsula, who persisted with their chant in tune and time. Men across the hall wearing frostflower surcoats lifted great pewter cups and sloshed black-gold mead onto the floor, oblivious to all but the rising call: *"Yot kuho! Yot kuho! Fiv pla sfuka yot kuho!"* Their collective energies, Gregor noted, were centered on the dais. For a confused second the Sagekind thought that they were encouraging Cato to kiss Wulfess, but then, to his surprise, Wren Ollspaer rose from her seat, and the chant exploded into cheers.

Lord Horos Ollspaer's sister swept down from the dais, looking like a cross between a soldier and a lady of grace. Gregor, as perplexed as the other non-natives in the hall, watched in silent wonder as Wren moved purposefully toward the moonbear, her steps falling in time to the beat of the steady clap forming on Kalandragotan hands. Watching her, Gregor couldn't help but think that she was Beoliotius in the flesh, come down from Owoervyrn to walk Ragar Or. Oh, how she made a show of it! Every step exacting, no sign of fear on her face, drawing ever closer to the beast.

A kiss for the moonbear? She couldn't possibly— Gregor's thoughts were interrupted by the inexorable reality of what was taking place. The beast had by now taken note, and was watching Wren approach while sitting back on its haunches; Gregor could not tell if the bear was perplexed or simply being patient. Worried where this was heading, Gregor gently reached out to the bear in the jeyedoshi manner, but the bear gave him nothing, or had nothing to give.

Wren was yards away now. The clapping ceased. The last few steps, it seemed, were hers alone to take. But no…the goateed lutist brought his instrument into the game, striking up an exotic flourish of notes, and, in a rush, moved closer to the moonbear with soft, swift steps. Wren Ollspaer moved with him, and together they swept into the bear's orbit. Wren leaned in, the bear leaned down, while the lutist stood to the side, weaving the musical magic that stitched the scene together…and then the kiss, delivered to the moonbear's nose, followed by the crashing thunder of huzzahs and applause.

Wren turned her back on the bear and retreated out of the animal's reach with a confident unconcern. Back on the dais, she turned to the roaring hall and soaked in their adulation with a face of stone. A bow seemed in order, but she did not give it, which only fueled the frenzy. Thirty seconds of this and she gave the hall her back, the same as she had the moonbear. The roaring persisted even as she retook her seat.

The second course arrived amid the hubbub. It was a salad of sorts in the Kalandragote fashion, thin slices of moonbear meat over a bed of rutabaga, cabbage and radishes, with a crushed ilkberry glaze. Gregor passed over the moonbear meat but made a smear of the ilkberry with his fork. A new chant was growing in the hall, the same as the old one, only this time the non-Kalandragotans were joining in. *"Yot kuho! Yot kuho! Fiv pla sfuka yot kuho!"* There was a manic madness brewing, Gregor knew, some sickness of the mob, but he was determined to try the ilkberry before the illness manifested. Its bruised colors did not disappoint, enrapturing his tongue with its cosmic sweetness. He had read in books that it was Owoervyrn's own fruit, planted by Beoliotius beneath the snows of Kalandragote even in the time before her sons Daguss and Ropske arrived.

The chant intensified. The energy of the benches once again focused on the dais. Gregor leaned forward between mouthfuls of the salad and looked down the table. Cato Ollspaer was in conversation with his bonded-to-be, the future Lady of Kalandragote, Wulfess Salk. A moment later, Wren Ollspaer joined in the conversation, and a decision was reached.

When the startling beauty from High Osgood stood, the benches exploded. More sloshing mead, fists pounding tables, standing salutes. The only indifferent being in the hall was the moonbear, who had settled once more onto his hindquarters.

Unlike Wren, Wulfess did not sweep down from the dais. Instead, she made a study of the benches, surveying the room with spellbinding blue eyes before teasing out a smile. The effect was more feminine than Wren's but no less powerful. The deliberateness with which Wulfess went about her business brought the moment under her control. A hush fell over the hall. Without a word, Wulfess stood and removed the cloak of black fur that she was wearing and placed it on the back of the chair. Then she descended from the dais in front of the table, presenting herself to the moonbear like a sacrifice with a bowed head.

The energy seemed to turn. "Don't do it, my lady!" came a shout from the crow camp. Wulfess paid it no mind. Even in her riding leathers, Wulfess was a vision. She wore tall, burned-brown leather boots that emphasized her above-average height. Her dark-blond hair was braided, plait after perfect plait, coming to rest at the deep small of her back. The wear of the journey north was on her, though it had done little to diminish her ineffable essence. The effect was one of rugged refinement, captivating precisely because of the contrast, the raw beauty of her being not at odds with the moment but infused with an uncertain friction. The friction being: was the future Lady of Kalandragote equal to the city's bizarre customs?

Wulfess approached the moonbear with a greater caution than Wren. The bear seemed unnervingly attuned to her; it dropped from its hindquarters onto all fours, waiting on her arrival with the lead of its snout. When it did this, Wulfess raised her head, and for a second it seemed that the sight of the bear had stopped her in her tracks. But the halt was only a hiccup. For in the next moment, Wulfess continued apace, determined on whatever destiny the moonbear had in store for her.

Gregor could not see Wulfess's skull, but his heartbeat galloped nonetheless as she entered the moonbear's orbit. He feared that disaster would befall her. But then, in a rush, the previous pattern repeated itself. The lutist followed Wulfess into the moonbear's circle, striking up the same hypnotic collection of notes. Wulfess arrived at the bear, the beast's eyes glazed in a musical haze…lips met snout, like a grazing arrow…and then it was over, the lovely wonder of Wulfess Salk striding confidently out of harm's way, into the warm shower of the great hall's approval.

The third course was a stuffed capsquash loaded with sausage, sage, pomegranate seeds, cheese, apple slices, and mushrooms. Gregor removed the cap and set to eating the contents sitting inside the perfect bowl of the capsquash's hard casing. While Gregor ate, he watched the goateed lutist, who had retreated out of the bear's reach and was playing "Winter's Lament," a traditional Ontish folk song. The moonbear, untethered to this particular number, lay down on the floor like a dog, its head between its front paws.

"I daresay, Sagekind, this lutist is not only braver than yours, it seems that he plays a greater role in the fate of nobles, no?" A needle of laughter escaped Dante Heron's thin lips. "What do you think? If the lutist misplayed a note, would the moonbear break from its spell and set to slaughter?"

Gregor was loath to speak with Lord Dante but inclined to agree with him. "The bear dances to the lutist's song, Lord Dante. That much is clear."

Out among the benches, a general bonhomie was on display. From all appearances, the sight of Wren Ollspaer and Wulfess Salk kissing the moonbear was helping forge bonds of friendship among the many different factions in the room. But included in the bonhomie was also a sliver of unfulfilled desire, the collective sense that one additional kiss was necessary to seal the pact. A new chant began to build, starting in the section of the double suns. Struvans shouting in Old Ontish. Gregor scarce believed the men could be so stupid.

"Yot kuho! Yot kuho! Fiv pla sfuka yot kuho!"

"A kiss! A kiss! Give the moon a kiss!"

There was only one woman remaining on the dais who had yet to participate in the ritual.

Queen Anjay.

Gregor looked down the table, trying to capture the attention of either the king or the queen. *This must not happen,* he thought, but already a sense of helplessness was setting in. Neither of the skulls looked his way, but instead conferred with Wren Ollspaer and Wulfess Salk. Gregor's thoughts grew frantic. *This is a setup. The lutist will play the wrong song, setting the moonbear on the queen, and then the massacre will begin…*

Queen Anjay stood. The great hall cheered, and chanted, *"Yot kuho! Yot kuho! Fiv pla sfuka yot kuho!" I have to put a stop to this,* Gregor thought. He pushed his chair back and rose to his feet, at last drawing King Micah's attention. His brother read his thoughts in an instant and responded with a glare full of fire, fury and self-evident meaning. Lord Dante, attuned to the interaction, chimed in darkly.

"Sometimes not even the Sagekind can stop events from unfolding."

Gregor stood frozen. He watched as Queen Anjay, like Wren and Wulfess before her, transformed into the version of herself that rose to the occasion. She was a relatively short woman, the compactness of her being reflected in the way she bundled up her emotions, becoming, within the span of a few short seconds, the epitome of equipoise. Her hard, hazel eyes gleamed like golden chaff within the deep-set sickle of her face, promising that she, too, could put on a performance.

The impending moment sprang into motion. Gregor, knees buckling, mind whirring, sat back down and tried to formulate a plan. His thoughts went first to the three great hearth fires, and the damage he might do to the moonbear with the flames, but the beast, perhaps sensing his thoughts, gave a disconcerting growl, causing Gregor to retreat. The growl gave

Queen Anjay no pause; she was already committed to her course. The energy of the great hall was behind her.

Gregor thought Queen Anjay looked like a sennequi piece moving across the floor, the hem of her cloak gliding over the gray stone. There was fear in her eyes, but also confidence that she would prevail. The moonbear reverted to its rocking step while awaiting her, a more ominous posture than Wren and Wulfess had encountered.

But that was before the lutist intervened. With Anjay's last few steps the goateed musician constructed for her a bridge of moonbear-soothing music…the beast's eyes softened, lulled once more under the spell…and Gregor's heart relaxed as it became clear there was no ploy, no plot, at least not so far as the moonbear was concerned.

Queen Anjay moved in for the kiss.

THAWOMP!

A thrown capsquash exploded against the moonbear's head. The sight was surreal, confusing: for a brief second Gregor thought that a large beetle had flown into the moonbear's head and exploded. The bear, its snout only inches from Queen's Anjay's lips, reared back in a stunned confusion, enraged at being awoken from its lute-wrought dream. Orange foodstuff colored its face. The moonbear whipped its head side to side, looking for the perpetrator. Overwhelmed by the choices, it decided that the person before it must be the culprit.

Gregor reached for the flames in the hearth fire. His work had to be done quickly, too quickly…in his haste he didn't channel the heat from the flames so much as hurl it…fire found moonbear flesh but didn't settle, caroming off into the ether. The moonbear roared, less in agony than in compounded rage. The beast's great claw came crashing down. Queen

Anjay was sent spinning like a top, two times around before falling to the ground. The moonbear reeled, staggered, stumbled to its left. Gregor kept his eyes on the queen, grasping at the best way to intervene, while the moonbear, alive in the wake of a fading pain and at last returned to its own mind, ran into the lutist with the black goatee.

Gregor, watching the queen, didn't see the start of the mauling. But the musicless screams of the lutist were too powerful to ignore. Gregor looked up to see the lutist's face in the moonbear's jaws, his instrument fallen from his hands. Around the hall, men from assorted houses rushed forward with their swords drawn, hurrying to plunge their fire-gleaming blades into the moonbear's flesh.

Johanna Salk

Johanna paced the ribbon of morning sunlight that split the room in two. She had been expecting Lady Wenavere to return Easton to her for hours on end, but now night had become morning, and still the Dayborn prince was gone. She hated how she felt, cooped up in the room. It was like she was in the Cherry Tower again, a prisoner to others' plans.

Be patient. And trusting. Easton is your bonded now. Lady Wenavere can say what she will; when all is said and done, Easton will talk it over with you.

But as the morning blossomed, so did Johanna's fears. It didn't help that Johanna had heaps of memories about the way Lady Wenavere used to manipulate Nicholas into doing her bidding. Easton Dayborn was no Nicholas Raleigh, but all the same Johanna wasn't excited to relive the experience of following up with her bonded after the formidable Wenavere Raleigh had spent time alone with him.

Damn her. I should have insisted on coming along, I should not have sat passively by while she whisked him—

A knock on the door interrupted her line of thought. She shouted "Come in!", and the door opened: a slow, creaking, almost apologetic aperture. Johanna rushed over, hopeful, but by the time she reached the door, the reason for the diffident opening had revealed itself in full.

"Your Light?"

"My dearest Johanna." Shupert Press was all soft smiles and magnificent eyebrows, a warm wash of benevolence. "I hope that my visiting you is okay. I thought that we might talk, while the prince and Lady Wenavere are away."

"Away?"

"Yes. She took him to the encampment outside of town."

Johanna felt her face go flush. Lady Wenavere and her retinue of armed men hadn't explained where they were taking Easton; Johanna had drawn the conclusion that they were nearby on her own. *How foolish of me.* Her ungenerous side wanted to blame Easton, but the more rational side understood that Lady Wenavere had likely given him little choice. *And to think that that woman is at the head of an army now,* Johanna thought, suppressing a shudder.

Shupert sidestepped Johanna's discomfort. "My dear, it is so good to see you! I apologize that I was unable to express my sentiments more fully yesterday, but, as you might imagine, your sudden and unexpected presence caught me off guard. Not to mention my shock at discovering that you are now bonded to a prince of the realm!" He moved deeper into the room. "You must tell me how this came about!"

Johanna knew that he would report everything she said back to the Lady Wenavere, but all the same, she wanted to share her story. Or at least parts of it. "The decision was made back at Coffyn Castle that we would be bonded. By my father, and his."

"And you were amenable to the idea?"

She smiled on the inside as she replayed her memories of their first few days together. "At first, I thought him a scamp, truth be told. But with our bonding a seeming inevitability, we made use of each other the best we knew how. We decided to flee Coffyn Castle together and bond on our own terms. And in the course of our journey south, we fell in love along the way."

The smile that was in her heart made its way to her lips. Shupert, conversely, pursed his lips into a small frown. "When you say that you are bonded to the boy, what exactly do you mean? Was there a…ceremony?"

She fought the red from returning to her face. "Yes."

"With witnesses?"

Bitterboy. Cloudy. The birds in the trees and the animals of the forest. "We bound our hands together and we said the words. We may have been alone in the woods when it happened, but there are many who have done the same, and they are no less bonded for it."

Shupert chuckled. "Yes, that may be true, but I daresay those couples don't have the surnames Salk and Dayborn." He brought his palms together as if in prayer. "No matter. It is a problem easily rectified. I will speak to Lady Wenavere, and we will bond the two of you again in a Stavusian temple, with witnesses on hand. It would be my honor to perform the ceremony for you for a second time." Shupert lowered his head and leaned toward her. "I have always hurt for you, my lady, after what happened to our beloved Nicholas. To see you in love again, and with a man born to the faith…it does my heart good."

A man born to the faith. Is he talking about Easton? Johanna fought to keep from laughing. She knew that what the old priest really meant was that Easton was Struvan born, and therefore Stavusian by default, but the thought of her beloved as a true believer was almost too ludicrous to let pass. *And what do you think about me, dear priest? That because I am Ontish-born,*

I am a heretic? Upon reflection, she realized that Shupert had always treated her like a convert. She supposed it was simply because he liked her. *And because he has never heard me defend the faith of the Twins.* The truth of her feelings about Ragar Or's two faiths were, like Easton's, infinitely more complex, but she saw no advantage in having that conversation at this particular moment.

"When Easton returns, he and I will discuss what you've said together." She could see the wisdom of a public bonding ceremony, though in her mind, Union was a more fitting locale than Hornwell.

"Yes. Of course." Shupert held her gaze with a peculiar intensity. "You will follow up on Easton's discussion with Lady Wenavere, and we will go from there."

He thinks he knows more than I do about what will happen next. Still, she saw no point in correcting him. Shupert was a kind old soul, and no doubt believed that he had her best interest at heart. *He will learn…just as Lady Wenavere will learn…that Easton and I are a team.*

Shupert moved over to the bed. "Do you mind?" he asked, ever polite, motioning that he wanted to sit. "My faith is as strong as ever, my lady, but my knees are weak."

"Certainly," she replied.

The Hawk's-Eye, a below-average-sized man, looked even smaller once seated: his white robe with its blue piping bunched up to reveal birdlike ankles. Below the ankles, the priest's sandaled feet barely touched the floor. Johanna hadn't noticed it yesterday in the waning sunlight, but His Light's white-colored beard had patches of gray, giving his face the appearance of a cloudbank precipitant with rain.

"It is a terrible thing to grow old, Lady Johanna. Life is a giving, but it is a taking as well. Some days all I see before me is the great reaping of my vigor and vitality, harvested in service of my approaching death."

Johanna was taken aback. The Shupert that she remembered did not dwell in negativity. "You do not look *that* old, Your Light."

The priest gave Johanna a grin that reminded her of Easton's shit-eating smile. "Then you are not looking closely, my dear. I have always had an old look—bald and bearded and stamped with crow's-feet at the corners of my eyes—but when we first met, it was half a disguise. I still had strength back then, hidden beneath my priestly robes. But now…now…"—he pointed to his temple—"Stavus has stripped me of all save my mind. I believe it is because he wants me to focus my energies there."

Johanna smiled, not knowing what to say. She was wearing the beige cloak given to her by Mariva, but not the hood. Unconscious of her actions, she angled her body so that the priest was facing the side of her head with the full length of hair.

"You have fought your own battles in life, have you not?" Shupert continued. He gave Johanna a heartfelt look of the utmost sincerity. "I hope you know that I have long admired you, Lady Johanna. To be born a twin in that pagan land, to be branded a lesser twin by your own father…why, it is a sign of an impressive inner strength that you have managed to retain a sense of self in spite of these trials. When Nicholas died, and you were made to return north, I prayed to Stavus that he would not forsake you, that he would shine a light down a path that would return you to us. And now…here you are. Returned at a time when Ragar Or seems headed toward a showdown between the pagan forces of Twin worship and the true light of Stavus. I can't help but think that Stavus has chosen you to help convince the people of this land to turn away from Twin worship once and for all."

Hearing the image of her that the Hawk's-Eye had in his mind made Johanna feel uneasy. "Your Light, I am *Ontish*-born. And while it is true that I hold little stock in the faith of the Twins, that does not make me—"

"I know you, Lady Johanna," Shupert interrupted, the flame of passion in his eyes. "You are a good person with a good soul, a creature of the light. I have known this about you from the instant I first laid eyes on you in Goldleaf Keep. Stavus sees it too… I feel it in my soul that he intends to use you—"

"Your Light, please—"

"—as an instrument—"

"ENOUGH!" Her voice was tinged with thunder, her body aflame with the same frightening energy that she had conjured the day she killed the woods witch. For the briefest of moments, she felt the elements flying to her, awaiting her command. But then she looked at the astonished priest and the moment passed. On an impulse, she reached over and took Shupert's hand in both of hers. "Please forgive me, Your Light. I do love and admire the Stavusian faith, truly…it was a comfort to me when I first came to Thistleton. It is only…"

"It is only what?"

It is only that I am a jeyedoshi. "It is only that my surname is Salk. I could not possibly be what you are asking me to be. It would rupture my soul."

Shupert recruited his free hand and placed it on top of Johanna's. He claimed that he was a frail, old man, but she could still feel the strength in his grip. "My Lady, I say to you now with all my affection: your attachment to your birth family is a luxury that you cannot keep. The time draws near when the people of this land will have to choose between the two religions. I know you, Johanna Salk. In your heart, you have already chosen. Save yourself a good deal of suffering, and make the change in your mind as well."

They rode out together to the Raleigh encampment. Johanna felt like herself again on Bitterboy's back, sitting high above the priest on his mule. A bold gust of wind tugged at the hood of her cloak, daring Johanna to show the truth of her hair, but the strength Bitterboy had imparted to her only went so far. She kept the hood on tight.

The air was crisp and clean, full of sunlight and birdsong. Outside of the Stavusian temple, Winged Women were cleaning the stained glass. As they worked, they infused the glasswork with the lifeforce of the sun, making an alchemy of light and color. When Shupert passed by, the women acknowledged him by joining their voices in song. Johanna recognized the hymn from her bonding day to Nicholas Raleigh: "Into the Blue." Despite Johanna's best efforts at resistance, the melody wormed its way into her brain and continued playing there on a loop even after they had moved out of hearing distance.

Once on the main road, they made their way south, opposite the gate where Johanna and Easton had entered the town. The citizens of Hornwell gathered in growing clusters as they went. *Word has gotten out,* Johanna thought, glimpsing at the gawkers. Only twice, however, did the onlookers vocalize their thoughts. The first came from a woman who shouted "A great blessing on the Houses Dayborn and Salk!" She was met with no response. The fellow who yelled "Show us the favor of your face, my lady!", however, was greeted with murmurs of approval. When Johanna put the people at her back without a response, it sounded as if some of the murmurs turned to hisses, though it was difficult to discern with the hood pulled tight over her ears.

Inside the camp, the Raleigh soldiers were equally curious. They pressed close in their red chevron surcoats, looking up into Johanna's hood, trying to identify her. She thought she recognized a few faces from her time in Thistleton. "Make way!" Shupert said again and again. The soldiers did as they were told, although Johanna had a feeling it was the swaggering Bitterboy that they moved aside for, and not Shupert Press.

In the center of the camp was a grand red-and-white pavilion. Off to the side of the pavilion, a quartet of men stood opposite an archery butt. Johanna noted, with some surprise, that Easton was one of the four, though, upon closer inspection, he looked like a man apart, his stance somehow in opposition to the trio. Johanna's former mother-in-law, Lady Wenavere, was standing back from the group, taking in the competition with apparent concern. As Johanna and Shupert drew close, a large man wearing a red-and-black-mottled overcoat loosed an off-target arrow, followed by a nasty imprecation. The oath was strong enough to make the priest flinch.

"Fuck all to the Bottom Black!" He tossed his bow and quiver of arrows to the ground and stormed off.

"And the vulture flies away!" Easton announced with false cheeriness. Johanna's couldn't help but notice that his words belied an expression of grim determination. Something serious was afoot. But then all was put on pause as everyone noticed the horses and looked up.

"Good morning, my beloved bonded," Johanna said to Easton, trying to strike a note of unconcern.

"Johanna?" Easton looked surprised to see her there. He walked over and helped her down from Bitterboy. Lady Wenavere followed him. The two remaining archers held back, studying Johanna from afar.

"What have I happened upon? An impromptu archery tournament?"

Easton broke out his signature smile, although Johanna couldn't help but notice that it was abnormally tight around the edges. "Something like that. I'm in the process of winning back a horse." The faintest whiff of alcohol was on his breath.

Johanna cast a quick glance at Lady Wenavere. The ever-present haughtiness in her bearing was complemented by a rather pointed expression of disdain.

"Winning *back* a horse?" Johanna asked, confused. "When did you *lose* a horse?"

Easton shook his head, then turned and gestured at his two remaining opponents. One was wearing the gold and brown of House Chesterly, and the other a stylish brocaded green. "Lady Johanna, allow me to introduce you to Richard Chesterly, the scion of his house, and Philemon Yurk, a swindler in exile from all reputable parts of the kingdom. Philemon owes my brother Ajax a horse, a debt that I am on the verge of collecting." He turned to the two men. "Lord Chesterly, Philemon, meet my newly bonded: the Lady Johanna, daughter of Lord Daguss Salk."

Richard Chesterly gave Johanna a reluctant half bow. Philemon, seemingly unfazed by the accusations leveled against him, put down his bow and walked over for a more personal greeting. He carried himself with a genteelness that was at odds with his crooked spine and spongy, outward-growing ears. The odor of alcohol was stronger on him, but not egregiously so.

"The Lady Johanna Salk," he said, reaching for her hand. "I must say that the only that thing could exceed my surprise at finding Easton Dayborn in Lady Wenavere's camp is being introduced to a Salk as his newly bonded." She noticed him eyeing her hair, although he didn't comment on it.

Johanna struggled to parse Philemon's tone. She gave him her hand for a cursory moment, then took it back.

"What's this about a horse?"

Philemon gave a tactful smile. "An old accusation. And a false one. It concerns a now rather infamous horse race through the streets of Union involving Lord Dante Heron and Easton's brother, the crown prince. Prince Ajax's horse had the misfortune of collapsing before completing its circuit, costing Ajax a certain victory. In the ensuing fallout, I took the blame."

"The horse died from eating snakegrass," Easton added. His voice had acquired a hard edge. "We found the poisonous weed in Silverwing's stall afterward. Just a handful of snakegrass and a horse's heart will explode. Two separate servants testified that they saw Philemon sneak into the horse's stall in the hours leading up to the race."

"Circumstantial evidence," Philemon stated. "Lord Dante sent me into the stables with sugar cubes for his steed."

"The king found you guilty," Easton rejoindered.

"Not formally. My exile from the capital was a matter of prejudice, not evidence. Your father admitted as much."

"He made clear what his opinion was."

"Yes…well…someone must take the fall when the royal family is involved."

"No one thought to question Lord Dante?" Johanna asked.

Easton answered with a clenched jaw. "My brother wouldn't hear of it. And when it was discovered that Philemon had placed a sizable bet on Dante's horse to win the race, that was deemed motivation enough for him to have acted alone."

Philemon gave an insouciant shrug and a grin that stopped just short of being apologetic. "Prince Easton has the right of it there. I did win an impressive amount of money that day. But I fear we risk boring Lady Johanna with our digressions. Come, Prince Easton. Let's finish this."

Easton gave Johanna a quick kiss. "Bear with me, my love. It's been a long night, but I'm on the verge of righting an injustice." Then he turned and walked back to the firing line, leaving Johanna with Lady Wenavere.

The scowl on Wenavere's face failed to dissipate at Easton's leaving. If anything, it deepened. "Fools. Your bonded, especially. I bring him into a camp full of allies and he has the temerity to treat them like foes. It's no wonder the Dayborns are losing their grip on the realm." She sighed and cut her gaze away from Johanna. "But I should be careful talking to you, shouldn't I? Who knows where your loyalties lie?"

Johanna felt her face go hot. "My loyalties lie with my bonded."

Wenavere scoffed. "I might believe you were you not once a part of my family. Your loyalties were certainly never with my son."

Johanna felt the keen sting of the attack. "That is unfair! I was loyal to Nicholas from the day we were bonded until the day death parted us!"

"Not with your whole heart, you weren't."

Johanna had to stop herself from saying *It's different with Easton.* Stifling the impulse, she measured her words. "You and I have the same goal, goodmother. We want to protect the Dayborn dynasty and to preserve Union."

Lady Wenavere tossed her head, and with it her braid of red hair. "Time will tell," she responded with a snort of derision. She then looked up at Shupert Press, sitting atop his mule. Something passed between them, but Johanna could not ascertain what it was. A second later Lady Wenavere moved away to watch the remainder of the contest by herself.

"Your goodmother carries a heavy burden now that Lord Wessel has passed," the priest said in a sober voice once Wenavere was out of hearing distance. "Moving an army north on the basis of a letter from the Sagekind, when Thistleton is hounded by pirates from Thralk-Braktur…she treads dangerous ground. She is trying to follow the light, Lady Johanna, but it is difficult when so many around her are touched by the dark."

Johanna saw no point in responding. The priest had a bell to ring, and it was clear that he intended to make it heard.

Over at the firing line, Philemon Yurk retrieved his bow. It was of a princely quality, five feet long and made from harriswood, the exceedingly supple timber found in the scattered forests of the east. Philemon, with his bowed shoulders and crooked spine, looked like the weapon might be too much for him, but when he stepped to the line and drew, it was with a surprising stability. He teased the release for longer than Johanna expected. When at last he let the arrow fly, it flew straight and nearly true, striking the butt a mere three inches off the center target.

“A damn fine shot,” Richard Chesterly barked, making his rooting interest clear. The Chesterlys took the eagle for their standard, but with his golden-brown beard, Richard Chesterly looked more like a lion than a bird.

Easton said nothing. Instead, he moved to take up his position. There were moments when Johanna nearly forgot that Easton was a prince, but this wasn’t one of them. He drew his arrow with a powerful ease, bringing the fletching beside his ear and then holding it there with a perfect stillness. Johanna thought that he looked like the archetype for the model archer, closer to a sculpture than a living, breathing human.

SWOOFT!

Easton’s shot struck the left-hand side of the center target, just inside of Philemon’s effort.

Johanna resisted the urge to cheer. Chesterly frowned. Lady Wenavere didn’t react at all. Only Philemon Yurk responded, with an equanimity that suggested a coolness even in the face of defeat.

“Impressive, Prince Easton.” He turned to Chesterly. “It appears that we are bested, Richard, unless you can skin the prince’s arrow with your own.”

Chesterly offered up a grimace. Johanna worried that he was the ringer of the group, held in reserve until the end, but the instant he stepped to the line, her fears vanished—from the look of his stance, the scion of House Chesterly possessed little natural inclination with a bow. Seemingly aware of his shortcomings, Richard Chesterly settled into his stance over and over again, hoping to get it right. But in the end, his efforts were for naught: his shot struck the butt a good foot wide of the center target.

All eyes turned to Philemon, who gave Prince Easton a generous bow.

"Bested by the Dayborns again. A fate I can only aspire to one day change. You have your choice of steed from my stable, Prince Easton. Or, if you prefer one of the equines belonging to Chesterly or Desighart, they are yours for the taking as well."

"Good," Easton responded. "You may rest assured that I will take care to deprive you of your most valuable steed."

"As you say, my prince."

Johanna felt a twinge of embarrassment for Easton's behavior. Past conflicts aside, didn't he need these men on his side going forward?

Lady Wenavere stepped into the ring of men, the white-and-red-chevron surcoat on her shoulders falling around her like a monument. "The matter of the horse is settled?" She didn't wait for an answer. "Good. Let us retire to the pavilion and continue planning our foray north."

The Lady Raleigh began to walk away, but before she had taken two steps, Easton addressed her. "I am happy to listen to what you have in mind, Lady Wenavere, and I am pleased that you intend to make me privy to your planning. But the Lady Johanna and I will not be traveling north. It is our intention to return to Union and hold my father's seat there."

Lady Wenavere bristled visibly. Before she could respond, Richard Chesterly interjected himself into the conversation. "You intend to hold Union? Ha! With what army, prince? While you have been on your *sweetmarch*, other Struvans have been in the field, working to save your father's kingdom. Perhaps the king's *second son* would be wise to follow the lead of those who have spent these last weeks fighting for the Struvan cause."

The Struvan cause? Before she had fully processed the decision to speak, Johanna found herself entering the fray. "The *Struvan* cause? I believe you mean the cause of Union, don't you? And if I may: why are the two of you here? My understanding is that the Raleighs mobilized after receiving a letter from the Sagekind. That in no way explains why so many easterners are present."

The short but uneasy silence that ensued made the hairs on the back of Johanna's neck stand on end. Philemon ended it with a reply of perfect composure. "We are here thanks to the foresight of Lord Dante Heron, my lady. Before going north, Lord Dante insisted that the eastern houses remain on guard in case our… northern brethren turned on the king. To that end, patrols were organized to keep watch over Struvan lands. We are small in number, but we travel quickly. A short while back, we intercepted the knight returning with Wessel Raleigh's reply to the Sagekind. Armed with the knowledge from that letter, we moved quickly west to meet up with the Raleighs and offer our assistance."

Easton responded darkly. "How dare Lord Dante command armed men to move about the country without my father's leave."

"And yet the wisdom of it seems self-evident now, does it not? Forgive me, my prince, but your father is lacking of late when it comes to making decisions that are in the best interests of the realm. It is only natural that men of quality like Lord Dante have stepped up to…bridge the gap."

Johanna was taken aback by the brazenness of it all. She was long accustomed to hearing Ontishmen speak dismissively of the Dayborn king, but to hear the same from Struvans was deeply unsettling. It suggested that the position of the Dayborns was more tenuous than she had imagined.

"You forget that I know you, Philemon," Easton said, his voice cold now as well as dark. "You and Lord Dante. I am not my brother or my father. When I hear a hiss, I see a snake."

To Johanna's surprise, Shupert Press weighed in from his mule. "My prince, please, we are friends here, sons and daughters of Stavus—"

"Kings and princes have no friends," Easton interrupted. "Only loyal and disloyal subjects."

"You're the one gallivanting around the country with the Ontish traitor's daughter at your side." Chesterly again. His comment was clearly meant to draw blood. Easton took it in kind, moving his hand to the pommel of his sword.

"You will take that back, sir. Or you will pay for it."

Events were spiraling out of control. Johanna felt the need to do something before blood was spilled. "Enough!" she shouted. She quickly made her way to Easton's side and placed a hand on his sword arm, both in a show of solidarity *and* to keep him from drawing his weapon. She then turned to address Chesterly. "I understand your concerns, Lord Chesterly. If what the Sagekind wrote was true, then I *am* the daughter of a traitor. It is no reflection of where my loyalties lie, but I understand your apprehension."

From the unchanged look on his face, her words hadn't moved Richard Chesterly. But they did compel Shupert Press. "Oh, my dear. My dearest dear." The priest climbed down from the mule and hurried to Johanna's side as fast as he could with his old-man's shuffle. Before Johanna knew what was happening, Shupert had taken up position beside her in a show of support. "Loyal you are, my dear. Loyal indeed. And a true child of the light, as our good friends here will come to know once they are in your company for a time."

She was tempted to protest—particularly the part about her being a 'true child of the light'—but her words combined with the priest's had so effectively stamped out the possibility of violence that it seemed unwise to undercut them. She had put Easton off balance, while the priest's intervention seemed to have quieted Richard Chesterly. As for Philemon Yurk, it was impossible to tell what he was thinking, but, for the moment at least, he was holding his tongue. Slowly, the energy shifted to Lady Wenavere, who appeared poised to weigh in on the matter.

She measured her words carefully. "By all means, gooddaughter, prove the priest true. Stay with us, and talk sense into your bonded. Or continue on your sweetmarch. It's naught to me. But know this: if you and Prince Easton do leave, I will leave too. And if I leave, I'm taking my men with me back to Thistleton." She turned and made for the pavilion, loosing one last volley as she went. "It's past time the Dayborns understand that if they have no use for their allies, their allies will have no use for them."

Silas O' the Songs

Not again.

Wulfess, gloriously naked above him, stopped moving at the sound of the knock on the door. A different woman would have panicked. But not Wulfess Salk. Instead, she savored one additional stroke of their joined bodies before pushing off him. Then, with glinting blue eyes and a devilish smile, she whispered, "Off to the wardrobe with you," before addressing whoever was at the door with characteristic authority. "A minute. Mind your knuckles!" She moved unhurriedly from the bed and began to dress, with all apparent unconcern for morals and guilt and what might happen if Silas was discovered.

Silas displayed no such calm. He fumbled at his breeches, fumbled at his shirt, and nearly fell as he stumbled for the safety of the wardrobe. The inside of the wardrobe was as he had left it two days before, a sensual pleasure of the finest silks and furs and a heady hint of Wulfess Salk's ineffable scent; but all the same it was a hidey-hole, the place where Silas would meet his end if the wrong person discovered him there.

Two days ago, the visitor had been Wulfess's father, Lord Daguss Salk. The horror of that half hour—the fear Silas had felt while in hiding and the unnerving conversation he had heard between daughter and father—

remained imprinted on his psyche. That same day, he had resolved to end his tryst with Wulfess. And but for the potential repercussions, he would have.

If I make an enemy of Wulfess, then who will be for me? He was already out of favor with the Dayborns. After the moonbear attack on Queen Anjay, the king had raged against him. "It's not you, it never was you! The lutist the leaf prophesied is now dead! And Anjay soon to follow! Damn you to the Bottom Black, Silas O' the Songs!" Were it not for the Sagekind's intervention, Silas was fairly certain the king would have had him executed. Grateful as he was to Gregor Thorn, it was of little consolation. Silas could see for himself how hated the Wraith in Red was. In the long run, Silas saw little advantage in tying his fortunes to a pariah.

The door to the wardrobe opened. Silas, his stomach a coil of agitated snakes, thought for a second that he had been discovered. Any second he expected sharp steel to probe through the fabrics in search of his tender flesh. But instead, Wulfess sat Silas's boots inside. *My boots!* The Yubriy leaf was stuffed into the toe of the left boot. He could hardly believe his carelessness.

Calm yourself. Outside the wardrobe he heard Wulfess crossing the room. Opening the door. *She hasn't even let them inside yet, you fool.* He listened for the sound of a second voice over the hammering of his heart. But it was Wulfess who spoke first.

"My bonded-to-be. Dare I hope that you've come to my room to renege on your vow to be chaste until our bonding ceremony?"

Silas's heart leapt into his throat. *Cato.* The man was a mountain made flesh, the sort of individual it was impossible to look at without imagining the violent sufferings he was capable of inflicting on others. Cato's demeanor was enigmatic enough that it was difficult to ascertain his inclination toward violence, but the ambiguity of his outward behavior was more than offset by the sheer ferocity of his look. This stood in contrast to someone like Madrig. The mute may have been a slightly bigger man than Cato, but the sight of him didn't cause Silas to instantly imagine the sound of bones breaking.

"Stop tempting me, woman. It's as I've said. Until our bonding day, I will remain pure. But then, rest assured, I will take what is mine."

"That's a shame," Wulfess responded with a cheeky boldness. "And here I am so ripe to be taken."

Cato ignored her overtures. "I come from my *hestrum*."

"And what did Wren Ollspaer have to say?"

"She said that my father is planning a surprise for our bonding ceremony. She wanted to warn me."

"Warn you? You Kalandragotans do surprises differently. Tell me, what manner of surprise does Horos have in mind?"

"A twin-death ceremony. One in which I will be expected to fight. He has an opponent in mind, but Wren doesn't know who. There are dealings going on…talking… Wren says that my father and Lord Heron are meeting regularly in private. My father was upset when he discovered that your sister and King Micah's second son were given permission to be bonded. I thought you and your father should know."

Silas didn't like the sound of that. If he had learned anything from listening to Wulfess's conversation with her father, it was that the powers of the realm were eager to move against one another. It seemed only their mutual distrust of each other's motives that was keeping the knives at bay.

"What is your father trying to do? Have you killed?"

Cato gave a disdainful snort. "If he means to kill me in a twin-death ceremony, then he'd have best summoned the Firewalker from his jeyedoshi grave. No, there's something else going on. Some scheming with the Heron."

Another short silence. Silas detected the soft sounds of Wulfess on the move. When next she spoke, it sounded as if she had moved to the bed. He had little difficulty imagining her lying in a seductive repose. "Your *hestrum* is wise to confide in you. Wren sees what is obvious. Your father lost Kalandragote during the Blackstar Rebellion. It's all but yours now." Silas could almost hear her smile. "All but ours."

A silence yet again, this one sexual in nature. Cato crossing the room. The sounds of kissing. Silas's hammering heart burned with a sudden jealousy. He knew more than he cared to about Cato's refusal to have sex with Wulfess before their bonding day, but that made it no easier for Silas to accept that they were indulging in different physical pleasures at that very moment.

At last, the exchange of affections ended. Cato's voice claimed the air. "My father was half a madman before I left Kalandragote. Wren assures me that his condition has worsened. He's weakened and wounded, angry at being made a lord, obsessed with what it means to be a Twin Ascendant. He once saw in me the continuation of his legacy. But now that I've succeeded in saving Kalandragote, he sees only betrayal."

There was pain in Cato's voice. The note was subtle, but it was there.

Wulfess heard it as well. She modulated her tone accordingly. "Your father is a sad and angry fool. His son, however, is strong enough to see the world for what it is. That's why you made an alliance to save your people. That's why you are bonding a woman who will be your partner in bringing about a new Kalandragote."

"Yes. I have made my choices. But what of your father?" The sudden anger in Cato's voice caused Silas's butt cheeks to clench. "Now that we have reached the crucial moment, does he have the guts to make a choice? There are days when I cannot determine if he is the strongest man in the kingdom or the weakest. He stands in the middle of all, seeming never to move. I can no longer tell if he is poised and patient or a coward."

"Lord Daguss Salk is a man apart. When he makes his move, others scarce see them."

"So you say. But what I see is the man I have allied myself with undermined, again and again. Dunning Harbor was a disaster. Your father with Ontish blood on his sword, fawning to that Struvan travesty of a king. I'm not joking when I say that I was half tempted to join in with Reginal Burntree's rebellion. He was at least a man who died on principle, defending the Twin Ascendant. Unlike me. I stand adrift, caught between my father's madness and your father's supposed cunning. For all I know that's where I'll be left when the dam breaks, waiting for your father to *make his move* while swords are plunged into my back."

This was new. Cato Ollspaer's stone-faced public demeanor had given no hint to his private dissatisfactions.

"Answer me this, beloved," Wulfess said in a soft voice. "Who threw the capsquash at the moonbear at the welcome feast? The one that has the Struvan queen at death's door?"

The question seemed to throw Cato off his footing. "How should I know? Some say it was a drunk cloaked in the garb of the double suns, others a man of the Garstrings, and yet others that it was one of my father's retainers, a servant of Winterworn Castle who took offense to the Dayborn queen participating in our ritual."

"It was one of the three, yes. *One*. Why the false allegations against the other two?"

"I'm not sure. It was crowded in the great hall. Chaotic. Many of the men were drunk, and—"

"My father knows who 'the one' was. While others were rushing to plunge their swords into the moonbear, he got to the bottom of that most pertinent question. Then, even before King Micah's investigation had begun, my father muddied the waters."

"How?"

"Silver. The power of suggestion. Convince one man to testify to a sight, and chances are the five friends standing nearest him will testify to the same. My father has men who are masters at spreading false rumors. They know who to pay, and who to pressure."

"Tell me, then, daughter of Lord Daguss Salk, who was the one?"

"Drop your breeches, and I will."

"Careful, woman. When you make mock of my principles, you make mock of Kalandragote."

"And you make mock of my needs with your piety," she shot right back. "I might remind you that you weren't so stingy with your affections before we entered the peninsula. We Salks don't suffer being spurned. I am no serving wench to be plowed and then ignored."

The silence that followed confounded Silas. *Are they truly angry with one another?* Without seeing their expressions, it was impossible to know.

Cato laughed at last, a hearty, if uncertain, cachinnation. "It's good to know that I'm getting in bed with someone so…fiery."

Wulfess's voice remained barbed. "But since you're not getting into bed this very moment, I think it best if you leave my chambers. Though before you go, know this. The invisible hand of my father will soon move again. As he assured you after the Blackstar Rebellion. As we planned. Don't mistake his distance from the deed for his noninvolvement."

"When? If your father truly considers me an ally, then entrust me with the details. I won't be left out of the loop."

"Come closer, Cato Ollspaer, and in the loop you will be."

The ensuing minute was full of hushed grappling and whispered words, the specifics of which Silas could only guess at. In truth, he was grateful that he couldn't hear. His soul was already overburdened by the many troublesome knowledges in his possession. The last thing he needed was to know what the Salks had in store for their rivals.

Out in the room, it seemed a bargain was struck. Silas heard a sound he had heard a half dozen times before, the trilling, thrilling sound of Wulfess Salk's teasing, tantalizing laughter. It had something of a mockingbird's lilt: edged with an aggressive energy but no less of a delight because of it. She was a woman who tied men up in knots. He wondered if Cato Ollspaer was as tied up as he was.

"Good. I am for it," Silas thought he heard Cato say, followed by footsteps and the sound of the door opening. "Until the morrow, then."

"Until the morrow," Wulfess replied. Then the door closed and quiet fell.

A full minute passed in absolute silence. Silas remained still, not trusting himself to move. Cato might return, or Lord Daguss Salk...or even worse, the Dayborns might somehow discover his perfidy. He imagined what the Sagekind would do to him if he learned that Silas was sleeping with Wulfess

Salk; the memory of Lumpy Head screaming in immolating agony at the Sea Swoon flashed in his mind. *That man is a jeyedoshi, never forget it. He will kill you if he ever learns the truth of what you've done. Burn you alive from the inside. And don't forget: you've done worse than sleep with her.* In his mind's eye, he pictured the Sagekind spying on him while he sung the Yubriy Tree's true message into Wulfess Salk's ears. The thought of it made him shudder.

The wardrobe opened, and Wulfess's hand shot inside. Her nails were sharp as a blade's, stinging against his chest as she grabbed at his shirt, pulling him back out into the room.

Her nails had no more let up with the assault than she pierced him with her eyes. She looked like a feverish warrior-queen, fully surrendered to the spirit of battle. "Now, where were we?"

She exhausted herself on him. Circling high above, distant, detached, transcendent; then finding him with her ethereal blue eyes, grounding, grinding, connecting, melding their skins into one; then leaving again, going wherever women like Wulfess Salk go, leaving Silas to grapple with all the delightful sensations she imparted to his skin while she laughed, high and away, daring him to retrieve her. His hand could not help but try and bring her back, climbing the tower of her ivory torso to lay claim to her breasts. She didn't fight him, and there they rode out the final wave, together and apart, cresting and then crashing on the same shoreline where they had begun: Silas a simple songwriter in the room of a dangerous and powerful princess, trapped by song and circumstance and the pressing wants of the skin.

When it was over, Wulfess rolled off him but didn't go far; she lounged on an elbow and traced distracted circles on his arm, thinking private thoughts. Silas lay in silence and let his mind meander as well. His thoughts went down the line of his former lovers: Abigail and Tess and Anna Josephine Arc and Gay Gracie and Merjy the woods witch and now Wulfess. Wulfess was the second highborn woman that he had slept with, but Silas knew that it was a danger to equate the daughter of Lord Daguss Salk with Anna Josephine, no matter the situational similarities. Anna Josephine's designs on him had always been ephemeral. He sensed that Wulfess's physical attraction to him was destined to be fleeting, too, but he feared she would take far more from him before they were through, the least of which was his song and the most of which might include his soul.

"We make a good music together," Wulfess said suddenly, breaking the silence.

Instead of responding straightaway, Silas looked around the room. They were in a room at the top of Bloodbone Tower, the highest point in Winterworn Castle, even higher than Lord Horos's solar in the Black and White Tower. Unlike the other towers, Bloodbone had an eclectic, eccentric quality, with parts of it outfitted for highborn guests and other parts neglected, broken down. Wulfess's room was the most opulent in the tower, although Silas had heard that Lord Daguss's quarters, commonly referred to as the red room, had a far richer history.

"We do," Silas admitted at last, still refusing to meet Wulfess's eyes. Now that their afternoon tryst was over, he was scared to look at her for fear of the conclusions she might draw from his expression. He had heard too much in the wardrobe these past two days, and he worried of the accounting that might take place if Wulfess stopped to consider all that he knew.

"Still, you're concerned about the position I've put you in." She moved her elbow to his chest and pinned him with a smile that dared him to deny her.

"I-I…" he stuttered, "I don't know what to think, my lady. I know that I enjoy this! And I know that I know how to keep my mouth shut. About this…about everything."

Wulfess gave a little laugh. "You sing a pretty tune, Silas O' the Songs. No one can deny it." She slipped from the bed and crossed the room to the wardrobe. Despite himself, Silas couldn't help but follow the lovely glide of her body as she walked. *You damn fool,* he chastised himself. *You're ogling a lioness. She'll be a stunning sight right up until the moment she devours you.* When he saw that she was donning furs, he stood up from the bed and went for his shirt and breeches.

He had his shirt halfway buttoned up when she spoke again. "The Dayborns have distanced themselves from you entirely since…the queen's mishap?"

Cold beads of sweat formed on Silas's brow. *Yes. Yes. The answer is yes. Tell her what she wants to hear, one simple word.* But when he opened his mouth, he said too much, as always. "The king wants nothing to do with me. He either no longer believes in the Yubriy leaf prophecy, or he's convinced himself that the prophecy was about the other lutist, the one the moonbear mauled. But the Sagekind…feels differently. He still believes that the prophecy…both prophecies…may be referring to me."

"This other prophecy…did the Dayborns reveal to you specifically what it said?"

"No, my lady." It was the truth. The Sagekind had read the prophecy stolen by Gorgostrine Betrard in front of a hundred souls at Saltbend Castle—*a song first sung in the Vake, prolongs the line of the suns*—but the other prophecy, the one that had predicted his arrival, Silas still didn't know the specifics of. He was only told that the leaf suggested that his arrival and his song would help save the life of the queen, and perhaps even the king.

Wulfess finished donning bronze-colored furs, striking pennywolf pelts gifted to her by Cato upon her arrival in Kalandragote. The harvested wolves used to make the furs came from the ancient forests high in the peninsula. It was said that the wolves were nearly as dangerous as the men who hunted them. Silas had heard Cato brag that three men in his hunting party had died before the pack surrendered their skins.

Clad once more, Wulfess crossed the room to Silas. He slipped on his boots just as she reached him, the toes on his left foot compressing against the Yubriy leaf. When he was finished, she reached up and touched his face, cooly caressing his cheek. The pearl-and-onyx necklace given to her by Cato dangled from her neck. "You are my secret, Silas O' the Songs. Fortunately for you, I'm a woman made for secrets. And you are a secret I intend to keep. Do you hear me? You and the song you sing. Your song is mine. Not my father's. And not my bonded-to-be's."

"Thank you, my lady." He laughed a nervous laugh. "I don't understand the song. The words simply came to me." In Silas's mind, he heard Wyn Dunkin laughing along with him to the lie, setting fiddle to chin, making a tune out of his misdirection. "I do not understand this prophecy business, nor how I am caught up with it. I only want to make my music, to play, to sing, to laugh, to love. I am not made for the madness of politics."

"I am," she responded, taking her hand away. Her grin returned, a cutting slice. "I was born to it, and made for it. Since you were not, I think it would be best if you entrusted your actions to my advice until the madness of the moment has passed. A madness, as I'm sure you've gathered from your time in the wardrobe, that may soon commence."

"As you say, my lady." What else was there to do but go along with her? He wondered if Wulfess was leading him to his doom or his salvation. Wyn would know, but Wyn wasn't there; he had gone wherever woodkins go, to do whatever woodkins did.

"I do say, Silas O' the Songs." She continued standing close to him, unbearably so, the distance working like a spell on him. Her words were a breeze upon his face. "Now listen to me, and listen to me close. Stay away from the Wraith in Red. Today and tonight."

Silas felt a prickling of fear. He recalled Daguss Salk's words to his daughter, two days prior. *There's no shortage of Ontishmen who would love to see the Wraith in Red to his grave.* "What if he sends for me? He likes to hear 'The Queen's Burning Heart.'"

Wulfess considered this. "We'll make sure he doesn't find you. I'll see to it that someone else sends for you. Grocian Mock, perhaps. That way you will have the excuse of being indisposed. But whatever you do, you will stay away. At least for today." She paused. "I hope you won't take this the wrong way, Silas, but I have someone watching you. For your own safety. So make sure you do what I've said."

Silas suppressed a shudder. Was he on a side now? He didn't want to be on a side. What he wanted was to be loved and respected for his music. That, and to have the secret of his song back…to have evaded Wulfess's wiles…and for Cato Ollspaer to never *ever* learn what he had done. *If you're going to make wishes, you might as well wish Queen Anjay to recover and the other lutist alive.* But the presupposition of his wishes was that they could set things right, when it was beyond clear that the madness unfolding around him had long ago taken on a life of its own. All he could hope to do was survive it, and if that meant avoiding the king's jeyedoshi half brother for the remainder of the day, then that's what he would do.

He nodded in reply.

"Good," Wulfess said, interpreting his nod to mean that all was settled. Wulfess's look turned wolfish, and for a second Silas thought she wanted him again; but then he saw that it was a deeper need, the desire to unravel the mystery between them, the one connected to the words pressing up against his toe. He knew what she would ask of him before she spoke. "One more thing before I let you go.

"Sing your song to me."

Gregor Thorn

Queen Anjay had never been one to accept the vicissitudes of fate without a fight. This held true even in her death throes. Her thrashing and groaning lessened near the end, but they didn't stop entirely until death claimed her. Gregor, attending bedside, bore witness to the battle, including the last word that escaped Anjay's lips: a defiant *No,* offered to the wind with the penultimate breath of her life.

King Micah said nothing once she was gone. Gregor watched him with concern. Since the moonbear attack, the king had been a black fury of misery and blame. Gregor, responsible for the queen's care—he hadn't dared entrust Anjay's ministrations to Kalandragote's dubious men of medicine—had pleaded with the king to take breaks, to go into the castle and politick, but the sovereign was obsessed with matters over which he had little control, beginning with healing Anjay and ending with identifying her 'killer,' the man who threw the capsquash. When Micah failed in his efforts, he grew insensate with grief. Now that she was dead, he looked dead as well. A corpse sitting upright, with a sharply visible skull.

"I must go into the castle and make our presence known," Gregor said to his grieving brother. He didn't mean to sound uncaring, but their position was precarious. Anjay's dying had isolated them for days, and there was no telling the machinations that had taken place in their absence. "I must get a sense of where we stand, of what's been said."

The king didn't look at him. "Go, then. Damn you. Go divine more falsehoods. Go try and make a different meaning of these senseless prophecies. Go pretend to be of use."

Gregor knew better than to respond. He gave a curt nod and left.

He passed Stryder—the king's personal guard—at the door. Tired of seeing skulls, he refrained from looking at the man. The greyhounds fell in with Gregor as he departed. After the queen's mauling, Gregor had brought the hounds into Winterworn Castle. They had attended the queen's dying with a peculiar grace, sitting vigil on their front paws like statues, infusing the occasion with an odd dignity. No one, not even the king, had protested their presence. But with the queen gone, Black and Tan seemed to understand that there was different work to be done.

Gregor talked to the dogs as he walked. Not aloud, but in his mind. They didn't respond, but he was certain that they understood him. *I did all I could. I poured boiling wine on the wounds, to decrease the chances of infection. I made a poultice of nettle, mustard seed, and bread mold for the injury. I played sennequi with the queen to take her mind off her suffering. I kept the wounds clean and I dressed them with care. By all rights, she should have lived.*

But she hadn't lived. *I did all I could,* Gregor thought again, feeling the need to justify himself. Had the claw marks been somewhere other than the queen's torso, Gregor might have taken more drastic measures to ward off infection, like cutting away the potential for corruption. But with the wound where it was, all he had been able to do was clean the wound, and tend the wound, and clean the wound, and tend it. Ultimately the wound turned—who knew what nastiness was embedded in the moonbear's claws—and the infection spread, and the queen died.

Simple as that.

I did all I could.

A memory flashed in his mind, from the day before. The queen was suffering greatly by then, hazed with pain, but there were also moments of startling lucidity. During one of those moments, when the king was absent from the room, Anjay awoke with bright eyes and a soft smile, which she gifted to Gregor.

"My cousin saw you differently, didn't she?" she asked him, apropos of nothing. "In all the years that you were bonded, I don't think Sephery once mentioned your powers. It must have been a great joy to you, to be loved by someone so unconcerned by that part of you on which the rest of the world fixates."

He struggled to respond. Gregor had suffered terribly after Sephery died, but Anjay, who might have shared in that suffering, made it clear that they were to mourn separately. For Anjay to recognize his pain, and on *her* deathbed no less…he couldn't find the words. "It was a great joy to me. *She* was a great joy to me. She cared not one whit that I was a jeyedoshi. But had I been a better jeyedoshi, I might have saved her."

The dying queen found the strength to pierce him with a powerful stare, like she was seeing straight through to the center of his tortured jeyedoshi soul. "I should have loved you better, Gregor, in honor of Sephery. I see that now. We ask too much of you. We always have."

She faded as soon as the words were spoken, back into the bleary mists of a fitful sleep. And he was left to do what he would with her late-given gift, for whatever it was worth.

I did all I could. And you did ask too much of me. It's what the Dayborns do. But I understand what I am. A bastard half brother, bound to serve.

And I will give all, if need be.

Including my life.

Gregor made for the great hall. He had one intention: to go to the place that would gather the greatest number of eyes. News of the queen's death would spread quickly enough; while it did, it was imperative that the Dayborns reestablish their presence. And no one had a presence like the Wraith in Red. Like it or not, Gregor knew that if there was anyone who could put a stop to potential plotting against the king, it was him.

Leaving the Black and White Tower, Gregor was accosted by a vision. One that he had seen before. Stepping through an arched doorway, snow fell near the top of his line of sight and turned to sand at his feet. *What is this? A Delilah herb flashback?* He recalled the original vision, back in Low Osgood, at the Three Dragons Inn. Repeated visions were usually a warning, but he didn't have time to stop and ponder the vision's potential meanings.

He had a dynasty to save.

He continued on to the great hall. Entering, he saw that many hearths in the hall were ablaze, in defense against the chill. The weather had turned numbingly cold the past few days, with no signs of a letup. As always, there was a motley collection of men-at-arms strewn throughout the hall, conversing and drinking. The interregional comradery on display at the welcome feast, however, was no longer in evidence: the pockets of men gathered round the hall were divided mostly by house, with what few cross-interactions there were falling along the Struvan/Ontish divide. On the right-hand side of the hall, a handful of Dante Heron's men stood admiring Jakastor Weylcoin's sword; in the back, Garstring men sat with the Mocks, quaffing mead; while nearer to the front of the hall, Larin Dove held court for a contingent of double suns, telling what appeared to be an uproarious joke. Gregor's presence generated the customary share of death-wishing stares, but they were flitting and unexceptional, all things considered.

Gregor took a seat on one of the benches. In turn, Black settled onto his haunches, tearing into a loaf of bread that he had somehow procured, while Tan took a lap of the hall, charting a course that kept him out of reach of any who might pet him. Gregor lost sight of the greyhound for a second on the opposite side of the hall, only to discover that the dog had picked up a walking companion when he came back into view.

Deglan Whisk.

The dog made his way back to Gregor with the young, black-haired knight in tow, looking like the entire purpose of his venture had been one of retrieval. When they were halfway across the hall, a man sitting on the benches with his back to Gregor stood and lowered his shoulder into Deglan, nearly sending the knight spiraling to the ground. Tan answered the assault with an angry nip at the man's heels, turning the broad-shouldered fellow so that Gregor could see who it was: Seydron Qorl. Or at least Gregor thought it was Seydron: the Qorlish lord's skull was a nightmare, making it almost impossible to place his face. Seydron swatted at Tan in retaliation but took it no further. Shooting a mean-eyed glance at Gregor, Seydron exited the hall.

Deglan regained his balance with grace. He made his way to Gregor without further incident and took a seat beside him on the bench, ignoring the guffaws elicited by his near-fall.

"It seems that we made an enemy of Lord Seydron back in Low Osgood," Gregor said. "He appears to harbor resentment over being drugged. And here I thought your assistance in helping him learn the truth of what happened to his falcon might have smoothed things out."

"To be fair, Revered Sagekind, all the Ontish seem to hate you. Whether you've drugged them or not."

It was a fair point. "True." Gregor sighed. "You do yourself no favors, young Deglan, being seen with me."

"We must all cast our die. I cast mine with you. What will come will come."

Gregor chose to accept Deglan's reasoning. He tried his best not to stare at Deglan, but it was hard not to gape at one of the few people in his inner circle who didn't aggrieve his eyes with the sight of their skeleton.

All around the hall, the different factions were breaking up, leaving. *Yet another power that I possess: the ability to clear a room.* A handful of Frostflowers entered the hall, saw Gregor, and immediately exited, sneering at him as they slipped out the door that led to the southern yard.

Gregor thought little of the affront. It wasn't anything that he wasn't accustomed to. He turned to Deglan. "Queen Anjay is dead," he shared with the young knight. There was a catch in his voice when he spoke. Pain lanced his heart, and for a second the feeling of it was so intense that he thought he had summoned death itself to his body.

"Revered Sagekind." The boy didn't know what to say, but he was doing his best, Gregor knew, to share in the Dayborn family's pain. "What might I do to best serve the family in this time of mourning?"

Gregor stuffed his pain away, possibly into one of the chambers of his already overtaxed heart. He faced Deglan, knowing exactly how the boy could best serve the Dayborns.

"Tell me, how go your ventures outside the castle walls? What have you learned?"

A smile played on Deglan's lips before disappearing, fast as a sorcerer's trick. Gregor had meant for Deglan's venture outside the castle walls to be a one-off, but the boy had clearly met someone, and made a trip of it most days. Fortunately, whomever he was seeing, they were a wealth of information. "The people here are like the people everywhere. What they desire most of all is someone to blame when things go wrong. Lord Horos caught the brunt of it during the Blackstar Rebellion. But now that the Blackstar blockade is over and bellies are once again full, they're not sure if they like the idea of it coming at the expense of their independence."

"Who stands in their favor?"

"The son, Cato. And to a lesser degree, Lord Daguss Salk. The people saw for themselves the heraldry on the ships that cleared Skithin Harbor of the Blackstar fleet. In most of their eyes that makes Wulfess Salk a suitable bond for Cato, but they'd as soon not bend the knee to a hawk worshipper when the ceremony is said and done."

"They are against us, then?"

Deglan shrugged. "Maybe? Mostly, they don't know what to think. They are a lost people. Ask anyone on the street and they'll tell you that Kalandragote isn't the city it once was. The Blackstar Rebellion brought home just how reliant the city has become on trade with greater Ragar Or. This isn't the same city that fought four wars for independence. Everyone seems to accept that something had to change. But I think they're reserving judgment on the direction matters will take."

Gregor stroked the top of Tan's head now that he had come to sit by his side. "You're certain you've captured the pulse of the city? Nothing's been lost in translation?"

"*Na hlyun mis ontish sfar supliv. In ni kram yot wruhu kat wru pla lomu ekwifi na.*" The boy's Old Ontish was spotless. Gregor made the translation with ease. 'I speak Old Ontish well enough. And I have a friend for when the language confuses me.' *I should practice with the boy,* Gregor thought. *He might improve my own feel for the tongue.*

"This friend of yours? You're certain that they're trustworthy?"

Deglan's cheeks pinked ever so slightly. "Yes," he replied simply.

The Uncle Bones in Gregor wanted to press Deglan for information, if only for his own amusement, but he resisted the urge. "Good. What about inside the castle walls? Have you learned anything here?"

Two crows cawed high in the rafters, fracturing Deglan's reply. "No, not as much. People will speak to me in the city, but inside Winterworn Castle, everyone knows that I'm your man." Deglan paused for a moment, readjusting his position on the bench. "I *have* spoken with the mute Madrig, and his bonded Jacy. I know you don't trust them because they're Salks, but I must tell you that I find their concern for the safety of the Dayborns to be genuine. It might behoove you to bring them closer. If the situation is as perilous as it seems, keeping two warriors of such renown at arm's length would be a crucial mistake."

My, how the boy's confidence has grown. This wasn't the earnest, eager-to-please boy that had ridden with Gregor into Low Osgood; no, this was a worldly, once-stabbed man unafraid to offer advice. A part of Gregor thought that Deglan was still too wet behind the ears to grasp just how dangerous bringing Madrig and Jacy into the Dayborns' inner circle could be, but another part of him thought that perhaps the boy had a point. "Thank you, Deglan. I will take it into consideration."

From high above, a dollop of crow shit fell onto their table. Looking up, Gregor could see the birds hopping in the rafters directly overhead, like they were searching for the correct launch angle. "That's our signal to move," Gregor said. He stood up from the bench and Deglan followed suit. "Two crows. Makes you wonder where the third one is, doesn't it?"

"You mean Johanna Salk?" Deglan followed smartly.

"I do. One can only hope that Prince Easton is faring better with the feathers than we are."

They moved at a languorous pace toward the front of the hall, the greyhounds trailing behind. Gregor wanted to lay eyes on a number of people, which meant it was time to take his leave of the hall. "What of Silas O' the Songs? Have you seen him today?"

"No."

No surprise there. The lutist had recently been going to great lengths to avoid the Dayborn contingent. Gregor could scarcely blame him. The way King Micah cursed his name, the lutist was undoubtedly scared for his life. "If you see him, bring him to me. With his instrument in tow. Recent setbacks aside, it's important that we keep him close."

"Yes, Revered Sagekind."

Two wet snoots grazed the back of Gregor's hand. Gregor sighed. As much as he liked the idea of Tan and Black accompanying him around Winterworn, they might hinder his ability to access his next point of call. "Keep a lookout for Silas. And take the hounds with you.

"They won't be welcome where I'm going."

Gregor walked the grounds of Winterworn Castle with a fearless verve. He had been at Winterworn for eight days, but, because of Anjay's injury, he was still familiarizing himself with the grounds. Somewhere, he knew, the king's enemies were plotting. But where? The most likely locales were the high reaches of the castle's two storied towers, the Bloodbone and the Black and White. These were the lairs of the Salks and the Ollspaers. Awkward places to arrive unannounced, but Gregor would if he thought it necessary. Another locale was the throne room, the secret beating heart of Winterworn. It might behoove him to see if Horos Ollspaer was still sitting on the Winterworn Chair. Nothing could be a surer sign of troubles to come.

In many castles, the great hall and the throne room served as the same space, but in Kalandragote the throne room stood separate. Located in the center of Winterworn's five towers, the throne room was, from the outside, an odd if arresting building: on the throne room's western side, towering windows surprisingly evoked the stylings of a Stavusian temple, while on the eastern side, one large arched window was framed by gorgeous timbers from the peninsula, a testament to the Kalandragotan ideal of splendor. Steps of stone—twelve in total—led to the great kurmenhi wood doors, fifteen feet high and banded with bronze.

Gregor approached the throne room from the southwest. A couple of intimidating men with a peninsular look were loitering near the steps, making a poor effort at inconspicuousness. *Frostflowers, standing watch,* Gregor surmised. Their biggest tell was the way they pretended not to notice Gregor: elsewhere on castle grounds, the Wraith in Red couldn't walk ten steps without feeling the fires of a hateful stare, but here his presence somehow went unnoticed. Gregor feinted, pretending to go far afield of the throne room steps, then at the last second, he reversed course and took the steps by storm.

They might have stopped him had he not spooked them so. One of the men, who had a long, sloping forehead and a shocking absence of a chin, tried to get in Gregor's way, but in the process managed to choke on something, saliva or shock or perhaps day-old chicken freed from his back teeth. Whatever it was, the coughing that followed hampered his ability to run interference; Gregor first sidestepped and then shoved the Frostflower aside, redirecting him into the path of a yard dog who had no patience for choking fits. While that fellow dealt with the twofold problem of the dog and regaining his breath, the other—a dirty-blond-haired brute—hurried up the throne room steps, presumably to warn of Gregor's arrival. Gregor dealt with him in the jeyedoshi manner. As the fellow howled in pain, Gregor drew close and issued an ominous warning: "Another step and I'll turn your insides to ash."

The fellow curled into the fetal position. Gregor could feel scores of eyes on him from those gathered in the yard, but it was no matter. He stepped over the Frostflower and pushed open the throne room's kurmenhi wood doors, bursting into the chamber.

From the far end of the cavernous hall, two souls looked up at him. A study in contrasts. Sitting the Winterworn Chair, with his pitted face and ungodly gray-black beard, was Lord Horos Ollspaer. He gave the impression of a roosting vulture, or perhaps a wizard gone to seed. Standing beside Horos, in a triumph of white, was Lord Dante Heron. Upon seeing Gregor, they donned different expressions: Dante grew a smile that threatened to swallow his head, while Horos retreated into a bitter frown, the line of his lips seemingly reinforced by the strength of his grip on the Winterworn Chair.

"Revered Sagekind! You are most welcome here," Dante proclaimed.

Bullshit, Gregor thought. But instead of responding, he continued his advance. The many turrets carved in relief into the throne room walls made Gregor feel as if he was advancing on the heart of Fortress Kalandragote. He stopped when he reached the foot of the tiered steps that led to the throne. *It's no longer a throne,* Gregor told himself, though he could see for himself that Horos didn't view it that way.

"I met two of your men on the way in," Gregor said, addressing Horos. "They made a mockery of Lord Dante's assertion."

"I don't encourage unwelcome disturbances," Horos responded. "Maybe it's different in Union. Maybe down in Union you open your door to any fig eater that desires the pleasure of your presence. Here, power means something."

Gregor nodded, as if in agreement. "In that case, I must confer with Lord Dante. He's no *fig eater*, and yet he seems to have made it past your men with ease."

Dante pursed his wormy lips. He shifted his body in Gregor's direction, taking up the cause of the defense. "You must forgive us, Revered

Sagekind. We *lords* manage among ourselves. We were just speaking of our desire to converse with the king, but we know how distracted he is, after what befell the queen."

"Queen Anjay is dead. She passed away from her wounds not one hour past."

The former king of Kalandragote and Lord Dante Heron were careful not to look at one another. "A tragedy," Dante said. Dante's words and the tone of his voice didn't quite match. "You must give our deepest condolences to the king."

"One would think Horos could speak for himself."

The barb was overly aggressive, but that was Gregor's intention. Provocation was the surest and quickest way to learn where Horos Ollspaer stood.

Horos shrugged. "Life carries on without a woman. I learned that lesson long ago. Your master will learn it soon enough."

"King Micah is your master too. In case you've forgotten. The way you're sitting in that chair, I worry that you have."

Horos looked fit to spit, but he swallowed whatever it was he wanted to say and instead slouched deeper into the chair, listing to his right. Settled, he stared a ten-count of daggers at Gregor. "You mistake me, *Sagekind*."

Gregor met Horos's ambiguously fuzzy response with silence. Feeling that the silence might work to his benefit, Gregor took a moment to look around the room. The famed Ontish austerity was at play, most notably in the crude stone flooring and the room's relative lack of adornment. But to the discerning eye there were also flourishes of wealth, from the thickness of the window glass to the massive candle chandeliers overhead, floating towers of fire. Behind the Winterworn Chair, the bronze pelts of six pennywolves hung from the wall. *Cato's kill,* Gregor surmised. The story of the hunt was a popular one in Winterworn; Gregor had heard it at least thrice since his arrival.

Horos noted Gregor's line of sight. "Six is nothing. I took twenty my first hunt as king. With half the number of the men in my son's party." The former Kalandragote king's gaze wandered back in time. "When the hunt was over, the pennywolves tracked us all the way back to the city. They would howl all night, then sweep silent behind us during the day, trying to pick us off. You couldn't stop to take a piss without a man guarding your back. I set out on the hunt with fifteen men, came back with ten." He gave a snorting laugh. "Never crossed my mind to make a gift of them for a woman. I wore the skins myself, till they turned to dust."

Of course you did. The pressing circumstances of the present moment made it easy for Gregor to forget who Horos was, but the story reminded him. *You're the man who killed your brother to become king.* If the rumors were true, Horos Ollspaer had done worse than that. *You had a second son. Cato's brother. You sacrificed him on the altar of the twin-death rite for the glory of the Twin Ascendant.*

Gregor's thoughts stayed clear of his tongue. Looking out the western windows, he saw the infamous Circle of Stones in the courtyard, the place where the twin-death rite was held. In an instant, two visions flashed before him: one of a boy mounting a great blue-and-white dragon, followed by a vision of the Dayborn prince, a deathly pallor on his face, preparing for combat. The visions faded in an instant. *What was that?* he thought helplessly. Like nearly every vision he had, there was nothing to be done about it. *Focus on the here and now. It's all that you can do.*

He returned his attention to Horos. "Have you made your peace with it?"

"Made my peace with what?"

"The fact that you are no longer a king."

Horos struggled to control his temper. "You've come to disparage me? It's not enough that I've bent the knee, you want to ensure my ego is bloodied too?"

"I am here for a lot of reasons. One of them is to secure simple answers to simple questions. And so I will ask you again: Have you made your peace, Lord Horos, with the fact that you are no longer the king of Kalandragote?"

An internal conflict played out on Horos's face, one that for a moment Gregor thought Horos's judicious half would win. But then Lord Ollspaer snarled and sneered. "I won't give you the pleasure, Wraith in Red. I'll answer to your half brother if that's what he wants, but I won't answer to you. Struvan bastard. Woodkin whelp. Fuck you and your bad magic. If you want proof that I'm no longer king, there's no proof better than the fact that you stand alive before me. If I were king, you'd be dead."

Horos's outburst appeared to shock Dante Heron. Gregor glanced over to see that the young lord's face had turned nearly as white as his clothes. "This discussion has naught to do with me." Seeing an opportunity to make his exit, Dante left in an affected huff, traveling the length of the hall and exiting through the same kurmenhi wood doors where Gregor had entered.

Gregor let the Heron go in silence, keeping his stare fixed on Horos. He didn't trust Lord Dante's performance—the Heron was as slick as they came, capable of all manner of deception. Horos, on the other hand, seemed incapable of backhandedness. Gregor had the feeling that if he stayed and pushed the matter, he might goad the man into giving away his true intentions.

He waited to speak until the kurmenhi wood doors closed shut. "The king who surrendered Kalandragote," he said softly. "Hate me all you want, Horos, but when I look at you, I see a hero. A true leader. A man willing to do what is in the long-term best interest of his people."

Horos retreated behind the hedges of his dark, bushy eyebrows. Hatred was pouring from his gaze, but at the same time he seemed to have gotten hold of himself, in growing awareness of who he was speaking to. "Be gone from here, Wraith in Red. Leave my sight."

Gregor ignored his command. "There were four failed invasions of Kalandragote, weren't there? Your ancestor Begwo Ollspaer fought off the first one. The only man to stand down Daguss the Unifier, they say. Then there was Reuel I's great go, and I believe the Traveling Queen tried twice, didn't she? All for naught. But now…well, it's like you said: I'm here, aren't I? The world has turned on its head. Your world, at least."

It helped that Gregor could see Horos's skull. *If it's an Ontish supper you mean to serve to your guests, it appears you'll be eating too.* A surge of confidence shot through him. If there was truly a conspiracy against the Dayborns, he would get to the bottom of it, here and now.

"You know little and less of this world, jeyedoshi."

"I learn more and more by the minute. I know that you're a man for the old ways, but that your people have grown soft. Trade does that. Once a people get a taste for foreign riches, it's hard to return to being self-reliant. When the Blackstar blockade cratered your economy, you made a pact with Lord Salk, one sealed with a bonding ceremony between Cato and Wulfess. A conversation we Dayborns weren't privy to. I imagine you've had many conversations in our absence. Some with Lord Daguss, some with Lord Dante. Not to mention the conversations you've no doubt had with yourself. But since you and I are having a conversation now, I'd like to hear from your own mouth where you stand."

"*Na kram henstu iflel kat kli, yedosh.*" I have no words for you, jeyedoshi.

"In my brother's absence, I speak with the authority of the Twin Ascendant. And as the Twin Ascendant, I require a response."

That did the trick. Horos jumped up from the chair, reaching for the baselard at his belt. His face seized in a paroxysm of hate. "Sacrilege! Blasphemy! Your Struvan perversion of our faith will not stand. A true Twin Ascendant pays the blood price of the lesser twin. A price I've paid in full many times over. Call yourself the Twin Ascendant once more and I'll gladly pay it again!"

Gregor remained calm. "The perversion you speak of is Union, is it not? The idea that the ruler of Ragar Or is both the Twin Ascendant and the Holy Son of the Air? What I want to know, *Horos,* is whether you are truly ready to accept your change in station. Because if not, then we had best resolve the matter here and now." He directed his thoughts to the candleflame and singed Horos to put a scare in him.

The heat brought fear to Horos's eyes, but it paled in comparison to the hatred. Horos unsheathed the baselard at his belt and prepared to fly from the throne, the ermine white of his great black coat billowing behind him like a snowy squall. Gregor, taken aback, readied to fight. Conflict seemed a foregone conclusion, but before Horos could fly from the dais, a man stepped from behind the anteroom door near the right front of the throne room and yelled "Sire!", freezing Horos in place.

Gothred. The commander of the Ascendant Few. Gregor had only seen Gothred a few times, but, knowing the importance of his position, he had made sure to commit his appearance to memory. Gothred, his white-and-gray-speckled beard looking like dirty snow, presented himself with the heightened awareness of a man attuned to Horos Ollspaer's particular form of madness. "Leave the jeyedoshi, my king. Leave him to his lesser fate."

Gothred's words ran cold up Gregor's spine. *Lesser fate? That's rich coming from the keepers of a dying kingdom.* Still, the cold stung, like a frostbite. He shook it off, saying what was on his mind. "Leave him? Yes, leave the jeyedoshi lest he end *your* life for treason." He tried to clear his thoughts. He had come to the throne room for the purpose of ascertaining Horos Ollspaer's intentions, but now that he had confirmed that the man couldn't be trusted, he didn't know what to do.

Go to the Salks. Daguss Salk could hardly be trusted, but he was at least a more rational actor than Horos Ollspaer. Gregor remembered his father's words. *When your enemies surround you, turn them against one another.*

It was time to climb the Bloodbone.

Horos, his baselard still in hand, looked suddenly uncertain of himself. With wild eyes, the Lord of Kalandragote looked to his left and to his right, like a man on the verge of coming undone. *Perhaps his madness isn't figurative,* Gregor considered. It seemed to Gregor as if Horos was listening to a far-off voice that only he could hear. But then the spell snapped, and Horos's gaze narrowed, becoming beady-eyed once more. He turned on Gregor, as if remembering that he was in the room.

"Be gone, jeyedoshi. Before one of us kills the other." Horos laughed a dark laugh. "When I look at your face, I see death."

Gregor responded in turn, and in truth. "I see the same when I look at you."

The timbre of Horos's laughter grew even darker. With his see-through flesh, the old king's jawbone was a horror. "Good. Then you've seen me for what I am.

"The true Twin Ascendant."

Gregor made his way to the Bloodbone Tower in a blind huff. His thoughts full of poison. *How did I ever let events go this far?* The north was the graveyard of monarchs, and here they were farther north than any royal before them, in the festering heart of old Ragar Or—Kalandragote, that land where beauty and civility and all the great and glorious things the Struvans had brought to Ragar Or came to perish. *They mean to kill him. They mean to kill my brother. That's what they've planned to do all along. They're in cahoots, the stinking lot of them. I should have insisted that we return directly to Union the instant the Blackstar Rebellion was squashed. I should have heeded the dark interpretations of my dreams.*

But returning home would have been a different sort of death, wouldn't it? An admission that Micah Dayborn was the ruler of Ragar Or in name only, not in reality. *Enough hand-wringing. The die is cast. The only option is to see it through. We must master the world around us or go to our deaths. And if Micah hasn't the will or the power to master Ragar Or, then I must be the one to do it.*

His steps lightened. Yes, this was the way. He, the hated jeyedoshi, would bend them all to his brother's will. Through their deaths, if need be. He would force the lords of the realm to show their hand, one by one, and if there was any doubt as to their ultimate loyalty, he would make them pay with their lives. *I should have left Horos dead and stinking on his chair. Demonstrated to the others the price of even suspected plotting.*

For a moment, he considered reversing course and returning to the throne room to finish the job. But for all he knew the old king was already gone, and Gregor was more than halfway to the Bloodbone. *On to Lord Daguss, then. I will pin the crow-hawk's feathers to the board, see how he squawks.*

As he crossed the northern courtyard toward the Bloodbone Tower, the castle grew quiet. A gentle wind blew in from the west. On its back a crow crossed over the battlements, flying directly over Gregor's head before landing in the center of the Circle of Stones. *Cursed spot,* Gregor thought, glancing over. He feared what he might see. *What good have my visions ever done me?* he thought, trying to forget what he had seen through the windows of the throne room only moments ago.

Black's commanding bark interrupted his thinking. The greyhound and his brother were approaching Gregor from the base of the Black and White Tower, cutting diagonally across the yard. Three humans followed on their heels: Deglan Whisk at the lead, followed by the wiry warrior-woman Jacy and the mighty mute Madrig.

The greyhounds came to a stop before him and retired to their haunches, with the peculiar dignity akin to their kind. Deglan comported himself similarly, with an air of formality. Behind him Jacy and Madrig wore resolute but world-weary expressions. The mute, dressed in boiled leather and black wool, was a commanding sight; he collected stray courtyard stares the way a cistern might water, funneling them into his keep.

"Did you find Silas O' the Songs?" Gregor asked Deglan, ignoring the bonded pair.

"He's playing his lute for the Mocks this evening. At Lord Grocian's request."

"Hmm." Gregor found that he cared little. The lutist, if he still served a purpose, could wait. "Why are *they* with you?" he asked, gesturing at the bonded pair.

Jacy stepped forward. She gave an uncertain look around the yard, as if worried about being overheard. When she spoke, her voice was a careful whisper. "We are here to request that you put us to use. The pledge we made in Dunning Harbor to protect King Micah was made in good faith. We understand your hesitancy, but you're making a mistake. And now, with Queen Anjay dead…use us, before—"

"Before what?" Gregor interrupted with an accusatory air. "What do you know?"

Madrig made motions with his hands, but Jacy was already responding. "We know the same thing that you do, Sagekind. That Kalandragote isn't safe for the king. This castle stinks of conspiracy. You can smell it everywhere."

Gregor looked up at the mute. "Tell me, do you smell it on your cousin, Lord Daguss?"

Madrig frowned down at him. The mute made a reply with his hands. "Madrig says that the whole of the castle is a pigsty," Jacy translated. "His cousin is one of the pigs, but he can't say for sure that Daguss Salk smells the most like shit."

A burst of laughter escaped Gregor. One of his father's old adages returned to him: *Laughter rarely follows lies.* He looked the bonded pair up and down, up and down. His rational side told him not to trust them, but his instincts said yes. "The two of you are out of favor with Lord Daguss?"

Jacy shrugged. "He keeps us at a remove. To some degree, he always has. But more so since Dunning Harbor."

"Bringing you into the king's inner circle won't be an easy thing. Micah already has a personal guard." Gregor paused, thinking of Stryder and his skull. *Another on death's doorstep.* His gut told him that he *did* need to bring Madrig and Jacy closer to the king, but his head couldn't rationalize what was so obviously a risky choice. "Remind me again why you want this? Because you're for the cause of Union?"

Madrig moved his hands with deliberation. Jacy continued to interpret. "Madrig says that he knows what horrors lie on the other side of an Ontish/Struvan schism. He would rather die in the hopes of preventing that schism than live to see such evil manifest."

"And you?"

"I feel the same. Plus, where he goes, I go. With all my heart."

Deglan chimed in. "We need our fiercest fighters closest to the king. If the stories from the Blackstar Rebellion are true, there are no two warriors of greater renown."

If I can't trust my own judgment on the matter, perhaps it's wise to trust the boy's. "I'll talk it over with King Micah later this evening. By the morrow, I'll have a reply."

"Thank you," Jacy replied. She shared a look with her lover. "Between now and then, perhaps we should guard *your* back? You have no small share of enemies here."

Laughter escaped Gregor's lips again. "You seem to have forgotten *why* I have enemies. It's precisely because I need no protection." To Gregor's surprise, however, the thought of having an honor guard amused him. *And the sight of two armed Salks walking by my side around the castle might have other benefits.* "But suit yourself. I'm on the way to speak to Lord Daguss now. Don't follow me up the Bloodbone, but if you'd like to wait for me at the base of the tower, I'll allow it."

He didn't wait for a response. Daylight was fading, and his work wasn't done.

The scar of red brick running up the Bloodbone looked like a lightning bolt cast by a blood-red god. Behind the Bloodbone, Wrepta Mountain hung over the tower like a shadow. Ominous-looking in the most flattering of lights, the Bloodbone appeared especially foreboding in the afternoon, when the sun was at Mt. Wrepta's back. *There's too much history here,* Gregor thought. If what was written in the book with the blue boards was true, Roop Ollspaer had once shared the secret of calling down a dragon from the sky with his jeyedoshi son in the red room near the tower's top. *And they killed him for it. They cut Roop down in the Circle of Stones and then they felled his jeyedoshi son from dragonback with an arrow.* The remembrance of what was in the book with the blue boards slowed Gregor's approach to the Bloodbone, but only for a second.

Now is not the time to be faint of heart.

The tower was ungodly large, the stairs switchback rather than spiraling. Gregor took them with gusto, two at a time, barreling toward the top. He felt half mad with bravado. He didn't know what would happen when he confronted Lord Daguss, other than that he meant to learn whether Daguss mistrusted Horos. He could already see himself staring down Daguss. Lord Salk had played a clever game in Dunning Harbor, but that was when he'd had the Gorgostrine Betrard to offer up as a sacrifice to an eager-to-forgive king. But this time Gregor was confronting him alone. And this time Gregor would get the answers he needed. All of them.

Gregor had ascended to the landing between the second and the third level of the tower when the vision returned in full force: snow falling from above, great white flakes of it swirling down from the third level, where, at the head of the whiteout, a figure was standing, looking larger than life. "Yedosh," the figure said, naming Gregor with the Old Ontish inflection. *Lord Daguss,* Gregor grasped, but otherwise his thoughts were muddled, trying to ascertain why snow was falling inside the tower. He waited for the Lord of High Osgood to say more, but Daguss simply stood there. It was then that Gregor awoke to the reality of the vision: if there was snow at his head, there must be sand at his feet. He took a step back and looked down the stairs, to see the sand—

—the first arrow took him in the shoulder. The impact of it nearly pinned him to the tower stone. He kept his eyes open, and with them he saw the fellow at his feet, Seydron Qorl, standing on a blanket of sand, drawing another arrow. Gregor knew that he needed to summon his jeyedoshi powers, but the arrow had knocked the senses out of him. All he could do was watch as Seydron sized him up, making sure of his aim. *Funny,* Gregor thought, *I'm the one about to die, and I can see Seydron's skull as plain as day.* Then everything happened at once, so fast that Gregor couldn't process the order. Seydron loosed the arrow, steel flashed in the shadows, Seydron's skull went flying from his body, the second arrow slammed into Gregor, and all went dark.

Johanna Salk

After weeks spent traveling as a duo, Johanna found moving at a pace with the Raleigh army a slog. To add to the frustration, Easton now had a horse capable of keeping up with Bitterboy, a stallion recently familiar with the rump of Richard Chesterly. The horse wasn't the equal of Bitterboy, but he was far superior to the majority of the horses in the procession, including Chesterly's drab replacement dray.

Not that the stallion—named Brazen—was permitted to show it. Along with Bitterboy, Brazen snorted and stomped enough to make his desire to run free clear, but Easton and Johanna ignored both horses' signals and held the reins tight. "Believe me, we'd like to make a break for it too," Johanna occasionally whispered into Bitterboy's mane, but a decision had been made. Logic dictated that they could ill afford to offend Lady Wenavere when her army might be King Micah's saving grace.

But logic couldn't quell Johanna's doubts. Nor Easton's. The Dayborn prince made his feelings known every time he and Johanna had a quiet moment together, tossing out phrases such as 'den of snakes' and 'Bottom Black bargain' to describe their present company. Johanna was inclined to agree with him, but the way she saw it, now was the worst possible time to burn bridges with their ostensible Struvan allies.

The second day out of Hornwell, Johanna's misgivings multiplied. At first, she thought it was to do with her place in the procession: Lord Doneg Desighart and his giant warhorse were in front of her, and the disgusting man, as was his wont, kept expectorating stream after stream of messy leaf at an angle that threatened to hit Bitterboy. Johanna resolved to ignore it, and instead turned her attention to the scenery. But pewter-gray clouds in the sky had dulled the day's colors, making it impossible to enjoy the endless succession of rolling, treeless hills. Whether due to Doneg or the scenery, Johanna's heart was seized with a sudden terror. *Where are we going? Where are they taking us?* She looked at the strangers around her. *We've given ourselves over to the enemy,* she thought, panicked. Glancing left, right, ahead, behind, she felt hemmed in on all sides, not only by the red-and-white chevrons but also by the birds in their midst, the vultures and the eagles and who knew what else—

"Watch your spit, sir."

Easton's words were a smacking hand, searching for Doneg's cheek. Johanna only then noticed the hocked glob of red and white that had landed on Bitterboy's muzzle. The horse clearly didn't like it, but, being a proud breed, made a presentation of being unbothered.

"What the fuck are you grumbling about?" In his frilled, black-leather cloak, Doneg looked the part of a vulture, albeit an oversized one. When he turned in his saddle, Johanna could see the red of Doneg's bulbous face. He was the sort of man whose face turned red when his ire was up, which was always.

"Your spit," Easton growled. "Watch it. You sullied Lady Johanna's horse."

Doneg turned further in his saddle, facing behind him. He took a good look at his handiwork. Pleased, he snorted in satisfaction, and returned his attention to facing front.

Easton's complexion turned apple red. Johanna could see that he was seething. Worried what he might do or say, Johanna reached out a hand to calm him. Brazen, however, took offense to the suggestion, and nipped at her fingers. She barely pulled them back intact.

"Damn! Almost got recompense for losing my horse in the form of finger flesh," Richard Chesterly laughed, chiming in. The Lord of Wellings was riding at a languid pace behind them. "Knowing Brazen, he'll be sure to try again."

"Recompense! You lost the horse fair and square when you demonstrated your paucity of skill with a bow and arrow." Easton's response, quick as it was, was somewhat undermined by his struggle with Brazen; he was doing all he could to guide the temperamental horse's head away from Johanna.

"Your issue was with Philemon. Not me."

"And yet you were more than eager to defend Philemon's claim by adding your *skill* to the wager. It's naught to me that you regret the decision."

"Rest assured, I'll get what's mine in due time, *Prince*," Chesterly said, apparently uninterested in the finer points of Easton's argument.

"That's enough, Richard," Philemon Yurk interjected, entering the conversation. He brought his horse up alongside Johanna's. Smiled at her with an unctuous ease. Of all the wealthy persons present, he was the one most conscientious of it in his clothing. Philemon's doublet was made of dark green silk lined with gold, while below the waist, olive-green breeches covered boots of black velvet. Keeping with the verdant theme, oversized emerald rings burdened the majority of his fingers. While the others were dressed for horseback, Philemon's attire seemed more suited for court. "A dreary day, is it not, Lady Johanna?"

"I would welcome a little sun," she admitted.

Philemon nodded somewhat absentmindedly. "Though perhaps the clouds are fitting considering where we're heading."

She looked at him askew. "And where is that?"

"That sad place where the Salk brothers cried and died," Philemon answered.

She studied the bland landscape. *Does he mean Hevengrow?* Two battles had been fought there during the War of the Three Brothers, battles that had brought about the end of the Salk dynasty. In the first battle, Silas Salk shocked the realm when he took the head of his older brother and king, Brogan III. One year later, with the corpses from the first battle still fresh in the soil, the youngest brother Xeuel avenged Brogan's death while suffering mortal wounds in the same contest. Xeuel ruled Ragar Or for a month from his Hevengrow deathbed, rallying the realm to unite around his right-hand man, Cedric Dayborn. Johanna's branch of the Salk tree—the Crimson Salks, as they were sometimes called, for the way they had subsumed the Redd line—were pushed aside, mainly for political expediency, but also because the Dayborns had an equal amount of royal blood in their veins.

"I have never seen Hevengrow. I had never *thought* to see it."

"It's fascinating," Philemon said, adjusting a moleskin glove. "It has the weight of a place marked by history. Silas Salk commissioned six sculptures of the heroes of the battle to commemorate his victory, but they were later smashed to bits. Now six bells stand in their stead. Commissioned by—"

"Orius Dayborn. My grandfather."

Philemon acknowledged Easton's interruption with a sly smile. Then he leaned closer to Johanna. "Do you know that when I passed through, I found bits of marble piled near the bells? The very detritus of Silas Salk's short-lived kingship, still lingering in the soil. Being a good Struvan, I cleaned it up." He gave a discomfiting little laugh. "I thought you would be pleased to know, seeing how devoted you are to your bonded and his house."

Johanna wasn't sure how to respond. *Is he trying to drive a wedge between me and Easton?* The old stories of the Salks and their bitter, brotherly war meant little to her. Johanna was a Salk, yes, but she also knew that the name was in large part a construct. Had Caeress Salk I been born the second daughter of Portia I rather than the first, Caeress's bonding would have made her a Redd, and Johanna's great-great-great-grandfather Theron Salk (Theron Redd's grandson) wouldn't have had the Salk name when he inherited High Osgood, the Redd family seat. (Everything traced back to Theron Redd. Johanna had worked out the math: it was in the person of her great-great-great-great-great-grandfather that Johanna's blood met Easton's). The surname fluidity afforded the royal line made for interesting history; in a world where the patrilineal line dominated, the exception made for the firstborn daughters of the Salks couldn't help but create controversy, and confusion.

"I *am* devoted to my bonded. And my bonded is devoted to Union. From the sound of it, that's more than I can say for the three of you." She tasted fire on her lips. With her voice, she fanned the flames. "Tell me, and tell me true," she said, growing louder, "what is the desire of the Desigharts and the Chesterlys and the Yurks of the realm? To keep this kingdom together, or to tear it into its Ontish and Struvan parts?"

The accused looked to each other to see who might respond. Doneg took up the call. "She certainly sounds like a shitting Salk, doesn't she?"

The ugly laugh that issued from Richard Chesterly's mouth had scarce reached Johanna's ears before Easton dug his heels into Brazen and brought the horse alongside the vulture. Doneg Desighart, slow on the uptake, turned to find the Dayborn prince gaining purchase on his cloak. For a second it seemed that Easton might topple Doneg from his mount, but then Lord Desighart, with a butt nearly as big as the horse's hindquarters, found his center of gravity and brought his massive arms outside of Easton's, grabbing *him* by the shoulders of *his* blood-orange cloak. A great grappling commenced. An egg formed in Johanna's throat as she watched. It wasn't long before Doneg's bulk started to tell. The vulture lord estranged Easton from the vertical plane that connected him to his saddle, priming him for a fall.

Johanna's jeyedoshi powers rushed to her. Dark and coiled, unapologetic, the distilled energy of a thousand passions. Somewhere, her conscious mind screamed *No!,* but in the moment it was made subservient to instinct. The wind, ever ready, leapt to Johanna's still-forming command. Then it moved with the fury of a hundred horses, knowing what her hidden heart wanted before she did, slamming into Easton and Doneg both. The wind reversed the two men's positions with such force that Doneg toppled off his horse onto his broad, vulture back, while Easton caught himself on Doneg's newly empty saddle, somehow staying atop Brazen.

The madness didn't end there. Lord Desighart's destrier, frightened out of its wits, stomped on Doneg's legs. Then it bolted away from the procession, running unchecked toward a hill. Meanwhile, Easton was restored to verticality. Fortunately for him, the stallion didn't follow the destrier's lead.

A second of stunned quiet. Up ahead, the Raleigh faction turned, trying to make sense of what had taken place. Their ears were greeted by an eruption of black thunder curses. Doneg, lying on the ground, made his pain into a nasty stew of swearing, one everyone in hearing distance was forced to swallow.

"Fucking fuck! Fucking cunts!" His eyes searched wildly. "What the Twin-fucking fuck was that?"

Johanna had never felt so exposed. In the fury of the moment, the hood of her cloak had slipped from its place, and now all that hid her jeyedoshi whorl was a downy layer of fledgling brown hair. She tried not to look guilty, tried to keep from rushing to hide her hair once more beneath the hood. For a brief moment she thought that she was in the clear, that what she had done was beyond the ken of all present save Easton. But then a perceptive stare fell upon her: that shrewd Yurk gaze. She tried not to look at Philemon, but the pull was too strong. One glance and she could see the dawning understanding in his eyes, an understanding further reinforced by the inadvertent look she gave him in return, that of the discovered.

She tore her gaze away. Found Easton. The look he gave her didn't help. Her bonded knew what she had done, and in the commingling of their eyes the guilt compounded, creating an unbearable pressure that demanded release. Fight or flight. Bitterboy, sensing the pressure, snorted in favor of the latter. Without thinking, Johanna gave the Rugarder her heels. Bitterboy responded with a forceful haste, rearing and bolting away from all that had occurred.

Within seconds, she had them all at her back. She passed Lady Wenavere last, catching a glimpse of the Raleigh matriarch's judgmental expression as Bitterboy ran by. Then it was only the Rugarder's thundering hooves and the gentle curve of the rising road.

The road that led to Hevengrow.

She was bringing Bitterboy to a trot when she saw the column of bells off in the distance. Six great bronze bells in six separate towers of gray-white brick. Cyclopic sentinels, standing guard over the city. Seeing the bells, Johanna's breath caught in her throat. *I'm trapped,* she thought. Some irrational part of her had thought she might run Bitterboy to a distant safe haven, but even before she had had the chance to fully indulge the notion, the dream was being ripped away. *And now Philemon knows. Which means they'll all know soon. The eagle, the vulture, the red-and-whites.* She tried to breathe, tried to clear her mind, but her fears were too powerful.

Behind her, bold hooves. Easton, approaching on Brazen. She turned to find his brown hair all a tousle, his clothing disheveled, his expression flustered. The boyish charm he possessed was still there, but it was hidden behind the concern of a man for his woman. "Are you okay?" he asked.

She didn't know what to say. For the moment she let Bitterboy and Brazen's clip-clopping hooves answer for her. On her thigh, the sennequi piece said hello.

"That…was a grievous mistake," she said at last. "I fear Philemon made the connection."

Easton's silence was admission enough that he agreed.

They kept the horses on a straight line. *I can run any time I want,* she told herself, feeling Bitterboy's massive power beneath her. *I can run and Easton will follow.* But she also knew that there was no running from what she was. She would be a jeyedoshi till the end of her days.

She glanced up at the empty sky. "Where do you think the dragon is?"

They hadn't spoken of the dragon once since leaving Shayla the wood witch's forest home. Or, to be more specific: she hadn't spoken of the dragon, and Easton had honored her silence on the matter. But now that the topic was broached, he gave the query its proper due.

"Nearby, I think," he answered with all sincerity. His voice softened. "Waiting for you."

A chill went up Johanna's spine. They had been carrying on for weeks with all manner of unspoken understandings between them, most of which were connected to their time with the woods witch. Johanna still wasn't ready to talk about what it all meant, but knowing that Easton wasn't in denial about her true nature soothed her soul.

"We were wrong…*I* was wrong…to encourage you to give in to Wenavere's demands. Lady Wenavere doesn't need us. We need her…or, more specifically, your father needs her. But she doesn't need us. What she needs is to prove a point. Perhaps if we were to give her what she wanted in some other way, she would let us continue on our way without reneging on her promise." She paused. "If you're going to go north in defense of your family, it should be with your own men. Not with this…rotten flock."

"*Rotten flock*," Easton repeated, chuckling. "Well named." He sat up straighter in the saddle. There was a leanness to him that was accentuated on horseback. She felt near feral riding alongside him, their power increased now that they were no longer stuck in the procession. They rode in step, close enough to touch. "What could we give her? What does she want?"

The muted clopping of a hard-ridden mule interrupted their discourse. Turning, they saw Shupert Press bearing down on them, his expression near as strained as the beast of burden he was riding. The priest reined up before them with pinked cheeks, short of breath. But his face, ever avuncular, still managed to convey love and concern and deep Stavusian conviction. "My dear Johanna. Prince Easton." He took a moment to collect himself. "Pray come rejoin the procession. There is no damage done that cannot be set right."

Johanna made a face. "Tell me, Your Light: Do you believe the men that we are riding with are good men?"

Shupert winced. "Good men? I…um…" He looked around uncertainly before seeming to find the answer. "…I believe that they are servants of Stavus. Instruments. Traveling north, we walk a dark path. Stavus must use what he will to bring Ragar Or into the light. If he used only the pure among us, little would get done."

"Your answer is 'No,' then."

The priest laughed uncomfortably. "They lack a certain moral refinement, I will admit. But Stavus loves all who seek the air and the light. And these men are Stavusian to their very core. Of that, I am certain."

They are against Twin Worship, you mean. And for you, a Stavusian priest, that is enough. "We are not made to walk this path, Your Light. Not with these men. And not with Lady Wenavere. We must go our own way. To Union. With the unrest and uncertainty in the north, a Dayborn is needed in the capital. Surely Lady Wenavere can be made to see that. If she is the friend to the crown that she claims to be, then she would not be so petty as to refuse King Micah her assistance simply to prove a point."

Shupert reflected on Johanna's argument. Together they traveled three abreast. A riot of colors played in the roadside grasses—chickweed white and buttercup yellow and thistle purple and sunpowder orange—a myriad of colorful weeds surfing the sea of green. The red of the realm's blood was there too, Johanna knew, soaked in the soil.

"You make a fair point, my dear. But you must also consider what is being asked of Lady Wenavere. In bringing an army north, she leaves Thistleton lightly defended against the Thralk-Brakturian menace. In bringing an army north, she risks incurring the wrath of Ontish lords who will not look kindly on her crossing their lands. In bringing an army north, she ties herself to a king who is—begging your pardon, my prince—*not* at the height of his popularity. She needs others to bolster her cause. These *bad* men, as you name them, are a boon to the venture, visible proof that Struvan might stands beside her. Having Prince Easton in tow further justifies her decision. Viewed through that light, she is hardly asking too much."

Johanna hated how reasonable the priest sounded. Easton, fortunately, had a readymade retort.

"Begging *your* pardon, Your Light, but who is Lady Wenavere to forsake the king—the Holy Son of the Air—simply because she had a difference of opinion with the king's wayward second?"

Shupert nodded, conceding the point. Keeping one hand on the reins, the priest brought the other to his white-bearded jaw and pinched his chin in contemplation. "Are you a student of history, my prince?"

"I am no Wandering Tongue, but I know my kings and queens."

Shupert continued with his nodding. "Have you ever stopped to consider why the power of the Salks was seen as legitimate, even by the Struvan nobility? And why your family, the Dayborns, has struggled to command the same respect?"

Easton pursed his lips and furrowed his brow. When he didn't respond, Shupert continued in a careful, tender tone.

"It is because the Salks emphasized the paramount importance of the Stavusian faith. Sure, they gave lip service to the faith of the Twins, but they knew, being Ontish, that the Struvan culture—and thus, Stavus—was what truly held the realm together. Daguss I, Portia I, Johanna I: when people think of these Salk monarchs, they think of them in temple, on their knees before Stavus. The Salk monarchs who sowed disunion in the realm were the ones obsessed with being the Twin Ascendant. The most notorious of all being Silas Salk, who ripped the realm apart."

Johanna crinkled her nose. She knew *her* history, and she thought that Shupert was oversimplifying matters. While it was true that some Salk monarchs were partial to the Stavusian faith, none of them had denied the title of Twin Ascendant.

"I don't follow your reasoning," Easton answered. "If my family is distrusted by parts of the realm, it is for being *too* Stavusian."

"Yes. Because the Dayborns are Struvan. *Born* Stavusians. Yours is the harder task. If the Dayborns want to truly rule Ragar Or, then they must take the final step to make the realm whole. It is time for Ragar Or to put aside the demonic business of Twin worship once and for all. We must unite as one under the light of Stavus."

Easton laughed. "You are being foolish. What you are suggesting would incite a civil war."

Shupert continued undeterred, his eyes blazing with the light of the true believer. "No…with the right leader…the realm is ripe for the change. And I, for one, can think of no better symbol to represent where the realm must go than of a bonding ceremony between a Dayborn and a Salk, in the pure light of a Stavusian temple. A ceremony that forgoes all allusions to the Twins. It would send a clear message—both to the realm and to Lady Wenavere—that a blessed new day is dawning in Ragar Or. It would send a message that the true faith is recognized and cherished above all others."

Like Easton, Johanna thought the priest was being naïve about the realm. But regarding Lady Wenavere, she hoped that he was onto something. "You think that a bonding ceremony in a Stavusian temple would convince Lady Wenavere to change her mind?"

Shupert beamed. "Let me speak to her. I know my lady well; she only wants what is best for Ragar Or. There is a temple in Hevengrow"—the priest broke off, looking like he was struggling to contain his excitement—"oh what a message we would send, with a ceremony so pure, so full of air and light. Yes, let me go and speak to her." He reached over and grabbed Johanna by the wrist, giving it a squeeze. "And then I will return, and we will plan anew. All will be set right. You will see."

The priest and the mule were gone before Johanna realized that she had not given Shupert her blessing. Before she could ask Easton what he thought of the gambit, he offered up his opinion on his own. "Bonding you anew would be worth it if we could take our leave of them without risking my father's prospects. Once we are in the capital, we could reassess. Rally an army of our own, if need be."

Yes. A temple ceremony is a small price to pay for our freedom. Johanna nodded absentmindedly while bringing her hand to her scalp, running her fingers through the fine layer of hair that covered her jeyedoshi whorl. Catching herself, she dropped her hand and gave Easton a lighthearted smile. "Bonding you again wouldn't be the worst decision I ever made."

Easton smiled. "We might stop at every temple between here and Union and bond each other anew. We'd be pretending to do it for Stavus, but really, we'd be doing it for us."

She felt a laugh rising, but it died in her chest, cresting instead as a melancholic smile. They could make light of their circumstances all they wanted, but this bonding ceremony wouldn't be like the one in the woods. This one would require a performance.

One where she had best not slip up and play the jeyedoshi.

A naked man stood beside the bells of Hevengrow, looking disoriented. He wasn't entirely naked—strips of gray cloth hung from his body like the tattered remains of a storm-ravaged sail—but his obscene bits were on full display, and made more vulgar by the man's seeming unawareness of his state. Johanna, trying not to look, nearly missed the full picture, but with one final glimpse she saw that between the strips of cloth the man's back was bloody from a scourging.

"I…I…" They were nearly past, but somehow the man had become aware of their presence, and was reaching toward them with a grasping hand. "I reject the Twins, I reject the Twin Ascendant, I do! Please don't…please don't…tell them…I want to be a servant of the light…" Johanna saw the glyphs on the man's fingers the same moment that he did. Giving a cry of despair, the man brought his hand before his face and stared at the glyphs in horror. Then, with a desperate savagery, he began clawing at the glyphs with the fingernails of his opposite hand in a brutal and bloody attempt to excise the glyphs from his skin.

"Sir! Please." Johanna steered Bitterboy toward the man, not knowing how to help but wanting to. He stopped at the sound of her voice and looked at her with terror, the whites of his eyes like two dirty, cracked eggs. It was clear that he no longer remembered calling out to her, and now was weighing whether she was a friend or a foe. He made his determination clear by turning and running. His gait was a broken thing—a dragging half step with one foot and a lurching stride with the other—the whole of it painful and shameful to watch, what with the blood slicking down his back and his testicles jostling between his legs.

"Who did he run afoul of?" Easton wondered as the man fled. "It's no crime to be a gorgostrine in the Struvan parts of Ragar Or. Or at least it wasn't when I left."

Johanna didn't respond. She didn't know the specifics of why the man had been bloodied, but there seemed little question that it was connected to his faith.

The mood inside the town was subdued. The streets weren't empty, but everyone out and about had their heads down, like they were in a hurry to get back inside. The weather played a role. The pewter-gray clouds above had begun to weep, quiet, pitter-patter tears of no great consequence, but they dulled things all the same.

In reality, Hevengrow was little more than a holdfast on a small hill surrounded by simple houses, but the history of the place required that it be more, so it tried. On the southeastern outskirts of the town, a Stavusian temple preened, its gleaming white walls and vibrant stained-glass windows a striking contrast to the many buildings made of cheap, timber-reinforced plaster. There was a large pond too, down below the holdfast, with crooked piers running out into the water. The two great battles of Hevengrow, Johanna knew, had been fought in the fields and the gently rolling hills outside the town, but soil couldn't tell a story the same way that manmade structures could, so it was only inside of the bells that a person felt the town's burden.

A half mile back, the Raleigh army had begun setting up camp. The nobility, however, were continuing on toward Hevengrow. Johanna and Easton watched with interest as one figure pulled ahead of the others: the priest, on his mule, presumably bringing Lady Wenavere's reply.

"Let's go to the inn," Easton said. "The priest can find us there."

Although lacking the charm of the Green Tree, the inn at Hevengrow—called the Black Board, for its ebony timber—was surprisingly full of life. There was a caged mita bird in the corner, singing a bright song. A nattily dressed crush of folk crowded round the common room, drinking and laughing and eating skewers of meat being rushed into the room by two servers. A graceful woman with chestnut-brown hair and perfect posture seemed to be at the center of the group's attentions; she possessed an unquestionable gravity, no doubt owing to the combination of her carriage and the introspective expression on her face, a look that managed to reflect a healthy sense of self rather than aloofness. *Wulfess's true twin,* Johanna thought, feeling uncharitable with herself.

While she was studying the brown-haired woman, a wizened, white-haired member of the female sex sidled up next to Johanna. The old woman had a mean, no-shit-taking mug, not to mention a spryness that seemed at odd with her wrinkles. Her voice bit like a snake when she spoke. "You two with Yurk's lot?"

Easton looked at her askance. "Yurk? Philemon?"

"Who else?" the woman asked. But noting Easton's tone, she studied them more carefully. "You are nobility, aren't you? Why else would you be here? Stavus save you if you're Twin lovers, what with *these* around."

Johanna looked at the woman intently. "We saw a bloodied gorgostrine near the bells. But we've only arrived from the west. What's happened here?"

The old woman retreated into her wrinkles, suspicion suddenly clouding her face. "Ah…I've run my yap too much. You say you know Yurk?"

They nodded reluctantly.

"Then ask him. Or better yet"—she jerked a thumb at the perfect-posture beauty—"ask his bonded-to-be."

His bonded-to-be? Johanna looked across the room at the woman. She had a refined manner to her, but all the same, Johanna would have wagered a silver Salk that she wasn't nobility. "Have you ever seen that woman before?" she asked Easton.

An equally perplexed Easton shook his head.

The old woman used the cover of their confusion to slip away. Tired of feeling at a loss, Johanna decided to take matters into her own hands. She walked boldly across the room, nudged a few drunk revelers out of the way, and planted herself in front of the woman at the center of things.

The woman looked up at Johanna in confusion. Perhaps a flash of fear. Johanna studied her in full. The woman's ears were a little large, but instead of detracting from her looks, they seemed to accentuate the slimness of her face. She gave the impression of possessing a talent, though Johanna didn't have the foggiest clue what it might be. One thing was clear: whoever she was, she hadn't quite yet mastered the noble art of giving unwelcome visitors the shrug.

Johanna made her voice neutral and smooth. "Hello. They say you're to bond Philemon Yurk?"

"Yes. That's true." The beauty's postured stiffened. She brought her abnormally long and elegant hands together. "And who are you?"

The drunks grew quiet. They wanted to know too. The whole room was quiet save for the mita bird, which continued with its bright whistling.

Johanna felt the old Salk pride. She wasn't Wulfess, but she had always had a presence. And she was enough of her father's daughter to know how to use it to effect. "I am Johanna of House Salk," she stated plainly. "And there, across the room, stands my newly bonded. Easton Dayborn."

The inebriated held their collective breaths. The same wordless question formed in every eye: *Is she telling the truth?* The smell of uneasiness—or was it guilt?—wafted through the air, mixing with alcohol and sweat. Only the beauty held her poise, though not without difficulty. "Lady Johanna! How did you come to be here? My bonded-to-be is on the road. Perhaps you crossed him in your travels?"

Johanna had hold of something. She could feel it. She needed to shake the girl with questions like a dog would its prey. "We met a bloodied gorgostrine near the bells," she pressed, ignoring the question about Philemon. "A wretched sight. We couldn't make sense of it. Perhaps, once you've shared your name with me, you might have some insight into why we found this gorgostrine in such a state?"

They knew. They all knew. It was writ plain on every expression. The woman didn't want to say, but glancing at the others in the room, it seemed that someone might. Johanna centered in on a foppish young man with a trembling lip. His thin brown moustache was too weak a dam to hold back the torrent of words trying to escape. "Forgive us, Lady Johanna! *They* said it was a new day. A dawning of air and light. We only looked the other way because we thought they were telling the truth. We did what we thought good Struvans *should* do. But now that you're here—"

A sputtering coughing fit interrupted the young man.

Johanna turned to find Shupert Press striding inside the common room.

With a fervent sweep of the room, the priest took in everything. If he caught wind of the contention, he didn't show it. Putting away his cough, Shupert grew a grand smile. "My dearest Johanna. Prince Easton. The Lady Wenavere is agreed. We will hold the ceremony on the morrow." His voice was loud, and he let his eyes roam the room as he spoke, making it clear that he was speaking to the assembled just as much as he was speaking to Johanna and Easton. "A bonding ceremony between our good Dayborn prince and the Lady Johanna Salk, in the light of Stavus. Right here, in Hevengrow."

The revelers in the room were at first slow to react. But then one person began to applaud, and was copied shortly by the others. Before long, all were smiling and clapping, save, Johanna noticed, the wizened old woman, who stood off to the side wearing a scowl.

The priest, taking to the role of town crier with good humor, continued. He pretended to address Johanna, but the unnatural tenor of his voice made it clear that he was addressing everyone there. "Yours, however, will be the second bonding ceremony of the day. Before you, I have the honor of bonding Philemon Yurk to a woman whose talent, beauty, and devotion to the Stavusian faith precede her." Shupert's gaze latched onto the brown-haired beauty. "Hello, my dear. You must be the wonderful harpist that I've heard so much about.

"Isbel Wicker."

A weightless drifting. Black becoming sky…night becoming light…the drifting now shifting, speeding up, becoming a *soaring*. Then, the nebulousness coalesced… Johanna was roaring across the backs of thick white clouds toward a distant, sun-kissed horizon. At first, Johanna thought the roaring was the very sound of the speed with which she moved. Then she realized that she sat astride the deafening din: a terrible and monstrous creature, the base of its long neck between her thighs, its scaly form enmeshed in the endless cloud bank, the guttural roar coming from deep within its gullet.

A dream. I'm dreaming. But it was damnably real, this dream, with none of the detachment she usually experienced when she slumbered. *I'm riding a dragon. I'm—* For a second, she seemed to remember that she was Johanna, but the force of the dream demanded that she consider again. *I'm—* The reality of who she was washed over her like a wave. *I'm the dragonfeeder. I'm the sennequi piece in my own damn pocket.*

And with that thought, the dragon dove. Down through the gauzy white before exploding into the pristine past, high above Lake Wyglass. A shimmering, serpentine body of water. The dragon—*Teriquay, its name is Teriquay*—hovered over the water, gargantuan wings flapping, seeing, studying. And the dream Johanna who was not Johanna studied too, seeking out the water below, locating the gilded vessel that could only be the boat of King Reuel I and his family.

Johanna knew from history what happened next. The Shayla shadow inside of her knew too…not only knew but wanted it above all else…Johanna could feel the fire of the dragonfeeder's desires burning, all twisted and tied up with the dragon's own nature, the want for blood and fire. Together they dove yet again, down toward Wyglass with one end in mind: the death and destruction of the royal line.

Teriquay's musculature rippled when she threw back her wings, reversing the descent. There the beast hovered above the boat, horrible and hot, flame gathering in its gorge. *Now!* the Shayla shadow commanded. Johanna resisted, wanting to see the faces of the family first. She craned her neck and looked past the dragon, down at the boat where Reuel and his brood stood.

But when the faces came into view, she didn't see her Salk ancestors.

She saw herself.

And Easton.

And a small male child.

Her child.

She brought all of her being into stopping Teriquay. She had never felt more like a jeyedoshi than she did in that moment: a primal *NO!* surged through her and passed into the dragon, the force of her will so strong that it stayed the beast's flame. Feeding off her energy, the powerful green-and-black dragon spun and flew away, faster than Johanna imagined was possible. She tried to look back at Easton and the child, to no avail. She and the dragon were already too far gone.

The flight was a thunderbolt of redirected fury, low to the ground across the rolling hills of Hevengrow. The miraculous distance they covered made real by the dream, Low Osgood and Lake Wyglass lost behind them. The Shayla shadow, Johanna noted, was gone as well. *Where are we going?* Johanna thought. The answer came to her instantly.

To battle.

She was a Salk, after all. And this was where the War of the Three Brothers had been fought. *Whose side do I fight on?* Johanna wondered. It was an important choice, she knew, one that could change the entire tide of history, for she was bringing all the might and power of a dragon into the fray. *Do I support Silas Salk, who believed he was the true Twin Ascendant? Or do I support his brothers, Brogan and Xeuel, who stood for Union?* While she considered the question, Teriquay flew faster, into a hard wind that came suddenly alive with leaves the color of honeyed orange, seven-pointed with silver scrawlings. *Yubriy* leaves. They slapped her hard in the face, obscuring her vision, the many messages written on their bodies turning into a cacophony of whispers, none of which Johanna could make sense of. Teriquay, blinded, roared in frustration.

But still they flew, into the leaf-obscured unknown.

Johanna closed her dreaming eyes. Stilled her mind. In doing so, she stilled the dragon beneath her. When she opened them again, the Yubriy leaves were gone, and she and Teriquay were gliding over flat grasslands, looking for a place to land. In the far distance, she heard the dulcet tones of a talented singer and lutist. She had never heard the song before but it was instantly familiar to her, like a remembered dream. But soon the song faded away, and she and the dragon came to rest at a green-white borderland, the abundant green grass giving way to a frostflower-dotted blanket of snow.

She looked up. She felt the form of the mountain before she saw it: a jagged tower of rock, cold to the core and cloaked in the finery of winter, snow and sleet and ice. The mountain made Teriquay seem small. Johanna breathed in the coldness, letting it sting her lungs.

A person was standing halfway up the mountain's face. A woman. Staring down at Johanna, as Johanna was staring up. The dream became a tunnel, their gazes at either end. They drew closer to one another, despite neither of them moving. Johanna could see every facet of the woman, every detail. The rich golden pour of her glorious, dark-blond hair. The blue eyes like bottomless pools. The bold curves of her body. And last but not least, the frightening power in her possession, stored behind an enigmatic half smile that seemed to suggest that their father's selection of her as the Twin Ascendant had not only been correct, but inevitable.

Johanna spoke her sister's name. "Wulfess."

"Johanna," Wulfess replied, the distance between them no impediment to hearing. "My beloved twin." The briefest shadow of sadness passed over Wulfess's face. "I hate that we must war against one another."

"War?"

Wulfess laughed an incredulous laugh, one that echoed off the mountain rocks. "It would seem that way. Why else bring your dragon? Or your son?"

My son? She turned back toward the endless bounty of grass. A young man stood some distance behind her. He had a face that hurt her heart, for in almost every way it was the face of her beloved Easton, except younger. The longer she looked at him, however, the less like Easton he seemed. The look of his face was close to the same, yes, but the expression on it hued to a darkness that the father didn't possess. In addition, the young man held a sword at his side with the languid gravity of one at unnerving ease with the instrument. "My son," she whispered. She didn't know if she was calling to him or mourning his grave expression.

He opened his mouth to respond. When he did, a leaf came flying out: an orange, seven-pointed Yubriy leaf immediately joined on the wind by thousands of others, the lot of them rushing toward her, whispering a name.

Weston.

The name filled up her ears with increasing pressure, until even the dragon joined in the cry—

—Johanna awoke with a start. Tried to get her bearings. Flames swam blue-orange in the hearth, providing the room's only light. Easton was curled beside her, breathing soft and steady, his right hand on her hip. She took hold of it and moved it to the soft swell of her belly. Breathed slowly. *Was the dream true?* The thought that she might be with child hadn't crossed her mind. But the dream felt like a revelation. *But if I'm pregnant, I should know, shouldn't I?* The dream had given her many clues to unravel, but what she needed to know this very moment was if she was with child, if her body was concealing—

"Something's different."

Easton. Awake and moving, he propped up on one elbow, finding her face in the firelight. His hand guarded the gentle swell of her stomach with all the protection his five fingers could afford.

"You're with child."

The entity within her, connecting to its father's voice, chose that moment to reveal itself to her body. Johanna didn't understand how the moment transformed her, but it did. She knew beyond a shadow of a doubt that she was pregnant, and that it was a boy too.

"I am," she responded. "A boy, I think." She paused. "No. I'm certain."

Easton's face filled with joy. She should have been happy, but Easton's expression filled her with sadness, for she remembered the look of their son, with his face so grave.

She told Easton the rest.

"And I know his name."

Silas O' the Songs

Grocian Mock, the big boar of a man, wanted to dance. The woman wearing the blue-and-white shawl was leaving by then, taking the secret she had whispered into Grocian's ear with her. Silas watched the woman go, plucking his rosewood lute all the while, wondering but not daring to inquire what the woman had shared.

"The rhythm, the rhythm, you must keep the rhythm!" Grocian shouted at Silas while taking a serving wench in hand. This Silas did reflexively, falling back on an old river song, "The Ragknot Trout," a song that he could play without thinking. Up-tempo and driving, the song soon had Lord Grocian spinning the girl silly, back and forth across the stone flooring while the rest of the room laughed, caught up in Lord Grocian's reckless joy. The dancing was a dangerous thing: the large but surprisingly agile lord was deep in his cups, and with every drunken step he took it seemed he was on the verge of crashing to the floor and crushing the wench, who had a look in her eyes that suggested that she was either frightened out of her wits or feeling fully alive for the very first time.

But Grocian did not fall. He released the serving girl at song's end with a flourish, twirling her into the arms of a young man wearing the emblem of his house, the mast and hull of a bow-facing warship. Then he called for a horn of ale, sat down, and resumed drinking.

Silas watched Lord Grocian intently. His wide, inebriated smile. His gleaming, good-news-getting eyes. The way his attention bounced about, the eager tug of his lips. Before long the gregarious lord bellowed at Silas to play another song, and then he was up out of his seat, parading around the room, pulling a confidant close. Spilling the secret. Silas watched as the secret spread around the room, fast as wildfire, until it became less a secret and simply news, albeit news that Silas still didn't know.

Though perhaps he did know. He certainly suspected what was being shared.

Somewhere in Winterworn Castle, the Sagekind, that bony fright, was dead.

Silas tried to imagine the jeyedoshi's power gone from the world. It made his head spin. It made him feel sick. Most disorienting of all, he didn't know if he was glad of it or sad.

You don't know who you are, do you, Silas O' the Songs? You don't know yourself in the fucking slightest.

Still, he played his instrument. Every song upbeat, to match the mood of the room. Lord Grocian, the ringleader of the festivities, spurred the room to revelry, calling out song request after song request. The others in the room—Lord Grocian had brought with him a stable of cousins up from Dunning Harbor, not to mention a tenner of soldiers—sang and danced by the light of the hearth fire, stopping only to lean close and continue in their whispering, the great game of it. Mock men wearing warship surcoats, their peninsula-grown beards sopped in ale, eyes alight;

a smaller gaggle of women, servants mostly, but some with Mock blood; celebrants all, whispering, whispering, whispering, whispering…

"WHAT NEWS?! I…I MUST KNOW!"

Was that his own voice? Shouting? Trembling? Silas looked down and saw that the rosewood lute given to him by Merjy the woods witch was no longer in his hands but down by his side. He recalled for an instant the stinging wisp, and he wondered anew what the woods witch had taken from him. But the silence of the room brought him back to the present. The Mocks were looking at him as if he'd gone mad. Lord Grocian especially. The pumpkin-faced lord of Dunning Harbor shouted back at him.

"Never mind you! Play another song, lutist!" Grocian gave his hands a sharp clap. "Play!"

There was no mistaking Lord Grocian's order. The logical thing for Silas to do was to hop to, and play. But Silas refused. No one in the room was more surprised than Silas himself, who, on some level, kept waiting for his body to spring into action and do what it had always done: the bidding of the patron. But instead, Silas asserted himself once more.

"No. I would know what's taken place."

A question hung from Lord Grocian's wasted face. *Who are you?* it asked. Silas watched as Lord Grocian suddenly recalled that Silas stood in good favor with Wulfess Salk. The Lord of Dunning Harbor turned cheery, and with a good-natured bonhomie brought Silas into the fold. "The lutist needs a break!" He grabbed a serving girl by the arm. "Bring the man ale. I'll bring the news."

Grocian walked over, strutting like a bull, and leaned in, serving up the same whisper so recently served him. "The Wraith in Red is fallen. There's your news. Feathered by Seydron Qorl. Dead, they say, though word is the big mute carried off the bastard's corpse for safekeeping. Qorl's dead too, a pity, his head hacked off by the mute's bonded, but I say Seydron's life's a worthy price to pay for ridding the world of that jeyedoshi."

First the queen. And now the Sagekind. Only earlier this evening Silas had learned of the queen's passing. The double blow suffered by the Dayborn dynasty was difficult to fathom.

Not knowing what to say, Silas held his tongue. In return, the Lord of Dunning Harbor held Silas in his gaze. Silas didn't dare look away. Trying to focus on Grocian's glassy, ale-swimming eyes was like tracking the movements of fish beneath the surface of water. When at last they stilled, Silas could see that the Lord of Dunning Harbor was attempting to fix Silas's allegiances.

"I trust you're with us, songsmith?"

Who's us? he wanted to ask. He supposed that Lord Grocian meant the Ontish houses. But he also remembered Grocian saying goodbye to Prince Ajax and his bonded Greta Worrint at Dunning Harbor, speaking small pleasantries and playing at good graces. *What a terrible game the nobles play,* he thought. "It seems that I am," Silas answered vaguely. *It seems that I'm on the side of whoever claims me.*

Grocian's fish eyes focused in. "Good," he said, seconding the word with a hearty back slap. The wench, newly arrived with Silas's tankard, hesitated in handing it over. "See to your drink, then see to another song." An idea occurred to him. "Why not play that prophecy song of yours? Huh? The one that served the Dayborns so well." Lord Grocian left laughing at his own cleverness.

Silas bit his cheek to keep from responding. Everyone knew that Silas's version of "The Queen's Burning Heart" referenced Queen Portia I, who had died in the flames of the fire at the Three Dragons Inn in Low Osgood a century and a half prior. But Silas knew exactly what Lord Grocian meant. Silas's song—in combination with his presence—was supposed to have been the magic that kept the Dayborns safe. *A song first sung in the Vake, prolongs the line of the suns.* But at the moment, Dayborns were dying left and right. There was a second leaf back in Union, Silas knew. He had no clue what was written on it, but the combination of the two leaves had convinced the Sagekind that Silas and his song were essential to fulfilling the prophecy.

For all the good it did him or the queen. The song lives, but they're both dead.

A different thought sent a shiver up his spine. *But you never played the true version of the song, did you? Maybe the magic was in the words, the ones you kept to yourself.*

The thought settled on him like a dark cloud. Sitting back down, he drank the ale, but instead of easing his burdens, it sat heavy in his guts. *What is your role, Silas O' the Songs?* He turned the thought over and over, wondering how he had waited until now to consider his responsibility to the realm-shaking events he was caught up in. *It was fate that brought me here.* The image of a pox-scarred, stringy-haired rodent of a man popped into his thoughts. *Fate and Wyn Dunkin.* Surely the woodkin knew Silas's true purpose. Wherever the thrice-damned fate tinkerer was.

Memories of the little man came flooding back. His mad shenanigans, his artful wit. But also darker images, like the red workings of his dagger. *I would have died multiple times were it not for him.* He remembered the fight in the forest near the Yubriy Tree, against the Desighart vultures. The way

Wyn had whipped in and out of the trees, delivering death. *He saved my life, though I showed little gratefulness for it.*

But Wyn hadn't been the only one in the forest that day. Madrig and Jacy had saved him, too, nearly at the cost of Madrig's life.

They who were holed up in the castle, possibly guarding the Sagekind's corpse.

I should go to them. The notion came to Silas with a gut-driven urgency. He owed Madrig and Jacy his life, after all. And now they needed allies. An odd chirrup of laughter escaped his lips. It was ludicrous, he knew, to think that he might make it to their side. *And what help could I give them, even if I made it?* But the rightness of the feeling wouldn't leave him. It was as if he was suddenly being swept up in the same mystical energy that had guided his hand into the tree hollow to discover the Yubriy leaf.

That's it. I'll go to Madrig and Jacy. That's what I'll do.

The front of the room exploded with a sudden infusion of men. Mactus Garstring at the head. Black ringmail shirts on the lot of them, swords at the ready. Until now, every time Silas had seen Mactus Garstring he had looked like a man preoccupied by a different moment in time—namely, the place where he'd rather be. Now it appeared he'd found it. Mactus had a large, rectangular-shaped head and angry-sea curls of salted-black hair. Spotting Lord Grocian, Mactus beelined across the room and shared yet another secret, sharp and stinging.

Silas didn't have to wait nearly as long to learn this one.

"Horos Ollspaer, with the help of the Heron, has seized the Black and White Tower!" Grocian shouted to all and sundry. "They've taken the king prisoner. Lord Daguss is rallying the Ontish to the Bloodbone Tower. We will go to him now with arms."

Silas tried but failed to grasp the full implications of what was occurring. *Was there fighting? Did the Dayborns resist? Where was Cato? Was he on the side of the Salks? Or was he on the side of his father?* There was no way to know. All around Silas, Mock men were fast sobering themselves up, some by slapping their faces and others by worrying at their weapons, the long knives and short swords hanging from their sides. And then, a collective exodus, Mocks falling in with Garstrings pouring out the door, while a few of the women cried, confused and afraid.

Hang back. Then slip out. Go to Madrig and Jacy. Now's your chance.

Silas waited patiently for the room to clear. Preoccupied himself by putting the lute away in its case. Kept his head down. The sounds of men on the move faded quickly. Thinking that he was in the clear, he looked up.

Mactus Garstring was standing over him. Looking the epitome of command. Wearing an expression that made it clear he would brook no argument. "Silas O' the Songs. Come with. I'm bringing you to the Bloodbone."

Silas did as he was told.

The night was long and full of rumors. Silas was brought to the red room, Lord Daguss's chambers, where he sat in a corner on an orphan chair, made from the unyielding wood of the kurmenhi tree. He took his lute from the case but didn't play it, assuming that if music was wanted, someone would request it. No one did. So instead, he pricked his ears and primed his eyes, to hear what he could hear and see what he could see.

The room itself was a marvel. Painted the color of a dark ruby, it had an otherworldly quality that acted on everyone who entered it. In the center of the room, a forever-flower water fountain recycled itself endlessly, creating gentle ripples around the silver-gray *milu sfal* blossoms that floated atop the water. The elevated engineering behind it was a mystery. Gray stone pavers flowed away from the fountain, circling ever outward. A massive candle chandelier hung from the ceiling, made from black iron and dancing with flame, the scores of candles like fingers formed into a perilous half fist of fire.

Ontish power players came and went. The imperturbable Daguss Salk at the center of the storm. The Lord of High Osgood rarely moved from his spot near the door but directed the evening's events with a word here, a nod there, and occasionally, a pointed gesture. Looking at Lord Daguss in his moonbear coat, Silas couldn't help but be reminded of the beast at the welcome feast. He wondered if Daguss's words were his claws, reaching out to strike at his enemies in the castle.

Wulfess stood by her father's side. She radiated a warmth that Lord Daguss lacked, but the warmth wasn't entirely comforting; like a fire it licked, threatening to singe those who didn't respect its power. She stepped away from her father's side now and again, sometimes to share a private word but otherwise for the effect of being seen alone. She was dressed like a highborn Kalandragotan: she wore one of the pennywolf pelts gifted to her by Cato, complemented by gold bracelets on her wrists and brown calfskin boots that reached to her knees. Her dark-blond hair, ever spellbinding, made mock of the pennywolf pelt, shimmering with the life so recently deprived of the creature upon which its golden pour rested. Only once did she make eye contact with Silas, and then with customary verve: she looked at him with the bold intensity of a woman with nothing to hide, holding his gaze until he looked away, which didn't take long.

The room was as notable for who wasn't in it as it was for who was. The most conspicuous absence being Cato Ollspaer's. With an eye on the door, Silas kept waiting for Wulfess's bonded-to-be to make an appearance. But only Ontishmen walked in and out, reporting whispers into Daguss's ear.

An hour in, the energy of the room shifted to the door. Mactus Garstring entered, but Silas could tell by the reaction of those standing post that a more compelling person was following in his wake. Silas watched, expecting the towering Ollspaer heir to follow Garstring inside. To his surprise, a woman entered instead.

Wren Ollspaer. Horos's sister.

On Wren's heels were two ladies-in-waiting, a fat man in gray robes, and a gruff-looking soldier wearing a frostflower surcoat. Wren wore a frostflower-embroidered indigo cloak that brushed against the stone as she made her way to Daguss. The cloak, it seemed, was the only soft thing about her. Otherwise, she was the picture of severity, from the inexpressive line of her lips to the steely look in her eyes. She wasn't an ugly woman by any means, but what beauty she possessed had long forgone its claim on her personality, the contest having clearly been won by her stoical side.

Lord Daguss greeted her wearing a similarly dour expression. Looking at the two of them, Silas worried that something truly terrible had occurred. But then, just as Silas was certain that a disturbing proclamation was imminent, Lord Daguss and Lady Wren joined hands. A second later, Lord Daguss bent over and kissed Wren on the forehead, after which she brought her lips to his white-bearded chin. The fat man in gray robes, watching nearby, took the exchange of kisses as his cue to come and stand before them.

Someone closed the door, sealing the red room shut. A tense silence fell. Silas made a count of the room. Twelve souls in total. Lord Daguss Salk. The Lady Wren Ollspaer. Wulfess. Mactus Garstring. Grocian Mock. The fat man in the gray robes. The gruff soldier in the frostflower surcoat. Wren's two ladies-in-waiting. Two Salk knights. And Silas made twelve. No Darryn Coffyn, and no Cato Ollspaer. *Someone has to be out there defending the Bloodbone, I suppose.*

Lord Daguss cast his gaze about, taking the measure of every person in the room, Silas included. Finished, he spoke, a bite to his baritone. "We have arrived at a perilous moment. Horos has turned his back on his fellow Ontish and aligned himself with the Heron. When the Wraith in Red fell, Lord Dante convinced Horos that it was part of a larger plot. Together they moved quickly to take control of the Black and White Tower. Birds and Frostflowers were brought inside the city and castle gates. Blood was shed. Micah Dayborn—I will no longer call him king—is now in Horos's possession. Now Horos sends his sister to me, to demand that I and the other Ontish lords swear fealty to him as the new king of Ontish Ragar Or."

Silas's breath caught in his throat. He could sense the spirits of the newly dead floating around him. The extinguished suns, the felled birds, the wilted frostflowers. The game the great lords played was afoot.

"What arrangement does Horos have with the Heron?" Grocian asked.

"They meant to split Ragar Or between them. An Ontish half, and a Struvan one. But the Heron has overplayed his hand. A realization Darryn Coffyn is helping him come to grips with this very moment. When the fighting began, Cato Ollspaer took control of the castle gates. There are more of the Heron's men outside of Winterworn's walls than within, and Cato intends to keep it that way. Lord Dante understands that he cannot safely get to his men. Not without"—he glanced at Wren—"*our* leave. Tomorrow, as has been planned all along, Cato will bond my daughter Wulfess. And tonight, I will bond Wren Ollspaer."

Silas struggled to process the enormity of what he was hearing. From the sound of it, the Heron had won over Horos, but while that battle was being fought, Daguss had made allies of the other Ollspaers. *Who truly commands the Frostflowers?* Silas wondered. *The father? The sister? Or the son?*

Wren stepped forward. Against the candle-washed red walls, her blue cloak was an ethereal sight; she seemed on the verge of slipping into a different dimension. Her face, however, was a perfect stone mask, hiding whatever emotion she was experiencing underneath. "By bonding Lord Daguss of House Salk—and by my nephew's bonding of the Lady Wulfess—House Ollspaer pledges itself to the *Ontish* cause. Tonight, I turn my back on my brother Horos and join with Lord Daguss to usher in a new era. My nephew, I assure you, stands with me. Tomorrow, Horos will learn the truth of our loyalties." Her stare somehow became harder. "When the time comes, every person here will attest to what they are about to witness. But until then—not a word."

Silas thought he understood the gist of the matter. Ontish custom dictated that unbonded women remain loyal to their families at all costs. If Wren meant to rebel against her brother, she needed to be freed from familial obligations. And the only way to do that was to join a different family.

Lord Daguss and Wren settled into the ritual stance. The gray-robed fat man—only now did Silas understand that he was a gorgostrine—cleared his throat, ready to begin. But at the first note from his oddly high-pitched voice, Wulfess interrupted him.

"Father. Not like this. On my new lady mother's behalf, I must insist on a bit of ceremony. A song, perhaps. 'The Binding Cloth.' Every bonding ceremony, even a rushed one, should have a song."

Lord Daguss didn't look particularly thrilled by the idea, but all the same, he bowed his head in deference to his daughter. Wulfess ran with it. She was on Silas instantly, closing in on his corner of the room with a predator's quickness, motioning and saying, "Up, up!"

Silas fumbled over the rosewood lute as he stood, nearly dropping it. *I shouldn't be here,* he thought, but, as was so often the case, his thoughts and circumstances weren't aligned. He glanced up at Wulfess, thinking, somehow, that she might recognize the wrongness of his presence and send him on his way. But there was no love in her gaze, only the surety of possession, the slightly dead-eyed stare that said *you belong to me.*

He supposed he did. Because he certainly didn't belong to himself.

He readied himself to play the song.

Interlude

Snow fell all through the sleepless night. An infinity of white tapestries hanging from the heavens. The snow made form-fitting coats for the castle's gargoyles and laid heavy hands upon its crenellations. Down in the courtyards it did different work, covering bloodstains and purifying the air and burying the corpses of the fallen where they lay. But soldiers unmade the last, rooting out the corpses to take them down into cold dungeons beneath the Old Tower, where they would keep until more pressing issues were settled.

The snow carried with it a song of stillness, the tune sung with such gentle insistence that the same men who had recently been caught up in the mad cacophony of murder heeded its message. Who were these men? Why, they were the victors: a mesh of Kalandragotans and Struvans, smuggled inside the castle gates to kill nearly fifty men loyal to the Dayborn king. At best, they were uneasy allies. At worst, they were foes as yet undeclared. The Struvans in particular had reason to be anxious: word was that a group of Frostflowers under the command of Cato Ollspaer had closed the castle gates behind them, cutting them off from their comrades. But Lord Dante had signaled no alarm, and the great swordsman Jakastor

Weylcoin walked in their midst, so they kept their calm and continued with the steady work of relocating the corpses.

One man, a Wandering Tongue in the service of Lord Dante, brought a torch to the dungeons and made a list of the deceased. *Erasmus Stryder. Larin Dove. Braxton Walshing. Percy Moon.* Weylcoin had done for Stryder, everyone knew, expertly running him through with one short sword while parrying blows from the king with the other, a display of fighting prowess that still had tongues wagging. Afterward, Weylcoin unhanded Micah Dayborn of his weapon, and with it his rule. The Wandering Tongue wished he had been there to see it. But his was the job of double-checking, and so he did it, reporting back to Lord Dante in the dead of night that yes, every last Dayborn loyalist inside the castle walls save the king was dead.

The Heron accepted the news with a nod. Then he returned to huddling with Horos Ollspaer. Lord Dante had spent the night trying to keep the rage-filled once-and-future king of Kalandragote from doing something rash; it was clear to Dante that the parasite of paranoia had entered Horos's system and was eating him alive. Horos railed against his son Cato most of all, stalking to-and-fro in front of the wall of pennywolf pelts, swearing vengeance and jabbering nonsense about what it meant to be a true Twin Ascendant. *He's forgotten that I'm Struvan,* Dante thought more than once. But most of all, Dante concentrated on ushering Horos through the night without letting events spiral out of control. The Dayborns were finished. That was the paramount thing. Aligning himself with Horos had been folly, but there were understandings and there were understandings, and after his shadowy tete-a-tete with Darryn Coffyn in the armory, it appeared that the one he had struck with Daguss Salk might still be salvaged.

Despite everything.

It helped that Dante had an ace in hand. One that he had confided to Darryn Coffyn, and would reveal on the morrow.

Up the winding steps of the north tower, in a barricaded room, the mute Madrig and his bonded Jacy sat vigil over the still-breathing body of Gregor Thorn. Together, the pair had used their rudimentary medical knowledge to extract the two arrows that had pierced the Sagekind's body. But the damage to the Sagekind's body was substantial, and worse, his breathing had changed over into a death rattle. If there was any chance of saving Gregor, they needed to get him help, and quick.

Leaving the room, however, seemed a certain death. In choosing to take possession of the Sagekind's body, they had made enemies of every faction in the castle, enemies that, based on the difficulties they had encountered barricading themselves in the north tower, were intent on butchering them at the first opportunity. Their enemies were waiting outside, eager to lay them to waste.

In the peeling-black hour before dawn, a disturbance at the window. Jacy, drawing her short sword, identified the grappling hook and moved quickly to cut it free. But before doing so, she tried to see who was climbing. A familiar voice emanated from the first of two ascending shadows.

"It's me, Deglan. I have someone with me. And a medicine that might help."

The cold break of dawn brought an end to the snow. Gray-bellied snow clouds fled in full retreat from the sun, like an army broken by the calvary charge of sunrays. Below the fleeting clouds, in the back courtyard of Winterworn Castle, stood the Circle of Stones, the ancient Kalandragote site of the twin-death rite. The center of the circle was an immaculate blanket of unbroken white. The stones stood sentinel around the circle, stoic and quiet.

Servants frightened by the previous night's fighting awoke to learn that the bonding ceremony between the heir to the Kalandragote kingdom and the daughter of Lord Daguss Salk remained scheduled as planned. Warily, they began the work of preparing for the day's ceremonies. Mostly the work was confined to the kitchens and the great hall, but a score were sent to the Circle of Stones to prepare the field.

They went about their labor in a deep and foreboding silence, exchanging uneasy looks, but never saying a word.

Silas O' the Songs

Silas awoke to the gurgle of the forever-flower water fountain, soft fingers pushing the hair from his eyes. Wulfess. He was sitting on the stone pavers, leaning against the side of the fountain, the back of his olive-green doublet damp with spray. Wulfess looked calm, alert and rested. Impressive, because if she had slept, he didn't know when. Her dress was the same: Wulfess's already wild mystique was enhanced by the pennywolf pelt hanging from her shoulders, intensifying her powerful aura.

"It's time," she told him.

He pushed away from the fountain. Made a quick check of the rosewood lute for water damage.

"Time for what?" he asked, frightened of the answer.

She stood. Looked down on him. "Time for my bonding ceremony to Cato Ollspaer. Time to discover what fate has in store for us."

He moved to his feet. Though taller than Wulfess by a few inches, there was something about the angle of her chin that made it seem as if they were looking eye to eye. Glancing around the room, Silas confirmed that it was empty. The room's red walls suddenly seemed a swirling cosmos, making him feel nauseous.

"I have made a decision," she said. "About you and your song."

Silas tightened his grip on the rosewood lute's neck. "What decision is that, my lady?"

"I have decided that you will make the song…about me."

Silas could hear Wyn Dunkin laughing in his head. "But Lady Wulfess…the lyrics don't fit."

"They will, once you're finished with it. You'll mold them to me the way you do your body when we're abed."

"I…I don't think—"

Wulfess interrupted him with a little burr of a laugh, her hand reaching out to cup his cheek. "And bless Beoliotius for that! Listen to me, Silas O' the Songs. I mean to give you the life you've always wanted. A kept life, in my court at Kalandragote. This song you've written is a powerful magic. A changed word here, an altered phrase there, and I'll become the queen in the song. No? Together we'll tell the story of how I came upon you singing the true lyrics in the snow. As for the name in the song…it's a fitting moniker for my future child, don't you think? You'll write a song that affirms my rights as the queen of Kalandragote, and of my future son as its heir. Then, when he's born, he'll have the legitimacy of a Yubriy Tree prophecy behind him."

Silas's insides twisted and turned like the braided silver-brown bark of the Yubriy Tree. "Lady Wulfess, I would not go down that road again! I would not have the song do to you what it did to the Dayborns—"

Wulfess smirked. "The song did nothing to the Dayborns that they did not do to themselves. Nor did the prophecy. These…*prophecies*…are little more than shadows cast by a long-dead deity. If the Yubriy Tree knew what it wanted, it would have achieved it long ago. All that matters is how those with power make use of the words."

Silas remembered the feel of the Yubriy Tree's twining, silver-brown bark against the palms of his hands. The breathing soul living inside the tree, infinitely patient. If the tree knew how to do anything, it knew how to wait.

"As you say, my lady."

Wulfess studied him carefully. "Yes. As *I* say. That's what I want from you, Silas O' the Songs. To do as I say." She lifted a finger and brought it to his sternum, traced a path down the center of him with the sharp of her nail. "You think me a wicked woman, I know. Perhaps I am." She paused. "I knew another wicked woman, once. We met when we were girls, on tour with our fathers. In Qorl of all places. There we became fast friends. We had much in common." A strange grin grew on Wulfess's face. "When we returned to our respective homes, we began writing letters to one another, letters that traveled back and forth between the deep woods of the Vake and the mountain passes that led to High Osgood. When she told me in her letters that she had taken a handsome young lutist as a lover, I was envious beyond compare."

Anna Josephine? Silas looked at Wulfess with shock. He could tell by her eyes that it was true. In an instant, the old wounds reopened. In his mind's eye, Silas could see Anna Josephine Arc's black ringlets and soft doe eyes, hear her teasing laughter. She who had chosen him for his talent, and spurned him for the same.

Wulfess's roaming finger found its way back to Silas's face, where she caressed his cheeks. "I wanted the man she described in those letters. Wanted him for my own. A man who would play songs for me, and make love to me, a man who would do as I desired. If given such a man, I knew that I would never give him up."

Silas's heart hammered hard in his chest. "My lady…you are to be bonded. Today! Were Cato to learn the true nature of our relationship…he would kill me!"

She took her hand away. Beheld him with her beatific blues. "Do you know what it means, Silas O' the Songs, to be a Twin Ascendant?"

Silas shook his head.

"It means simply, that in the end, you win. You overcome. You get your way. What most people don't understand is how that sort of selfishness is a burden. Because to win…why, then others have to lose, don't they? And who truly has the strength to inflict the suffering of defeat? Who wants the responsibility of fashioning a world according to their own vision, when the price is constant vigilance against those who believe that they ought to have their way as well?" She paused, pinning him with her stare. "I do. When you look at me, Silas O' the Songs, you are looking at a true Twin Ascendant. And lucky you"—she reached out yet again to touch him on the chest—"I have given you a glimpse of my vision and the role I want you to play in it. The only choice you have to make is whether to accede to its inevitability or to resist and reap the consequences."

She took her hand away. "One hour, Silas O' the Songs. When I return, I want my song. Then we will go down together, to welcome the new world that I intend to make."

Wulfess returned for him an hour later. He followed her out of the red room without a word. Together they descended the Bloodbone Tower.

Servants with bristle brushes moved aside as they crossed the landing between the second and third levels. Chins pinned to their clavicles, eyes on the floor. The bristles were red with the blood the servants had scrubbed from the stone. The Sagekind's blood, telling the story of his death.

The tower was cold, but it was nothing compared to the bracing shock that greeted Silas outside. Sunlight strained high above, failing to provide warmth but blazing against the snow-white ground, assaulting the eyes. Feathered inkblots *qorked* and hopped in the blinding white. *If not crows then black-feathered toads,* Silas decided.

An honor guard of the crows' upright cousins, all wearing the beige and black of House Salk, formed around Wulfess. Men who hadn't slept a wink. Silas could see in their eyes that they didn't know if they were going to a bonding ceremony or to their doom.

The Salk men fell in with the other Ontish, Coffyns and Garstrings and Mocks and Qorls. *Enough men to fight, too few to guarantee victory.* The leading men—Grocian Mock, Darryn Coffyn, and Mactus Garstring—surrounded Lord Daguss, until he extricated himself and fell back with his daughter, taking her arm in his own. The father wore a moonbear coat; the daughter was dressed in bronze pennywolf fur. The group moved across the yard en masse, boots crunching on snow, steel resting on hips.

Ahead, Struvans and Kalandragotans. The Heron's and Horos's men. They stood still as statues outside the Circle of Stones. The stones reminded Silas of seven minor deities, cold slabs of rock jutting up from the ground without explanation or apology, stones that predated the structures built up around them. The snow in the center of the stones had been shoveled away, revealing the coarse ghost-green grass that lived on the peninsula. Scattered about the grounds were frostflowers. A handful of renegade blues tunneled up through the snowbanks, but most of the flowers had been plucked and brought into the yard, their slender, funnelform bodies arranged with a kind of wild intention.

Silas continued taking inventory of the yard. Looking up, he saw a sight that made him gasp. Overlooking the circle, on a stone platform caked with snow, sat Micah Dayborn, the king of all Ragar Or. His legs were bound to a wooden chair. A kurmenhi wood tree stump had been placed before him, to serve as a makeshift table. Upon the tree stump, an untouched slab of bloody beef rested on a pewter plate. The king sat listlessly, with a drawn and tired expression, the color leeched from his face. His once proud gray-black beard resembled a dried-up bramble of thorns.

Standing on opposite sides of Micah Dayborn were Horos Ollspaer and the Heron. An ugly crown of black iron pronged with white rested on Horos's head. His eyes made angry stabs at the Ontish as they approached, while his hand patted at the baselard on his belt. Dante Heron, too, looked frayed, though, unlike Horos, he made every effort to hide his nerves behind a façade of equipoise, presenting himself in a pristine white cloak and with an everyman smile, as if to say *we are all friends here.* Jakastor Weylcoin stood off to the Heron's left. At the back of the stone platform were Gothred and the Ascendant Few, the king of Kalandragote's honor guard. Wren Ollspaer stood next to the warrior faction, a dispassionate expression on her face.

On the far side of the stones stood two lines of teenaged men. Clad in fur, with spears and swords and shields in their hands. They had an air about them, like ones before battle. Silas didn't have the first idea who they were, or why they were there.

Silas searched for Cato. He was nowhere to be seen.

Lord Daguss escorted Wulfess to the perimeter of the Circle. Together, they looked up at the platform.

"Today, I bring my daughter, Wulfess Salk, to be bonded to the heir to Kalandragote, Cato Ollspaer." Daguss gave a cursory glance around the yard. "Tell me, Horos: Where is your son?"

Horos ignored the question. "I am *King* Horos, of Kalandragote," he growled. "As long as you are in my kingdom, you will address me as such."

"As it pleases you," Daguss responded. "Though I am curious: What title do you give your prisoner on the platform? He, too, was a king recently, wasn't he?"

Horos's face fixed in a sneer. "I give him the title of *dead man.* A title we had all agreed upon. No? Or are you as false as I always feared you were, Daguss? You who gave Seydron Qorl permission to kill the Wraith in Red."

Daguss's face betrayed nothing. "Seydron Qorl's quarrel with the Sagekind was his own. Though I won't deny that everything that's transpired since last night might be in the best interest of Ragar Or. You won't hear me protest Micah Dayborn's fall." Daguss's eyes went to the Heron. "But this so-called dead man before us has two sons. Neither of which are here." Daguss broke off his gaze from Dante and gave another searching look around the yard. "We're missing many important sons, it would seem. Perhaps if more of them were present, we might get a better handle on how to proceed."

Silas experienced a Dunning Harbor flashback. He was once again watching the great lords taking part in a play, reciting their lines.

But the play had gone wrong in Dunning Harbor.

It wasn't difficult to imagine the same happening here.

The voice of Dante Heron made itself known. That preening, supercilious tenor. "I have a bonding gift for the couple. Outside the castle. A gift that speaks to the subject of…sons. If I might pass through the castle gates, I believe I could address Lord Daguss's concerns."

The first off-script lines. Or at least that was Silas's impression, based on the way Horos spun on the white-cloaked lord. Lord Dante tried to ease Horos's concerns by bringing a hand to his shoulder and whispering in his ear. This seemed to placate Horos without putting him entirely at ease.

Daguss Salk waited patiently for the whispering to stop before weighing in. "By all means, Lord Dante. Go and retrieve your gift."

Dante worked his thin lips into a wry smile, then turned and crossed the castle yard with a premeditated swiftness, making for the arched passageway between the armory and the throne room that led to the front courtyard. A befuddled Horos watched him go with mounting alarm. Horos was so preoccupied by Dante's leaving that he didn't notice his sister Wren crossing the yard. When at last he turned and saw that Wren was standing next to Daguss and Wulfess, his face contorted into a knot of emotion: disbelief and horror and anger all a tangle.

"What is this?!" Horos shouted at his sister. "A betrayal? Do you betray me?!" With its pits and ridges, Horos's red face looked like crusting magma.

Wren kept silent. All around the yard, a dangerous sizing-up was taking place.

Horos drew the baselard from his belt and pointed it at Gothred. "Return my sister to the frostflower fold!" he commanded.

Gothred took a halting step forward. Then, thinking better of it, he looked to Wren.

She addressed his unasked question. "Cato will be here in a moment, Gothred. With men loyal to him. Then it will be for you to decide whether you want to die for the old Kalandragote or live for the new one."

Gothred froze. The Ascendant Few followed their commander's lead.

Horos, beside himself with anger, charged forward with the dagger held high as if he might fly from the platform and take the matter in his own hands. He stopped and screamed before reaching the edge. "You treasonous bitch! How dare you betray your family! How dare you betray me!"

Wren met her brother's accusation with words of ice. "This isn't a betrayal, Brother. This is a long-awaited reckoning." She paused for effect. "You should know that I bonded Lord Daguss last night. In the red room. There are many here who will attest to the fact. Once Cato bonds Wulfess, the Ollspaer clan will be made anew. We will be a family without you."

Wren's response put Horos on his heels. Silas could hear the ragged edge of the Kalandragote king's panicked breathing. Fighting a visibly mounting fear, Horos attempted to reshape the narrative of his rapidly crumbling reality. "When the Heron returns, we'll gut the lot of you!"

Daguss Salk put an end to the farce.

"Dante Heron isn't returning, Horos. You see, that's the thing about birds. They fly away."

Horos's face twisted in shock and anger. His wasn't the only one. The Heron's men looked to one another in fear and confusion. A handful even reached for their swords. Lord Daguss interrupted them with a booming voice.

"LISTEN TO ME, MEN OF HOUSE HERON!" The strength of Daguss's command brooked no dissent. The Heron's men quieted as one, and gave Daguss their attention. "Lord Dante and I have struck an agreement. Once Cato Ollspaer arrives with Dante's gift, you will be free to follow Lord Dante out of Winterworn Castle unmolested. You have my word. A fight inside the castle walls would only bring ruin to us all." Daguss paused to let the Heron's men consider his offer. Silas watched as the soldiers quickly came to the unspoken agreement that Daguss's proposal was a far preferrable offer to the alternative.

But will they stay gone, Silas wondered, *once they are reunited with the Heron and his greater army outside the walls?*

Silas's wondering was immaterial at the moment, for the hastily struck accord between Dante Heron's men and Daguss Salk made a madman out of Horos Ollspaer. "YOU CRAVEN, STAVUS-FUCKING STRUVANS!" Horos screamed. Horos stabbed wildly at the air as he stalked the platform, laying to waste an untold number of phantoms.

The king of Kalandragote's performance might have gone on forever, but it was interrupted by a squall of black laughter. A laughter so jagged and uneven that it sounded alien, unnatural.

A laughter emanating from Micah Dayborn.

When all eyes were upon him, the Dayborn king's laughter turned to words.

"Take a seat, Horos. It appears that you and I will be served our Ontish supper together."

For a moment, Horos lost his senses completely. Raising his dagger with one hand and grabbing a fistful of his stringy, gray-black hair with the other, Horos spun around on the stone platform with the dagger raised as if in search of Micah's voice, the way a haunted person might search the air for spirits. He looked so crazed that for a moment Silas thought that he was going to plunge the blade into his own chest. But then Horos stilled, and settled his gaze on Micah.

An instant later, he charged.

It happened in a blood-soaked flash. Horos kicked aside the kurmenhi wood stump and stabbed Micah Dayborn, not once but a dozen times, a bloody flurry that fought through the king's blocking arms to find his chest, sending spouts of blood leaping into the air.

When the frenzy was over, Horos stepped back like a painter to appraise his work. King Micah, the deep cuts on his body puckering a dark crimson red, resembled a butchered carcass. But still he breathed, his broad and heaving chest giving rise to a dropped chin. It was a ghastly scene. Silas, trying to make sense of all the blood, wondered if Horos had cut himself in his fury. But it was impossible to tell. The only thing Silas *was* certain of was that the king of Ragar Or was dying, and that Horos Ollspaer had dealt the killing blows.

"I am the Twin Ascendant," Silas heard Horos say. The words rose from the platform like a dark humor. Horos turned and slashed at the air, sending a spray of blood flying from the dagger. "I am the Twin Ascendant! No one else!"

The soft percussion of boots on snow interrupted the madness. At the archway next to the armory, a line of men came marching into the courtyard. Cato Ollspaer at the head. A full head taller than everyone else, the heir to Kalandragote strode like a colossus into the yard. He led a prisoner by the arm, a well-dressed young man with a noble carriage and stubble-covered jaw, a man that Silas recognized at once.

Prince Ajax.

Ajax, squinting against the snow-reflected sunlight, looked everywhere but the platform, trying to make a mental map of his environs. Other than the fact that his hands were bound, the prince's body looked whole. Neither, it seemed, had his will been broken. But then the prince's eyes went to the platform, and Silas watched as fractures to Ajax's psyche formed in real time.

"Father!" cried Ajax. He thrashed with all his might, trying to get away. But there was no escaping Cato Ollspaer. "My king!" he cried out, changing tact, as if calling Micah by his royal designation would shake the traitors in the yard from their treasonous stupor. When still nothing changed, Ajax's voice began to fade. "My father, my father, my king…." Ajax fell to one knee, collapsing in grief. Cato dragged him back to his feet. Together they made their way to the edge of the stone platform.

Cato freed Ajax with a rough shove. "A gift from Lord Heron," he announced. Freed, Ajax scrambled onto the stone platform and made his way to the feet of the blood-soaked king. There the crown prince knelt and wrapped his arms around his father's legs, and sobbed and sobbed.

Cato never took his eyes off his sire. Horos, calmer now that he'd stabbed Micah, met his son's stare with an equal intensity.

"I was warned that you would betray me," Horos spat, addressing Cato as if they were the only two people in the yard. "The woodkin told me. Now that woodkin lies dead beneath the Old Tower. By my own hand." He took a moment to study his blood-soaked hand. "In my time, I have slain many. Kwelkis, of the *heki plasuk*. My brother Tesken, the ten-day king. The dying man you see before you: Micah of House Dayborn, the lesser king of Ragar Or. And today, I will kill you too, seed of my loins, for your treason. You and your *hestrum.* I will prove once again that I am the true Twin Ascendant. No one else."

Given the difference in the size and age of the two men, Horos's suggestion seemed laughable. But the conviction in his voice was real.

Cato's voice boomed like a roll of thunder. But it wasn't his father that he addressed. "Stand with me, men of Kalandragote!" he shouted at the other Frostflowers in the yard. "You see for yourself the depths of my father's madness! Join the Lady Wren and I in making a new Kalandragote!"

Horos laughed at his son with contempt. "To think that I thought you could follow me as king! Your brother Onav at least had the stones not to deny his birthright. He who died by your blade." With a sneer, Horos turned and addressed the other Ontish. "This is Ragar Or, you fools! The land of the Twins! Those who deny the danger of the lesser are destined to be corrupted by them. The true Ontishman knows this in his very bones! When the Struvans came and all of Ragar Or capitulated before them, Kalandragote stood alone. A bastion against the Corosian-cursed weakness spreading across the land."

He pointed his blade at Daguss. "You want to steal my family from me, Daguss Salk? Then do it by honoring the old ways. Come dance in the circle. The song of steel will tell us who the true Twin Ascendant is, and who is the lesser."

Daguss gave Horos a look that suggested he wanted nothing more. But when he opened his mouth, it was the Heron's men that he addressed, not Horos. "It is time for the Struvans to leave. We Ontish have a matter to settle."

Dante's soldiers did as they were told. Following Jakastor Weylcoin, they departed the yard through the archway. Some struggled to hide their curiosity over what would happen next, but the majority kept their heads down, happy to depart Winterworn Castle without having to fight their way out. Lord Daguss waited until the last man had disappeared under the archway. Then he turned to Cato.

"The gate is in hand?"

"I control the castle gate and the gate at the city walls. My men can close both in an instant if needed. But that won't be necessary. The greater portion of the Heron's strength is visible from the towers. At the moment, they're too far away to pose any danger. The birds can leave, but they won't be coming back."

Daguss nodded. The chin wag of a commanding man. Satisfied, he returned his attention to Horos. "You would lecture me about the old ways? You, who made common cause with Dante Heron, a Struvan lord? You, whose harbor I cleared during the Blackstar Rebellion? You, who cannot hold the loyalty of your own family?"

"The true Twin Ascendant walks a lonely road. I have walked it my whole life."

Wren weighed in. "The road is at an end, Brother. As is the old Kalandragote."

Horos laughed a nasty laugh. "Yes, if there's anything you love, Sister, it's making Kalandragote anew. Remember the first time we did it together, when we killed our brother Tesken? I gave you a boon for siding with me, didn't I? That's right. I saved the life of your priest lover. Do you remember?"

Wren said nothing, but it looked to Silas as if a shadow passed over her eyes.

"Of course you remember," Horos continued. "You remember everything. All these years, you've stood by my side, but don't think I didn't see the judgment in your eyes. You've always wanted me dead for bearing witness to your crimes." Horos opened his blood-painted arms, as if readying for an embrace. "But I won't die easy, Sister. Beoliotius bless me, I mean to go like the Twin Ascendants of old, with steel in my hand and the corpses of the lesser at my feet." He pointed the baselard first at Daguss, and then at Cato. "I'm ready whenever the two of you are."

A charge in the air made a promise of the madness to follow. But before it could unfold, Wulfess stepped forward and shouted, "Wait!"

She gathered attention like the sun. Leaving her father's side, Wulfess walked toward the platform. A spellbinding, breath-stealing journey, for with every step she drew closer to Horos Ollspaer's dangerous orbit. When it was clear that she had no intention of stopping, Cato gave an audible growl of dissent. He stepped forward as if to protect her, but Wulfess stopped him with a raised hand and an oddly warm smile. Then she turned to face Horos.

"Was there to be a twin-death rite today? At the bonding ceremony?" She gestured at the line of armed, teenaged men standing on the far side of the circle.

"Yes," Horos replied. Silas half expected the Kalandragotan king to fly from the platform and attack Wulfess with the dagger, but Horos looked as stunned by her closeness as everyone else.

"Then we should go forward with it. As planned. The bonding ceremony first. Then the twin-death rite. And after that"—her fingers fluttered through the air—"all the rest." She fashioned an enigmatic smile, made a gift of it to Horos. "The king of Kalandragote has it right. If we are to make Kalandragote anew today, we should honor the old ways first.

"After all, we are Ontish."

Greta Worrint

"We found it first," Short Paul reported with red-cheeked pride. "O'er in the woods. The Dayborn men, not the birds." He was young, Short Paul, and plucky, and driven. When a competition was proposed to see which side might find the wooden sculpture of Breta Barton that the townspeople of Crelk were known to keep, he led the charge. Now that the double suns had won, he wanted the accompanying honors. "I'll take you to it, my lady. If…it pleases the prince."

"Never mind the prince," Greta responded, taking umbrage with Short Paul's presumption that she needed to ask Prince Ajax for permission. "It pleases *me* to see the sculpture, and that's quite sufficient."

Ajax raised *I-should-have-warned-you* eyebrows at Short Paul. "You heard the lady," he said. Ajax had an ease about him now that he was out of King Micah's and Queen Anjay's orbit, a relaxed self-assuredness that hinted at the ruler he might someday become. *He'll come fully into his own once we've returned to the capital,* Greta thought. *Give him charge of Lord Saylet's men, let him disperse the birds to deal with the Thralk-Brakturian threat, and all will be well.* She still felt uneasy in the midst of so many birds, but there was naught to be done about that at the present.

“I understand,” Short Paul answered. He was the sort of fellow who responded to gentle rebukes with increased diligence and attentiveness, traits he already had in buckets. The sight of him drawing up straight in his saddle almost made Greta regret needling him. “Shall we go now, before it gets dark?”

Greta stopped herself from saying yes. Seeing the forbidden sculpture of Breta Barton was something she had long wanted to do—her lifelong fascination with the Yubriy-leaf thief of yore bordered on the obsessive. But there were larger concerns at play, and she needed to make certain that she and Ajax were on the same page. “Yes,” she answered. “But give the prince and me a moment first.”

Short Paul nodded, then trotted his white-and-tan palfrey a short distance away.

Ajax waited to speak until Short Paul was out of earshot. “I would go with you, but—”

Greta leaned over from her mount and kissed him to stop the apology. She knew that Ajax’s place was in the midst of the men, where by sight and sound they would know him as their leader. In the three days since leaving Dunning Harbor, he had spent every evening thus, making the rounds of the camps and taking stock of the procession of men he was leading south. Ajax didn’t personally believe that Dante’s men were plotting against him, but on the off chance that they were, both Greta and Ajax agreed that his being in their presence was the best way to put a stop to it.

“Okay,” he said, releasing from the kiss. He made a face of faux concern and changed his voice to playfully stern. “You go and visit the sculpture of the heretic, and I’ll consider what your punishment should be when you return.” A dark little joke. Salk kings and queens of yesteryear had arrested—and sometimes executed—an untold number of folk for paying homage to the shrine of Breta Barton, but neither the arrests nor the executions had stopped people from visiting the sculpture, nor the citizens of Crelk from sculpting new likenesses of Breta Barton when prior versions were destroyed. The policing of Crelk had stopped with the Dayborn dynasty, but the history of the area was well known.

Greta made brassy doe eyes at her bonded. "A good spanking might suffice."

Ajax returned her stare long enough to charge a spark. "Then a good spanking you will have, when later we meet."

Had Greta known this was the last time she would see her beloved, she would have held his stare and softened her own; she would have cupped his cheek, or perhaps kissed him again; she would have stubbornly refused to release him to his doomful fate. But she didn't know, and being that they were playing a game, she whisked the horse away, granting Ajax one last flirtatious look as she went.

The cook's daughter, Tyna, accompanied Greta into the woods.

Tyna, who thought that they looked like sisters, which was one of the reasons why Greta loved her, because no one save Tyna would have dared tell Greta that she looked like the common daughter of a cook. But it was the truth, and Greta knew it. They shared the same coal-black hair, the same fractured blue eyes, the same spirited dispositions, the same robust waistline. They got along like sisters, too, which was why they had become fast friends. For Greta, part of the appeal of being with Tyna was the simple joy of talking to a common person again. She loved Ajax more than she could say, but her time among the lords and ladies of the realm took a toll on her soul.

Riding a short distance behind Short Paul and two other Dayborn men-at-arms, Greta and Tyna entered the hardwood forest chatting up a storm, only to fall quiet once beneath the trees. Greta delighted in the arboreality: before them stood ash and alder and beech and black oak and a bevy of other trees, including a wicked little stream-adjacent willow that bowed its branches in a pretend show of shame. Behind the trees, a glorious riot of bruised late-afternoon colors filled the sky. The effect was melancholy-inducing: the feeling took hold of Greta and, for reasons she didn't fully understand, brought a tear to her eye.

Tyna noticed. "Don't cry, lovey, you'll make me cry too! Though when we're done, you will need to explain to me why we're crying!"

Greta chuckled. "I cry for fleeting beauty. The color of the sky…it won't last." She gave a sad sigh. "I should warn you, there'll be more tears when I see the sculpture. The story of Breta Barton…do you know it?"

Tyna's voice turned singsong. *"She found a leaf and lost her head, told the truth and now she's dead."*

That old song. Greta had heard it a thousand times growing up. Every kid in Ragar Or had. "That's the short of it. What I'm interested in is the *long* of it. Like why she's revered in Crelk. Back when the Salk dynasty was trying to stamp Breta's name out of history, there was a secret order in Crelk that refused to let Breta's story die. If soldiers came through and destroyed a sculpture, another one appeared in short order. Baron the Redd went so far as to raze the town to the ground. But within a fortnight a new sculpture was standing in the ashes."

Tyna tossed her hair. "Why do they love her so? She was naught but a foolhardy young girl who stuck her nose into matters better left alone. Messing with Yubriy leaves and the like. What kind of fool does that?"

"There was a time when all sorts of fools did that. The Salk dynasty had been sending holy men and women to collect the leaves since before the reign of Caeress I, but in those days, there were no soldiers guarding the tree, and onlookers could get as close as they liked. Commoners came away with leaves more often than you might imagine. The thinking was that most of the writing on the leaves was unintelligible, so losing a leaf here and there wasn't a catastrophe."

High above, a hawk shrieked. Seconds later, a stiff wind blew through the forest, making it seem as if the bird was commanding the heavens.

"But all that changed with Breta?"

"Yes. After Queen Portia died by fire at the Three Dragons Inn in Low Osgood, word spread throughout the kingdom that a young woman had predicted the queen's death. Worse, she was making other predictions, ones that didn't bode well for the Salks. Caeress I had Breta arrested for treason. When the other prophecies failed to come true, she had Breta executed."

"What were the other prophecies?"

"Wars between brothers. Crows flying into suns."

Tyna's eyes widened. "Truly? She predicted the War of the Three Brothers and the rise of the Dayborns?"

Greta shrugged her shoulders uncertainly. "Only Union and White Walls know for sure. But that's the legend." She paused. "When Ajax and I return to the capital, I intend to find out what secrets are kept on Breta Barton in the Crow Keep." She paused again, worried that she was revealing too much of herself, but feeling too impassioned to stop. "And if I discover what I think I will, when Ajax becomes king, I'm going to have him draw up a writ posthumously absolving Breta Barton of her crimes."

Tyna stared at Greta dumbstruck, before laughing so hard that her shoulders heaved. "You're not lacking for ambition, are you? I've often wondered how a common lass convinced the bloody prince of the realm to bond her, and now I know. You're a force of nature!"

Greta's cheeks burned beet-red. She was well aware of her *bold* nature. "My mother always told me I was a bit extra." In truth, Greta was as proud of her *extra*-ness as she was embarrassed by it. Without the *extra,* she would have never stepped forward when Ajax asked for the hand of a woman to dance with at the Orange and Red Festival. Without the *extra,* she would have never convinced herself, let alone Ajax, that the notion of bonding each other shortly after they met was a good idea.

"I can't help it. So I might as well own it." The secret truths of her heart were pouring out of her like a fountain. "I think I have something to offer him…to offer to the whole family…that another woman couldn't. Because I'm a commoner. It's terribly arrogant of me, I know…but it's how I feel." She paused. "It's how I've always felt."

Tyna nodded thoughtfully. "It's good you feel that way. What you're doing isn't for the faint of heart. Sometimes I think that I'd *kill* to be you for a day, but if I had to do it for any longer than that I'd kill myself."

Up ahead, the horses came to a halt. Short Paul shuffled the palfrey off to the side, revealing a slant of sunlight pouring into a clearing. A pinewood sculpture stood in the midst of the clearing, life-sized and solemnly still, looking like a stunted tree that had turned human but was trying not to draw attention to the fact. Piled at the sculpture's feet were a dozen faded-yellow sunset flowers.

Greta drew closer to get a better look, only to be distracted by a different sight. Standing twenty feet away from the sculpture, beneath the boughs of a black oak, was a middle-aged man. He held sunset flowers in his hands and a cross look on his face. Squat and sturdily built, he reminded Greta of her father, who was a blacksmith. He gave a mean glare to any who wanted it, one that landed on Greta and stayed affixed.

Short Paul snarled. "I'll make him leave if it pleases you, Princess."

"No," Greta answered. "Leave him be." Dismounting, she acknowledged the man with a gentle look, then stepped to the sculpture. Tyna dismounted as well and stood behind her.

Greta studied the carving. Weather and time had softened Breta Barton's features, emphasizing the carving's androgynous qualities. Determined to see through to the essence of the woman, Greta studied the sculpture in detail. The large forehead. The round, fleshy face. Ringlets upon ringlets of hair. The hint of a smile that could have as easily been a frown. A broad, bird-beaked nose. The bowed, contemplative neck, but with the eyes and chin up, future facing. Oversized hands. A simple tunic covered the body, cinched at the waist with a rope. Sandals. Greta wondered if it was Breta Barton that she was looking at or someone's idea of the woman, writ in wood.

"What do you want of her?"

It was the maybe-smith who asked the question. His voice half a growl, half curious. When Greta turned to look at him, the two halves of his face were smushed together like loaves of bread, perhaps to stop himself from saying more.

"No more than what she would have me know."

The man spat. "And what if she tells you something you don't want to hear? Huh? What then? Will you burn her down? Chop her up?"

"No," Greta answered, thinking it best not to protest too strenuously. She knew the history of the place. She knew why the man was suspicious.

The maybe-smith scoffed. "So you say." He turned on his heel, muttering, "A pinch of salt, bread in my pocket, an apple, the truth—" His voice faded away.

Greta finished the saying, loud enough that he could hear. "—my lying lord, a sword, the place fates meet, the courage to keep."

That stopped the maybe-smith in his tracks. She was sure that he was going to turn around, but instead he kept his back to her and laughed, a hardy har-har. Then he disappeared into the woods.

Tyna gasped behind her. "My lady," she said, aghast.

Greta ignored Tyna, and looked instead to Short Paul. He, too, was aghast, perhaps doubly so due to his black-and-white worldview.

"Lady Greta, that was…the Gray Fog's credo!"

"Part of it," she admitted. "The gentleman started the rhyme, so I felt compelled to finish."

"All the same! I have half a mind to run that bastard down for daring to voice the credo in the presence of his betters, but I'm too flummoxed by…your role in the affair!"

Greta sighed. She looked up into Breta Barton's wooden eyes. She thought she saw a glint of rebellious mischief in the carving's empty pupils. Or maybe she just imagined it. "Tell me, Short Paul. In Union, when a commoner enters the kingswood, what are they required to do?"

"They have to pay tribute."

"Well, we're in Crelk. These are his woods. And that was my way of paying tribute."

Short Paul was at a loss for a response. Which was fine by Greta. As far as she was concerned, it would do the young knight good to grapple with the princess's 'treason.' Peter Scarl, a.k.a. The Gray Fog, a.k.a. The Noblekiller, had been alive during the reign of King Reuel II, during which time he traversed Ragar Or killing nobles in their sleep. Struvan, Ontish, it mattered not to the Gray Fog: by the time a young Manfred Salk hunted Peter down in 162 A.U., the Gray Fog had murdered the heads of four major houses and lain waste to the scions of three. Like Breta Barton, Peters Scarl lived on in legend, and his credo was oft quoted by commoners wishing to thumb their noses at nobility.

It was a credo Greta had heard all her life. One she had even recited on occasion.

Savoring the silence, Greta gave the sculpture her full attention once more. An intense desire to touch Breta Barton overwhelmed her. Feeling sacrilegious, she made a study of the carving with her fingers. The smoothness of the wood delighted her. *How many times have they sculpted her? A hundred? More?* She wondered if the maybe-smith belonged to the order that brought Breta Barton back to life. She wondered if he had carved this particular likeness.

She looked at the sculpture with earnestness.

What would you have me know?

A splinter of wood slid into Greta's finger, taking her breath away.

A brightly painted red-and-white toadstool swung from the sign that marked Toadstool Tavern. Not that it was necessary. Smells and sounds alone made the place known: raucous laughter; a wild, spirited singing; and an effluvium of alcoholic vapors poured out of the daub-and-timber building.

Greta turned to give Tyna a conspiratorial look, only to discover that the cook's daughter had beaten her to it. "Here!" they shouted at Short Paul together.

Inside of the tavern, Crelk was accepting the passing-through army with open arms. Familiar faces from the march meshed with a healthy helping of Crelk citizenry to make for a lively atmosphere. A band was playing, and all were stomping to the martial rhythm of "The Broken Arrow," the percussive elements of boots on the floor accompanied by sloshing drinks, silver Salk clinks, clapping hands, and lusty ass-slaps. Leading the revelry were three players at the front: a drummer, a lyrist, and a fiddler. Characters all, especially the fiddler, who with his short stature and ragged ropes of silver-brown hair looked strikingly similar to the impish musician who had played the part of the prophesied lutist's sidekick in Dunning Harbor.

Greta studied the fiddler. Her mouth went slightly agape. She gave a second look, and then a third.

That is *the fiddler from Dunning Harbor!*

The fiddler pivoted in his playing and stared directly at Greta. Rewarded her a conspiratorial wink.

She stared back, stunned. *Wyn Dunkin. That was his name. But why is he here? Why isn't he on the way to Kalandragote with Silas O' the Songs?* The little man had made her laugh in Dunning Harbor, but seeing him in Crelk had the opposite effect: every nerve in her body came alive at the wrongness of it. She shivered and blanched in short order.

Tyna grabbed her by the arm. Shouted over the music, "Lovey, what's wrong? You look as if you've seen a ghost!"

Greta gestured toward the front. "The fiddler! He was in Dunning Harbor. He shouldn't be here. He should be on his way to Kalandragote."

Tyna looked at her with confusion, either because she didn't know who Wyn Dunkin was or because she couldn't hear Greta over the din. By then Short Paul was sidling up and pressing a pewter tankard into her hand. She took a sip of ale and the sharp end of her worry dissolved.

The song came crashing to an end. The crowd howled their appreciation. Wyn danced a devilish jig in response, back and forth, all the while strangling his fiddle the way a farmer might a chicken. More cheering, more howling. Greta smiled in spite of herself. She decided that when the show was over, she would approach Wyn and get to the bottom of why he was here. If it suited her, she might even have Short Paul bring the little man before her bonded. As the second woman of the realm, it was, after all, her prerogative.

Greta softened her eyes. Tried to sink into the here and now. Breta Barton immediately popped into her brain. She could still feel the sting from where the splinter had punctured the top of her finger. Was that Breta's way of rejecting her, or of giving her warning? For all of Greta's life she had felt an affinity with the Yubriy leaf prophetess, but standing before the sculpture, Greta hadn't known if she was Breta's natural successor or an insult to everything she stood for. *I want what's best for the realm, just like Breta did, right? It's why Breta tried to warn the Salks, and why I'm trying to—*

The stuffy room suddenly felt even more compressed as a large group filed into the tavern. They were a hard-looking lot of birds: seven men wearing blue steel ringmail, grim expressions, and capes of gray. The swallow-tailed sigils on their shoulders marked them as kites. Days ago, the sight of the men would have unnerved Greta, but now she was too familiar with the look of sour-faced, steel-carrying soldiers from the east to be undone by the likes of these.

"Sober Stavus, draw these mean-mugging newcomers drinks afore they kill us all!" the fiddler shouted. The comment bought laughs and a scurrying of activity from the two servers drawing ale from the kegs. Greta, glancing back and forth between the musicians and the kites, noted that Wyn's quip brought nary a smile to their lips.

They'll relax once they have drinks in hand, she thought.

"It'll take more than alcohol to bring joy to the likes of those," Short Paul said, as if he'd been waiting to refute her thoughts.

Up at the front, Wyn Dunkin continued needling the kites. "While these ugly gents are waiting on their ale, I've got something that will shake their sullen dispositions! A song fit for a princess." He paused for dramatic effect. "Like the one in the room."

The fiddler turned to look at Greta. The eyes of everyone else in Toadstool Tavern followed, settling on her like a swarm of flies. At first, she was embarrassed, but then, a second later, confused: looking at the fiddler, it seemed that his gaze—and the gazes of the patrons at the Toadstool—were slightly askew. It stayed that way as he started up a song, the bow settling into the strings with a mid-tempo lean.

She was the rarest of women
She was a gem to find
At the beginning bitter truth, at the end the sweetest lie

The fat-handed drummer joined in with a steady rhythm. The lyrist followed suit, her elegant fingers scaling the horizontal ladder of strings like a clever spider. Greta didn't know the song. Neither, it seemed, did anyone else, but still the music did its work, weaving an additional layer of reality into the fabric of the collective experience. The fiddler began moving through the room, still playing, still singing, his gaze remaining slightly askew of Greta, parting the patrons as he charted a path to the princess.

She prayed with all the commons
She dined with kings and queens
She made a fool of prophecies, and other thorny things

Greta could see the fiddler clearly now in all his ugly glory. He wore a ragged cut of a tunic, brown and belted, atop faded brown breeches and black boots. Gray hair like a rodent's coat covered his arms. His face was pox-scarred, save for his nose, which with a hint of unblemished prominence seemed to be having a laugh at the rest of him. His eyes, beady and black, bore in on Tyna. The way he looked at her made it clear that he considered her the princess in question.

Wyn Dunkin stopped directly before Tyna and belted another verse.

She drank from the cup of wealth
She begged the poor to shine
She disappeared without a trace, and there made a new line

Tyna brought a hand to her mouth and giggled. Wyn lowered his fiddle and bow and, to Greta's surprise, handed Greta the instrument without looking at her. Too confused to refuse it, Greta accepted the fiddle and then watched with bafflement as Wyn took Tyna's hand and brought it to his lips, sealing her identity as the princess with a gentle kiss. The sound of the drum and the lyre faded away. The world rested on a pin.

Then all hell broke loose. It started as a roar in the back but quickly spread through the entire establishment. The kites were crashing through the crowd, brandishing steel, a shout of 'Death to the Dayborns!' on their lips. Screams. Tankards of ale flew through the air like foaming stones. Everywhere bloody tussles, a confusion of fighting.

Short Paul reached for his sword and got it up just in time to meet the first blow from an oncoming Kite, but it drove him backward, up against a wooden bench, while the other kites closed in. Greta, reeling away, clutched the fiddle to her chest. She didn't understand what she was seeing. Wyn Dunkin had a nasty dagger in his hand and he was pointing it at Tyna like a demon's finger, screaming 'Here she is! The princess! Take her! Take her! Take her!' Then the kites had hold of Tyna, wrenching her arm and dragging her through the tumult, away, away.

"NO!" Greta shouted in protest. She was the princess, she was the one they wanted, why had the fiddler confused Tyna for her? One of the kites whirled at the sound of her shouting. Greta choked down her fears and shouted the truth. "She's not the princess, I—"

Wyn Dunkin jumped between Greta and the kites, waving a dagger, a mad gleam in his eyes. "Shut up, servant!" he screamed, poking the steel in Greta's general direction. Behind him, the kites hauled Tyna toward the door. Greta, desperate, swung the fiddle at Wyn's head, but the fiddler nimbly dodged the effort, dancing in place without advancing. She left herself exposed in the trying, but Wyn didn't cut her. She took another swing. The fiddler slipped the blow once more, content to keep their standoff at an impasse.

Adrift in confusion, Greta glanced to her right, where with horror she saw Short Paul slumping to the floor, the sharp end of a longsword lodged between his ribs. Beside him, the foul labyrinth of a Kite's intestines unspooled on the floor: Short Paul's only kill, far short of what was necessary. Greta watched as Short Paul's killer wrenched the sword free and turned to follow after his gray-caped brethren.

"NO!" Greta wailed. *Where are they taking Tyna? What's happening?* A terrible truth hit home. *If they've come after me, what are they doing to Ajax?* Furious and flustered, Greta reared back and, instead of swinging the instrument, hurled it at the fiddler. Wyn ducked the toss with a frown. The fiddle smashed into a wooden bench and exploded into pieces. Greta followed suit with the bow. It clipped the side of Wyn's head and went spiraling off. Out of things to throw, Greta made up her mind to charge the fiddler. Some distant part of her brain knew that it was madness, but her thoughts and emotions were too far afield to reconcile.

She was lowering her head for the charge when two powerful arms slipped round her from behind and lifted her off the floor. Certain that a Kite had her, she screamed and flailed. Unable to see her captor, she watched with horror as Wyn now charged at *her.* A gutting and certain death seemed imminent. But before the little man could close the gap, Greta's captor spun around and made for the kitchen door. Hoping to impede his progress, she pushed her heels against the doorframe to keep from going through, but while she was doing that, Wyn whisked by and opened the door instead. All obstacles removed, Greta's captor turned with his back facing the door and carried her through.

The kitchen was a madhouse. Screaming people. A skinned, parsley-pasted rabbit and a big bowl of barley stew hovered over a hearth fire. Greta's captor transported her to the back of the kitchen and tried to set her down in a corner. Seizing on the opportunity afforded by his shifting grip, she bit his finger to the bone. He dropped her for a quick second only to grab her up again even tighter, cursing and screaming and then repeating something over and over and over and over. Greta couldn't make sense of what he was saying over the roaring sound of her heartbeat. Wyn was dancing in front of her, the dagger gone, and he was saying something too. It took her a second to realize that the mood was different, still frantic but no longer violent. Finally, her beating heart quieted sufficiently enough that she could discern what was being said.

"We're trying to help!"

Greta stopped struggling. The man didn't release her, but he did loosen his grip enough that she could turn her head to get a look at him. She took in his face with a shock.

It was the maybe-smith from out in the woods.

The fiddler's voice cut in, sharp as a sickle. "Listen to me, Greta Worrint. Time's precious. It won't be long before the birds realize they flew away with the wrong worm. Before that happens—"

Greta spat at Wyn Dunkin, leaving a gob of white on his cheek. "Tyna wasn't a worm, you ass!"

Wyn wiped up Greta's spit with his finger, tucked it into his mouth. Grinned. Rejoindered. "There's not been a princess alive whose continued existence didn't result in injury to at least a couple of common folk. That's the price of playing the game, Greta. You want to go and get yourself killed like your heroine Breta Barton, rest assured, you'll have the chance. But if you want to live and give birth to the twins in your belly, then you'd best play along."

The twins in my belly? Greta staggered under the weight of Wyn's intimation, all the fight gone out of her. "I'm…I'm not pregnant."

"You are. Survive today, and there'll be time aplenty to protest your change of fate with the gods of the wicked and wild. But all's a moot point if you don't live."

The maybe-smith released his grip on her entirely. A smear of his finger's blood traced the edge of Greta's mantle like a comet's tail. "We know how to hide people here in Crelk." His breath was a hot mash of whiskey and apples. "Come with me, and I'll take you someplace where you won't be found. Somewhere you can whelp your pups. You were a commoner once. We'll make you a commoner again."

No, she thought. She was meant to go to Union with Ajax, to live out the rest of her life with her beloved, to become the common *queen.* She was meant to remedy the ills of the realm alongside her bonded, to reverse aristocratic entropy with a dash of common vigor. She was *not* meant to go into hiding to give birth like a rodent. She was *not* meant to shrink away from the great battle of being alive.

The fiddler sighed. At the end of it, he unsheathed his dagger. He stared at the blade for a second like it was an old friend. Then, in a blur of sharp steel, the dagger flicked out like a serpent's tongue and touched Greta's cheek, where it made a line that would last for all time.

By the time Greta gasped, it was over. Reflexively, she brought a hand to her cheek. She was shocked when it came away red and sticky. While she stared at her hand, the pain started in, running the length of the cut like a river of fire.

"Make your decision, Greta," Wyn said flatly, with no sign of his customary humor. "But don't delude yourself into thinking that the path you were on before is still open to you."

Reality bit at her like the cold steel of the dagger. She gave a short nod. Girded herself.

"Okay. Let's go."

Johanna Salk

Johanna lay with Easton in the still of the morning, awash in the sunlight and the birdsong filtering in through the window.

Hevengrow and all its heaviness outside.

They had been awake for hours. Recounting Johanna's dream. Making sense of it. Dulling its edges. Easton's fingers tracing the smooth plane of Johanna's stomach, speaking a tactile language to their unborn child. Johanna drifting in and out, anxious to avoid dreaming but otherwise content in Easton's arms.

Occasionally they whispered a name to one another.

Weston.

Finally, a rising bubble of human voices drifted up from downstairs, followed by the tempting smells of bacon and bread. And with that, consciousness claimed them fully. They began to shift back and forth on the bed, the blood quickening to their extremities, the need to stand upright becoming increasingly urgent. Johanna heeded the call first, only to have Easton pull her back to bed and wrap her in a warm embrace. She laughed as she fell, in spite of herself.

"We bond again today, my love," Easton said.

Johanna responded with sarcasm. "A Stavusian ceremony for the good Struvans of the realm."

"I suppose it's only fair. Our first bonding ceremony did have a decidedly Ontish character."

"And what do you mean by that?"

"I can only assume that witches, woods, and wolves are standard for an Ontish bonding. Am I right?"

Johanna laughed again. It felt good to laugh at their trauma.

Easton continued. "I did think the *dragon* a bit much. Perhaps we should leave him off today."

Johanna twisted in Easton's arms so that she was facing him. "*Her*," she corrected him. "Leave *her* off."

A renegade lock of Easton's brown hair curled over his eyes. "*Her*," he repeated, nodding with gravity. He tucked a strand of Johanna's hair behind her ear.

For some reason she didn't fully understand, Johanna had withheld the particulars of her experience on Halfhead Mountain with Easton. Why she chose now to open up, she didn't know. "Shayla the woods witch said that the dragon was Teriquay. Do you remember?"

The vanguard of a V formed on Easton's brow.

"Teriquay," Johanna repeated. "The same dragon that burned King Reuel I and his family on Lake Wyglass." She remembered the feeling of seeing the green-and-black dragon when it first appeared overhead on Halfhead Mountain, the way its size and power made mock of her senses, the way she struggled to accept that the beast before her was *real*. Even now, weeks later, the interlude existed in the hazy space of her mind where old dreams were stored, rather than the stable shelf where memories were kept. "The woods witch told me that Teriquay was mine but for the asking. She thought that I could speak dragon. She didn't understand why the ability was beyond me."

Easton opened his mouth to speak, then closed it again. His hesitancy, so thoughtful and attuned, loosed something in Johanna, causing her to say the rest, all the fears and half-formed thoughts weighing on her. "I don't know why I failed. Don't get me wrong…I know that I can't speak dragon, but I don't know if it's because of fright, or hesitancy, or because I'm unwilling. It might even be wisdom. Because I *know* that I'm a jeyedoshi. We both know it. If the power to speak dragon *is* latent in me, it could be that I can only call it forth if it's necessary to protect you, or, if needed"—she brought her hand on top of Easton's, which was resting on her stomach—"him."

"Weston," Easton said, whispering the name with reverence.

"Weston," Johanna replied.

They made space for the ensuing stillness. The exigencies of the day were bearing down on them, but it seemed vital to put them off a little longer for the purpose of honoring the sacred now. Inside of that silence, they could feel their love growing, creating a light that might see them through the coming murk.

Yesterday's rain was gone, the gray-bellied clouds replaced by a sprightly sprawl of bright white tufts. The tufts marched along the skyscape to the whooshing sound of a lively wind. Beneath the clouds, hearty crowds gathered, lining the road to the temple.

Johanna rode Bitterboy at the front of procession. Isbel Wicker rode alongside her, sitting astride a striking white stallion. Behind them on his mule came the Stavusian priest Shupert Press, playing the part of the town crier. "Make way! Make way! We bond couples in the light of Stavus today!" Seeing the priest, many in the crowd opened their hands and raised them to the sky, making a symbol of Stavusian devotion. Shupert signed back at the commons, and, on occasion, so did Isbel.

Johanna kept her fingers to herself.

Easton rode Brazen a little farther back, in the company of Philemon and the birds. Like the others, he was dressed for the ceremony, the rough-and-tumble quality of his character buffed away by the shine of a new outfit. Glancing back at him, Johanna's only thought was that he didn't look like himself. Easton wore a slashed velvet doublet of orange and black, of a quality that rivaled Yurk's attire. Philemon, as per usual, was dressed in green, only today his doublet was a creamy green and silver, over which he wore a moss-green cloak pinned at the shoulder with a silver broach in the shape of a coin. Desighart was done up in red and black, Chesterly in proud mahogany brown. Behind the men, the Raleighs marched in red, Lady Wenavere at the head: she wore a cloak that was white on the top half and red on the bottom. The cloak billowed off her shoulders against a suit of red-enameled armor, unapologetically martial.

Fitting for the head of an army, I suppose, Johanna thought. Johanna envied Wenavere her armor. Johanna and Isbel were to be dressed for the ceremony at the temple, where, Johanna did not doubt, they would be appareled in gowns of the finest material. For now, she wore the same beige-and-black cloak that had been her constant companion since Hornwell, with the hood pulled over her half-shaven head. She shuddered at the thought of putting the cloak aside for the ceremony. She shuddered at the thought of everyone staring at her whorl-scarred, half-shaven skull.

The route from the inn to the temple gently declined traveling east by southeast. The crowd fell in with the host along the way, news of the two bonding ceremonies heralding an impromptu Hevengrow holiday. At the temple, a dozen Winged Women and two Hawk's-Eyes greeted them in two lines leading to the temple doors, the Hawk's-Eyes mimicking Shupert's open-handed salute and the Winged Women singing the temple song "We Breathe the Purest Air." The wind played thief with the women's voices, snatching parts of the song away only to deliver it up seconds later with energetic abundance. It made for a surreal feeling as Johanna dismounted Bitterboy and went inside, following the Winged Women, whose voices came in and out of the ether like ghosts.

Inside the temple, the Winged Women led Johanna and Isbel to a room off the Hall of Air and Light. The white-clad Winged Women lined the room six to a side, servile smiles affixed to their faces. Johanna and Isbel stood awkwardly in the middle of the room, waiting. His Light Shupert Press and the two Hawk's-Eyes entered shortly. Shupert, palms beneficently open, moved to where the light was filtering in through the room's stained-glass windows. He stood awash in the refracted colors of a red-tailed hawk.

"A glorious day," he said. "Glorious." He turned in a slow circle, taking in everyone, his voice an ecstatic mumble. His ever-conspicuous raised white eyebrows looked like albino caterpillars contemplating metamorphosis. The revolution complete, he stared at Johanna and Isbel with pride. "The Winged Women will help you prepare. When it is time for the ceremony, I will return for Isbel. She will bond Philemon in the light of Stavus. Then, my dearest Johanna, you will bond the prince." Shupert's speech hooked on an unexpected snag of emotion. Johanna watched as tears welled in the priest's eyes. He used his thumb to wipe the tears away, chuckling at himself. "Glorious," he said again. "A glorious day."

Shupert and the Hawk's-Eyes left. The instant they were gone, the Winged Women sprang into action, flying around the women with speed and precision, changing them out of their clothes and helping them into silk and samite. Johanna's gown was the color of desert sand at sunrise. Black satin lined the dress. The sleeves were long and dagged, coming off her arms like the wings of a warrior bird. She felt the loss of her cloak but relaxed as the Winged Women ignored her half-shaven skull, their attentions fully absorbed by the task at hand.

"You look beautiful."

Johanna had nearly forgotten Isbel. She looked across the room to find the Winged Women dressing Isbel in a heavenly yellow, the color of the silk gown a few shades shy of diaphanous.

"Thank you." Johanna took the opportunity to study Philemon Yurk's long-spined bonded-to-be. The taxing nature of the past twenty-four hours had been the cause of much distraction, but Johanna suddenly remembered something Shupert had said about Isbel back at the Black Board Inn. "His Light said that you play the harp?"

Isbel ran an uncommonly long hand through her hair. The Winged Women continued primping the dress. "Yes. I do." An odd, frightened flickering in her eyes. "It's how I met Philemon, actually. He saw me playing the harp."

"Where was this?"

The tops of the Winged Women's heads suddenly seemed to interest Isbel greatly. "The Vake, I think it was." Her anxious fingers worked the air like spider legs. Appearing to recognize the absurdity of not knowing where she had met Philemon, Isbel firmed up her answer with a smile. "The Vake. We met in the Vake."

That's odd, Johanna thought. Her instinct was to press ahead with further questioning, but, seeing that the Winged Women were almost done, she waited. All at once the Winged Women stepped back in concert, satisfied with their work. Johanna hoped they would leave. Instead, after a moment's quiet, they started up another temple song.

Johanna cut them off quick. "Sweet sisters, please!" The white-clad women quieted in confusion. Johanna explained herself. "I think you would agree that a moment's reflection is called for before such a momentous occasion. While we are grateful for the music, I must request that you give my sister and I time alone so that we may pray to Stavus and gather our thoughts."

The looks on the women's faces conveyed that they weren't enamored of the suggestion, but all the same, they gathered themselves and left the room. When they were gone, Johanna crossed over to where Isbel stood. Gathering up her dress in her hands, Johanna took a seat on a wooden bench in the room's center, and, patting the bench, motioned for Isbel to do the same.

Isbel did as she was prompted, although she sat as far away from Johanna as the bench would allow. Some false expression took possession of Isbel's face, a vacant twist of a smile that suggested she was retreating to a distant place in her mind. Following an impulse, Johanna reached over and took Isbel by the hand. The harpist consented to it in the same way a dead fish gives itself over to being handled.

"Tell me about the day you met Philemon. I would love nothing more than to hear how your love began."

Isbel nodded absentmindedly. "There was a fire," she said numbly. "Philemon…rescued me."

"A fire?"

"People died," Isbel said, looking down and shaking her head. "We were playing at the Golden Pear. For the Swans. The king's players. I thought I'd lost my harp. There was so much panic, so much commotion…" She snapped out of the reverie. "But in the end, Philemon saved me." She gave a weak smile. "Me and my harp."

Only you? Did he let the others die? Johanna caught herself. *You weren't there. You aren't in a position to judge.* "What a terrible ordeal to endure."

Isbel seemed not to hear her. Instead she slid her hand out from under Johanna's and bunched up her dress, gathering up enough of the fabric to expose her ankles. "What do you think is the most important trait for a man to possess?" she asked, apropos of nothing. "I used to think it was strength, before I met Philemon. Now I think…" She trailed off, the smile on her face changing into an expression Johanna couldn't decipher. "Philemon's not a strong man, but he knows how to keep me safe. He is, I think—and I mean no offense…" she said, suddenly switching out her right hand and grabbing Johanna by the arm, "the smartest of them all. And in the end, intelligence wins, doesn't it?"

Johanna's heart struck a clanging note against her breastbone. *What's happening here?* "Why would I take offense? The way you're talking, you'd almost make me think that we're in danger."

"Aren't we always in danger?" Isbel responded. Her eyes went roaming again. "I learned that the night of the fire. If it hadn't been for Philemon, I wouldn't have survived. If it hadn't been for Philemon, I…I…"

Johanna found her strength. There was a disturbing message lurking in Isbel's wordy morass about the fire and Philemon, she only need coax it out. Johanna reversed positions with Isbel, grabbing *her* by the arm. "Tell me about the fire. Specifically. I want to know what happened that night."

Guilt flashed on Isbel's face like a gleam of light in the blade of a knife. There and gone in an instant. Then Isbel pursed her lips. Whether the expression was a precursor to a stubborn silence or the beginnings of a confession, Johanna would never know, for the door to the room opened, and in stepped Shupert Press.

"My child," the priest said, addressing Isbel. "It is time."

Johanna kept an ear to the door. Outside, in the Hall of Air and Light, the ceremony began with a heavenly chorus of singing. Straining to hear the Winged Women, it dawned on Johanna how ridiculous it was that she wasn't out in the hall watching the ceremony. She opened the door to remedy the situation, only to discover, with some shock, that a Hawk's-Eye was standing guard, the dumpy one with the dough-pressed chin. "Back in with you," he demanded, shooing her. "It's inappropriate for a woman to see her bonded-to-be before the ceremony."

She went, but not before catching a glimpse of the outside. The temple in Hevengrow possessed the simple but effective magic inherent to all Stavusian temples throughout Ragar Or: the ability to transform light refracted through stained-glass windows into a place of reverence and awe.

The guests in attendance—birds upon birds, Raleighs, and a smattering of Hevengrowans—stood arrayed in pious, contemplative poses. None looked so beatific as Shupert Press, who, standing behind the marriage altar wearing an expression of the utmost beneficence, gloried in the sunlight streaming through the wings of a mighty stained-glass hawk.

But it was Easton that Johanna wanted to see, not Shupert Press. She looked desperately for the love of her life, to no avail.

He's waiting outside the temple, Johanna assured herself as the door closed. *They will bring him in when it's time for our ceremony.*

The word *they* bothered her. There could be no mistaking their position: in agreeing to be bonded in the Stavusian fashion, she and Easton had given themselves over to the Struvan contingent.

Stop fighting it. You've made your decision. The only thing to do now is to see it through.

Taking a deep breath, Johanna restationed herself at the door. Pricked her ears. She might not be able to see the ceremony, but she could damn well listen to it.

The singing ended in an angelic hush. A second's pious quiet and Johanna heard Shupert's genially authoritative voice, underlining his role as the enthusiastic ambassador for the blessed institution of Struvan bondings. His voice was made faint by the door's bulk.

"Children of the Light. Blessed are we this day to bear witness to the sacred—joining—of not one, but two significant couples of the realm." Johanna's skin crawled at the way the priest aborted the word *Union.* "It is always a blessed event whenever a man and woman join their lives together, but *especially* so when they make their vows in the light of Stavus. More than ever, our realm needs to turn away from false Ontish doctrines. More than ever, our realm needs to look to the hawk. To the sun. To the sky. To Stavus."

Would he be saying this if I were standing before him? Maybe that was why she wasn't allowed in the congregation: she couldn't take offense at what she hadn't heard.

His Light continued. "And what better place to begin healing the realm than in Hevengrow? For what part of Ragar Or knows better the folly of following the cult of the Twin Ascendant? It was here that a young prince, driven mad by the false beliefs of a foolish religion, murdered his brother and plunged the realm into civil war. But that was long ago. Today, thank Stavus, Hevengrow rejects the false doctrine of the Twin Ascendant. And today, we bond two powerful and blessed young couples in the light of Stavus. Let us pray that as today's ceremonies bind the couples together, so, too, will they go forth and use their power and influence to bind the realm to the Stavusian faith."

You would not have dared preach this way the first time I was bonded. A vision of Shupert Press at Johanna's bonding day to Nicholas Raleigh formed in her mind's eye: the bushy-eyebrowed priest acting mild and mannered, the very picture of diplomatic circumspection. No Twin-bashing, no pontificating; in fact, if Johanna remembered correctly, Shupert had even given a nod to religious pluralism. *But then my father was sitting in the front row, wasn't he? And Daguss Salk isn't a man to give offense to.*

Her father.

Wulfess.

Johanna's thoughts flashed on her family. She wondered what they were doing in Kalandragote. She wondered if they were bringing the realm to its knees.

Out in the Hall of Air and Light, the ceremony transitioned. Shupert began speaking in lower tones. *He's addressing Isbel and Philemon.* Johanna struggled to envision Philemon and Isbel standing before Shupert, their hands bound together by the ceremonial cloth. But then she remembered her own awkward ceremony with Nicholas, and suddenly she could see the bow-shouldered Philemon leaning over the harpist, calm and sly and two times too clever, Isbel's long and elegant hands imprisoned in his own, tied tight by the cloth. She felt a pang of sorrow for the girl in the yellow dress. *She's like me when I bonded Nicholas.* But that wasn't right. Her bonding to Nicholas had been a mismatch, that all-too-common affliction among noble pairings. What was happening between Philemon and Isbel was an abomination, even if Johanna didn't fully understand why.

The vows bled through the door. Johanna wanted to weep at the wrongness of them.

'We are become one, you and I
Standing in the light, beneath the eternal sky
Our lives intertwined, willingly
We make the knot
That bonds us to one another.'

Johanna stepped away from the door. Returning to the bench in the center of the room, her thoughts traveled back in time to the glistening waterfall at the base of Halfhead Mountain. The place where she had bonded Easton.

The memory of the day was a sunspot blinding her brain. What overwhelming joy. What life-altering trauma. The dead woods witch, the disappeared dragon, the sensation of *milu sfal*—the forever flower—threading through her veins, stitching on Stavus knew how many additional years to her life. And…Easton. Standing before Johanna, swearing his devotion to her for now and for always, his voice crisp and honest. She could still hear the waterfall roaring its approval. *Did we say the oath the way it's said in temple?* She couldn't be sure. But if they had failed in exactitude, they had more than made up for it in feeling, the passion of their oaths far surpassing whatever dogma the temple required.

We were bonded that day. If not in the light of Stavus, then in the light of love.

Johanna contracted the muscles of her body. Released them. *We shouldn't be here. We shouldn't be doing this. Not for these people.* She ground her back teeth in frustration.

A wave of applause broke upon the shore of the door. It was over. Philemon and Isbel were bonded. Johanna lengthened her sitting spine, bringing her body alive. *At least Easton will be out there waiting for me,* she thought. A smile came to her face as she imagined Easton walking through the front doors of the temple, making his way down the aisle to the altar. *At least we're going through this together.*

Seconds passed. Minutes. She continued waiting, believing that at any second one of the Hawk's-Eyes would open the door and see her out. But nothing changed. Growing frustrated, she moved once more to the door. Listened. On the other side, a low murmur of voices reigned, incomprehensible.

Then: Music. A bright stirring of strings, the melody spreading through the temple like a roost of beautiful birds put to flight. *The high harp,* Johanna recognized. She had heard the instrument before, but never like this: the sublime quality of the playing infused the air with an ecstatic grandeur.

What song is that? It was a temple song, but, try as she might, Johanna couldn't place it.

Time bent to the power of the music. Alone in the room, untethered to the sight of all that was occurring in the Hall of Air and Light, Johanna slipped into its soft embrace. The song made an unspoken promise: *How can anything go wrong in a world where music like this exists?*

But go wrong it did. The song collapsed in the middle of a fitful arpeggio, broken in half by a shouted, gasping "No!" Johanna recognized the voice immediately: Shupert's, all sanctimony and softness stripped away. The *No* was shortly followed by a countermand. "Keep playing!" Johanna registered Philemon Yurk's voice on a delay, unaccustomed to hearing it sound so strident. Next, Richard Chesterly demanded, "Grab him!" and then all was a cacophony: the harp started up again, but its beauty was gone, undercut by anxious playing, garbled orders, and a flurry of footsteps.

The door to Johanna's room flew open. A wild-eyed Shupert Press stood on the other side. He tried to enter, but Doneg Desighart, hot on his tail, grabbed hold of the priest's arm and wrenched him away. The Hawk's-Eye with the dough-pressed chin stood off to the side, arms up, too frightened to intervene. Realizing that his efforts to reach Johanna were in vain, Shupert Press relayed with frantic haste the heart of what he wanted to communicate. "I didn't know, Lady Johanna! I didn't know! Had I known, I would have never—"

The rest of whatever Shupert was trying to say was lost in the ruckus of Doneg dragging him away. The doorway cleared, and Johanna glimpsed the holy hall: what had once been a staid and solemn place was now a madhouse of moving men. A lone Winged Woman screamed. The doorway filled with men carrying crossbows. Birds: three eagles, two vultures. Philemon following after them. The son of Lord Delton Yurk wore an unconvincing expression of contrition on his face, as if he'd come to confess a sin that he was secretly proud of.

"Lady Johanna."

Outside, in the Hall of Air and Light, the harp stilled.

"Where's Easton?" Johanna asked, her voice cracking with fear.

Philemon gave a sham grimace of pain. "That's a question for Lady Wenavere, I'm afraid. One I have every intention of learning the answer to."

Philemon really did kill Silverwing. It was a ridiculous thought to have at the moment but it was the one that popped into Johanna's brain. *And I need to kill him. Now. I need to reach for the terrible power that resides deep within me and bring it to the surface. Before…before…*

"I know what you are, Lady Johanna." Philemon voice was subtly different, like the change in a snake's hiss after shedding its skin. Philemon gestured at the crossbowmen. "And you should know this. I'd like to keep you alive, but, if need be, I won't hesitate to kill you. Going forward, the crossbowmen before you will be your constant companions. They have my permission to put a bolt through your heart at even the slightest suspicion that you're using your…gifts."

She scarcely heard Philemon. She was looking beyond him, looking for Easton, the valiant love of her life. *He will show. Lady Wenavere cannot keep him from me. No one can keep him from me.* The idea that she and Easton had been undone was unfathomable, they had killed a woods witch and driven off a dragon together. This was nothing, nothing at all…

"I must admit, my lady: your power, it fascinates me. You are wise not to risk your life. But perhaps, with time, we might reach an agreement where you might demonstrate your abilities."

A wild panic raked its claws against Johanna's soul. *What evil is this?* She glanced at Philemon and then back at the doorway, hoping against hope that Easton would appear and save her, only for it to dawn on her that he was almost certainly in a worse position than her. She was the one, after all, who possessed the powers of a jeyedoshi. But what could she do? Aside from the fact that five crossbows were trained on her, she had scant knowledge of her powers and less control. Using them here and now would only get her killed. What she needed was practice of the sort that Philemon was suggesting, but the thought plunged her into a nightmarish headspace. *I'm evil. An accursed jeyedoshi. It'd be better for me to die than to turn into that hellish woods witch.*

The other side of her rejoindered.

But what about Easton?

What about Weston?

Despairing, she put her head in her hands and cried.

Philemon intervened, picking up from where his drifting query had left off. "Of course, there will be plenty of time to discuss such matters later. We must travel many miles together, you and I."

Johanna struggled to catch her breath. "Where are we going?" she asked through her tears.

Philemon answered with scarcely suppressed glee. "If all has gone according to plan, we are going to meet the new king of Struvan Ragar Or.

"Dante Heron."

Gregor Thorn

In the deep of Gregor's dark dream, Sephery was waiting for him. She stood on the shoreline of the beach at Dunning Harbor, the wind making a flag of her raven-black hair. Farther down the beach, at the grasping edge of Gregor's vision, the sea fingers feasted on the last of the whale. The knowledge of it disturbed Gregor. Sephery, sensing his distraction, cupped Gregor's chin in the palm of her hands.

"Look at me and only me, my love."

He did as he was told. A part of him resisted, knowing it was only a dream, but the longer he looked at her the more she seemed to sharpen into the fullness of the woman he had so dearly loved. Her shining black eyes like a gentle night. Her saucy nose a little too small for her face, the only impudent thing about her. The sweet calm she exuded, a calm that carried the love she had for him through the storm of life, and now, into this dreaming death.

"It's really you, isn't it?"

"It is."

Movement at her feet. Sephery looked down and laughed. The two greyhounds, Black and Tan, had taken up position on opposite sides of

Sephery, sitting on their haunches in the surf. They looked the way greyhounds always look: elegant, regal, and slightly goofy.

Gregor asked Sephery the question that had haunted him since first making the greyhounds' acquaintance. "They're the Twins, aren't they?"

In lieu of an answer, she grinned.

Gregor nodded. For a dream, the world around him seemed incredibly stable. *Perhaps I'm dead,* he thought. He vaguely remembered taking an arrow in the shoulder. *No. That's not right. There were two arrows. Not one.* He considered asking Sephery to clarify his condition. Perhaps she knew. But he also knew that if this *was* a dream, and the asking broke the spell, he would never forgive himself.

Sephery addressed his line of thinking without Gregor having to say a word. "If you're meant to return to that place, it will wait for you."

He was grateful for the reprieve from that place and all its attendant responsibilities. "Why am I here?"

She gave him a look that only Sephery would give him, a sideways cock of the head coupled with a teasing twist of the lips. "Come now, Uncle Bones. You're here because you have questions for me. Out with them."

Her straightforwardness was almost cruel. Sephery, for all the care and kindness she bestowed upon him, had never been anything less than direct. She held him in her stare with a heartless strength, heedless of his discomfort.

Tears welled in Gregor's eyes. "Do you blame me for your death?"

"Not half as much as you blame yourself."

"I failed you. I'm the Sagekind; it's my duty to see through to the truth of a prophecy, to the truth of a vision—"

"No, it's your duty to *try* and see through to the truth. And try you did."

He *had* tried. If anything, he had tried too hard, and in the trying become so narrowly focused that he missed the bigger picture.

"Don't leave me, Gregor," Sephery said. "You don't have to relive it."

But Gregor was already tumbling from one dream into another, into that cruel place where his mind loved to reside. *What might I have done differently?* In an instant he was back in the great hall at Union Palace, the vision of the poisoned feather at the forefront of his mind. Dorjav the Eloquent, adorned in a coast festooned with rainbow-colored plumage, stood at the front of the hall with the king, signing the treaty that no one thought would come to pass: Thralk-Braktur agreeing to a cessation of pirating off Ragar Or's southern and western coasts. An occasion for celebration, but Gregor was on his guard. *Any moment now and the bastard will try and kill the king,* Gregor thought for the thousandth time since Dorjav had arrived, certain that the ambassador and the vision were connected.

The hall filled with a great and mighty cheering as the crowd reacted to the king holding the signed parchment aloft. With the signing completed, the celebration began in earnest. Marrows wine, dark as oxblood, filled every cup. Gregor knew it wouldn't be long before the color of the wine made its way to lips and tongues. Gregor took a nominal sip, but no more: he had no intention of letting down his guard until Dorjav was on a boat returning to Thralk-Braktur. All the same, Gregor untensed a little as the emissary moved away from the king and out into the crowd to cavort with the nobility.

His eyes were still on the emissary when the first scream rang out. *A ruse to draw my attention away,* Gregor had the hubris to think, so certain was he that his original interpretation of the vision would prove right. But then came a second scream. Startled, Gregor scanned the hall, searching for the tragedy. To his great surprise, he discovered the king's fool—a bumbling imbecile named Rags—choking, Marrows wine spewing from his mouth like a fountain. And, to Gregor's horror: a large red feather falling from Rags's loosened grip.

Gregor was the first to reach Rags, not that it did the fool any good: Rags was deep into his death throes by then. With his right arm, Gregor gathered Rags round the torso and propped him onto his knee, hoping to give the fool the dignity of an elevated death. With his left hand, Gregor grabbed the feather. He tried to put the pieces of the puzzle together. *It's a feather from the Wasting Bird,* he realized. A gift from the kingdom of Clyesia, the Wasting Bird had long been a part of the king's menagerie. Gregor remembered reading somewhere that the bird's barbed quills were poisonous if ingested or exposed to liquid.

"Did anyone see what happened?" he asked, holding the feather aloft.

A page boy rushed forward, looking like he might have answers but scared to speak.

"Go on," Gregor prodded. He felt guilty for feeling relieved. If this was the great tragedy his vision had tried to warn him of, the realm and the royal family could bear it.

"Yes, Revered Sagekind. The fool grew excited during the s-s…signing ceremony," the boy sputtered. "All the cheering, I think. He left for a bit and came back with the f-f-feather. Next thing I know he was dipping the quill into unattended cups and trying to sign whatever he could lay hands on. He drank from his own cup, but it wasn't the only one he dipped the feather into—"

Gregor would never again know the like of the fear that seized him then. "DON'T DRINK THE WINE!" he shouted with a booming voice, the jeyedoshi in him somehow commanding the air to compound the effect. For a brief moment, time came to a standstill. Then, across the room, Lord Starrs fell to the floor. The crowd, seeing Lord Starrs tumble, gasped. But not Gregor. For Sephery had swooned into his field of vision, looking at him askance, a dull lolling of her eyes.

Gregor was bargaining with the fates before she even dropped, begging his own life for hers.

"Gregor."

He was back with Sephery on the shoreline. The loving touch of her fingers on his face. It was time to tell her the rest. Time to come fully clean. "After you died, I revisited a Yubriy leaf prophecy. One of the leaves had forewarned me, although I didn't have the foresight to see it."

"What did it say?"

"*A fool drinks the words he cannot write, spreading death.*"

Sephery was unimpressed. "You tried, Gregor. That's all that you could do."

"I always try. I try, and I fail. And I try. And I fail."

"Such is life," Sephery responded. "Come. Walk with me."

Hand in hand, they strode across the sand, the far reach of crashing waves caressing their feet, the greyhounds following behind. Day turned to night. They walked under the watchful eyes of the Jailer, standing eternal guard over Werring in the Sky Ends. The sounds of crashing surf faded away, and so, too, the water at their feet. In the western sky the Gatherer brought in the last of the crops.

Solid ground. The stars in the sky suddenly dimmed, torchlight and tallow candles the culprit. Small fires like dancing cat's eyes stared from the windows of the mighty castle that appeared before them. Union Castle. The Crow Keep. Home.

"What would you have me see here?"

"The rest of it. Who you are."

"I know who I am. My father told me everything. Who I am has never been a secret to me."

"There are secrets and there are secrets. Come and see."

Black loped ahead, eager. They passed through the castle gates and under the barbican, into the sprawling labyrinth of the Union Castle complex. Gregor assumed that they would make for the Crow Keep, but instead they worked their way past the barracks and the great hall toward the servants' quarters, nestled against the castle walls beneath the West Tower.

Gregor knew well the room they entered. The smell of cloves and lavender, of ground herbs and goat's milk, flooded Gregor's senses, affirming the place. His eyes shot to the corner of the room and there she sat, cooing a song to a breastfeeding baby.

His ostensible mother. Meg Barret. The infamous crofter's daughter, dead these many years.

"It's a shame I never met her," Sephery said. "She sings a compelling song. Listen."

Gregor perked his ears. Meg Barret's voice was a sound that oft played at the edges of his memory, teasing at a grand truth that Gregor could never quite discern. But here, in this dark dream, Meg's voice was crystal clear. She sang to an audience of one with treasonous abandon, fitting lyrics of her own to a familiar melody.

They bring you here to suckle
This babe they mean to change
Your brother takes the mantle
And you the bastard's shame

Gregor looked to Sephery. She gave him a sad smile in return, and squeezed his hand.

Meg's made-up song churned along.

And I your never mother
Forevermore will be
The one who tells the truth to you
Regardless of the fee

Gregor shook his head. This was too much. Already another voice was pressing in on this space, a timeless entity that knew no bounds: his father's. "*Who are you*?" it demanded. He murmured his response aloud. "A bastard half brother." The pressure eased.

"But you're not a bastard," Sephery corrected. "And you're not a half brother. If the song has the truth of it, you might not be the second-born son."

Gregor frowned. "She wouldn't have known. They brought Meg in from the village and made a pretend mother out of her after I was born. My father explained everything to me after she died. It was an open secret in court that Orius Dayborn's first love had been a crofter's daughter. When the queen, *my true mother*, gave birth to twins, one a jeyedoshi, they brought in Meg from the country and told everyone that I was her illegitimate get. The secret wasn't perfect, but it was passable. There would have been no reason to tell her the true birth order. Who would have even told her?"

"Orius?"

The dream blossomed into daytime. A gust of spring air ushered Orius Dayborn into the room. In Gregor's mind's eye, his father was an eternally staid and serious man, beset by the responsibilities of governing the realm; but here in the dream Orius Dayborn's face was the picture of joy. *He is not yet king. He is still the crown prince.* Gregor realized something else with surprise. *He looks like Easton.* In all of Gregor's memories, Orius's face morphed into Micah's. But not in the dream.

"You're here," Orius said to Meg, who was sitting in the corner. "You're really here."

"I am," Meg replied. "As the mother of your son, I would expect to be." There was a warning in her voice. The dark black hair falling from her head looked like a river at night.

Orius responded quietly. "I would make you the mother of all my sons and daughters, were it up to me. You know that."

Meg walked to the nearby cedarwood crib. Peered inside. Gave her hand to the child, whose feet were carefully covered with little velvet shoes. "No. You would make me your whore. In the eyes of the kingdom, you *have* made me your whore." She kept her eyes on the baby, refusing to look at Orius. "Before you sent for me, we had the memories of our time together. It was less than what we wanted, but those memories were sacred. By bringing me here, you've opened a new chapter. Everything from before is changed."

"You've *seen* the child. You understand why it had to be done."

"And you thought: why not solve two problems with one solution?"

Orius grimaced. "No. People knew about us. The lie would have been transparent if I claimed a different woman was the mother. But with you…people will believe that I made my way back to you in secret. People will believe that the child is *yours.*"

"If that's the story you want people to believe, then it should be *the* story. You returned to me. And I, being your whore, refused to turn you away. And this"—she looked back down at the babe—"…this is the child that resulted from our tryst. The little boy with the bastard's name of Thorn."

"I'll give you another child, if that's what you want. I would do anything for you. You know that."

"Except make me your bonded."

"I am the crown prince, Meg. You *are* the whole world to me. But you can never be my bonded. Who I am doesn't allow it."

Meg looked at Orius Dayborn and nodded, tears spilling from her bright blue eyes. "I understand. And I agree to it all. As you knew I would. But I must have something from you as well. You must make a truth out of the lie. Do *you* understand? If I am to be the whore that you are madly in love with and cannot resist, then I *will be* the whore you are madly in love with and cannot resist. And this child…he will be my child, in complete. Do you hear me? Gregor Thorn is my child now. And I will not betray him. Not ever. But I will know the truth of him, and you, being a man who cannot resist me…you will give me that truth."

The joy fled Orius Dayborn's face. *Now he looks like Micah. Now he looks like my brother.* "You will have everything you ask for," the future king of Ragar Or responded. "I promise."

A wild wind entered the room and swept it clean of spirits, ushering Orius Dayborn and Meg Barret into the ether. Fear seized Gregor's heart: for a moment he feared that the wind had taken Sephery with it as well. But when he turned, she remained standing beside him, with Black and Tan loitering at her feet.

"How well do you remember her?" Sephery asked.

"I remember the *feeling* of her love. But I don't remember her face, or anything she ever said to me. I only remember…the feeling."

"You were five when she died."

"That's right."

"What did your father say to you when she passed?"

"He said that he was sorry that she had died. He said that I had a difficult path ahead of me, and that she would have made the journey easier. But there was nothing to be done about it, except press on."

"And your real mother, the queen?"

"She never once acknowledged me. Even after Meg was gone. This might sound strange, but her refusal to acknowledge me actually made it easier for me to believe that I was her son."

The dream shifted again. It was time to leave the room. They stepped into the outer yard. Orange-and-black streamers flew from the turrets of the castle in abundance. Servants crossed the yard in good cheer, dressed in handsome apparel. The sun above was a peeled orange, bursting with color.

"What day is this?" Sephery asked.

A pit of unease settled in Gregor's stomach. "Father's coronation day."

The yard emptied. Far away, in the bowels of the throne room, trumpets blared and a great hurrah sounded, marking the moment of ascension. *What joy. But it doesn't last.* Only ten years and two days later, Micah Dayborn would ascend to the same throne. A different sort of day entirely. On that day the sun hid behind a dark cloak of the blackest sky, spitting rain and throwing bolts of lightning from the heavens.

From the direction of the throne room, a boy came streaking through the yard. *Where do you think you're going, lad?* Gregor wondered, seeing the much younger version of himself. *There's nowhere to go.* The boy flew past in a blur of legs, intent on getting away. A voice boomed behind the boy, sonorous and swelling. It wasn't the new king's commanding baritone, but rather the decadent foreign tongue of the soon-to-be Sagekind: Zust, the eccentric Thralk-Brakturian who had worked his way into Orius Dayborn's inner circle.

"Gregor! Gregor Thorn!" Zust shouted, calling to the boy. Zust, who always sounded like he was half laughing, made Gregor's name a booming chuckle.

I don't remember this at all. Had Gregor tried to run away on his father's coronation day? The memory seemed real in the seeing of it, but it was impossible to differentiate between his faded recollections and the current death-dream.

Gregor the boy continued running with a resoluteness that suggested there was no stopping him. *Go,* Gregor thought. *Don't stop.* Zust was too far behind the boy to make up the ground. *If I make the castle gates I might make my way to a different life. Whyever do I stop?*

Zust's voice boomed. "King Gregor of House Dayborn, the first of his name, the Holy Son of the Air, the Twin Ascendant, and the rightful ruler of Ragar Or!"

Gregor the boy stopped dead in his tracks.

Gregor the man turned to Sephery. "I don't remember this. I don't—"

Sephery shushed him.

Gregor the ten-year-old lad turned around. The boy stared at Zust with confusion in his eyes. Gregor the grown man surveyed the entire dream tableau, watching the boy, watching Zust.

The greyhounds barked. Black and Tan. One crisp bark apiece, Tan first, then Black; Daguss, then Ropske. The barking crossed the borderlands of the dream. Gregor watched with amazement as Zust turned, spotted the dogs, and laughed. *Can he see us as well?* Gregor wondered. He thought for a second that Zust was staring at him, but that certainty faded as the Thralk-Brakturian's eyes followed Black and Tan.

Gregor the grown man, needing to confirm that he was invisible, shouted, "Hey!"

Neither Zust nor Gregor the boy looked his way.

Zust greeted the dogs with genial good humor, dropping to one knee and cradling their faces in his hands, one at a time. The greyhounds endured the big man's affections with good-natured gentility. Finished, Zust nodded at Black. As if heeding a prearranged signal, the greyhound loped toward Gregor the boy, gathered the young fellow in tow, and brought him back.

Gregor the boy, looking as though he was drifting in the slipstream of his own dream, approached the new Sagekind with caution. The greyhounds, content that their work was done, took up together and went away, exiting under the castle portcullis and disappearing out of sight.

"You named me king," Gregor the boy said to Zust, with an air of bewilderment. He looked like a younger version of Gregor the man in every way but one: his flesh had a fuller aspect, in no way suggesting the

Uncle Bones nickname that would one day claim him. "But I'm not. I'm not even the crown prince. I'm the king's bastard son, and forevermore will be."

Zust, still on one knee, was eye to eye with the ten-year-old. From Gregor's vantage, the Thralk-Brakturian's back looked like a mammoth turtle shell: large, hard, and curved. "As you say," he responded, in a tone of voice that made it clear that he believed no such thing.

"I know what *I* say," Gregor the boy retorted with verve. The stalwart boy squaring off against Zust seemed a far cry from the lad who only moments ago was fleeing the castle. "What I'm interested in is what *you* had to say. You named me king. Why?"

Zust didn't respond straightaway. Instead, he took a moment to study Gregor the boy like he posed a particularly interesting problem. He broke the silence with a sigh. "Isn't that what you want, boy? To be king? In your deepest heart of hearts?"

Gregor the boy shook his head, not entirely convincingly. "No. I want to be a good son. A good brother. I want to be an asset to my family."

"No. What you want is to know your place in this world."

Zust's words struck a chord. The boy's lips trembled, and he looked at Zust with fear.

The Thralk-Brakturian reached out and put a hand on Gregor the boy's shoulder. "Your place is under your father's wing. Your place is by your brother's side. But should the day come when all the necessary lies fail you and your family, you should take the mantle that is rightly yours. You will know your birthright, and all will tremble before you. The truth will be as plain to you as peering into a looking glass. When you see what you were meant to see, you will know what to do."

Is this real? Gregor had no memory of the conversation with Zust. In reliving the dream, he seemed to have the faint recollection that he had fled the castle on the day of his father's coronation, but even that was uncertain. Perhaps the dream was true, and Zust had been the one to stop him. Or perhaps in his death-dreaming he had fallen under the influence of greater powers.

The dream faded instantly, violently. Gregor was spinning through space and time, shooting through the cosmos. He couldn't see Sephery but his hand was held tight to hers. The stars were no longer distant pinpricks of light but rather blinding forms and figures: the Moonbear's massive head filled the northern sky while to the east the Jailer stood stern and diligent, keeping watch on red Werring. There were many and more figures—an archer, a pack of pennywolves, a distant princess, a copse of half-cut trees, far-off dragons, layers upon layers of figures and creatures deepening into space. Some Gregor recognized, others he did not. Suffusing everything was the all-permeating black, the stuff of existence. *Owoervyrn, the sky-black palace.* Owoervyrn was here, it was there, it was all around them.

Fire burned through Gregor's body. The poison of life, filling him up like a cup. He fell from the firmament, holding tight to Sephery's hand, her name on his lips. "Sephery, my love, Sephery, Sephery." He didn't know if she could hear him, but he could feel her hand tightly gripping his own, refusing to let go. *When we land, when the cup is full, we'll be rent asunder*, Gregor sensed. He willed himself toward her, gripping and pulling. He sensed that she was doing the same, their free hands grasping and then grabbing, finding, drawing into one another, turning away all the rest. He was on the verge of losing her, he knew—life had him in its talons—but before the break they wrapped each other in an embrace and came face-to-face, fixed in a sacred space.

"I love you," she said.

"I love you," he replied.

Sephery smiled sadly. "Now go do what's left to be done."

Silas O' the Songs

Wulfess Salk and Cato Ollspaer were bonded in the center of the Circle of Stones. An Ontish bonding, stripped of all Struvan pretense. Like Daguss Salk and Wren Ollspaer the night before, they said the vows, stringing together the meager run of words that passed for joining two lives together in the north. Were it not for the ceremonial cloth binding their hands together, Silas would have scarce thought the bonding official. *Is the hand binding an Ontish tradition? Or a Struvan one?* Silas didn't know. It crossed his mind that perhaps hand binding was the one custom that had managed over the course of Ragar Or's history to transcend the Struvan/Ontish divide.

A renegade snow cloud refreshed the courtyard in white. The gorgostrine conducting the ceremony—the same gray-robed fat man who had bonded Daguss Salk and the Lady Wren the night before—promptly fled the circle the instant the ceremony was finished, casting wary glances at Horos Ollspaer. The blood-soaked king of Kalandragote watched everything from the stone platform, dagger in hand. Never moving. Beard a bramble. Eyes red-ringed and wild.

Behind Horos, King Micah Dayborn sat slumped over, dead. Ajax, the seemingly not-for-long new king, sat at his father's feet, listless. It made

Silas feel sick to look at him. Back in Dunning Harbor, Ajax had in every way been the dashing young prince, with his whole life in front of him. Now, it appeared that he was staring at the reach of his existence: the distance from the platform to the Circle of Stones.

"Your gorgostrine is finished, is he?" Horos inveighed from the platform, addressing his sister. "Best call on mine to commence the twin-death rite." He didn't wait for a reply. "Bernsward!" he barked. "Bernsward!"

A beak-nosed gorgostrine stepped with reticence from out of the grouping of Frostflowers standing near the platform. He didn't look like a true gorgostrine to Silas: the fine quality of his robes seemed to mark him as an impostor, a fraud. But he came forward all the same and moved to the center of the circle. Despite the cold, Bernsward looked feverish: either a teardrop or a bead of sweat had journeyed down the priest's face to the hook of his nose and was hanging there, refusing to plummet. The gorgostrine had lines to say, but appeared, for the moment, to have forgotten them. Horos helped him remember.

"Vengeance, priest! Say it!"

Bernsward jumped like a man snakebit. The bead of water flew from his nose. Once resettled, he began to speak in a reedy, quavering voice, reciting one of the four prayers of the faith of the Twins: the Prayer for Vengeance.

Whole, we shall be cleaved
And ever after strive against our whole selves
For who is the other but an impostor
Deserving only of death

Mother Beoliotius

Daguss, Ropske

Grant me vengeance

Against my friends, my siblings, my enemies.

Silence fell like an axe when the prayer was finished. Only blood could follow a prayer like that.

When the prayer was over, Bernsward moved swiftly from the Circle of Stones. The two teenagers at the front of their respective lines replaced him, squaring off with weapons. The larger of the two, a dirty-blond-haired boy wearing a black cloak, cut an impressive figure, the effect of which was magnified when he took a sword to hand, guiding it through the air with masterful control and lethal grace. His opponent, a lean, bordering-on-scrawny boy with a patchy beggar's beard, tested the sword with a spear, not without skill but noticeably less fluid than his counterpart.

The soldier standing next to Silas snorted. One of Grocian Mock's men, an old hand from the looks of him. "Name the winner, singer," the soldier leaned in and whispered. "And quick, afore it's over."

"The swordsman," Silas replied.

Silas was lucky to get the words in. Seconds later, the spear-thruster took a wild stab and overreached. Turning aside the point of the spear with his shield, the swordsman stepped inside of his opponent's perimeter and made a bloody ruin of the spear-thruster's bowels, plunging the steel deep. An efficient and brutal departure from the artistry of his opening moves. For a suspended moment both men surveyed the damage. Satisfied with his handiwork, the swordsman withdrew his blade from the spear-thruster's stomach and kicked him over. The dying youth fell without protest, dropping his spear and losing his grip on the shield he had failed to use. Entrails spilled through grasping fingers. The blond-haired boy spun his sword with a flourish. He completed the arc by cutting off the dying boy's head, drenching the snow in crimson.

A second for the dead, and then all a movement. Gorgostrine acolytes hustled into the circle and carried the body away, setting it on a pyre outside the Circle of Stones. Bernsward returned to the circle and marked the victor with black ash and talcum, a horizontal line over each eye. When the priest was finished, the blond-haired boy walked away, trembling with adrenaline. A middle-aged Frostflower emerged from the Kalandragote side to wrap him in an embrace.

"As I suspected," the Mock soldier muttered. "That's a nobleman's son, that is. Trained from birth for combat, then given the opportunity to prove himself against the *heki plasuk*. Nine times out of ten it's no contest."

Silas's couldn't recall his Kalandragotan. "The *heki plasuk?*"

"Orphan fodder. Young Kalandragotan men without prospects, promised a chance at social advancement if they'll risk the twin-death rite. Given just enough training to give them hope. But make no mistake, singer, they're meant to die. This isn't a true twin-death rite, like the days of old. Two hundred years ago, every male in Kalandragote had to prove his ascendancy by defeating an equal. Further back, before the arrival of the Struvans, the twin-death rite was common practice throughout Ragar Or. *This,* I'll have you know, is slaughter for show." The soldier leaned in. "They say old king Horos has always hated it. He wanted to bring back the old ways, but the nobility wouldn't agree to it."

Silas believed it. The Kalandragotan king looked like a man eternally disappointed that there wasn't more death in the world. "If they really wanted to do things the old ways, only twins would fight one another," Silas said to the soldier. Silas's uncle, a Wandering Tongue named Krayton, had shared the secret of Ragar Or's true history with him long ago. "That was the true purpose of the twin-death rite when it began. Stopping potential jeyedoshi from coming fully into their power. The Onts believed it was the duty of the Twin Ascendant to stop the Corosian curse from ever again afflicting the land. Only later did it become a marker of manhood."

The soldier nodded at the line of *heki plasuk* while spitting a red stream of messy leaf onto the snow-covered ground. "I promise you this: There's no Firewalker in that bunch."

There wasn't a Firewalker, but in the last match, the *heki plasuk* surprised his counterpart with a spirited flurry of hard blows from an axe that splintered the noble boy's shield and inflicted a terrible cut on his left arm. Despite searing pain, the noble boy kept his wits about him: the underdog, shocked that his wild assault had borne fruit, hesitated in his attack, and that was the moment the young noble lunged forward and ran his sword through the *heki plasuk's* neck. The fourth and final *heki plasuk* joined his poor brethren on the pyre. Four up and four dead.

The last of the victors shared an embrace with Gothred. *Is that the commander's son?* Silas wondered. Now that Silas looked closely, he could see a resemblance.

"Your son is bleeding like a stuck pig, Gothred," King Horos bellowed from the platform, confirming Silas's suspicions. "His fighting shamed all of Kalandragote."

Horos has lost his mind, Silas thought. *He has no hope of leaving here alive without Gothred's support.* It seemed to Silas that Gothred's earlier betrayal of

Horos was situational; if circumstances changed, Silas could envision the commander of the Ascendant Few going back over to Horos. But Horos was too intent on burning bridges to let any advantage develop.

Gothred's face pinked in fury. He spat his reply. "Say what you will, Horos."

"I always do. That's what a true Twin Ascendent does. I'll say it again. Your son shames us. As do you. Traitor."

"I am no traitor. I stand with Kalandragote. Kalandragote simply no longer stands with you."

Horos laughed. "The Ascendant Few. How we've misnamed you. I still remember the weakling you killed at your twin-death rite, Gothred. A runty thing, through and through. No wonder my kingdom has grown frail. I'm the only one who's ever had to kill an equal." He glanced back at the stone platform, at the dead King Micah. Another peal of laughter rolled from his mouth. "Two kings I've killed now. Who else can boast of such?"

"Perhaps your son, before the day is through."

Wulfess, entering the fray. *She is nothing if not bold,* Silas thought. Her teasing lilt was unnervingly lighthearted.

Horos gifted his new daughter-in-law a chilling grin. "And what kings are these?"

"It's true that you've killed a Dayborn king. But at his feet, I see a second. The current king of Ragar Or. Cato will kill him inside the Circle of Stones. As a bonding day gift to me." She paused, unmoving, collecting energy, fixing the moment. "The second king is you. The self-proclaimed Twin Ascendant."

Horos's grin grew horns. "I'm agreed to fight him. But you can't set the sennequi board and not play the game, girl." He brought a finger to his chin. "Grant me this. When my son lies dead at my feet, you'll offer up your neck to my blade. Then you may go together, the newly bonded couple, to the grave."

Silas felt the specter of Horos's prediction settle in his spine, a needling chill. It seemed incredibly unlikely that the old, gray-black-bearded king with his face full of pits and ridges could overcome his man-mountain of a son, but the certainty and quickness with which Horos summoned the vision of Cato and Wulfess lying dead in the snow rattled. Even Daguss Salk shifted uncomfortably.

"We agree," Wulfess said simply. She turned, stood on her tiptoes, and brought her face to Cato's, bringing him in for a long and showy kiss. She brought her hand to the hilt of his greatsword as she kissed him, letting it linger, letting everyone see. When she broke away from Cato she brought the sword with her, withdrawing it from its scabbard in all its gleaming glory, showing off its fearsome length. Sword in hand, she turned and stared down Horos, sending a wordless message. Satisfied, she handed the sword over to her newly bonded and took a step back.

Cato grabbed an oaken, iron-rimmed shield from one of his men, then moved into the center of the Circle of Stones. His footsteps the only sound in the yard, *crunch-crunching* in the snow. The greatsword looked normal-sized in Cato's gargantuan paws, but in comparison to other swords its massiveness was evident. Everything about Cato seemed designed to instill martial fear. In addition, the heir to Kalandragote possessed a blunt confidence separate from his size; he had the mean assertion of a man who knew how to kill.

For mercy's sake, I hope he kills the prince quickly, Silas thought. Four gray-robed priests had moved onto the platform and were attempting to bring

Ajax Dayborn to his feet. Ajax resisted, sconcing into the stone and pushing the gorgostrine away. The gorgostrine, growing more assertive, appeared to have hold of Ajax and were about to heave him to his feet when, in a burst of fury, the prince exploded from his seat and shoved the lot of them away, toppling one priest who in turn toppled two more, sending three of the four gray-robed gorgostrine spiraling to their asses.

Horos fingered the fiasco with his blade. "I'll bring him to you, Son, if you need me to. But if I have to prick him to do it, I'm adding another king to my tally."

Cato sheathed his sword. Started for the platform. Silas felt sick watching it transpire. *I should do something. I should—* The thought was interrupted by the old fears. *Who am I to stop it? Who am I to change anything? I'm good for nothing but my songs. And even those I use to wrong ends.*

Silas tried to look away. Tried to put what was happening to Ajax out of his mind. But the pain of standing silent in the face of what was transpiring lanced his soul.

What would Wyn Dunkin do, if he were here?

Cato crossed the stone platform in a boot-stomping huff. Upon reaching Ajax, Cato hauled the prince to his feet by the scruff of his shirt, then dragged the Dayborn heir to the platform's edge and threw him over the side. Ajax tumbled into the snow, crushing the Frostflowers beneath him. Leaping down from the platform, Cato was on him again in an instant. Ajax, dead-eyed and numb to the world, let Cato grab him up again and shove him into the center of circle. Ajax stumbled and fell on the blood-splattered snow.

"Get him a sword and shield!" Cato commanded. Cato's words were accented by the hiss and pop of the burning pyre. A Kalandragotan hurried forward and threw a longsword and a black-painted oaken shield at Ajax's feet. Silas watched it all numbly, not knowing what to do. The smell of cooking corpse meat filled the air. *This must be what it's like in the Bottom Black,* Silas thought. He was in hell and his song had brought him here. It was more than he could bear.

Apropos of nothing, his mind trailed to the woods witch and the stinging wisp. *What did she take from me?*

The answer dawned on him at last. The woods witch had taken from him the ability to care only about himself.

"Stand and fight!" Cato yelled at Ajax. It was clear that if the Dayborn prince didn't move, Cato would butcher him where he lay.

Silas thought of the one song that might stir Prince Ajax from his stupor. Before he thought better of it, he belted out the first line.

Three broken kings and a rip-torn land, still they say the sun forever rises!

The choice of song was so incongruous to what was taking place that the response was one of stupefaction. Silas continued, his voice quavering but insistent.

Three charges with a lance from the Dayborn man, now Ragar Or knows the sun forever rises!

In the center of the Circle of Stones, Ajax Dayborn stirred. Silas watched as the prince rose to his feet confusedly, like a man uncertain about his bearings. But even from a distance, Silas could see the energy building in his eyes.

Three words from King Xeuel as he goes to his grave, in Union's name the sun forever rises!

In some far-off sector of his brain, Silas knew that what he was doing was madness. But now that he had begun singing, he could not stop. He was being driven by a force beyond him, toward an end he could not predict. But the choice had been made, and he would see it through.

In the center of the Circle of Stones, Ajax Dayborn picked up the sword and shield. Returning to upright, he rolled his shoulders and pumped his legs. Ajax was smaller than Cato by far, but now that the prince had set aside his apathy it was possible to see his potential for defending himself. There was a fluidity to his movements that bespoke his aristocratic upbringing, and the sense that, were he to go to work with weapons, he would acquit himself with honor. *If I can keep his spirits up.* Silas knew that it was the Dayborn anthem—"The Sun Forever Rises"—that had roused Ajax to defend himself. *I must sing until the battle is over, regardless of the consequences. I must sing for Ajax's soul, and for my own.*

The two men began circling each other. Unlike the young men in the earlier fights, who had charged at each other straightaway, Cato and Ajax were inclined to feel each other out, for fear of the consequences of making a mistake. Cato wore a shirt of light mesh chainmail beneath a tunic and a frostflower-emblazoned surcoat, but otherwise neither man was armored.

If he's quick and lands the first blow, Ajax might have a chance.

The Dayborn prince, perhaps thinking the same, attacked first. He darted in with a serpent's speed, striking Cato's shield with a harmless left-sided half blow that flowed into a fatal-minded follow-up on the right. For an instant Silas thought Ajax's sword had slipped through, but Cato was equal to the attack, dropping his shield with an incredible speed to catch the blade. The big Kalandragotan shifted his body as he moved, keeping his balance.

Safely repositioned, Cato launched a forceful counterattack, hammering down on Ajax with his greatsword. Ajax barely caught the attack with the borrowed black shield. The force of the blow cracked the wood, splintering the shield near its iron edges. Driven to his knees, Ajax tried to parry, but Cato easily turned aside Ajax's sword and swung the greatsword again, this time with death in mind.

Ajax rolled smartly away. As he did so he dropped his shield, for need of speed. The hair-shaving narrowness of his escape proved the wisdom of his choice. Ajax scrambled to his feet with a feral quickness, caked with snow and short a shield but still alive. He moved to recover the shield, but Cato had already beaten him to it. The odds of Ajax winning the fight, already slim, decreased significantly.

Silas had reached the song's chorus. He felt as if he was of two bodies: one was watching the fight and the other was singing. Frigid as the morning was, the cold did not touch his voice. Every word coming from Silas's mouth was fire and honey, infusing Ajax Dayborn with the courage to meet his foe.

And now the war is broken
And new the day is born
Union for all Ragar Or
The Sun Forever Rises!

A whip of wind lashed freshly fallen snow back into the air, painting a crystal glimmer inside the Circle of Stones. Ajax gathered himself, breathing heavily. Now that the prince was short a shield, Silas worried that he would lose hope. But no… Ajax gathered himself and sang the chorus back at Silas, his voice strident with defiance.

And now the war is broken
And new the day is born
Union for all Ragar Or
The Sun Forever Rises!

When the chorus ended, Ajax and Cato charged into the fractal field, swords burning through the snowy mists. Ajax, garbed in orange and black, looked like a dark sunbeam. When the Dayborn prince swung his sword, it seemed for a second a fatal sunbolt. But once again, Cato caught the prince's steel on his shield. And then Cato's greatsword came hammering down, hard and heavy.

This time the Dayborn prince could not stop it.

The blow took off Ajax's arm at the left shoulder. It sent the prince twisting to the ground, screaming in agony. Silas could only watch in horror as Ajax writhed on the ground, a dying man on the fast track to dead. All that remained was for Cato to deliver the killing blow.

Sing, Silas commanded himself. *Sing.*

One king to rule the land, now as before, one king to show the world the sun forever rises!

Some demon of defiance had hold of him. Prince Ajax may have fallen, but the song wasn't over. And it was his job to sing.

Cato stood hulking over Ajax, surveying the damage. He ground his heel into the prince's right wrist, forcing Ajax to let go of his sword. Bending over, Cato picked up the sword and tossed it aside. Ajax, eyes adrift, blood shooting from his shoulder, did nothing to resist. Death had the prince in its talons.

One voice sings the song that binds all Ragar Or, with one voice the people sing the sun forever rises!

Cato wheeled in anger. Until that moment, he had seemed oblivious to Silas's singing. But now it was clear that the song was driving him mad. "Enough! Kill the blasted singer if he keeps at it!" Cato commanded anyone who would listen to him. "I won't hear another word. I won't…AAAARGH!"

A dagger sprouted from Cato's calf. Ajax's work. Silas wouldn't have believed it if he hadn't seen it. The injured, one-armed prince had summoned the strength to reach over and grab the dagger sheathed on the outside of Cato's boot, then redeposited it in the man-mountain's calf.

Cato clutched at the dagger in shock. In doing so, he lost his balance and toppled over, crashing treelike to the ground at an angle that jammed the dagger even deeper into his flesh. Howling in pain, Cato tried to work his fingers through the snow to the blade. Silas couldn't see clearly, but from the sounds of Cato's misery, his efforts at extricating the dagger were failing.

"THERE IS NO TWIN ASCANDANT BUT ME!"

The shout came from the platform. King Horos. Horos moved as he yelled, jumping from the platform with a shocking speed and crossing into the Circle of Stones, violence in his eyes. The sight caused Silas to stop singing. Everyone was spellbound. A spell that held until Horos wrapped his hands around the hilt of Ajax's dropped longsword.

Wulfess's scream broke the spell.

"STOP HIM! STOP HIM!"

Her screaming might have slowed a different man, but not Horos Ollspaer: what the Kalandragotan king lacked in youthly vigor, he more than made up for in violent decisiveness. With a merciless swing of the sword, Horos took Ajax Dayborn's head. Silas watched as the bloody pool surrounding the prince's butchered body expanded into a bloody lake. Horos stomped through the gore, paying no mind to the blood congealing on his boots.

He was too intent on killing his son.

Cato caught onto what was taking place. The son grabbed his shield from off the ground and threw it up in front of him as his father's sword came crashing down. But Cato's grip on the shield was poor: the shield buckled at the force of the blow, allowing the blade to slide off and deal a glancing blow to the side of Cato's face. The man-mountain scream-grunted in pain and turned away. Fortunately, he had the state of mind to regrip his shield and swing it up at his father with a tremendous force. The shield caught Horos hard on his left side and sent him stumbling backward.

Silas only now realized that he was no longer singing. A different voice now filled the courtyard, insistent and entreating, familiar but changed, its normally liquid tones turned to screaming stone.

"SAVE HIM, FATHER! SAVE HIM!"

Daguss Salk hurled himself into the fray, the white of his moonbear coat like a dirt-flecked phantom against the pure-driven snow. He drew his sword as he flew forward, the blade leading him toward his fate. He reached Horos with the speed of a boulder crashing down a mountain, too fast, too fast. *Stavus save us, they're going to collide,* Silas thought. But at the last moment Horos Ollspaer sensed Daguss and turned away, sword raised, slicing down, a blur of bodies and an exchange of steel, the stinging cry of a man cut. Gawping confusion. *Where's the welling red?* Silas swiveled his head between the two men, desperate to see the damage done. Then he saw it, bubbling up beneath the moonbear coat, like lava coming up through the cracks.

"NO!" Wulfess screamed again. Horos paid her no heed. As Daguss staggered backward, Horos turned his attention once more to his son, Cato. The man-mountain was half risen and fumbling for his greatsword. But he couldn't gather it in time. Horos fell on his son without mercy, driving his steel through Cato's ringmail and into his flesh, making a skewer of his shoulder. The heir to Kalandragote jerked away, separating from the blade and staggering five or six steps before falling backward into the snow.

"I AM THE TWIN ASCENDANT!" Horos shouted triumphantly. *The old madman's doing it, he's killing them all,* Silas thought with astonishment. But then...here came Daguss Salk plodding forward again, bloodied but unconquered, a grim, graceless set to his white-forest jaw. His movements were labored but measured, every step weighed with a deadly intentionality.

Horos, squaring on Daguss, tried to match his movements. But in slowing down, Horos's age seemed to show, the advantages accrued to him by impulse and rage no longer giving him the edge. "I am the Twin Ascendant!" Horos shouted again, shaking his sword. Daguss, however, refused to take the bait. Instead, he continued circling and measuring, circling and measuring, while something like fear settled into Horos's eyes.

This time, when Daguss Salk fell on Horos, he made a music of it. Measured steel clanging against steel, metronomic, one…and two…and three…and…Daguss's pace quickened, Horos struggling to hold the beat…and four…and five…and…seizing the half step, Daguss drove his sword inside of Horos's lagging cut, hard into the Kalandragotan's heart. Silas heard the crunching pop of Horos's breastbone. A startled "I…!" arrived on Horos's lips but was left marooned there. Death claimed the remainder of the assertion before the words could escape Horos's mouth.

The Lord of High Osgood staggered away, leaving his sword in Horos's corpse. Silas watched in astonishment as Daguss Salk sat down on the snow. The blood on his moonbear coat traced the arc of a falling star. Silas could see that Lord Daguss was badly hurt, but with his arms draping over his knees, it was difficult to gauge how bad.

Wulfess rushed forward into the Circle of Stones. Everyone watching. She hesitated over her father before continuing on to Cato. The colossal Kalandragotan was a horrid sight, blood-drenched and slumped over like a marionette with cut strings. Wulfess knelt beside him and cupped her hands over his shoulder wound. When she pulled them back, they were black with blood. She turned with a frantic look on her face, searching the yard. She stopped when her eyes fell on Silas.

"Singer! Come forward!" Her voice was wracked with sobs. "Sing the song! Tell them! Sing to them the truth of the prophecy, tell them of the child Cato Ollspaer and I are meant to have! The child who will be the heir to the Ontish kingdom. Sing the true version of 'The Queen's Burning Heart,' wrought from the words of the Yubriy Tree!"

Madness. Pure madness. Silas did his best to speak the truth. "Lady Wulfess. There is no child."

She stuck out her chin defiantly. Choked down her sobs. "Let all who are here bear witness to my testimony. Even now, I carry Cato Ollspaer's child. The natural heir to the Ontish kingdom."

Nonsense. You've only slept with me.

Wulfess answered Silas's thoughts with a hard and piercing glare. He sifted through her statement to get at the truth of what she was suggesting. *No. It can't be. You wouldn't know if you were pregnant, not yet. Not enough time has passed. And wishing won't make it true.*

But the truth, whatever it was, mattered little in the moment. What mattered was Wulfess. She had taken charge of the narrative, and woe be it to anyone who resisted.

"Come forward and sing the song, singer. NOW. Or I'll have my father's men cut you down where you stand."

Silas could see in her eyes that she meant it. If he didn't pacify Wulfess Salk, he was going to die. Here and now. In cold and cruel Kalandragote.

"Beoliotius bless us, save your skin, man. Do as she says!" the Mock soldier standing nearby whisper-hissed at Silas. Silas heard him, but from far away, as if in a dream. He knew that he should be afraid, but he wasn't. Something strange was occurring: time was rippling, bending, the world and the moment at hand fracturing. He sensed powerful forces gathering at the periphery of his senses. They would intervene to save him, or they wouldn't. But he would not sing Wulfess's version of the song.

Why? It didn't exist. All morning long he had refused to write it.

“No, Lady Wulfess. It’s true that I haven’t sung the true version of ‘The Queen’s Burning Heart,’ the one gifted to me by the Yubriy Tree. But the song is not about you, nor is it about any child you may or not carry.”

Wulfess’s fair white skin reddened in rage. She grabbed the pearl-and-onyx necklace at her throat and squeezed it. “Liar,” she proclaimed. She turned to her father’s soldiers. “Kill him! Now!”

Silas closed his eyes. He heard the bustle of men reaching for their weapons.

And then he heard a dragon’s deafening roar.

He opened his eyes, expecting to see the beast. But instead, what he saw was the Sagekind.

Gregor Thorn.

Gregor Thorn

Gregor awoke to a quartet of faces staring down at him. Three familiar, one unfamiliar. His mouth tasted like a dragon's anus and his body felt like it was holding fast to a comet's tail. At the fuzzy edges of the dreaming-death realm he sensed Sephery, and for a second it seemed he might return to sleep and find her there, waiting for him. But the flaming lifeforce burning through his veins wouldn't allow it. The waking world had him in its iron grip.

"I was a dead man. What did you give me?"

Deglan answered with a flat honesty. "*Yompto pew.* Poison life. My decision. It might kill you, but the way I saw it, you were already dying. And knowing that you are a jeyedoshi, I figured there was a decent chance you might turn the medicine on its head."

Yompto pew. Stavus save us. The plant was a known fatal poison, one that gave its user an incandescent burst of energy before finishing them off. How a jeyedoshi might respond to it, Gregor hadn't the foggiest. Jeyedoshi nearly always had reactions to natural substances different from the norm, but, so far as Gregor knew, there was no record of what occurred when a jeyedoshi ingested the plant known as "poison life."

Gregor took a moment to consider the young woman standing beside Deglan. Ribbons of sea-green were woven into her hair, and she had the skin color of a woman practiced in the art of absorbing salt and sun.

"Who are you?" he asked her.

"Tern."

"Like the seabird?"

"Exactly."

There was a story here, but he hadn't the time. Gregor stood up beside the bed, the fire from the *yompto pew* coursing through his veins. He sensed the four elements gathering on his fingertips, in his thoughts, on his tongue. He could move mountains if he wanted. He could bring the world to its knees.

"Seydron is dead?" he asked, looking at Madrig.

The big mute nodded.

"Elements of the castle took umbrage when we absconded with your body to the north tower. They're on the other side of that door," Jacy said, motioning at the opposite end of the room. "Waiting to kill us." Gregor heard voices outside, the timpani of footsteps.

"And what of my brother's men? They never arrived to claim my body?"

Jacy deferred to Deglan. "There was a coup overnight. Successful, so far as I know. Now the rival factions are positioning, possibly fighting. Your brother the king…if he's alive, it's only by the grace of whoever's captured him."

"We should flee, Revered Sagekind," Jacy said. "We could climb out the tower window. Leave the same way that Deglan and Tern came in.

Tern's father has a ship waiting in Skithin Harbor. We could sail far away from here until you've had time to rally allies to Union's side…"

Gregor shook his head.

"If my brother's still alive, it's my job to save him. To save and defend the Dayborn dynasty. And if he's not alive, it's my job to…" He remembered what Zust had said to ten-year-old him in the dream. *But should the day come when all the necessary lies fail you and your family, you should take the mantle that is rightly yours.* He felt a tremendous pressure building inside of him, demanding release. *Wraith in Red. Skin 'n' Bones.* He felt his destiny calling. *Bad Magic. Struvan Bastard.* He had spent his life as the Sagekind, but he should have been the king. *Jeyedoshi. Jeyedoshi. Jeyedoshi.*

The jeyedoshi king.

When he failed to finish his thought, Jacy finished it for him. "We understand. You must do what you must do."

He felt that that if he breathed with intent, all the walls of the castle would crumble, crushing his enemies. "Fight with me, and we will preserve Union." He looked at their faces. He saw no skulls beneath their flesh. "You will survive. I swear it."

Madrig worked his hands into a flurry. He made one sign repeatedly, bouncing fingers and then a closed fist from his right hand off his left palm. Jacy translated. "Madrig says that we fight for Union, Sagekind. Union. We care not that you are a jeyedoshi, so long as you are for Union. Union is all."

Gregor sized the giant mute up. *He is a cousin of Daguss Salk.* Gregor had the fleeting thought that he should kill the mute where he stood. *One less Salk in the world.* But the fervent earnestness in Madrig's eyes convinced Gregor that he meant what he had said.

"Good. To the fight, then. For Ragar Or. For Union."

When they removed the barricade and threw open the door, nine men—a mix of Qorls and Salks, every skull visible—stood on the opposite side, bemused expressions on their faces. A Qorlishman with a V-shaped goatee pointed a trembling finger at Gregor. "You're supposed to be dead," the man said dumbly.

Gregor strangled the man where he stood. He had stolen the wind from people's lungs enough in his lifetime to know the feeling, but this was different. He made the man's lungs collapse, then he fashioned a rope from the stolen wind and wrapped it around the fellow's throat. Every soul paused and watched the speed with which the man succumbed to the assault, the way his face changed colors, passing from purple to red to dead.

When the Qorlishman fell, the others looked at Gregor with a profound fear. For a moment, it seemed that they might turn tail and run. But the most frightened-looking of the bunch forced himself to mount a charge, and the others joined in.

Gregor called upon the cold, a deep and devilish laughter playing in his mind. He congealed the blood of three of the men within a three-step span, their movements faltering then failing. They died bloated blue. Madrig and Jacy moved around him as he worked his magic, their swift and terrible swords carving bloody paths through flesh. A lanky Salk drew a bead on Jacy, and might've skewered her, but Tern found the killing angle in time, driving a tapered blade deep into the attacker's kidneys. On the periphery, Deglan fought a Qorlishman. It was an even fight, but the distraction of the Qorlishman's dying companions cost him in the end; one too many sideway glances allowed Deglan to capitalize.

While waiting for Deglan to put him out of his misery, the man made an anguished plea.

"You must kill *him* (gasp)! The *jeyedoshi!* There is no greater (gasp) threat to us all! None. Coros's curse cannot be allowed to—(gaaaaaaaasp)!"

Deglan's sword ended it. Gregor shared a look with the young knight when it was over. The young knight who was faithful and true. The young knight who had nearly lost his life back in Low Osgood. Gregor told the boy his thoughts.

"If my kin are dead, I name myself king."

Deglan answered forthwith. "The realm would be the better for it."

You are loyal to a fault, he thought. But Deglan wasn't wrong. The realm *would* be the better for it if he was king. But first the realm would suffer. Starting with the men in this castle. *I will deal with these traitors now, while I am the Firewalker come again.* His blood was boiling. He remembered standing on the beach in Dunning Harbor, Tan by his side, imagining what it would be like to manifest the Firewalker's powers.

Now he need not imagine.

Now the powers of history's most famous jeyedoshi were at his fingertips.

He stepped over the bodies and made for the stairs. A crow perched upon the sill of a tower window gave a shrill caw and took flight. Reminded of the Salks, Gregor called upon a gust of wind with a horrid little half thought and sent it slamming into the bird. The crow went spinning out of sight. *I am crazed,* he thought. But what of it? The world was crazed against him. Always had been. Now, at least, he was on an equal footing.

The vortex of stairs spat him out of the base of the north tower, the others following behind. He stepped into the snow-covered courtyard and beheld a scene of the most excruciating intensity. Bodies burning on a pyre. Stupefied soldiers, staring at the carnage. The scattered battered and blood-soaked.

Gregor put names to the maimed. Lord Daguss Salk sat upon the snow, grievously wounded across the chest. Nearby, Horos Ollspaer lay dead. Wulfess Salk was kneeling beside Cato Ollspaer, helpless in the face of the horrors inflicted upon his body. She was issuing frantic commands and carrying on a strained conversation with Silas O' the Songs. An additional corpse lay in the center of the Circle of Stones, decapitated. Garbed in orange and black. *Ajax,* Gregor's eyes told him. How the heir to the throne had come to be there, he didn't have the first clue. There was no sign of Greta Worrint, but he assumed her dead as well.

His thoughts and eyes ascended, settling on the stone platform. There he saw King Micah of House Dayborn, the first of his name, Holy Son of the Air, the Twin Ascendant, and the Rightful Ruler of Ragar Or. Tied to a wooden chair, body bloodied, head slumped to one side.

Gregor's trueborn brother.

Dead.

Gregor closed his eyes. The fury of a thousand suns filled him up; the dread cold of an eternal winter enveloped his heart. Easton Dayborn flickered across his mind's eye, but the image was distant and blurred.

High above an otherworldly heaviness.

I am the jeyedoshi king.

Gregor opened his eyes at the same time a dragon let out a deafening roar.

He looked up. The green-and-black-scaled underbelly of a large dragon moved like a swift river of dark-plated armor above the courtyard, its tail lagging and lashing behind, cracking the air like a whip. When it was finished passing overhead, the dragon climbed and curved, belching fire, fomenting madness, bringing time to a panicked standstill. Every eye tracked it with wonder and fear.

Gregor drew the only logical conclusion. *It's a sign. All the Dayborns are dead. Easton too, wherever he may be. The dragon is here for me.*

The jeyedoshi king.

For a time, Gregor exacted revenge with impunity.

First, he called down snow from the crenellations and made a miniature blizzard, stirring the white into an angry maelstrom, blinding and bludgeoning all. He felt outside of himself as he did it. Godlike. A mischievous and spiteful deity. The chaos and confusion he sowed was exacerbated by the dragon, who made a second pass and unleashed a terrible spout of fire while swooping by, a rope of scorching orange red above the blinding white. Panicked soldiers howled in horror, uncertain what was happening.

But Gregor was blinded too. And there were people inside the all-enveloping white that he needed to punish.

No. Not punish. Kill.

He gave the snow back to gravity. Refocused. *Dante and Daguss. Kill them first.* But Dante wasn't here. All the birds were gone, in fact. *Daguss. Kill Daguss.* The Lord of High Osgood remained in the center of the Circle of Stones, knocked over onto his side. Gregor saw him and went blind with rage. Without thinking, he directed all of his energy into one of the larger stones in the circle. The stone was a dark gray green, the color of a tempestuous sea. It was at least seven feet tall and ungodly heavy. Gregor extracted it from the ground the way one might a tooth or a difficult weed. Normally, he wouldn't have been able to move it; too much energy, even for a jeyedoshi. But under the influence of the *yompto pew,* the stone felt as light as a feather.

A shocked silence met the sight of the levitating stone. It was a jagged monolith, bulky in the center and sharp on the ends, the bottom quarter caked in mud and snow. Gregor moved it across the courtyard with a steady speed. Straight toward Lord Daguss Salk.

The head of the line that had once ruled Ragar Or tracked the stone until it was hovering directly over him. Daguss Salk's bald head, usually fierce-looking, acquired a penitent aspect. Covered in stone shadow, Daguss leaned backward on a propping elbow. Gregor held the stone still, watching as Daguss's brown eyes grew white and wide. Like an animal, frozen in fear.

"STOP HIM!" Wulfess's voice rang out. "STOP THE BASTARD, THE JEYED—"

Gregor dropped the stone. It buried into the spot where Daguss Salk sat with a sickening *thud*, making an end of the man. Blood and bits of viscera escaped at the edges, but otherwise, it was as if Lord Daguss Salk had simply disappeared.

A great deal of screaming and shouting ensued, cut through with panic and horror and hate. Gregor felt the sting of it for a second, and the guilt. He had killed men before, but never outside of himself, never in bloodlust. The guilt didn't last. The *yompto pew* was burning through him like a wildfire, making demands of him before the fuel was spent. All of his life he had repressed his jeyedoshi spirit. Now he would give it full rein.

He looked for the dragon. *My dragon.* He didn't know where it had gone, but he felt a tether to it, an absolute certainty that it had come to Kalandragote for him. His certainty was so strong that he opened his mouth, thinking that he might call the dragon to his side—but that was when he remembered the book with the blue boards, and the knowledge it had imparted to him about how a jeyedoshi learns Dragon Tongue. *A Yubriy leaf. There must be one in the vicinity. I'll find it, burn it, inhale the smoke, call the dragon to me…*

An arrow zinged past. The enemy was in disarray, but not entirely: intrepid types were charging from various angles. *The dragon, if I could only call the dragon…*but there was no time to think. Gregor turned to his left to deal with four hard-charging Frostflowers. He opened the ground beneath their feet, creating a sizable gash that sucked in snow and tangled the men's feet and redirected their swords, some of the blades finding the backs of their compatriots running in front of them. The broken men screamed in pain.

Returning his attention to the forefront, Gregor caught sight of Madrig slamming his sword into Mactus Garstring's shield with a force that rivaled thunder. Behind Gregor, Jacy and Deglan and Tern fanned out. It dawned on Gregor with alarm how badly outnumbered they were, how much of the weight of the fighting he needed to carry.

He took the charge to task.

The ensuing minutes were a blur. Gregor became a vessel of magic and rage and revenge. He made an ungodly mayhem out of the courtyard, joining chaos to retribution. From the wan sun he made pillars of fire, and with them consumed the enemy; he hurled boulders of snow into the charging few, freezing his adversaries on impact; with the wind he kept control of the periphery, blinding anyone attempting to regroup on the edges of the courtyard with stirred-up snow. Power raged through him like a dragon. So consumed was he in the task that he lost track of his allies. He was too busy slaying skulls, left and right. He understood now why the sea fingers had shown him the skulls. *So I would know who must die.* He wondered how many skulls there were in Ragar Or. His mind went to the skies. *Give me the dragon, and I will kill them all.*

But the dragon didn't return. Its absence became a burr in Gregor's thoughts. *If I am to become what I am supposed to become, a true jeyedoshi king, I must have the dragon.* The idea became a haunting one. Soon, it was working on him like an enervating force. His power diminished with every passing second. And then, all at once, he could no longer fight. He stood at the north edge of the courtyard, undone.

Tens of dead surrounded him. The survivors were scattered across the courtyard, bewildered and unorganized, no immediate threat. Gregor turned his head to the left and to the right and confirmed that his four allies were still alive. At Madrig's feet, Mactus Garstring lay dead with a half-caved-in head. The hulking mute was breathing heavily but otherwise looked none the worse for wear.

Out of the carnage, a lone figure stepped forward. The lutist. Silas O' the Songs. The musician drifted over as if wading through the waters of a murky dream. Gregor stared at Silas with bewilderment. *You? Why are you still here? Why are you still alive?* The sight of the lutist sapped even more energy from Gregor. He buckled at the knees. *I feel as if I'm dying.* Only the power of the dragon could save him, only the power of the dragon could restore him to his full jeyedoshi might.

His four allies converged, huddling around him in a half-formed shield. Silas O' the Songs joined the shield wall. For a moment they stared at Gregor with a mixture of wonder and fear, amazed at what they had seen him do. Then their voices rolled off each other, an impromptu war council, the questions and the answers mixing and matching with little concern for order.

"Can you stand, Sagekind?" Jacy asked. The question sounded far away. Gregor did not reply.

Madrig made signing motions with his hand.

"I am with you," Silas O' the Songs said, addressing the mute. "I am…not for the Salks. Nor the Ollspaers. Nor the birds. Not after what they've done…"

"They're taking notice," said Tern, looking across the courtyard.

"The Ascendant Few," confirmed Deglan. "Gothred is eyeing us. They're going to attack. Revered Sagekind, you must…what's wrong? Is it the *yompto pew*?"

Was it the *yompto pew?* The poison life? No, he was a jeyedoshi, he was Ascendant, he possessed an unmatched power. Except…*the dragon, remember? You need the dragon.* He mustered all the energy he could. "The dragon will restore me. I am a jeyedoshi. The dragon has come for me. But to call it, I need…a Yubriy leaf."

Seconds ago, at the height of his powers, the universe had seemed a serendipitous place, making Gregor certain that a Yubriy leaf was in the vicinity. But now, with his lifeforce flagging, the great unlikelihood of there being a Yubriy leaf nearby became obvious. *The woodkin Wyn Dunkin stole your Yubriy leaf, you fool. All other leaves are in Union Castle, or lying latent in the Yubriy Tree's branches.* Despair gripped his heart. "A Yubriy leaf," he muttered. "I must have—"

"I have a Yubriy leaf. Hidden in my boot." Silas O' the Songs spoke with the blunt simplicity of the honest. "I've had it the whole time."

On the back of Silas's words, the rumbling roar of the dragon echoed off mountain stone and tumbled down into Gregor's hearing like an avalanche. Gregor could barely lift his own head, but he sensed the others shifting their gazes above him, staring up and out of the castle at Mt. Wrepta. He could have wept for joy. "Get me somewhere safe. We must burn the leaf. Then I will inhale the smoke. That is how a jeyedoshi learns Dragon Tongue. Then I will call the dragon to me."

There were no looks of doubt, nor of wild wonder. The day had done considerable damage to everyone's capacity for astonishment.

"They're going to charge at us," Deglan interrupted, eyeing the other side of the courtyard. The young knight turned to Madrig. "Pick up the Sagekind. We must retreat to the north tower. Now."

Gregor scarce felt the giant pick him up. He felt so weak that he was almost weightless, the very embodiment of his nickname, *Uncle Bones.* But it mattered not. He would soon inhale the smoke of a Yubriy leaf, and he would become a jeyedoshi king in full. The Firewalker born again.

Then he would call a dragon from the sky, and set Ragar Or to rights.

Gregor was half delirious with pain by the time his friends returned him to the room near the top of the North Tower. He slipped in and out of hallucinations as the others barricaded the door, his grasping Sagekind mind revisiting the mad array of images the universe had shown him these past months. There: the sorcerer, silver brown, no longer laughing but standing tree-root still, a thousand riddles written in flame in the sky behind him. Fading, then gone. There: the cordrix, that indescribable Clyesian beast. The animal gave a long and plaintive cry before slipping back into the shadows. There: the dragon from the dream. *The same green-black dragon now resting on Mt. Wrepta.* The dragon carried the Union crown in its claws, but unlike in the dream, when it was flying at a distance, it now flew directly overhead. Gregor looked up at the rider, expecting to see himself. Instead, he saw a woman. The lesser twin and rumored jeyedoshi who had caused the hubbub at Coffyn Castle.

Johanna Salk?

Johanna Salk and the dragon disappeared. In their place, Silas O' the Songs hovered above Gregor. The lutist was standing on one foot, taking off his boot. He looked different from the incomplete, half-formed man that Gregor remembered. This was a *new* Silas O' the Songs, formed in the fires of decisions made.

Silas withdrew a large, dark-honey-orange Yubriy leaf from the bottom of his boot. Gregor could see the looping silver scrawlings that adorned the leaf, words written in the common tongue.

"I found the leaf while traveling through the woods near the Yubriy Tree. It inspired my song. 'The Queen's Burning Heart.' But the leaf's true message…I don't pretend to understand it. I only know it's different from what I've let on."

Another puzzle, another trick, another prophecy with multiple meanings. Gregor remembered the silver-brown sorcerer laughing at him. *Is the sorcerer the Yubriy Tree? Or is the sorcerer the Firewalker? Or are they one and the same?* It mattered not. He was done with the deity and its foolish games. *I will burn the leaf and become the Firewalker myself. There will be no need to interpret prophecies when I myself am become a god.*

A terrible pounding erupted on the door, the furious fists of vengeance-minded men. The door, barricaded by a heavy oaken board reinforced by the room's furniture, didn't budge.

"Fire," Gregor forced himself to say. It hurt like the Bottom Black to speak. "Fast. Burn the leaf and bring the smoke to my lungs."

He heard his defenders moving around the room. Their bodies flitted at the edges of his vision. A rich and buttery voice, the one least familiar to him, spoke. "There are tapers in the corner. Use one to catch a flame from the hearth." Tern's voice. *Who are these people helping me?* Gregor would need to fashion a kingdom from their loyalty when it was all over. It seemed ludicrous, suddenly, that he would be king. *And who will be my heir? Deglan?*

The door at the front of the room jolted and shook under the force of an assault. Shouting on the other side. *A fire. Bring me the fire and burn the leaf. What is taking so long?* Everything seemed wrong. *I shouldn't be lying down. A king needs to see his subjects.* He felt frantic at the need to take in the room. *Madrig, Jacy, Deglan, Tern. And Silas. I need to see them. My kingdom of five.* He used all of his power to force himself to sitting upright.

Silas O' the Songs put a hand on his shoulder. "Easy. Rest until the leaf restores you." The lutist was looking down on him with grave concern. *He can see my bones.* Now that Gregor's family was dead, perhaps he'd give the five in the room the honor of calling him by his Dayborn moniker. *Uncle Bones.* He made a tour of the room with his eyes. Deglan, his true and faithful knight, knelt opposite the bed, bringing a flame from the hearth to the wooden end of the taper. Tern, dressed in a salt-stained jerkin, leaned over Deglan, watching him. *They're lovers. Thank Beoliotius I didn't get the boy killed before he experienced love's sweet taste.* He kept his head moving, fighting through the pain to find Madrig standing guard at the door. Gregor thought he could see through to the center of the mute, to where Madrig's giant heart beat steady and slow, warrior-ready. Jacy stood at his side, short sword in hand. A formidable pairing. *They will head my honor guard, in Union.*

He knew the thought was false the instant he had it.

Who else is here? He sensed a sixth presence in the room. *The last citizen of my kingdom.* He turned his head to the right, to the wall opposite the door, where a massive armoire rested. Beside the armoire, a vertical pool of darkened silver cut a portal to another realm. Inside of the portal, a skull stared out, sitting up in bed and reaching across space and time to bring home a terrible truth.

A mirror.

I'm looking at a mirror.

I'm looking at myself.

He started to unravel. *I'm a dead man.* He could feel it in his body, in his bones, in his blood. He understood that the *yompto pew* had worked on him like it did every mortal: one last burst of energy before finishing him off. He closed his eyes and it felt as if he was falling through the cosmos again, falling to his death. *I will be with Sephery soon.* He only needed to keep his eyes closed, and life would settle his accounts for him. He only needed—

"I have the flame, Revered Sagekind. I'm going to burn the Yubriy leaf."

The star of life exploded inside of him. Gregor opened his eyes and with a wild lunge grabbed the burning end of the taper with his bare hand, catching the flame before Deglan fed it to the leaf. He brought the flame to the bed, where it kissed his red cloak. "What are you doing?!" young Deglan asked, his voice full of confusion as Gregor snuffed out the flame with the hem of his cloak. Gregor wanted to answer, wanted to explain his actions to the young knight who was faithful and true, but his star was fading and he was dying…and he had only enough energy for a few words.

It's your duty to try and see through to the truth, he heard Sephery saying from the death-dreaming realm, that place where he would soon go. *Do your duty, Uncle Bones.*

He looked at Silas O' the Songs. "The leaf. It's not meant for me. Easton…my nephew…is now the true king. If he's bonded the Salk girl…she then is the true queen. They say she's…a lesser twin. A jeyedoshi, perhaps. It's up to you…it's up to *all of you*…to find them. To see. *The lutist…bears a song for the queen.* The true song. The gift. You must give the leaf to her…you must…*you*…"

Space and time collapsed around Gregor. He was returning to the sky, to Stavus, to *Owoervyrn.* Sephery took his hand in her own.

Uncle Bones.

Gregor Thorn, the trueborn brother of King Micah Dayborn, breathed his last.

Johanna Salk

Johanna could not think clearly for the emotions roiling within her. Anger. Despair. Anxiety. Rage. Hopelessness. And most paralyzing of all—shame.

Rage was the most dangerous of Johanna's feelings, tempting her over and over to tap into her jeyedoshi self and exact revenge on her captors. It would come over her like a wave, building slowly and then cresting all at once, and where seconds ago she wouldn't have had the first clue how to channel her jeyedoshi self, rage made it where she could scarce hold the powers back. The insistent voice of reason was the only thing that stopped her. *They'll kill you in an instant,* the voice screamed from deep within the gorge of her consciousness, louder and louder until she was released from rage's grip and handed over to shame.

Shame, conversely, acted as a soporific, using its quiet, repetitive voice to strangle her spirit. *You did nothing when they took Easton away. Nothing. You've shown who you truly are. There's naught to do now but accept your fate.* She would submit to the mantra for hours at a time, until rage rebelled and forced its way into her bloodstream, and the cycle would start over again.

Surprisingly, it was one of the crossbowmen assigned to guard Johanna who shook up the cycle. Norbert. An obnoxious, tree-bark-chewing, completely unprepossessing aggravation of a young man. As Philemon had promised, there were always five crossbow-carrying soldiers keeping watch on Johanna, but most preferred not to speak to her, and when ahorse retreated as far away as twenty yards. But not Norbert. He would draw abreast of Johanna's and begin chatting with a glib nonchalance that would have been galling were it not so unselfconscious.

"Have you ever been to Union, my lady? The capital city?"

"No," Johanna admitted. She was a noble, and she had traveled far and wide throughout Ragar Or, but she had never been to Union.

"Oh! To think it! You being who you are, and I being who I am, the son of a tanner and a washwoman, and I've been to the capital city, and you have not. There's a feather in my cap. It will be a changed city by the time you reach it, I think. Lord Philemon—"

Johanna knew that she should press Norbert on exactly why the capital city would be changed, but the title he had conferred on Philemon was too galling to let pass unremarked upon. "Philemon Yurk is no lord. His father Delton disowned him."

"Delton Yurk is dead, my lady," Norbert replied, chewing on a twig of beechwood. "A fortnight ago. And Philemon is *indeed* a lord. I swear this to you."

"By whose authority? Only a king or queen can confer lordship. And surely Delton Yurk named a different heir after disowning Philemon." Johanna wished she had better knowledge of the Yurk family tree.

"My lady, Lord Delton legitimized Philemon shortly before his death. There's a signed document. I've seen it."

What in the name of the Twins has happened east of here? She wondered how Lord Delton Yurk had died. She wondered if *someone* had slipped snakegrass into his soup. "You said the capital city would be changed by the time we reached it. Is that where we're heading? Union? And why would the city be changed? Lord Saylet remains the regent, does he not?"

Norbert laughed at that. He had a thin, pinched face, one made for mean comedy. When he laughed, his mouth looked like a burrowing hole. "My lady, I'm no lord to say what was or what will be, I only know that history is being rewritten as we speak, and that the eastern houses have the upper hand." He pointed at his surcoat, the proud gold and brown of the Chesterly eagle. "As for Lord Saylet, I'd wager that by now he understands the situation. If he's smart, he's gone over to the rising powers. If he's stubborn, the Heron will sort him out when he returns."

Johanna's heart sank. She wondered if her father's coup was in conjunction or in conflict with this one. "And if it's King Micah who returns? Or Queen Anjay? Or Prince Ajax?" she asked. "What then?"

Norbert scoffed. "My lady, if you'd seen what I'd seen, and heard what I'd heard, you'd realize just how unlikely the prospect of the Dayborns returning south actually is."

They rode in silence for a spell. Johanna and her crossbowmen were positioned in a severed segment of the procession, cut off from the lordly retinues at the front but a fair distance ahead of the rank and file following behind them. Since leaving Hevengrow, the high lords had given Johanna a wide berth, with only Philemon checking in on her from time to time. *They're frightened of me. Frightened of what I might be capable of.* She snagged glimpses of the front from time to time, the odd bend in the road revealing Isbel Wicker's long and lithesome back, Doneg Desighart's horse-sized rump, Philemon Yurk's bowed shoulders. Most infuriating of all was the sight of Richard Chesterly sitting astride a Rugarder that Johanna was certain was Bitterboy. She had asked about Bitterboy when they put her on a different horse, but no one had seen fit to answer her.

Though she didn't particularly enjoy conversing with Norbert, Johanna forced herself to keep at it, lest the opportunity for learning passed. "Do you know what's become of my bonded?"

"Easton Dayborn?"

She nodded.

"You weren't bonded yet, my lady," Norbert said, laughing. "I was in the temple. That part of the ceremony never took place."

I bonded Easton Dayborn in a stretch of woods at the base of the Edgeling Mountains, standing before a waterfall, with the blood of a woods witch not yet dried on my conscience. But she didn't correct Norbert. She knew his view would be the prevailing one.

Norbert continued. "That she-bitch, the Lady Raleigh, made Easton her prisoner and started south. Took us all unawares. She's headed to Thistleton, most like. The vulture wanted to pursue and plant your beau in the ground, but Philemon said Lady Raleigh was only hedging her bets, and would fold when the Heron returns. Heard him say that with my own ears, I did. A good call, I think. Our numbers are spread thin."

Surely Wenavere won't kill him, Johanna tried to convince herself. *The Raleighs are true friends to the crown. Aren't they?* She wondered how the Struvan south had become so full of false friends and traitors. *You know exactly how,* she forced herself to admit, sobering to reality. *Micah Dayborn lost control of the kingdom long ago. Even Easton admitted as much. This is merely the aftermath.*

Johanna breathed the day's cold air deep into her lungs. Readied another question.

"And what do you believe they intend to do with me?"

The query clearly delighted Norbert. "You will get me in trouble, my lady!" he said, leaning in like they were chums, oblivious to any distress on her end. *This is all a lark to him,* she thought. A part of her hated Norbert for his insouciance, but another side saw an opening, one that might not present itself again. "Lord Philemon has plans for you, I believe," Norbert continued, apparently unbothered about the aforementioned prospect of getting in trouble. "They're wary of you, yes, on account of you supposedly being a…" He looked at her expectantly, hoping for confirmation.

"I'm aware of what they think I am," she replied, turning in the saddle to face him full on, unabashedly showing Norbert the short-haired side of her scalp. She felt neither rage nor shame, and instead experienced a defiant confidence, shot through with the belief that she could handle this fool. She let go of the reins with her left hand and let it drift to her cloak pocket, where she touched the sennequi piece through the fabric.

Norbert's eyes filled with a hazy lust. "You could show me, if you wanted. You could…touch me with your power."

Was he suggesting what she thought he was? "My understanding is that you are under orders to kill me if I do that."

"What's a little secret between friends? Huh?" Norbert looked as hungry as a fox, though he kept his voice barely above a whisper. "Touch me, my lady. Let me feel your power. I won't tell a soul."

Johanna could scarce look at him, so repulsed was she by what he was suggesting. *What kind of sick desire is this?* But neither did she dismiss Norbert out of hand. She needed practice with her powers in the worst way, and, perhaps more importantly, she needed to know that she could call on them if the opportunity presented itself. *Take the offer,* she thought. *A chance like this won't come again.*

"I might kill you," she forced herself to say, keeping her voice below the wind. She was choosing to be honest for her sake, not Norbert's. "I don't have…perfect control of my powers."

Norbert chewed on his thoughts and the beechwood twig simultaneously. "I'd wager you won't. If I fall dead from my horse, the others will quickly put two and two together and put a crossbolt through your heart, so you'll find a way to stop short. But if you do kill me…to die at the hands of a jeyedoshi princess! Oh! I'd be immortal, wouldn't I? Wandering Tongues would spread my story through the realm. What a way to die! So do what you will, my lady. I'm ready."

He's mad. But does it matter? Johanna was tempted to glance behind her to see how close of attention the other crossbowmen were paying, but she feared that would instigate the very thing she was trying to avoid. *Focus. Inward.* She took a deep, cleansing breath. In doing so she felt a shift in the world around her, all of nature leaning in and attuning itself to her person. *What do you want?* the animals and the elements seemed to ask, from the cool, licking wind to the songbirds swooping through the air to the ground humming beneath her feet. She reached out to each one in turn, weighing nature's many wild magics, trying to assess which one to employ. But they were chaotic things to corral, and she feared none would give themselves over fully to her will.

Then, at a deeper distance, she sensed a supreme force, waiting patiently to be noticed. The pale sun, made indistinct in the wrappings of a terrycloth sky. Johanna knew with a sudden certainty that she could work its power through the sky like a sieve, sifting what she needed and shunting it into Norbert.

Closing her eyes, she went to work. It immediately struck her how easy it would be to burn Norbert to a crisp. The sun's rays were wan, but once she started gathering them their force multiplied, attracted to her power. The easy thing to do would have been to channel the full force of the sun's energy into Norbert and then cut off the supply, but instead she held a great store of it in check, keeping it in a container of concentrated will while she poured the desired amount into Norbert.

The exertion took a toll. Her will was the arm holding a never-emptying pitcher, the weight of which made the pour imperfect. The feel of her jeyedoshi power was invigorating, but the longer she tried to sustain it, the less control she had. *Cut if off,* she told herself, sensing that her control was slipping, but the part of her desperate for agency resisted, wanting, at almost any cost, to hold on to the *feeling* her jeyedoshi power afforded her. And then she was drowning in it, blinded, beholden—

"AAAAAHHHH!"

Norbert's scream sent Johanna slamming back into the present moment, severing the tether to her power. She felt instantly nauseous, but whether it was in reaction to channeling her jeyedoshi magic or an effect of harming Norbert, she didn't know. Beside her, Norbert listed in the saddle, half coherent and half cooked. *What have I done?* The thought was interrupted by hard-charging horses and mad-screaming men.

"What's happened here?! Is this the jeyedoshi's doing?!" The four guards surrounded her, crossbows at the ready. Horses stomped, snorted, tossed their heads. A sallow-faced soldier grabbed Norbert and held him upright, shaking him, while keeping his crossbow trained on Johanna. *This is how I die,* she thought. Instinctively she brought one of her hands to her stomach, to protect her unborn son.

Easton. Weston. My loves.

Forgive me.

"Knowll, know, no," Norbert slurred. He gave a sort of strange cackle and came fully to life. "It was my doing, not hers. Let her be, let her be."

The crossbowmen looked at each other with fear and confusion. The one with the whiskered chin vented his ire. "You're half fucking mad, you are. I've been saying it all along." He turned to the others. "We should have put a stop to him talking to her soon as it started." He about-faced to Johanna. "Is this your doing?" he asked pointedly.

She was trembling on the inside, but that didn't stop her from forming a haughty face and adopting a tone of disdain. "You said it yourself. He's mad. That's no fault of mine."

"That's no answer," whisker-chin replied angrily. All four men looked upset, but Johanna noted that their postures had eased from provoked to peeved.

The hard sound of hooves brought everything to a standstill. Philemon—nay, *Lord* Philemon—was riding down on them, looking with his bowed shoulders like a gargoyle that had managed to mount a majestic steed. His gaze fixed on Johanna as the horse cantered forward, but before coming to a stop, he took in the others, lingering the longest on Norbert. As per usual, he was the picture of equipoise, though for him it was a greedy bearing, tied to his ambitions.

He settled his gaze last on Sir Whisker-Chin. "Arvis?"

Arvis responded in a low growl. "Norbert here's been chatting with the jeyedoshi…erm…Lady Salk, my lord. You know how he is…well, I suppose you don't know, actually… Norbert's a talker, something of a fool, but harmless enough. All of a sudden, he starts screaming like a dragon's breathing on him. We rushed down to find him half loopy, and Lady Salk just sitting on her mount, and him saying 'forget it, it wasn't her,' or words to that effect."

Philemon held Arvis in a vise grip of stare and silence. Arvis shifted uncomfortably in his saddle. "We'll shoot her if you like, my lord. If that's what…you want."

Johanna's heart raged wildly in her chest. She reached for her powers. They were ready and waiting. She felt nauseous at the prospect of using them, but she would, she'd strike at Philemon, she'd defend herself and her unborn child, she'd—

"No," Philemon responded. "Don't shoot her. Shoot him."

With an unbothered ease Philemon Yurk fingered Norbert for death. Though still somewhat dazed, Norbert took the prospect of his demise more seriously than he had when Johanna used her powers on him, his eyes bugging wide and halting words of protest coming to his lips. "No…no…I…kill her!…the jeyedoshi…not…not—"

Arvis's whisker-chin was trembling, but he redirected his crossbow at Norbert while keeping his eyes on Philemon. Johanna could see that Philemon's order and pointing finger weren't enough, Arvis needed an additional nudge. Philemon saw it too and nodded forcefully at Arvis, leaving no doubt that he expected Sir Whisker-Chin to follow through.

Arvis's crossbow *clacked* and a quarrel sprouted from Norbert's sternum. Norbert made an O of surprise with his burrowing hole of a mouth. Swayed in the saddle. Gravity called, but before Norbert could oblige, two more crossbolts took him in the belly. Unconsciousness claimed him then, X's in his eyes. As Norbert fell from his horse, a fourth crossbolt sailed wide, the last of the crossbowmen getting in on the act too late. The latecomer made up for it by reloading his weapon and depositing a final bolt into Norbert as he twitched on the ground, a kill shot to the heart.

Johanna wanted to look away but found she could not. A man was dead because she had used her *powers*. Killing Shayla the woods witch had been in defense, but this…this was the manifestation of the exponential unknown her powers brought into play, the consequences of which could not be predicted. She had nearly killed Norbert on her own, without meaning to…but even though she had stopped short he had died regardless, fate attaching itself to her powers and guiding Norbert to his doom.

"I suppose you'll need someone new to talk to," Philemon said to Johanna, as if she had been the one encouraging the conversation with Norbert. "I have just the person in mind." He turned and addressed Arvis. "If people start dying left and right, put her down. But if it's more fiddle-faddle, kill her new companion. He'll be along shortly."

Philemon trotted off without giving Johanna or the dead Norbert another look. Arvis and his crew retreated to their customary twenty-yards distance, eager to give Johanna space. One of the men led Norbert's mount away. Norbert, however, they left for the carrion birds.

A short while later a man riding a mule peeled away from the front and started toward her. Short and saintly. Eyebrows like pupating larva. Frosted beard.

His Light, Shupert Press.

The priest was pained to discover that Johanna would not speak with him, but that didn't stop him from justifying his actions and muttering his misgivings and opining on where matters were heading. It was all anxious babble, red-faced and short-breathed, but Shupert couldn't stop himself, not when the alternative was suffering the punishment of Johanna's silence.

"My Lady, you must know that I wasn't aware of what they had in store. I understand now that matters have progressed, and all is coming to a head, but that doesn't mean I would have gone along with...surely you know this, I am a man of faith, a true *Stavusian,* I thought we were working in concert to bolster the Dayborn dynasty, not...not...*dismantle it!*"

Straight ahead and to the east, lolling hills gathered on the horizon, apologetic clumps of mounded earth. Lethargic rises, green and going nowhere. *Beyond those hills, Lake Sparrot,* Johnna knew. *If we are headed to the capital, we must soon turn south.*

Shupert blathered on. "Though I may not agree with the methods of the eastern houses, it's as I've said to you...the two faiths of the realm cannot live in concert any longer. As a servant of the light, you must understand that it is my imperative to defend the Stavusian faith at all costs, *all costs.* These men are brutes, yes, but they are *Stavusian.* It's only...politics muddies the waters, the way it always does."

Johanna held out a slim hope that Lord Saylet still sat regent in Union. If he did, once she arrived, perhaps there was a chance she could work with him to turn the tables on Philemon and rally the Dayborn faithful to resistance. *That's presupposing Dayborn sympathizers can be convinced to trust an Ontish woman, and a Salk at that. Not to mention a jeyedoshi.* She sighed in frustration. *If Easton were with me, even if we were both in chains, we might have a chance…* She wondered if Easton was in chains now, traveling the road to Thistleton with Lady Wenavere. *He has to be. Either in chains or under heavy guard. Otherwise, he would have fought his way to me. Nothing could have stopped him.* She wanted to believe that Lady Wenavere had rescued rather than seized her beloved, but if that were the case, Easton would have never allowed Philemon's party to flee with her in tow. *Lady Wenavere had the greater number of soldiers in Hevengrow. She could have stopped Philemon had she wanted, she could have rescued me—*

"As for Easton, we'll simply have to put our faith in Lady Wenavere, won't we? I've known her for years and years, she's a woman of the light, she'll do what's right. I simply can't imagine that she would—"

That bit of drivel struck too raw a nerve. "Can't imagine what? That she would hurt Easton? That she would abandon you and me to the birds? That she would renege on her vow to take the Raleigh army north? Damn you, the least you could do is not give voice to your naivety. Not when it's been made manifestly clear exactly how *little* you knew when knowing might have made a difference."

That shut him up. She was tempted to glance at the priest but forced herself to keep her eyes ahead. Only the clip-clopping of Shupert Press's mule let Johanna know that he remained beside her. Ten minutes passed before he broke the silence.

"You're right. I'm sorry, my lady. I'm so very sorry."

Shupert's *sorrys* weren't worth squash, but they did dull the sharp edge of Johanna's ire. The quiet between them reasserted itself, but it was a softer quiet, opening a space for a potential reconciliation. She wanted to hate the priest, but that was a luxury her present situation couldn't afford.

The day ground along, stifled by the hush of an early-winter sky. Johanna hatched plan after plan in her head—*steal back Bitterboy, dash for freedom; try and kill Philemon before anyone can react; sweet-talk a second captor*—but each idea was equally foolhardy, more likely to end in failure or death than success. The real action was the choice that would be made for her: when they reached the first of the easy hills, would the procession bend southeast toward Union, or northeast toward the Vake? *Union. It will be Union.* She couldn't fathom why they would head north.

At the base of the hills, a road maneuvered like a river around the lowest points, the rougher path leading northeast while the southern route smoothed toward the capital. She watched the front of the procession as it joined to the road and veered left, sending a shock through her system. She ended her embargo of words against His Light. "We're not going to the capital?"

"I'm as privy to Lord Philemon's plans as you are, my lady."

Don't call Philemon 'Lord,' she thought, though she did not say it. "Where else might they be taking us?"

"I don't know. There's a hamlet nearby. Further on, a town. Beyond that, Lake Sparrot. If we keep traveling to the north and east, the Vake. Even farther east, Dagon. I doubt we're meant to go that far. But I could not say for certain."

They bypassed the hamlet and reached the outskirts of the town of Tuendol by day's end. Tuendol was bustling with energy, its citizens scurrying to-and-fro in the wheel-rutted streets like rule-following mice. Most of Tuendol's buildings were made of daub and timber, except for the Stavusian temple with its many faces of glass. The temple in Tuendol was smaller than most Stavusian temples, but also clearly a point of pride;

positioned at the town's western point, it was the first building visitors encountered.

The natural bend of the road gave Johanna a clear view of the front of the procession as it reached the temple. A greeting party emerged from the cobweb of Tuendol's streets and filed onto the exterior thread that abutted the temple, a score's worth of men and women. Full of fake smiles and false cheer, they approached Philemon and company with half bows and hesitant hand claps and other unnatural signs of welcome.

"The statue outside the temple, my lady. Do you see it?"

Johanna followed Shupert's pointing finger. Facing the temple was a small limestone statue of a kneeling woman, hands pressed together in prayer. *A Winged Woman,* Johanna thought at first. Then she noted the crown. "Who is it?" she asked.

Johanna heard the smile in Shupert's voice. "Your namesake. Queen Johanna Salk I."

That surprised her. "Why is there a statue?"

"Tuendol was the first place Queen Johanna stopped in her travels after she became queen. She needed to shore up support with the Struvan areas of Ragar Or, who worried she would take after her Twin-Ascendant-obsessed father and grandfather rather than her Struvan-sympathetic uncle. She put many a fear at ease when she stopped to pray. They say a host of Winged Women prayed alongside her, and that when she emerged from the temple, the people gave a great cheer, for they knew that their new queen was a holy queen."

Johanna knew the history. In the tumultuous years preceding Queen Johanna Salk I's reign, the future queen had lived in court under the custody of her uncle King Daguss II, the monarch rumored to have killed his twin brother Baron I (Queen Johanna's father), to acquire the throne. At the time, little was known about Johanna save her lineage, and there were many in the Struvan parts of the kingdom who worried her ascendancy would mean a reversion to the Redd family's focus on all things Ontish. (Theron Redd's influence over the reigns of Baron Salk I and Johanna's grandmother Caeress Salk I was well documented.) Queen Johanna I's pious actions in Tuendol were the first indication that she was aligned with her uncle's way of thinking.

"I wonder how she truly felt, in her heart of hearts?" Johanna questioned, letting the pull of history distract her from her troubles.

"Her actions spoke for themselves, my lady. She was a servant of Stavus, through and through."

Johanna snorted. "No. Her actions merely show that she was a pragmatist, and a politician. I can assure you that the only person who truly knew Queen Johanna's heart…was Queen Johanna."

That shut the holy man up yet again.

At the front of the procession, the three Struvan lords dismounted. Even at a distance, it was clear that Philemon was in command. Everyone, even Lords Chesterly and Desighart, deferred to the bow-shouldered dandy, adjusting their bodies in response to his every move. The townspeople kept a careful distance, a few of the leaders stepping forward to talk without encroaching on his personal space. Philemon listened to them with interest, hands clasped at his chest, index fingers pressed together and pointing skyward. With his compromised posture and elegant green attire, he looked a little to Johanna like an exotic plant, the expensive kind a Struvan lord might import from Clyesia.

When the conversation was over, Philemon cut a path in the direction of the statue. He walked with unhurried ease, but all the same it startled Johanna; she didn't like watching him approach a bust of her namesake. The others followed in his wake, Doneg Desighart beetle-heaving his giant ass forward, Richard Chesterly employing a walk imbued with arrogance, the townspeople content to fall a little behind. When Philemon reached the statue, he stood before it in an obscene position, Queen Johanna's prayerful head hovering near the level of his waist. Nothing he did was overtly lewd, but Johanna saw Isbel look away in apparent shame.

Johanna felt her own cheeks burning red. *Damn you,* she thought. But she kept her eyes trained, staring through the discomfort even as Philemon reached out a hand and stroked the statue's cheek and chin. He repeated the motion well past the point of propriety.

A white-hot rage ran through Johanna. She felt the urge to call on her powers then and there for the purposes of strangling *Lord* Philemon to death on the spot; only Philemon's hand dropped away and he turned and spoke to the townspeople, a simple sentence or two, words that, were they an order, gave the townspeople pause. *What did he ask of them?* After an uncomfortable interim, two of the men headed back into the village, seemingly to fulfill Philemon's wishes.

They returned with hammers. Big, stone-headed mallets, instruments of destruction. Philemon smiled when he saw the hammers and stepped away from the statue, motioning for the men to approach. The two men did so uncertainly, exchanging guilty glances; they looked to Johanna like they were hoping a higher power would intervene. But there was only one power on the scene, and that was Philemon Yurk, a man who wanted the statue of Queen Johanna Salk I smashed to bits.

"Look away, Lady Johanna," Shupert said, when he realized what was to be done.

But she didn't. She bore witness to it all. Clenching her teeth. Thinking: *If I don't manufacture my own salvation, this is what will become of me.*

Silas O' the Songs

Silas stared at the Sagekind with the same confusion as the others, struggling to wrap his mind around the dichotomy between the all-powerful jeyedoshi who had lain waste to his enemies and the corpse on the bed. "He's dead," Silas said, needing to vocalize the fact, for fear that keeping quiet would shackle him to a disbelieving limbo.

Deglan responded by punching the bed hard, the young knight's fist missing the corpse by inches. With the punch over and done, Deglan's self-possession quickly returned. The façade of calm, however, didn't last. Mere moments later, Deglan unleashed a volley of punches, a couple of which grazed the Sagekind's leg. The young knight punctuated the flurry with three sharp "No's!" *He thought the Sagekind would survive the yompto pew,* Silas realized. *He didn't believe that death could touch such a powerful man.*

Madrig stopped Deglan before he could do real damage by wrapping him up from behind in a bear hug, pinning his arms to his sides. Deglan struggled futilely against the giant's strength but stopped resisting when Tern stepped to him and kissed his cheek. "I've killed him," the young knight lamented, slumping in surrender. "I've killed the kingdom's best hope."

"Seydron Qorl's arrow killed him," Jacy corrected, her mouth a hard line. "Not any of us. And certainly not you."

Across the room, the oaken door made a cracking noise under the fury of a battering assault. Five heads turned to see signs of the damage done. No crack was visible, suggesting the stress was interior. But it was clearly only a matter of time before the northmen breached the room. And when that happened, slaughter was the likely outcome.

Tern scampered over to the tower window. Looked down. Shook her head. "No escape. There are northmen waiting on the ground."

Silas left the Sagekind's bedside and made his way to the door. "PEACE!" he shouted, speaking loudly so he could be heard. Working quickly, Silas slipped off his boot and stuffed the Yubriy leaf back inside, readying the one admission he knew would buy time. "THE SAGEKIND IS DEAD. WE WOULD SPEAK WITH LADY WULFESS AND LADY WREN."

Shuffles and murmurs in response. Then, a lone, scraggly voice. "THE SAGEKIND IS DEAD? TRULY?"

Silas felt compelled to look back at the bed and verify. A small part of him wouldn't have been completely surprised to find the Wraith in Red rising to life. But no: the red-cloaked body remained at rest, the last of Gregor Thorn's magic having fled along with his soul. "Truly. He's dead," Silas said a little softer, letting the words bleed through the door.

Silas didn't know if the northmen believed him—he could hear a handful of voices questioning the veracity of his claim—but whatever the consensus, it was clear that he had bought a little time. While they waited for a response, Silas's four allies crossed the room to join him: Deglan with a dark and downcast face, Tern wearing an enigmatic expression, Jacy grim-glowering and Madrig magnificent in his placidity, looking as if he was viewing the proceedings from a cloud high above.

They waited at the door in a somber silence. While they waited, Madrig placed a friendly hand on Silas's shoulder. *The big mute would make the world whole if he could. He's the best of us. It's why I need to save him. Why I need to save all of them. Even if that means sacrificing myself.*

Then he remembered the Sagekind's last command, and the press of the Yubriy leaf in the toe of his boot. *The Sagekind charged me with a task before he died. Find Easton Dayborn. Find the new queen. Give her the Yubriy leaf. I need to… I need to…oh, what would Wyn Dunkin do?*

From the opposite side of the door, Wren Ollspaer's voice rang like a chipped bell. "THE STRUVAN BASTARD IS DEAD?"

Deglan beat Silas to a response. "THE SAGEKIND DIED AS HE LIVED, DEFENDING HIS FAMILY, THE RIGHTFUL RULERS OF THE REALM! HIS FAMILY WHO WAS BUTCHERED AT THE HANDS OF VILE AND LOATHSOME TRAITORS!"

The young knight, usually stoic, looked on the verge of sobbing. His eyes were angry red brambles.

Getting everyone out of here alive is going to be more difficult than I thought, Silas thought.

"WHAT'S DONE IS DONE," Wren answered back. "AND IT'S NOT ONLY DAYBORNS THAT ARE DEAD. MANY ONTISHMEN DIED AS WELL."

"LIKE MY FATHER." Wulfess Salk's voice cut through the door like an axe. "I SHOULD KILL YOU ALL FOR BEING A PARTY TO THAT CRIME." The silence of her threat stood on its own for a second. "BUT THE SINGER OWES ME A SONG. THE TRUE SONG OF

THE YUBRIY LEAF, THE ONE THAT HONORS THE FUTURE HEIR OF THE ONTISH KINGDOM. GIVE ME MY SONG, SINGER, AND PERHAPS I'LL LET YOU AND YOUR FRIENDS LIVE."

Silas's heart filled with a black defiance. "THE SONG IS NOT—"

A different hand touched Silas on the arm, silencing him. Tern's. Madrig stepped away and Tern made a bridge, connecting Silas to Deglan with gentle hands and an inscrutable smile. The green ribbons in her hair gleamed like sunlight on the morning sea. With all eyes on her, she took over the talking. "NOW THAT LORD HERON IS REUNITED WITH THE REST OF HIS MEN, DO YOU THINK THAT HE WILL TRY AND ATTACK THE CITY?"

Tern asked the question in a light, offhanded kind of way, in a tone entirely at odds with the gravity of what she was suggesting. Still, the weight of her suggestion hit hard, as evidenced by the ensuing quiet.

A third voice on the opposite side of the door joined in. Masculine and direct. Gothred's. "IT'S A POSSIBILITY."

Tern shifted her gaze to Deglan. "WHAT IF I TOLD YOU THAT WE HAVE INFORMATION FOR LORD HERON THAT MIGHT SEND HIM ON HIS WAY."

Wren's flinty voice made itself known. "WHO IS SPEAKING? IDENTIFY YOURSELF."

Tern laughed a teasing little laugh. "I DOUBT MY NAME WOULD INTEREST YOU, LADY WREN. BUT MY FATHER'S NAME MIGHT."

A second of quiet confusion. "WHO IS YOUR FATHER?"

“A MAN BY THE NAME OF MARVIK,” Tern answered with relish. “HE’S THE CAPTAIN OF A TRADING GALLEY CURRENTLY DOCKED IN SKITHIN HARBOR. ALL MY LIFE, HE’S ENJOYED TELLING ME STORIES OF WHEN HE WAS A YOUNG MAN AND SERVED AS A GORGOSTRINE IN THIS VERY CASTLE. HE CLAIMS, MY LADY, TO HAVE KNOWN YOU.”

The silence from the opposite side of the door was of three parts. One part could only be described as gobsmacked, the kind of silence heavily credited to shock. Wren’s silence. The second part was wrapped up in confusion, and seemed to be emanating from everyone listening in. The third silence, Silas intuited, was the silence of a predator intent on her prey. Wulfess’s silence. A silence determined not to let any unexpected revelations stop her from getting what she wanted.

The silence was at last broken by Wren. “Open the door and let me in,” she said, standing close enough to the wood that she could be heard without shouting. “I would speak with Marvik’s daughter.”

Objections wormed through the woodwork. Gothred’s voice came through as the most insistent. “You can’t go in there, Lady Wren! They will kill you, or…they will take you hostage!”

“No they won’t. And if they do, it will simplify things, won’t it? If I don’t return, you are to follow Lady Wulfess’s orders. She will be the unquestioned regent of Kalandragote until Cato recovers. And if Cato doesn’t recover…make her queen.”

Silas didn’t like the sound of that, but he had more pressing concerns. “IF WE OPEN THE DOOR, HOW CAN WE TRUST THAT YOUR MEN WON’T BARGE THROUGH AND KILL US ALL?”

"YOU HAVE MY WORD," the Lady Wren answered. "WHICH IS ALL THAT I CAN GIVE YOU. IF MY WORD DOESN'T SUFFICE, WE'LL SIMPLY CONTINUE BREAKING DOWN THE DOOR. BUT INSTEAD OF GOING THAT ROUTE, I'D PREFER TO HEAR WHAT MARVIK'S DAUGHTER HAS TO SAY."

Silas looked at the others. Nods all around. Together they removed the massive iron-reinforced oaken board barricading the door. When the work was finished, Silas did the honors, opening the door just wide enough to create a person-sized aperture. Glancing out, he sensed a good two dozen Ontishmen scowling at him, but only one person caught his eye: Wulfess, her stare a skewer. Silas quickly looked away from her and stepped aside for the Lady Wren, who slipped into the room with all good haste.

Madrig barricaded the door back on his own.

Wren made the rounds with her eyes, taking in the living and the dead. She settled last on Tern. On the surface, she wore her customary expression, devoid of emotion. But Silas could tell in the way her stare lingered that beneath the surface, her emotions were roiling.

"You must take after your mother," Wren finally said, addressing Tern. It was either a statement or an accusation. She certainly wasn't asking a question.

"I do," Tern replied. "But only in appearance. I have my father's wanderlust."

Wren nodded, studying Tern a little longer. She seemed to reach a conclusion. "He didn't send you, did he? The fact that you're here at all is…circumstantial."

"You give circumstances too much weight, my lady. My father warned me that it was a failing of yours."

"My failings are manifold. They're so numerous, they even include my greatest victories." A sad little sigh escaped Wren's lips. Glancing at the dead man on the bed, she pivoted to politics. "The Sagekind is dead, and the four of you will soon be too, unless an agreement is reached. Tell me what information you have that might compel the Heron to be on his way. I'll determine if it's enough to save your skins."

"You had best find a way to save our skins, or you can be damn sure you'll lose yours," Jacy declared.

Another *humph* from Wren, this one harder. "The fact that I'm in this room at all should tell you how little concern I have for *my skin*." Her eyes were solid stone. "Now tell me what you know."

Silas assumed that Tern would be the one to speak, but instead Tern turned to Deglan, and with a gentle touch, coaxed him to talk. He shook his head, unwilling. "I won't tell her. The realm would be better off if the Heron returned and spent his strength on the walls of Winterworn. I say we allow it. Let them fight. Let them die. All of them. Ontish and Struvan alike."

Tern withdrew her hand, though not unkindly. "I would show you my home, Deglan Whisk. But for that to happen, you and I must live." She touched him again, ever so tenderly. "There's enough death on the horizon without you needing to clear it a path."

Silas watched as an internal struggle played out on the young knight's face. Anger and pain wracked Deglan's features. Trenches of aging showed on his skin. Biting his lip, Deglan looked back at the Sagekind on the bed, as if hoping the dead man might come to life and offer advice. When that didn't happen, his anger changed to resignation. "Okay," Deglan said. He faced Lady Wren. "When we were in Dunning Harbor, the Sagekind sent a letter to Lord Wessel Raleigh, asking him to bring an army north and seize the Brokebone Pass. In the letter, the Sagekind warned that he believed there was a conspiracy against the king, and that the Heron was involved. If Lord Wessel were to reach the Brokebone and close it before the Heron passes through…the Heron would still have the numbers, but his position would be disadvantageous, to say the least."

"That will suffice," the Lady Wren quickly concluded. "I'm inclined to believe that the Heron doesn't really want Kalandragote. Especially if it comes at a cost. His true designs are on the south. But on the off-chance he thinks it wise to capitalize on an advantageous position, learning that his position isn't as advantageous as it seems will be just the thing to send him on his way." She took a deep breath and closed her eyes. With her eyes closed, Silas could better see the young woman in her, the one Tern's father must have known.

When she opened them again, Wren was looking at Tern. "You want to return to your father's ship, I assume?"

"Yes. With my four friends." There was a taunt in Tern's voice.

"The Lady Wulfess won't like it. She'll let you and the young knight go easily enough, but she'll want justice against her father's cousin and his bonded. And as for the singer, I don't know if there's anything we can say that will convince her to give him up."

"Now that your brother is dead and your nephew is injured, you're the highest-ranking Kalandragotan in the castle," Jacy pointed out. "One would think that your people would do what you say."

Wren chuckled darkly. "I'm aware that you're not up to speed on everything that's transpired since you stole away with the Wraith in Red, but I'm a Salk now. Not an Ollspaer. Or at least that's what I was before the dead man on the bed killed my newly bonded. The Lady Wulfess, conversely, is an Ollspaer, not a Salk. She bonded my nephew in the Circle of Stones shortly before the four of you appeared."

All eyes went to Silas. He nodded in confirmation.

Wren continued. "And even on the off-chance that every Frostflower in the castle chose to heed my commands, I'm not certain I would have the advantage if Lady Wulfess gave a conflicting order. Neither am I of a mind to make an enemy of Wulfess. Depending on if my nephew survives, she may very well be the new Queen of Kalandragote. And if an Ontish-Struvan war is brewing, Wulfess may become the Queen of the North."

Jacy shrugged. "You're making our decision easy. It seems to me that our best option is to slit your throat and die glorious deaths fighting our way out."

Wren ignored Jacy. A softness seemed to overtake her, coupled with an effeminacy that had previously been missing. She tucked a braid of black-gray hair behind her ear. "Has your father forgiven me, after all this time?" she asked Tern.

"I honestly couldn't answer that. He did love you once. That I'm sure of. He may love you still."

Wren made her voice small. "And what of your mother?"

"My mother died long ago. My father loved her, he tells me. But I never knew her."

Wren smiled. "My Marvik. A ship's captain." The smile faded away and she looked at the floor, gathering her thoughts. "It's true that I have some power over the people outside. At least for the moment. Power that I'm willing to relinquish. That willingness may be my greatest bargaining tool. But I make no assurances. You're more than welcome to slit my throat and take your chances with combat, if you so desire. Or we can see what happens if I vouch for the importance of what you've shared with me."

Everyone nodded. Silas included. Wren shook her head at him alone. "You will be the snag in the negotiations. I guarantee it."

Wren moved to the door. Raised her voice. "THE SAGEKIND IS DEAD. AND THEY'VE SHARED WITH ME INFORMATION THAT WILL ENSURE THE HERON'S DEPARTURE. IN RETURN, I'VE PROMISED THEM SAFE PASSAGE TO A SHIP IN SKITHIN HARBOR."

Wulfess answered. "OPEN THE DOOR AND WE'LL FINISH THE NEGOTIATIONS."

"I'VE GIVEN THEM MY WORD, LADY WULFESS. THE NEGOTIATIONS ARE OVER." No response. When the silence persisted, Wren called to Gothred. "GOTHRED, WILL THE ASCENDANT FEW HONOR AND DEFEND MY WORD? THE WORD OF KALANDRAGOTE?"

Another uncertain silence. Then Gothred said, "LADY WULFESS MEANS TO HAVE THE SINGER, MY LADY. IF WE DEFY HER, IT MAY COME TO SWORDS. AND I BELIEVE ENOUGH BLOOD HAS BEEN SHED FOR TODAY."

Wren grimaced. Silas should have been worried, but strangely enough, he wasn't. He knew where fate wanted him. Knew what he had to do to get there. He looked at Wren and spoke with a surprising boldness. "It's okay," he said. "Open the door."

Tension filled the air. A word from either Wulfess or Wren and Silas knew the Ontishmen would gladly murder his little quintet. Fortunately, it was also clear that the Ontish faction had no desire to start a bloodletting that might end with them turning their swords on each other.

"What did they share with you, Lady Wren?" Wulfess demanded. She stood in the midst of the armed Ontishmen like a bold flower growing in rocky soil, petals of flowing blond hair fountaining over a billowy stem of bronze-colored furs.

"Something that assures the Heron will return south. We simply need pass the information along. In return, I've granted them safe passage from Kalandragote. I'm a woman of my word, Lady Wulfess. Once given, I intend to keep it."

Wulfess's lips curled into a wolfish snarl. Her next words were clearly intended for Madrig and Jacy. "By all means then, go. But know this: I will spare no expense in hunting you down. You betrayed your blood. Your family. And for that, there is no forgiveness."

Jacy snarled in kind and readied a response, but before she could, Madrig reached out and touched her on the arm, staying her. When it was clear no response was forthcoming, Wulfess turned to Silas. "You, however, are going nowhere. Not until you give me my song."

Behind the anger in Wulfess's eyes, Silas could see the fear. In the last hour, Wulfess's father had died and her newly bonded had been gravely wounded. What she needed at the moment was legitimacy. Something an heir would provide. Especially a prophesied heir, one foretold by the Yubriy Tree.

But Silas wouldn't be the one to give it to her. He had reached the conclusion that the song was sacred, intended for an audience of one. His charge was to find the audience and sing it to them, or die in the effort.

The latter of which seems the most likely outcome at the present moment.

"That won't be happening," Silas responded. He continued on, before Wulfess exploded and ordered him seized. "But what I will offer to do is relay the vital message to Lord Heron. Then, when he leaves Kalandragote, I'll go with him."

Behind him, Jacy offered a weak *no,* a withering protest that died on the vine. Silas refused to turn to look at her, or at any of them. He had his destiny to follow. A destiny that was now in league with his duty.

"Someone has to do the dangerous work of delivering the message," Wren seconded. "Let it be the lutist."

Wulfess scoffed. "Enough of this. Lady Wren, you owe nothing to these traitors. Tell me what they told you, and then we'll do with them what we will."

Wren Ollspaer shook her head, swinging her black-and-gray plait like a pendulum blade. "I've told you. I'm a woman of my word. I know that's recently counted for little in Kalandragote, but so long as I'm speaking, it will."

A dark shadow passed over Wulfess's face. She turned to the armed men around her—foremost of which were Grocian Mock and Darryn Coffyn—and appeared on the verge of giving a dangerous order, one that would spring the tightly wound stasis into an unspooled violence. But then Wren's voice rose again, quick and sharp, cutting to a different heart. "Listen to me, Wulfess. I intend to go with them. All I ask is that you honor the agreement I've struck. Send the lutist to the Heron. Once the Heron's army has departed and it's clear that Kalandragote isn't in imminent danger, I will leave with the others for the ship docked in Skithin."

That was unexpected. Wulfess, caught off guard, didn't seem to know what to make of it. A flummoxed Gothred broke in. "Lady Wren, you mustn't! With your brother dead and your nephew wounded, it would not serve if the one healthy Ollspaer fled the city in the hour of our greatest need!"

"After everything the Ollspaers have done to this city, it would not serve if we stayed," Wren responded coldly. "When I bonded Lord Daguss Salk, it was because I knew it was past time for Kalandragote to stop pretending that it exists independent of the rest of Ragar Or. And now that my brother is no longer alive to foster the fantasy that Kalandragote can relinquish its independence without giving up power, I have no desire to serve as a wretched reminder of the city-state that once was. The Lady Wulfess and my nephew Cato—Beoliotius grant that he survives—are more than capable of ushering in the new era." She turned her cold stare on Wulfess. "The only thing that would make me change my mind is if you were so foolish as to refuse to uphold my word. Do that, and I will stay in Kalandragote, if only to draw on every resource at my disposal to rob you of your power in its cradle."

A chill surged down Silas's spine. He wouldn't have thought it possible, but it seemed the Lady Wulfess had met her equal.

If Wulfess knew it, she refused to show it. Watching her, Silas grew convinced by her steely expression that she meant to refuse Wren and let the chips fall where they may. But then she turned to Silas and said the words that set him free.

"Be gone by sundown, Silas O' the Songs. By this time tomorrow, the Heron had best be on his way south. If he lingers in Kalandragote, your friends will die." She leaned toward him. "And pray our paths never cross again. Because if they do, I'll cut open your throat and find the song you withheld from me."

Silas said his goodbyes to Madrig and Jacy at the gate. Memories of meeting them at the Yubriy Tree flashed in his mind, reminding him of the many miles they had walked together. *I would have died at the hands of the vultures without their help,* he thought. He worried that Jacy was going to give him a piece of her mind for negotiating to be the messenger, but instead she grabbed his hand and pulled him into a strong embrace, whispering, "You're more than a singer, Silas O' the Songs. You're a warrior in your own right." When she released him, Madrig flashed fingers at him along with a conspiratorial smile. "Madrig says 'Go forth and share your gifts,'" Jacy interpreted. Silas nodded gravely at the giant, feeling the press of the Yubriy leaf in his boot.

Wulfess was ahorse behind him, but Silas found it easy enough to resist the temptation of exchanging a final look with his former lover before leaving. He wondered if she carried his baby in her belly. He wondered if he'd ever learn the truth of the game she was playing.

Outside of Winterworn's gates, the snow glistened in the evening sun, shining a path to the Heron's campfires. Silas rode slowly in the direction of the camp, breathing in sync to his steed's carefully placed steps. He had died nearly a dozen times today, and he knew there was a decent chance he'd die at the hands of the Heron, so he resolved to make the most of the short journey before him. Entranced by the snow, he resolved to make his mind as blank as the field before him. Every breath an infinity.

He managed it, for a spell. A perfect, pure, peaceful calm. But out of the drifting seconds of nothingness came an insistent something: the sounds of a song. His song. "The Queen's Burning Heart." The true version, the one waiting to be heard by the person it was intended for. Silas tried to acknowledge the song without fixating on it, but still it came, louder and louder, as if being played by a deity tucked away in the dark corners of his brain, a mischievous Wyn Dunkin, or perhaps a twisting brown-and-silver tree. He resisted it as long as he could, but eventually gave in, humming the melody for the last stretch of the journey.

An image of Wyn Dunkin appeared in his mind's eye. Silas said what was on his mind. *Okay. I get it. No more skirting the issue. I promise. When the time comes, I'll do what I'm supposed to do.*

Wyn, to his surprise, spoke back. *Not until I get there, you won't. Performed properly, 'The Queen's Burning Heart' takes two. I'm your partner, Silas O' the Song.*

Don't you forget it.

Jia Brinks

Her brother's friend was as brawny as an ox, with dark-red hair that looked like it had been licked all over by the same animal. Jia had her suspicions as to who he was, but she did not voice them. Instead, she sat quietly in the crook of a twisted beech tree, listening to her brother make his request.

"Come with us, Jia. There will be food to eat. As close to a feast as a humble person might hope for. You will meet our guest. You will sing your song. If you desire, you can leave after that. Or, if you'd rather, you can stay to the end."

This was the first time she'd seen her brother in weeks. But she'd heard his name mixed in with the never-ending stream of rumors that ran through the Vake these days, wild hearsays and half-truths and hard facts, all swimming alongside each other, impossible to tell apart. *The Dayborns have gone to die in Kalandragote, never to return. The Eastern Houses have taken control of southeastern Ragar Or. Your brother Ridgely is running with the bastard son of Lord Moren Arc, hunting birds. When the birds aren't hunting them.*

"You're serving your guest an Ontish supper, then?"

"That's right," the ox replied, the taut chords in his tree-stump neck vibrating. Jia fought the temptation to reach over and pluck them like a string. "We think it'd be fitting if the last song the plucked kite heard was the one you've been singing all over the Vake."

I've hardly sung it all over the Vake, Jia thought. But she also knew from the campfires and small villages where she had sung "The Flames" that the song had made an impression. The denizens of the Vake didn't have a perfect grasp of what was happening in the realm, but when Jia sang her song about what had taken place at the Golden Pear, they understood who their enemies were.

"I'm happy to do my part," Jia replied, staring evenly at Mintor Thorn. She'd never seen Mintor Thorn before, but she was certain: the man before her was him. The bastard of Castle Greenwell had become a legend the last few weeks. While his father and the rest of the Arc family sat holed up in the castle, waiting to see which way the political winds blew, Mintor had taken the fight to the birds.

"If you're coming with us, Sister, we'll need to blindfold you," Jia's brother said.

She made a cross face at him. "You're the one who asked *me* to come."

"It's for your own protection," Mintor interjected. Jia turned her cross stare on him. The bastard of Castle Greenwell's smile suggested he enjoyed being the recipient of Jia's attention, even if it was ireful. "And for our protection too," he admitted. "If the wrong sort got hold of you and tried to make you sing, well, you can't very well sing a song you don't know the lyrics too."

"Okay," she said, assenting to the logic. "Let me go home and get ready. I'll meet you back here—"

Ridgely shook his head. "Not with a Stavusian in the house. No way. You know as well as I do that Mom can sense when something's awry, and if she starts in on the questioning, who knows where it will lead. Nope. Too big of a risk."

Of all the regions in the realm, the Vake had the largest cross section of faiths, with slightly more Stavusians in the southern Vake and slightly more Twin worshippers in the north.

"You don't think Mom will sense something's amiss when I don't return home?" Jia countered. Ridgely was right about the risk their mom posed, but that didn't mean Jia didn't enjoy pointing out the flaws in his logic. Still, he made a fair point. "Fine. I suppose that means I'm leaving…now?"

The ox retrieved a strip of hempen cloth hanging from his belt and made a display of it for Jia to see. "We leave directly from here. Let me blindfold you and we'll go."

Jia gave Mintor a closer look. He looked every bit the bastard, thick-muscled with close-set eyes and a craggy visage that suggested a certain roughness of character. He wore clothes cut from good cloth, but he didn't wear them well—they were ill matched and roughly treated, stained with dirt and blood and ribboned with tears. His was a look that didn't normally appeal to Jia, but the times being what they were, she found herself attracted to him. She closed her eyes and envisioned Mintor Thorn cutting a bloody path through the birds that had torched the Golden Pear, leaving their corpses to rot in the shade-covered soil of the heavily wooded Vake. The thought made her smile.

Jia opened her eyes.

"Okay. Let's go."

The blindfold fogged Jia's perception of time; when Mintor lifted Jia from the horse and removed the hempen cloth from her eyes, she didn't know if one hour had passed, or two. She was standing deep in the heart of a dark and brooding forest, beneath an odd-shaped rise that wore a white birch tree for a crown, the tree's roots falling down the embankment like snowy tresses. It took Jia a moment to realize that the root system obscured the mouth of a cave cut into the hill. But then all became clear, and Jia could see the flames dancing beyond the roots, hear the sounds of men and women talking and laughing, smell the aroma of an Ontish supper. Instinctually, she listened for the sound of music, the river-running play of a fiddle or the stairway plucking of a lute or the melodic makings of a human voice. *Nothing,* she noted. *I'm the only performer.* Not long ago, she had lost her nerve performing at the Golden Pear and fled the establishment. That decision had saved her life. Performing since hadn't been a problem, and she thought she knew why. She was no longer singing for herself. She was singing for a story that needed to be heard, to an audience with the courage to listen.

A coarse cheer went up when they entered the cave, rough-throated roars for the bastard of Castle Greenwell. Intermixed were shouts of "Red Ridgely!" aimed at Jia's brother. She didn't know whether to be proud of or disturbed by his nickname. Looking around, Jia saw near twenty people, mostly bruising men but a few women as well. The man marked for death was easy to identify: a morose-looking fellow sat bound and bloodied on a long bench, before a pewter plate piled high with goose eggs and dried figs and fire-roasted yams, every item drenched in the blood from a thick cut of beef. As was often the case with the honored guest of an Ontish supper, he had yet to touch his food.

Jia was soon seated on the long bench and given a plate of her own. As intimated by her brother, it was as close to a feast as a humble person could hope for. Jia ate slowly, relishing the richness of the meal. She was given wine to drink and so she drank it, also slowly, washing the red over her tongue multiple times before swallowing it down. Eating and drinking centered her. These last few weeks had left her floating, untethered in a world coming apart at the seams. It was only when she slowed down and remained mindful of her actions that she felt fixed to the here and now.

The ox sat beside her. He, too, ate slowly, but it seemed to Jia that his attentions were fixed not on the meal but on the interplay between the parties in the cave. He gave his attention to anyone who approached him, but in the detached manner of leaders since time immemorial. Bastard or no, he was above these men, by nature of his bearing and actions. When he was finished eating, he rose to his feet. In an instant the cave quieted, scores of shadow-sunk eyes swinging to Mintor Thorn.

"We..." he began, letting his gaze roam into every corner of the cave, "...are the ones who resist."

Robust "ayes" and stamping feet. Jia wondered how many of the guests inside the cave were trained in combat. She knew her brother had learned the art while serving House Arc. *These are the ones who left Castle Greenwell when the fighting started,* she reasoned. Arc men whose loyalty to the Vake superseded their fealty to Lord Meric. *Men fighting for a reason above and beyond coin.*

"It's a damned dangerous thing we do," Mintor continued. "We know little of what is taking place throughout the realm. All we know for certain is that men from the eastern houses have fallen on the Vake and mean to subdue our people. The rest...who knows...some say the Dayborns have walked north into a trap, others that Lord Daguss Salk and Lord Horos Ollspaer mean to join armies and march south, others that only Lord Dante Heron can save us from northern aggression. My father would have me wait, see what unfolds, turn a blind eye to the present atrocities until we know for certain which houses have the advantage. But I say"—here he gritted his teeth and slammed a balled fist into the table—"FUCK THAT. If a man strikes at the Vake, he is my enemy. It's that simple. And right now"—Mintor showed his balled fist to the guest of dishonor—"every bird that walks these lands is an enemy of mine."

The stamping and shouting returned in earnest. A few men seated close to the guest of dishonor shook their fists in his face. One went so far as to lean aggressively into him until he toppled over. A laughing pair grabbed the man by his arms and jerked him back to upright. The man was restored to verticality for only an instant before the first fellow knocked him over again, this time intentionally. Guffawing joined in with the shouting and stamping. The process repeated itself. This time, when the condemned man was returned to upright, they let him be.

"Speaking of enemies, we have one in our midst." Mintor stepped toward the guest of dishonor with malice and menace. The sight of it sent Jia's spine to tingling. "A kite. He claims he's the nephew of Lord Conway Acton, and worth a fistful of brogan's-heads if only we'd get our heads out of our asses and ask his uncle for a ransom. He doesn't understand why we won't ask for a ransom, doesn't understand how a man can be accused of murder in a time of war, doesn't understand why we are feeding him an Ontish supper. *The east has a right to rule,* he says. *We've got the men and the money.*" Mintor, having reached the fellow, took the man's chin in hand and tilted his face upward. He then gazed down on the condemned with a surprising earnestness. "I say to him, time will tell on all accounts. But until that time comes, know that the bastard of Castle Greenwell and his companions mean to pluck the feathers of each and every bird that dares desecrate the holy soil of the Vake."

Stamping, shouting, a thrown cup, general ruckus. The way the bedlam was building, Jia thought for certain that the ox was about to reach for his knife and cut the man's throat. But instead, Mintor turned the man's chin with a violent twist and faced him toward Jia.

"We have a song for you, kite, to go along with your supper. The last song you'll ever hear."

Jia stood. She felt eerily calm, in full possession of her body. Once upon a time, she had used her fiddle as a barrier between her and the audience, a way to protect herself. But when she wrote "The Flames," she left the fiddle behind. All she had now was her voice.

It was all she needed.

They came, the dark flock
That murdering crowd
Into the night of our joy
Took a bite from the pear
Golden as day
Snuffed out the songs
And started the flames

Jia had closed her eyes when she started singing, but now she opened them. In the dim light of the cave, every person staring back at her seemed a low-burning flame. She imagined for the millionth time what it must have been like inside the Golden Pear when the birds put it to the torch. Not staring back at the scene in horror from up the street, moving toward the safety of the woods, trying to make sense of the unfolding madness. The shame she had felt over her performance had saved her life that night. The only problem was that she had spent every night since trying to find a way to forgive herself for surviving.

The cave nearly hummed with the intensity of its denizens' listening. Jia could taste it in her teeth. She continued with the song.

The flames, ever higher
The flames, a reminder
Our anger won't perish in the flames

Jia began crossing the cave toward the guest of dishonor, following in Mintor's footsteps. One step, two steps, in time to the natural pause that followed the chorus. On the third step, she began singing again, her voice rising in volume.

Now in the forest
Our enemies gather
Believing the Vake will be theirs
But the fire they started has spread to our hearts
And with it a terrible pain
And still our hearts beat, unbroken and strong
Fueled by the flames

She reached the guest of dishonor. Though his face was held tight by Mintor's hand, the condemned man tried to evade Jia's gaze. Seeing this, she cut off all angles of escape, bending over until they were almost nose to nose. She did so with a calmness that conveyed an incredible power, which she channeled into the chorus.

The flames, ever higher
The flames, a reminder
Our anger won't perish in the flames

The guest of dishonor went slack in surrender, as if the song had convinced him of his crimes. When Jia sang the chorus again, the rest of the cave joined in.

The flames, ever higher
The flames, a reminder
Our anger won't perish in the flames

Steel gleamed like a scything moon off to her side. Jia, sensing what was coming, quickly spun away. She knew it was over by watching the changed expressions in the cave, two-score eyes widening as the bastard's blade did its work. She sat down in time to the sound of the dead man's head falling to the table. Her eyes straight ahead. Silent as a stone.

She had played her part.

Now it was time to go home.

Johanna Salk

A knock on the door. *Shupert,* Johanna knew. It was always Shupert. Her life in Tuendol had been reduced to the company of six men, five of whom carried crossbows and wouldn't speak to her. The sixth was the priest.

"My dearest Johanna." Normally, the Stavusian priest said her name with the sincerest warmth, but ever since their arrival in Tuendol, Shupert spoke Johanna's name like an apology. An apology she refused to accept.

Johanna stepped aside and allowed Shupert to enter the room. He gave a smile that was half a grimace as he passed her by, the dolorous effect magnified by his cumbersome eyebrows. *He's in a predicament too,* Johanna reminded herself. *Who knows what Philemon means to do with him?*

Johanna glanced up. Arvis, the head crossbowman, was sitting with his legs hanging over the ledge of the loft, watching Johanna with customary intent. The attentions of the other crossbowmen drifted from time to time, but not Sir Whisker-Chin's. She had the impression that none of the men charged with guarding her relished the idea of putting a bolt through her heart, but Sir Whisker-Chin, she was certain, had steeled himself to the prospect should it come to it.

Shupert cleared his throat. Cast an upward glance at the men with weapons. The house Philemon had requisitioned for the purpose of holding Johanna captive was the home of a wealthy merchant, uniquely if unintentionally configured for keeping watch on a jeyedoshi. The men worked in shifts and kept their distance, staying in the loft. Johanna sensed that Shupert liked the presence of the crossbowmen as little as she did.

"A minute's rest for my weary bones, Lady Johanna, and then I'll pray." Shupert looked at her beseechingly. "Will you pray with me today, my lady?"

He asked the same question every day, and she always gave the same answer. *No. I will not pray with you. I have no desire to pray to the god of the men who have made me a prisoner.* But the days had grown long, and her refusals were growing stale. "Yes," she answered, surprising herself. *It will be worth it to shake things up. If any of these fools think that makes me a true believer, they are free to keep the misconception.*

The priest's eyes went wide with joy. "Oh! You make an old man happy, my lady." Johanna waited, expecting the next words to come out of His Light's mouth to be something about bringing Johanna into the light, but instead, with a glint of conspiracy in his eyes, the priest made a surprise suggestion. "You'll kneel beside me, won't you? Help keep an old man from toppling over?"

Suppressing the urge to insult Shupert, she gave an acquiescing nod.

The act of going to his knees was an ordeal for the priest. When it looked like he might falter, Johanna grabbed Shupert's arm and helped him the rest of the way, politely ignoring the chorus of creaking sounds that ensued. Shupert grabbed her arm in turn with a talon-like tightness, pulling her close to him as they descended to the hardwood floor. *That's unnecessary,* she thought. Growing angry, she was half a second from pushing away from him when she caught the whisper on his lips, threading the waterfall half of her hair. "Stay close to me, child. I've news you need to hear."

She momentarily froze, shocked by Shupert's subterfuge. Fortunately, following his orders was easy. A split second later, Shupert started up the prayer, alternating between a voice possibly audible in the loft and one soft enough to mask secrets. Shupert's lower register mixed religious phrasings with confidences, but his higher one never gave away the game.

"Holy Stavus, lord of the sky, bringer of light, spirit of the hawk, I pray to you now on behalf of your loving daughter Johanna of House Salk, brought from the north to this place for your purpose, they're bringing a woods witch to determine whether you are with child, may your light shine upon her as she navigates the challenges you have set before her, show her, Holy Stavus, how she might make peace with the path you have set her on, there's no word of Easton or Lady Raleigh but the news from the north is dire, may she learn that there is wisdom in looking to the hawk, to the sun, to the sky, for only there will Lady Johanna come to know the truth, they say the Dayborns are dead, killed in Kalandragote, and that the Heron is returning to take over the south, may she come to know that only you have the answers, and you can show Johanna her place, beside a Holy Son of Stavus, a blessed bonding in the holy light of a Stavusian temple, there are rumors they mean to bond you to Lord Dante, so long as the problems you pose can be circumnavigated, oh we pray that you will save and keep your daughter, show her the light and give her peace in all that is to come, and in the role that she must play."

Johanna tried to stay calm, but it was a struggle to suppress her emotions. *The Dayborns? All dead?* The news made Johanna hurt for her beloved nearly as much as she feared for his safety. Her hands having grown ice-cold during the prayer, she kept a frozen hold of the priest, hoping he would impart more information to her. *What of my father? My sister? What of the dragon that flies above the realm?* But Shupert's prayer was a performance, and the performance was over. Raising his bowed head, the priest made a soundless effort to communicate contrition, but even that gesture was of a piece with rising to his feet, a performance that Johanna joined in with, helping His Light navigate the gauntlet of discomfort between kneeling and upright.

Now standing, the priest patted Johanna's hand before pulling away. He ambled a few steps away and took up a new position, staring into the middle distance, forging a limbo. *What are we waiting on?* Johanna wanted to scream. She was grateful for what Shupert had told her, but it was all useless information if she couldn't *act* upon it. She needed to leave, *now,* needed to save herself and save Easton and then somehow the realm. She felt the terrible might of her jeyedoshi powers gathering, tempting her to conjure a story with a violent start and an uncertain end. She looked up and locked eyes with Sir Whisker-Chin. She watched as he repositioned his hand on the crossbow, sensing that he might need to respond to the story of her stare.

The door opened. A slant of sunlight and Philemon Yurk entered the room, followed on his heels by a shrew-faced woman wearing a brown-and-white peasant dress. The woman scurried inside, giving furtive glances, taking in the room without settling down. Her right hand was balled into a fist, enclosed with a secret. "Who are you?" Johanna demanded. That drew the woman's slippery-minnow eyes, but only briefly. *The woods witch,* Johanna intuited, remembering Shupert's warning. Johanna's hand instinctively went to her belly, but halfway there she realized the folly of drawing attention to her stomach, and forced her hand to her side.

"Never mind her, Lady Johanna," Philemon said, standing still save for a shifting smile. A blatant attempt at distraction, but it worked.

"Werring take you," Johanna responded, glancing at the bow-shouldered lord. In the time it took Johanna's eyes to return to the woods witch, the woman was dangling a thread-laced needle from her hand, which she faced toward Johanna. The witch began to mumble what sounded like an incantation. "And curse you too," Johanna countered. The woods witch, steady now and watching the swaying needle, ignored Johanna's curse and took a step closer, intent on finishing the job.

The wind. Johanna called on the element, coaxing it to dance around the needle. That was all it took to wreak havoc with the reading. The startled woods witch, sensing magic at play, looked up at Johanna with fearful astonishment. Seeming to catch herself, the witch swept the needle up into her hand and changed her expression to stone. Johanna watched as calculations played out on the woods witch's face. *She's going to out me,* Johanna surmised. But instead, the woods witch shocked her.

"The lady isn't with child."

Bless Beoliotius. Johanna's heart leapt in gratitude. Philemon, however, met the declaration with a skeptical silence. He looked first at Johanna, and then at the woods witch, before bringing his hand to his chin, measuring the room. "Do the test again," he commanded the woods witch, tapping a finger on his jaw. "And this time, think long and hard about who you should be more afraid of: the jeyedoshi standing before you with five crossbows trained on her? Or me?"

A mixture of shame and fear boiled the woods witch's cheekbones red. The witch seemed to weigh the wisdom of sticking with the lie, but then, deciding against it, she once more dropped the needle and resumed the business of divining Johanna's uterus.

Johanna's body surged with a terrible strength. The seawall of her self-control was collapsing; any moment now and her jeyedoshi side was going to take control, consequences be damned. The elements all begged Johanna's favor, *me, me, me,* the air around her and the sun in the sky and the ground beneath her feet, even faraway bodies of water. On a distant plain, Johanna had the vague sense of the dragon Teriquay tuning in. The jeyedoshi feeling was so overwhelming that it distorted all rational thought; it *felt* to Johanna like she could destroy all enemies in the room before a crossbolt found her heart, no matter how nonsensical the notion. The woods witch clearly intuited what was coming: the fear of a prey animal was in the witch's eyes as she desperately tried to finish her task without giving in to the instinct to flee.

Too late, witch. Too late. Too late for us all.

The magic pooled all around Johanna…

…only to drain away at the sound of a voice.

"What you're doing, Lord Philemon…is…is a disgrace. An affront to Stavus. Using a woman of the woods, hectoring the Lady Salk…it's a shame, an insult against everything good Struvan leadership is supposed to stand for. I condemn the action. Do you hear me, Lord Philemon? I condemn it."

The shock of hearing Shupert speak so forcefully distanced Johanna from her jeyedoshi side. She looked at the priest askance, mouth agape, scarcely able to process what he had done. *Philemon will kill you for this,* she thought.

But before Philemon could respond, the witch weighed in again.

"I was wrong the first time. Apologies, my lord. The jeyedoshi *is* with child. And…it's a boy."

Johanna whirled at the grainy sound of the woods witch's voice. The witch's words, however, were a parting gift: she was already giving the room her back, scurrying past Lord Philemon and out the door. Stunned, Johanna watched her go.

With the witch gone, Philemon cleared his throat. Looked up. "My loyal men in the loft. The ones with my silver Salks in their pockets. Are you listening?" Philemon's voice was as smooth as his green silk doublet.

The crossbowmen gathered round Arvis, their heads hovering over the railing like ugly moons. "Yes, my lord," Arvis replied for the group.

"Divulge what you've heard in this room under pain of death. Do I make myself understood?"

The moons bobbed like apples in water. "These won't talk," Arvis replied. "And if they do, I'll gladly take it upon myself to ensure those are the last words they'll ever speak."

Philemon judged that a response was unnecessary. With a slow turn of his head, he returned his attention to Johanna and the priest while using his thumb to rotate the large emerald ring on the middle finger of his left hand. There was no anger on his face, but rather a detached sort of philosophical deportment, the sort of look that precedes thoughtful sighs. When he spoke, Johanna was surprised to hear real passion in his voice, the blade of his sharp tongue stowed away.

"Would you believe me, Lady Johanna, if I told you that I was jealous of your gift? Well, it's true. I am." He laughed. "If I had what you had, Stavus himself couldn't stop me from working the world to suit my fashion. But alas, some of us are not so…blessed. Some of us must make do with other talents. Fortunately for me, I discovered my true talent long ago. Do you know what that talent is?"

Johanna held her tongue.

"My talent is that I can see through to the dark, twisted heart of the world. Without flinching. It's a talent that allows me to plan for the stark realities of life while other men and women sit waiting on a sun that never comes. That's the mistake you're making now. You and the priest. The both of you are waiting on suns that are never going to come."

It was a clever allusion to Easton and Stavus, deftly done.

Johanna hated the bastard for it.

Philemon pressed his point. "There are two dark truths the two of you must swallow." He pointed a ring-heavy finger at the priest. "A good Stavusian is simply a Struvan who knows the right words to say in front of his friends and neighbors. As a priest, you've become accustomed to telling people what the right words are. It's where you get your power from. But what you perhaps don't grasp, Your Light, is that at this moment in time, sensible Struvans understand that being a good Stavusian has very little to do with following the words of a priest, and everything to do with backing the Struvan powers taking control of the realm. If you were to speak out against those powers, or to try and work against them…why, I think they'd view any calamity that might befall you as the just retribution of a god angry at you for working against his servants. Servants like Dante Heron. Like Richard Chesterly. Like Doneg Desighart.

Servants like myself."

Philemon paused to let the priest chew on what he was insinuating. Then his finger found its way to Johanna. "You're upset that I've learned the truth of your condition. In truth, it's your saving grace. When the Heron takes over the throne, he'll need an heir to solidify his position.

Discovering that his soon-to-be-bonded is already with child will relieve him of the anxiety of needing to bed a jeyedoshi."

Johanna blanched with horror. "How does Lord Dante even know I'm here?"

"We've been sending messages to one another via our fastest riders. He was thrilled when I informed him that the Lady Johanna Salk had joined our party. He wrote back that he has every intention of bonding you forthwith."

"Did you tell him that you suspect me of being a jeyedoshi?"

A taunting, teasing grin. "I've shared my concerns."

"I would kill Lord Dante before I would bond him. I would…I *will*…kill myself."

"You could certainly try. Perhaps you'd be successful. Far be it for me to judge what a jeyedoshi of your caliber is capable of. But what is beyond certain is that you would die. As would your unborn child. And what a waste that would be." Philemon adjusted the hem of his doublet where it met his olive-colored breeches. "You are the daughter of Lord Daguss Salk. A descendant of the line of kings and queens that once ruled Ragar Or. And a possessor of the greatest magic known to man. If you would accept the difficult truth that you have been eternally separated from Easton Dayborn…if you would accept the truth that a new era is rising where the Heron and the houses of the east will rule this land…if you would accept the role history is fashioning for you…why, who is to say what the future might hold?" Philemon grinned in a way that made Johanna's soul shudder. "Accept your role, Lady Johanna, and you will find a most eager friend in me. In time, I might help you navigate this new world that we are entering." His grin sharpened at the ends. "In time, we might help each other."

Johanna was too disturbed to respond. She felt trapped, with no chance of escape. Resistance meant not only death, but also the end of hope. Hope that she'd be reunited with Easton. Hope that her unborn son would have a future.

But she also knew that going along with what Philemon was suggesting meant a different sort of death—the death of her soul.

"I see that I've given you a lot to consider," Philemon said. He rubbed his hands together in a praying mantis fashion, green from his doublet to his jewel-bearing fingers. "Lord Dante fast approaches Tuendol. He will arrive within a day or two. When he arrives, events will move fast. When he arrives, you need to be prepared to play your part." Philemon turned his gaze from Johanna to Shupert, and back again. "The both of you."

Dante Heron arrived late evening the following day. Pink-ribboned skies overhead. From inside the walls of the merchant's home, Johanna could sense the change in Tuendol, the weight of the army like an approaching storm front. Johanna's captors in the loft rotated in and out of the house in quick shifts, wanting to see the Heron's arrival, wanting to be a part. One returned laughing. "Philemon was right. With these numbers we'll storm the Struvan south. No one would dare oppose an army that size. Not the Raleigh bitch, and certainly not the old man sitting regent on the throne."

The general bonhomie intensified when darkness fell. Drunken shouts, raucous laughter, voices dancing up and down the streets outside the windows. Johanna watched shadows through the glass, caught snippets of conversations. "...that's when the moonbear went wild...." "...Weylcoin ran his sword through the king's guard like a knife through butter..."

"...who's to say what would have happened had we started a siege? All I know is that I for one was happy to leave the Stavus-forsaken place to the moonbears and the frostflowers..."

She stayed at the window as the darkness deepened. Her hand resting on her belly, thoughtful breaths for the child inside. Two names working on a loop, one on the inhale and one on the exhale. *Easton. Weston. Easton. Weston.* She poured all the love she possessed into the two names, tried to hold them in her heart. For a time, she thought she had stolen into a perfect space where she was alone with her beloved and their unborn child. But then her thoughts fractured, and other people appeared. She saw her father, Lord Daguss Salk, naming her the lesser twin. Her sister Wulfess, glorious and golden-haired, reigning above her. The Lady Wenavere Raleigh, stealing away with Easton, a knife at his throat. Philemon Yurk, bow-shouldered and broad of smile, seeing through to the center of her jeyedoshi soul.

Leave me, she pleaded with the spirits, tears in her eyes.

The spirits answered her thoughts with a knock at the door. "What now?" she mumbled, expecting the priest. But when the door opened, it wasn't Shupert Press. Instead, five men dressed in surcoats the color of the purest snow walked into the room. "Lord Heron's men," Johanna said. The truth of it was self-evident. *I will kill your lord if given the chance,* she thought.

The young man in the front with blue eyes glanced up at the loft. He smirked at the men with their crossbows, as if thinking them ridiculous. Took his time returning his eyes to Johanna. "Tonight is a celebration, my lady. Lord Dante has arrived in Tuendol, and he wishes to see you. There will be dancing. And music." The young man chuckled. "Lord Philemon insists that you require a retinue, so we are here to oblige."

Johanna sighed. She could fight the request if she wanted, but if she did, she knew it would likely be the last fight of her life.

Silas O' the Songs

"Nothing connected to you comes true, does it, singer?" Dante Heron laughed. "First, you made a mockery of a Yubriy leaf prophecy, and now the army you warned would be waiting for me isn't here!"

Lord Dante made a broad sweeping motion with his hand as he talked, surveying the Raleigh-free expanse of land south of the Brokebone Pass. The young lord was in a rising good humor this morning, a state no doubt influenced by the fact that his army wasn't having to fight its way off the peninsula.

"Perhaps you were led astray," Dante continued, reaching over from his stallion to lay an insincere hand on Silas's shoulder. "For mine part, I thought the news of the Raleighs coming north was a ruse the moment you told it to me. Still, it obliged me to go, or at least it made the decision to leave Kalandragote an easier one. What I find hilarious, however, is that *you* are made the false messenger yet again! Tell me, please, I must know…are you a deliberate patsy, or simply the unwitting fool of fate? Are your friends in Kalandragote having a laugh at your expense, or are you a sacrifice of your own making?"

Dante's insinuations couldn't help but prick Silas's pride, not to mention stir his paranoia. But he also knew there were many reasons why the Raleighs might have spurned the Sagekind's call, reasons that didn't make a liar out of Deglan Whisk. "The Sagekind sent a letter."

Dante patted Silas's shoulder. "Perhaps he did, singer. Perhaps he did. But the Raleigh army isn't here. Unlike you. You *are* here, under my thumb, for me to do with what I please. Tell me: should I have you killed for your many false pretensions? Or should I let you sing and play at my pleasure, all your pretensions stripped away, at long last revealed for the simple, stupid musician you've always been?"

Silas should have felt fear. Or anger. Historically, being threatened by a lord made him feel an amalgam of the two. But now he knew that his purpose was beyond Dante Heron's purview. The egoistic young lord would do with Silas what he would, but Dante's actions were subservient to fate, and Silas was certain that providence had its own plans in mind.

"You will do as you please," Silas answered simply.

Dante looked at him long and hard, surprised by Silas's lack of fear. At last, the white-clad lord forced a laugh, meant to be menacing. "That I will, singer. I will make a fool singer of you for as long as it pleases me. Then…I suppose time will tell, won't it?" The threat issued, Dante's expression changed. "Do you know, singer, that I was truly worried that you were the prophecy in the flesh? My ally, Philemon Yurk…excuse me, *Lord* Philemon Yurk…knew about the prophecy and was working to stop it from coming to fruition."

The mention of Philemon Yurk caused the hair on the back of Silas's neck to stand on end. "How did he…know about the prophecy?"

"Betrard the gorgostrine," Dante responded, forming an unctuous smile. "You remember Betrard, don't you? As it turns out, King Micah and the Sagekind were right about him. The old gorgostrine was more than keen to share the message of his stolen Yubriy leaf with anyone who wasn't a Dayborn. He first made Lord Daguss and I aware of the prophecy even before the Dayborns went north to deal with the Blackstar Rebellion. *A song first sung in the Vake, prolongs the line of the suns.* When I went north with the king, Philemon stayed behind to…address any problems the prophecy might cause."

Something in Dante's smile changed. "Do you know that I received a letter from Philemon shortly after we left Low Osgood? He wrote to say that he had razed a bar in the Vake called the Golden Pear where the Swans were recruiting talent. 'We killed every musician inside. None escaped,' he claimed." Dante laughed. "It wasn't long after that you and your little friend showed up at Dunning Harbor. Tell me, singer, were you there that night, at the Golden Pear?"

Silas remembered the flames dancing on the roof, the sight of Felix Fingers grasping for his lute as the soldier with the eagle helm ran him through. "Yes," Silas replied. "Philemon tried to poison me. I'm sure he thought me dead." Silas was tempted to tell the story of Wyn Dunkin and the birds they had killed while on the run, but he held his tongue.

"You don't know how much joy this brings me, singer," Dante continued, laughing louder, his thin, pale lips stretched to the point of transparency. "Nor how much this benefits you! Now I'm very much inclined to keep you alive, at least until I've seen the look on Philemon Yurk's face when he lays eyes on the ghost of Silas O' the Songs!"

South, south, ever south. Out of the peninsula passing east of Dunning Harbor, crossing the Cutback River by way of the Seven Spines, wooden bridges first built during the reign of the tall and spindly queen, Caeress I. Water the color of dark tree moss roiled beneath the bridges, agitated by a storm upstream. The current hungry and cold. A cruel body of water. Nothing like the languorous Holly River that ran through Ragknot.

Ragknot. Home.

Home was south and east. Past the cold, lolling hills and fields that they walked for days. Silas could smell the forests of the Vake before the trees came into sight, the comforting scent of winter woods. Ragknot buried somewhere at the bottom. *What I wouldn't give to go home.* But when at last the treetops came into view, the Heron's army veered south and west, keeping the woods on the distant horizon. Silas wondered if the birds could smell their dead brothers in the woods, the vultures he had slain with Madrig, Jacy, and Wyn. *These birds know better than to enter the woods.*

These birds, he decided, *are headed to Union.*

All, however, was speculation. Lord Dante checked in on Silas from time to time but did not divulge the specifics of where they were going. *He's taking you to meet Philemon. Remember?* Philemon, that crooked crook-backed scoundrel, the one who had tried to kill him at the Golden Pear by spiking his wine with Graywater Ghost. *Philemon will have a laugh at my expense with Lord Dante, then they will orchestrate my end.* But what of Johanna Salk? He doubted fate would be so kind as to deliver the Sagekind's deathbed-revelation queen up to him, but the only thing to do was wait and see. He had no means of escape. Brutish birds kept constant eyes on him. Escape was not an option.

Silas assumed that watching him was all the men were given leeway to do, only to discover one evening that this assumption was incorrect. The men were drunk, as they often were in the evenings, when they approached him for the purposes of making him sing and play. Had they asked, he would have assented, but it turned out that his opinion wasn't of particular importance to them. Instead, they grabbed and swore at Silas, with a laughter mean-spirited, forcing him toward a blue linen pavilion darkening to black in the day's dying light.

"A song, we'll have a song from you!" they demanded as they pushed and prodded him along. He clutched the rosewood lute to his chest, worried that he would stumble and destroy the instrument. But he didn't, and soon he was inside the pavilion, where on the other side Lord Dante saw him enter, and laughed and laughed, encouraging the men in their devilry.

"What song will we have from him?" a brawny man asked.

One of the primary jostlers, a blond-haired fellow with protuberant eyes, shouted in Silas's ear, "Yot kuho! Yot kuho! Fiv pla sfuka yot kuho!"

That brought a roar of laughter. Still, a different soldier pointed out the obvious problem. "That's not a song, you stupid dunce! That was a fucking Ontish chant!"

"It was too a song! It was the *moonbear* song!" the blond-haired fellow petulantly insisted. The man's veiny, bugging eyes looked on the verge of bleeding. "Don't tell me it's not a song! The fucking lutist played it to the bear!" The man turned aggressively on Silas. "Play it! Play the song!"

Not sure how to respond, Silas opted for ignorant confusion, hoping the other birds would come to his aid and shame Bug-Eyes into silence. But instead, they fell under the blond-haired man's sway. Shared looks soon transformed into a drunken chant as nearly every Struvan man in the pavilion took up the Ontish chant, "Yot kuho! Yot kuho! Fiv pla sfuka yot kuho!"

Across the pavilion, Lord Dante surveyed the scene with pleasure. With his pale skin and white raiment, he looked like an apparition let loose in the world of mortals. Framed between two candelabras, Dante waited until the chant was at its strongest, then raised his hand, directing the pavilion to silence. The drunks ceased chanting in sputtering fits, catching on at different speeds. Silas, having caught on quick, eyed Lord Dante with unease. He couldn't imagine the coming announcement being to his benefit.

"The men have made a request, singer," the Heron stated. "Oblige them."

Lusty, drunken cheers. The old Silas would have acceded on the quick, but the new one took a moment to check in with his soul, where he found a hard nugget of resistance forming. Usually, it was an easy thing to give the powerful what they wanted. But at the moment he found nothing so repulsive as the thought of singing a song, no matter the danger silence conferred on his corporeal person.

His resistance began to bear notice. "Play!" Bug-Eyes demanded, cupping the bottom of the lute and shoving it toward Silas's chest. *Play,* a tiny voice of self-preservation pleaded in the back of Silas's brain. But his rebellion held. Across the tent, Silas could see Lord Dante looking at him with growing displeasure, the onetime smile on his lips turning into a frown, sharp words readying behind it.

"THE BEAR, THE MOONBEAR, THE STUPID, SLAVERING, ONTISH BEARRRRRRRRR…" A melody like a strangled cat pitching in and out of tune came from near the pavilion's flap, every head turning to the sound, the *song* borne aloft on a wild wind of fiddling. Into the tent the player came a-bounding, ragged ropes of silver-brown hair bouncing, face

scrunched in ersatz effort, the reckless tune running forth. The wailing intro settled into a verse the way a wild boar settles into a meal.

Silas stared at Wyn Dunkin in disbelief. A remembered Wynicism jumped to his lips.

"Gods of the wicked and wild redeem us."

Wyn gave Silas nary so much as a glance. He was too busy performing.

In that far northern place
Kalan-dra-the-Ontish-like-to-fuck-goats
If you've been there a day
You've seen ladies who look worse than your nut-scrote
There they keep bears
Whiter than the spit of a snow-ghost
Why are the bears there?
Why, to kiss queens who desire to live…no mo!

Wyn's voice was as shrill and screechy as ever, yet it cut through the tent like a bracing wind, the words crystal clear and reaching every ear. The Heron's men, catching onto the subject matter, hung on every word. Their laughter built along the way, until, by the end of the first verse, every man was doubled over at the waist, gasping for air in-between laughing fits. A respite was offered in the form of a fiddling interregnum, during which Wyn caught Silas's eye and gave him a wink.

Silas stared back at Wyn in bewilderment. He couldn't believe that he was in the presence of the little woodkin once more.

Wyn forewent a chorus, making the second verse the last. Sticking with bawdy doggerel, he played to the crowd, casting the Dayborns as dead dupes and hailing the Heron as the hero of the tale. It wasn't until Wyn was halfway through the second verse that the obvious strangeness of what the little man was singing dawned on Silas. *He wasn't in Kalandragote! How does he know any of this?*

A roar of approval greeted the song's end. Wyn danced a little jig in lieu of a bow, a similar jig, Silas remembered, to the one he'd danced at the Golden Pear. The Heron's men ate it up. Silas, forgotten in the hubbub, moved to the side of the tent. Hoping to be forgotten.

Lord Dante stood clapping along with the rest. But the smile on his face didn't reach his eyes. When the din finally faded, the Heron spoke. "What a delight! Wyn Dunkin, isn't it? If I recall correctly, we last saw you in Dunning Harbor."

"That you did, my lord," Wyn replied, now giving the bow. "I was needed elsewhere on short notice. But now, I'm needed here."

That seemed to intrigue Dante. "Pray tell, why are you needed here?"

"Why am I needed here?" Wyn called back. A manic grin formed on his face. "Isn't it obvious? My playing partner needs me! The one and only Silas O' the Songs! We're a duo you see, in fact and in form. Two halves of one whole minstrel act from the Bottom Black! Ha! It's true that we're still perfecting our routine, but one day soon the two of us mean to put on a performance that will draw dragons from the sky!"

Scattered laughter. Lord Dante smiled but didn't laugh. *He's heard the rumors about Wyn,* Silas thought. *Even if he doesn't believe in such a thing as a woodkin, he'll be reticent to keep a man in his company who has made a fool of so many others.*

"How do you know the story of the moonbear? Seeing as you disappeared in Dunning Harbor?"

"Perhaps I heard it in the trees," Wyn answered mischievously, keeping a happy-go-lucky-grin in place. "Ha! Fine, I'll tell you the truth. The truth is that I learned all I needed to know about the goings-on in Kalandragote simply by hanging around the outskirts of your camp. Drink a mug of mead with a feathered fellow and the first northern story he'll tell you is the one of the moonbear killing the Dayborn queen. Every one of your men knows the tale, whether they were inside the halls of Winterworn on that notorious day or not. The story belongs to the masses now."

Dante's teeth gleamed in the torchlight. "What about the story of you being a woodkin? Have you heard that one?"

Everyone in the tent went silent. In response, Wyn took up the jig again. "I suppose I have," he replied while dancing. "Bound to have some truth in it. Only a woodkin could dance like this." That won him a few spontaneous laughs. "Mostly though, I chalk that story up to Ontish superstition. Any man that stands under five feet tall is like to get called a woodkin in the north."

This time, the Heron joined in with the laughter. Something in his smile relaxed. "You make a good point. We Struvans don't waste our time worrying about the old Ontish superstitions." Lord Dante's gaze then went wandering, searching for Silas. The singer was quickly spotted. "There's your man, over there," Dante pointed. "The songsmith extraordinaire. Being the loving lord that I am, I'll permit you to join him. Only know this: once you're Silas O' the Songs' partner again, you won't be leaving his side save at my behest."

Wyn Dunkin clapped his hands in pleasure. "Don't worry, my lord." Wyn began to cross the tent toward Silas, holding the fiddle by the neck in his customary way, like it was a chicken in need of wringing. Eyes dancing.

A secret hidden in his smile. "Silas O' the Songs and I…we're exactly where we need to be."

Wyn Dunkin's time spent away from Silas had made the little fiddler no less insufferable. In the days that followed their reunion, Wyn proved as incorrigible as before, his every word and action polluted with the malady of mischief. "It's as if the gods have sent you to test my sanity," Silas snapped at the little man on their second day together, when Wyn kept insisting that they work together on a song that hailed the Heron as the Stavus-sent savior of Struvan Ragar Or.

"They've sent me to distract you," Wyn countered, with a face so straight that Silas could almost see the little man's mask fitted in its place. "And to assist you in your clandestine duties." The fiddler danced his little jig, drawing attention to his thrusting, upturned toes. Watching Wyn, Silas felt the press of the Yubriy leaf at the end of his boot.

Silas looked around. They were relatively alone at the moment, given space beside a cookfire to practice their music at the end of another day of travel. Enough eyes were on them to raise the alarm if they tried to leave, but no one seemed particularly concerned that they would make the attempt. Silas figured it was as good a time as any to try and get to the heart of things.

"My clandestine duties? What, woodkin, do you believe my clandestine duties to be? Please, for once, stop speaking in allusions and say what you mean!"

Wyn gave a chirruping laugh. "Woodkin. Woodkin, woodkin, woodkin. Say the word enough times and it loses all meaning, no?" His beady black eyes locked suddenly onto Silas's. "Do you know what a woodkin is, Silas? Truly? Besides the rumors you've heard, and the things you think you've seen, and the fanciful flights of your imagination?"

Silas returned Wyn's stare without apology. He knew how dangerous the little man was: he'd seen firsthand the bodywork Wyn was capable of with a dagger, as well as the magic Wyn could resort to when the tables were turned against him. But Silas was a different man than the one he'd been when they were last together. He wouldn't be put off his line of questioning by vague threats. "I may not know exactly what you are, Wyn Dunkin, but I know that you're a creature working me to some unknown end."

Wyn's black eyes shone like obsidian. "Am I, now? And what end is that?"

Silas opened his mouth to reply but nothing came out. Now that the time was ripe to level Wyn with a devastating accusation, he didn't exactly know what he was accusing the little man of.

The little man watched him patiently. When it was clear that no reply was forthcoming, Wyn decided to answer on his behalf. "I'm here to help you sing your songs, Silas." A knowing glint in the little man's eyes. "Perhaps even help you find the courage to sing the one song you were destined to sing."

The wasp sting of Wyn's words made Silas flinch. He'd never heard the little man say anything so guileless, so direct. He couldn't help but reply with sincerity. "I intend to. Sing the song, that is. The one that I'm meant to sing."

Wyn showed off his collection of snaggleteeth, imbuing the moment with his customary unserious charm. Brought the fiddle to chin. "Good for you. Until such a time presents itself, I say that we write a song to wrap the Heron in his own hubris. The sort of musical abomination that only you and I could write together." He slashed the bow across the strings, filling the air with discordant sounds.

A small sigh of acquiescence escaped Silas's lips. Then he brought his lute to lap and played a dissonant string of notes in turn.

Johanna Salk

The sky was a black soup of stars, overlain with galaxy gauze. On the ground, the men and women of Tuendol were either cheering or jeering Johanna, she couldn't tell which, shouts of "Queen! Queen!" ringing the soft circus of her entourage. The escort of Heron's men, forming a loose circle around her, laughed hardily at the hubbub, treating the procession like a hilarious riot. Reaching a particular boisterous section of cheerers, one of the Heron's men shouted "Yot kuho! Yot kuho! Fiv pla sfuka yot kuho!" back at them. His words set the entire entourage to laughing. Johanna, adept in Old Ontish, made the translation.

A kiss. A kiss. Give the bear a kiss. Johanna knew of the Kalandragotan tradition connected to the chant. She didn't know what the men were on about, but seeing a collection of Struvan males having a laugh at the chant weeks after returning from Kalandragote sent chills down her spine.

The twisting streets at last opened onto the town's main thoroughfare. Thirty yards ahead, a great roosting bird of a building sat fat and heavy against the road. Painted a garish red, the many-windowed establishment was aflame with light, festive sounds within. Johanna sensed the many powerful people inside, Philemon Yurk and Lord Dante Heron undoubtedly among them.

Johanna eyed the house with resolve.

To my fate, then.

Another step, however, and her attention was hijacked. Outside of the house, beyond the competing penumbras of light, a servant was struggling with a horse. And not just any horse, but a Rugarder.

Not just any Rugarder. Bitterboy.

The proud equine didn't appreciate the way he was being handled. Tossing his head left and right, Bitterboy was giving the young man holding his reins a fit, while vocalizing a neigh that Johanna construed as either a fit of pique or a spate of mean-spirited laughter. Seeing an angle present itself, Johanna pressed toward the horse, the Heron's men lagging behind. She had one hand on the horse's reins and the other on its jaw before the young man knew what was happening.

Bitterboy gave a little snort, then settled at her touch. The horse handler, awed and confused, let go of the reins and backed away. Hot breath poured out of Bitterboy's nostrils, warming Johanna's hands. Without thinking, she led the Rugarder into the center of the street.

An anxious silence settled around her. The Heron's men were no longer laughing, no longer chanting Old Ontish. She ignored the quiet, and instead focused on removing the rein and the bit from Bitterboy's mouth. She stroked his jaw throughout. The horse gave a haughty permission, waiting like a king for her to finish. A silent, secret language passed between them, no words required.

From the formless black of the street behind Johanna, a voice fractured the silence. "Careful, Lady Salk. That horse no longer belongs to you." Johanna instantly recognized Sir Whisker-Chin's menacing, malignant tone. *He must have followed the Heron's men.* She visualized the crossbow in his hands, its bolt tracing an unseen line through the dark to her heart.

Johanna leaned forward and rested the crown of her head on Bitterboy's muzzle. Breathed in the rich animal scent. The aroma reminded her of riding through Ragar Or with Easton, Bitterboy beneath her. With a sad sigh, she gave Bitterboy a gentle kiss. Released his jaw. Trusted that he understood the words written on her jeyedoshi heart.

Go.

Bitterboy turned and disappeared into the darkness of the street at a blistering gallop, the sudden fury of his leaving drawing gasps from several of the Heron's men. Johanna set the wind at the Rugarder's back. With it, Bitterboy vanished into the void like a collapsing star. "After the horse!" Sir Whisker-Chin ordered, but the futility of such a course of action was self-evident. The only thing anyone could do was listen to the thunder of his leaving.

Johanna elected not to wait for the fallout. Instead, she drew up the hem of her dress and hurried toward the house with pace, ignoring the possibility that Sir Whisker-Chin might shoot her in the back.

It was a wine-soaked room that she entered. Marrows, no doubt, every face flush with it. Drops of candlelight floated in half-full cups like yellowed pearls bobbing in blood. Visages like hallucinations, distorted by wine and revelry. A mad, wild music rode rampant through the scene, driven by a lute and a fiddle. She'd never heard anything like it. Her eyes went searching for the source of the sound, and there found the first face in the place untouched by the gaiety. A strikingly good-looking fellow with his soul showing in his hazel eyes. Eyes that were transfixed on her.

The music crashed and fell in a huff. Raucous cheering, while at the same time people were becoming aware of her presence. Johanna pulled her gaze away from the lutist and went searching for the powers in the room. She found them on the dais at the room's far end. The white-appareled lord with the thin smile she assumed was the Heron, while Philemon she knew, clad as always in sumptuous green and rising bow-shouldered from his seat, a look of concern on his face. Beside Philemon sat his bonded, Isbel Wicker, looking detached, lovely, and long. Philemon seemed briefly disconcerted by her appearance, but then the Heron's men and Sir Whisker-Chin entered behind her, and Philemon relaxed.

The room quieted without surrendering to silence. Only then did Lord Dante rise. A cup of Marrows in his hand, up, up, and up, a toast forthcoming. "To Lady Johanna of House Salk." Every cup with him, cheers of "Hear, hear!" A half-hundred pours down a half-hundred necks. Dante continued, "I mean to bond Lady Johanna on the morrow, here in Tuendol." More cheers, though Johanna had the impression that everyone present already knew. Dante's eyes left hers, gathering in the room. "Then together we will go to Union, and remake Ragar Or into the land it was always destined to be." That thin-lipped smile. "A land ruled by me."

A waterfall of laughter. Johanna stared at him, not frowning but unsmiling. A moment more and Lord Dante motioned with his hand, inviting Johanna to join him at the high table. "Come, my lady. Sit. Eat. Be merry. We've been waiting for you."

She made her way across the room, weaving through tens of eastern drunks. Eyes on her hair, unspoken thoughts writ on the men's faces. At the high table Richard Chesterly and Doneg Desighart were on their best behavior; both men averted their eyes as Johanna approached. Only Philemon dared look at her, wearing an expression that she couldn't quite place: there was trepidation there, but hunger too, hunger like a question that Philemon wouldn't ask but all the same hoped Johanna would answer.

What does he want from me?

A wild thought occurred to her. *Is he secretly hoping that I'll kill the Heron?* It wasn't the most outlandish idea. Who else would benefit from the Heron's death more than his right-hand man? Still, it was pure speculation. Why? For one, Philemon had warned her explicitly against harming Lord Dante; for another, she hadn't the foggiest idea if Philemon was in a position to capitalize on the Heron's death. *For all I know, Dante's death could be the ruin of him.* Still, now that she'd had the thought, she couldn't shake it.

A liveried serving boy hurried forward and filled her cup to the brim with Marrows wine. The Heron appeared on the verge of shooting out his hand to stop the pour, but refrained. *I should drink it all down just to see what he would do,* Johanna thought. But she didn't. She needed to keep her wits about her.

A cheery voice rung through the air as Johanna settled into her seat. "My Lord Heron!" Johanna looked across the room and was surprised to find that the voice belonged to a ragged-looking rodent of a man holding a fiddle and standing next to the handsome lutist. Johanna worried that the man's informal tenor would incite the Heron's ire, but, to Johanna's surprise, the Heron grinned and shouted back.

"Wyn Dunkin! What would you ask of me?"

"With your blessing, Silas O' the Songs and I would play the song again. 'The Glory of White.' So that Lady Salk might hear it."

Dante didn't seem drunk, but the rosy hue on his otherwise pallid cheeks suggested that he wasn't entirely sober. "A grand idea!" And with that, the Heron started up a brisk clap. The rest of the room promptly joined in. In response, Wyn bowed his head, while the handsome fellow took up his lute and started to play. The clapping dissolved and a cheering commenced as the lutist's masterful fingers conjured the quickening song. Wyn joined in, striking his bow across the fiddle's strings with abandon.

The lutist closed his eyes when he opened his mouth to sing. At first Johanna thought that he was trying to connect to the essence of the song, but the longer he played, she began to wonder if it was in shame of the lyrics.

Oe'r the realm of Ragar Or
The people cry wanting more
They long for the glory of white
For they can see the setting sun
A gathering darkness sparing none
Less a Hero takes flight

The lyrics had something of the quality of a temple song, but the tempo, hectic and hard-charging, disabused the notion. The pace, already fast, quickened intermittently, threatening, like a runaway horse and carriage, to crash.

And blessings the hero appears

The blessings of Stavus are clear
In Lord Heron, the glory of white
The kingdom will be reborn
One by one, till all have sworn
To obey our most glorious knight

The song continued thus, obsequious and fawning. The speed of the thing struck Johanna as profane, as did the Stavusian-style lyrics. But if Johanna took offense to it, she was the only one: the Heron and his faithful delighted in the composition, hooting and beating their fists on the tables and grinning and drinking and acceding to general merriment, all with the permission of their lord, who, by the contented look on his face, approved heartily of what was taking place.

The song ended with the same crash that had greeted Johanna when she first entered the room. Another round of cheers. Lord Dante neither cheered nor clapped, but he did lean over and make his thoughts known. "The problem with most sycophantic songs is that they aren't good. But here we have a song that manages to both entertain *and* stroke my ego." The Heron pointed at the lutist. "A week ago, I had every intention of hanging Silas O' the Songs by the neck once I'd had my fun with him. He's a prisoner of mine, you see, from my time in Kalandragote." Dante gave an odd grin. "But then the ugly-looking one showed up and they wrote this gem of a song together and now, I don't know…could be I'll take them both to Union and have them perform for me at my leisure."

Johanna decided that now was the moment to test him. "And what will you do with *me*? In Union?"

Dante looked away, as if she'd said something untoward. "I will make a queen of you, Lady Johanna Salk." The Heron lowered his voice. "And a crown prince out of the babe Philemon assures me is in your belly. Your surname is priceless for when the time comes to retake the north. Surely you know that. Give me your name, and the babe, and your acquiescence…and your life is yours, to do with in Union as you please. Defy me, and your life is forfeit."

Johanna felt herself reaching for the candleflame that filled the room. She wondered if herons squawked when they burned.

"Has Lord Philemon told you what I am?"

The Heron laughed. "Yes. He says that you are a jeyedoshi. But from what I gather, not a particularly formidable one." A smirk formed on his face. "You must forgive me if I am unimpressed. *Lord* Philemon may fear you, but I do not. I've known a few jeyedoshi, and if experience has taught me anything, it's that they die as easily as the next person. You might ask the Sagekind, but he died in Kalandragote."

This was news to Johanna. Though she supposed it stood to reason that if the Dayborns were dead, so was Gregor Thorn.

The Heron sank into the chair, as if to emphasize his unconcern at the threat she posed. "However, if you do mean to try and kill me, you'd best go about your work quickly. And by quick, I mean quicker than the most-accomplished-killer-in-the-realm quick." Dante nodded at the nearest table below the dais, where a man with a stiff brown moustache and cold gray eyes was keeping an attentive watch. "Jakastor Weylcoin. My personal bodyguard. If your powers are beyond his speed, well, then, Lady Salk, I resign my soul to the Bottom Black."

My powers **are** *beyond his speed,* Johanna thought, feeling the surge of omnipotence that coursed through her blood when she tapped into her essence. But a separate feeling—the sense of the babe in her belly—pulled her back from the jeyedoshi edge.

Around her, the room was resuming its revelry. Most of the people paid Johanna little mind, but now that she knew Jakastor Weylcoin's eyes were on her, she sensed others keeping watch as well. She decided to make a careful tour of the room. Feeling a heat from the room's left side, she flushed a stare like it was an unsuspecting hare. *Shupert.* The Stavusian priest's cheeks blushed as he averted his gaze. *The old fool truly cares for me,* she thought. Studying the tortured soul behind the priest's crow's-feet-stamped eyes proved to be a balm for her troubles. She decided then and there that she forgave him for his sins. *Though if you'd like to keep making amends, Your Light, I could use every possible ally.*

Her breathing had slowed and the tight knot of tension wrapped round her spine had uncoiled by the time she looked away from the priest. She meant to continue her study of the room, she only needed a moment of peace, a clear head—

"My Lord Heron!"

An ambered tenor this time. Johanna's eyes went with the rest, alighting with ease on the handsome lutist. *What do they call him? Oh, yes. Silas O' the Songs.* Silas's face should have been easy to stare at, but there was something obdurate in his expression that made it difficult to settle into, some nugget of resistance, or possibly resolve. His eyes skipped quickly over to Johanna with an intensity that unsettled her.

"What do you want, singer?" Lord Dante replied. His voice had an undercurrent of dismissiveness in it.

"I would play a song in honor of the Lady Johanna."

Lord Heron struck a disinterested tone. "And what song is that?"

Silas O' the Songs made his voice strong. "A song of truth."

Dante smirked. "Sounds boring," he replied, bringing the room to laughter. When the laughter ceased, the Heron turned up his palms, as if to imply that the decision wasn't altogether his. "But I suppose since it's Lady Johanna's song, I should leave the decision to Lady Johanna." He addressed Johanna with the smirking look still plastered to his face. "What say you, Lady Johanna? Are you interested in hearing the singer's song?"

A song? No, I don't want to hear another song. I want to burn this house to the ground and you with it. Her thoughts went wild for a moment; in her mind's eye she imagined every person in the room aflame, their laughter turned to screams. *I could do it,* she thought, gauging her willpower. She forced herself to look at every person present, the entire rotten flock. *I could do it. I could destroy them all.*

Her eyes met Silas O' the Songs'. The intensity of the lutist's stare pulled Johanna from her reverie. In his gaze, a simple, straightforward appeal: *Please.* Johanna came back into her body. She took a deep breath.

"Yes," she answered Dante. "I would hear it."

The Heron nodded, granting permission. A smattering of cheers. Johanna, watching the lutist carefully, noted the trembling intensity of his movements as he tore his gaze from hers and turned his attention to the rosewood lute. *Something is happening,* Johanna thought. But no else seemed to notice, with the exception of perhaps Wyn Dunkin, who shared a whisper with his playing partner. Silas nodded at Wyn in turn. Then, looking like a soldier going into battle, Silas took up his lute and settled his fingers over the strings. The silver-and-brown-haired Wyn, smiling madly, brought the fiddle to his chin.

The notes that Silas first stirred from the lutestrings elicited surprised reactions from many in the room. *Has he played this song before?* Johanna wondered. It certainly seemed that way. She glanced over at Lord Dante and saw that he was wearing an expression tinged with the darkness of a man uncertain if a joke was being played on him. Irrespective of the reactions, the song was a golden rush of delicate notes ascending to the heavens. The fiddle underscored the lute with sublimity and grace, feeding the richness of the music. When the opening crescendo was reached, the song settled into its progression, a structure both expected and enthralling. Johanna's entire body melded to the music.

Then came the words.

They say
In the flames
Of the queen's burning heart
Lies the truth that waits on a name
With a song
From the one
Who continues the sun
By reminding the queen of her pain

Johanna's heart raced to the speed of a Bitterboy gallop. *He's singing to me.* As if hearing her thoughts, Silas O' the Songs locked eyes with her, a penetrating and apologetic stare that promised only the truth.

Around Johanna were mumblings, whispers, confusion. She heard the strange complaint that the lyrics had been changed.

The song continued apace.

When the chorus was reached, one word made the melody.

A repeated name.

Weston

Weston

Weston

Weston

Johanna felt herself coming undone. She swooned in her seat, fighting the urge to faint. Dante, noticing, grabbed her by the arm, angry and bewildered. "What's this about?" he asked accusingly. "Who is Weston?"

Johanna jerked her arm away. Something was happening, something vital. A flummoxed and frustrated Lord Dante stood and first motioned, then bellowed, for the song to stop. But the players were too engrossed in the music to heed him. A confusion of looks, gestures, motions, shouts. Richard Chesterly rose from his seat, Doneg Desighart behind him. Together, they started toward the musicians. Chesterly, the first to reach the singer, wrenched the rosewood lute away from him with a careless violence. Desighart went for the fiddle, but the little man called Wyn employed a sprightly step to evade the vulture lord's grasp.

All the same, it brought the music to a stop.

A split second of silence. Wyn Dunkin, his face full of glee, used the last fleeting seconds of his freedom to deliver a mock bow to the Heron.

"And that," he announced to all who could hear him, "is a performance that will be remembered for the ages."

Silas O' the Songs

Richard Chesterly handed Silas the smashed remains of the rosewood lute before leaving the upstairs room where the Struvan lords had deposited Wyn and Silas. "Try and play a song with this, you nit," the lord with the golden-brown beard remarked before taking his leave.

Wyn was tsking at Silas before Chesterly and Desighart were out the door, bothered, as per usual, about the wrong thing.

"Nimble movements, next time," Wyn lectured. "A hop here, a skip there. Buy time. Whatever it takes to protect your instrument." He held his fully intact fiddle aloft in demonstration of the fruits of elusive movements. Lord Chesterly had destroyed Silas's lute with enthusiasm, but by the time he and Desighart corralled and collared Wyn, the eagle lord's gusto for instrument destruction had passed.

Silas didn't respond, choosing instead to stand in silence and stare at the mangled lute. He couldn't help but wonder if he had played the last song of his life. He'd been living on a knife's edge with the Heron for weeks; now, with the true playing of "The Queen's Burning Heart," he was sure the cut would come.

"Don't fret. We'll find a new lute for you," Wyn continued. "A true Wrainish lute, with the Fruy Teech Guild label. We'll travel to Wrain if necessary to get one, you and me together. It'll be like old times!"

Silas laughed scornfully. "*I'll* be dead by the morrow. You'll use some woodkin magic to slip away, but there will be no escape for me." He straightened his posture, thinking of Johanna. From the moment he first saw her, he'd known that the Sagekind had been right about her. And when he sang "The Queen's Burning Heart," the look in her eyes confirmed it. "But I don't regret what I've done. Not in the least."

Wyn rejoindered with a laugh of his own, a high-spirited cachinnation. "You think fate is finished with you, Silas O' the Songs? I doubt it. Not while there are songs to write and leaves to clear out of your boots."

Silas felt the soft press of the Yubriy leaf in the toe of his boot. *Does he know?* Silas wondered. *Of course he knows,* Silas answered himself. *The bloody woodkin knows everything.*

The opening door interrupted Silas's thoughts. Dante Heron, Philemon Yurk, and a hard-looking fellow with a stiff moustache entered the room. The mustachioed man had his hands crossed and resting on the ornate hilt of a sheathed rapier, giving the impression of a lion drawing subtle attention to the power of his retracted claws.

Lord Dante faced Silas full on, glowering. The look, so uncharacteristic of the Heron, betrayed the man. Silas thought it strange seeing Lord Heron discomfited; even in the most trying moments in Kalandragote, the Dagish lord had appeared unaffected, a man certain all would work out for him in the end.

But here he looked upset. Angry.

Uncertain.

"A question for you, singer. Do you know how many times a man can be run through with a rapier before he expires of his wounds?"

The question chilled Silas. He shook his head, trying to resist the temptation to glance at the mustachioed man's blade.

Dante continued. "With a blade like the one Jakastor has here, the answer is dozens upon dozens. How do I know, you ask? When I want a man tortured, running them through with a rapier is my preferred method. You see, there are many meaty, non-mortal parts to a man, many places—feet, hands, arms, legs—where one can inflict suffering without cleaving the soul from the flesh. When I look at you, singer, I see all manner of places we might do damage."

Silas held his tongue, fearful that if he opened his mouth he would plead for his life.

Philemon Yurk, dressed in sumptuous green, stepped forward. Made a study of Silas. As Lord Dante predicted, Philemon had been shocked to discover that Silas was still alive when they were reintroduced in Tuendol. Shocked and disconcerted. "Silas, Lord Dante tells me that you were present in Kalandragote. You are aware then, that the Dayborn line is diminished, if not ended?" He paused long enough to interpret Silas's silence as an admission of knowledge. "Why then sing a lyric like 'a song from the one, who continues the sun, by reminding the queen of her pain'? Are you a Dayborn sympathizer? Is it your wish to continue the sun? And if so, for what reason did you involve Lady Johanna—Lord Dante's queen—in your foolishness?" He paused. "And who, pray tell, is this *Weston*?"

Silas summoned the courage to shake his head. "The song is the song. If the words mean anything, they speak for themselves."

Lord Dante erupted in a mocking laugh. "*The song is the song.* Spare me. Your Yubriy Tree pretensions have no purpose here, singer. I'm the one who has power over your life now. And unlike the Dayborns, I won't be taken in by the game you're trying to play."

"You think my friend is playing a game, Lord Heron?" Wyn Dunkin piped in, surprising everyone. Silas turned to find Wyn wearing a wide and sardonic smile that showed off every last one of his teeth. "You'd best hope *he's* the one playing the game. The gods of the wicked and wild help you if it's the Yubriy Tree."

The little man's words took the Heron and his friends aback. Lord Dante's counter was slow in coming. "No. The *gods* help the Yubriy Tree. When I am crowned king of Ragar Or—and rest assured, it won't be long before I sit the Union Throne—I intend to tear the Yubriy out by its roots and chop it into kindling. The days of kings and queens fretting over leaves with magic words written on them will soon be a thing of the past."

"Best hurry to the throne, then," Wyn shot back, fire dancing in his black eyes, "before the prophecy comes true."

It was obvious to everyone that Wyn had gone too far. Silas watched in fear as Lord Dante addressed the swordsman. "Enough of this. Do the fiddler first. The singer can watch. I want him to get a sense of what's coming."

The man with the stiff moustache drew his rapier from its sheath. Silas's heart began to gallop in his chest, a horse running at double the speed of war drums. Whatever horror he was in for before, Wyn had made it worse. He closed his eyes.

"NO, NO, NO, NO, NO, PLEEEEAAAASSSSE!" Silas opened his eyes. The shrieking plea was coming from Wyn, who, to Silas's utter disbelief, had fallen to his hands and knees. "Don't kill us! Make an example of us at the bonding ceremony! Tie us up for all to see! We'll recant the song, we'll proclaim you king, we'll be a testimony to your power, a testimony to the falsity of Yubriy prophecies! If you kill us now, the legend of the song will only grow, but let us make a show of self-abasement at the ceremony and all will see that your power supersedes that of a prophecy! I beg of you! *We* beg of you!"

Do we? Silas had been ready to die. Seeing Wyn change into a begging, sniveling wretch was the last thing he had expected. *Stavus save us, those look like real tears!* The fiddler had transformed into a fountain, his tears falling with a force that seemed to negate the existence of the snide little man who had been freely needling the Heron only seconds before.

Lord Dante raised a hand, stopping Jakastor from advancing. "Your about-face beggars belief. Why would I trust you? Why antagonize me one second and plead for your life the next?"

The little man was a blubbering mess. "The…the song! The song! I thought the song would save us! It wasn't until your man flashed his steel that I even considered the possibility that the Yubriy Tree would permit its servants to perish! I…I…you must forgive me, m'lord, I'm mad, and a fool, caught up in events far beyond the scope of my meager sensibilities. The same goes for Silas, I'm certain of it. But we take it all back, we do! Let us set this to rights. Please!"

Three pairs of eyes swung to Silas, to see if he concurred. But Silas's own stare lingered on Wyn, long enough to witness the startling mask-drop that occurred when Lord Dante and the others looked away: all at once the impish woodkin returned, wearing an expression that encouraged Silas to play along. And Silas, rather than fight it, surrendered to the flow, finding within himself the mask for the occasion.

"I will recant what I've said and sung, my lord, if you let me live. I'm…I'm…" He felt tears coming, unbound and of their own accord. "…I'm mad too, I must be, a mad fool caught up in a fever dream. Forgive me, please, spare me, I'm nothing, I'm a fool singer, you've always known it. I don't want to die! Truly, I don't! The song was nonsense, words rattling around in my brain, I don't know from whence it came. Keep me alive until the morrow and I'll set things right, I swear it! Please, my lord. Please."

The Heron tugged on the cuffs of his brilliant white doublet, straightening the sleeves. Something in him seemed to settle. He gave Philemon a questioning look. The bow-shouldered lord leaned in and whispered in Lord Dante's ear. A smile spread on the Heron's thin lips.

"You'll spend the ceremony in stocks," Dante announced when the whispering was through, "proclaiming me as the true king of Ragar Or to all who attend. You'll avoid the subject matter of the song you sang tonight entirely. It'll be as if it never occurred." His voice flattened. "If all goes well, I'll reconsider your sentence."

The Heron's final words rang false. *We're still dead men,* Silas understood. *Nothing's changed. We've only bought a little time.* But perhaps that was Wyn's intention. Buy a little time, and see what could be done with it.

Dante, Philemon, and Jakastor turned to go. Wyn's voice halted them in their tracks. "I noticed a Stavusian priest in your company, m'lord."

"What of it?" Dante responded, perturbed.

"Mightn't you send him our way? It'd do us good to confess our sins tonight. Put us in the right frame of mind for singing your praises tomorrow."

Silas knew that he wasn't alone in recognizing the returned levity in Wyn's voice. Dante furrowed his brow, looking like he meant to comment on it. But in the end, he threw up his hand and gave his answer walking away.

"I'll send the priest. Make it a good confession. In case it's your last."

Wyn moved to the moonlight-soaked window and sat cross-legged. The serene look on the fiddler's face suggested he was on the verge of meditation, or perhaps saying a prayer that would reveal his woodkin secrets. *I suppose I should trust that he is attuned to things that I am not*, Silas thought, watching as the fiddler took a deep, cleansing breath. That trust diminished, however, when Wyn withdrew a dagger from the inner folds of his shirt, and, leaning over, placed one hand flush against the wooden floor and with the other began dancing the blade twixt his fingers.

"Why ask for the priest?" Silas asked, simultaneously irritated and mesmerized by the quickening blade. "I'm fairly certain that you're not…a servant of Stavus."

Wyn's laughter failed to slow the speed of his knife. "Stavus? I've nothing against the far-off fellow. But no, I don't think I'm what you would call…his servant." Wyn stopped the knife-dancing on a silver Salk and spun the dagger into the air, catching it with his right hand and pointing the tip at Silas. "But *you're* Stavusian, are you not? Ragknot boy? Seems to me it might be in your interest to unburden yourself of your sins before the morrow, eh? Might feel good to walk a little lighter in your boots? No?"

Is he speaking of the Yubriy leaf? Or is all his wordplay happenstance? Why would I tell a Stavusian priest about that particular sin? Silas had all but convinced himself that Wyn knew about the leaf, but now he had doubts. *Enough with this riddling. Time to get to the truth.* "Are you suggesting that I tell the priest that I have a…a…"—he lowered his voice to a whisper—"Yubriy leaf hidden in the toe of my boot?"

"A YUBRIY LEAF IN YOUR BOOT! GODS OF THE WICKED AND WILD REDEEM US!" Wyn shouted in mock surprise, loud enough that Silas worried the guards outside would hear. Silas thought the fiddler would soon contain himself, but instead Wyn's laughter grew, causing his body to rock and the dagger in his hand to stab at the air before him.

Wyn was still laughing when the door swung open and the Stavusian priest entered the room. The priest was elderly, and slight, with white eyebrows so large and cumbersome that they appeared to be weighing down the rest of him. He bore the burden of his eyebrows on bird's ankles, knobby protuberances accentuated by priestly blue-and-white robes that failed to reach the floor.

Once inside, the priest closed the door behind him. Turning, the priest noticed Wyn's dagger for the first time, and for a brief moment his eyebrows found wings. But gravity soon restored the order of things, and the priest made no other movements except to sigh as if in acceptance of the situation.

"Your Light." Silas had never been a regular temple-goer, but he knew and respected the honorifics.

The priest seemed pleased to give his attention to the man not holding a blade. "My son. They say that you asked for me. That you want to…confess?"

Uncertain how to respond, Silas held his tongue. The priest waited patiently, respectfully, allowing the seconds to tick by without a show of expectation. When it became clear that Silas wasn't ready to respond, the priest commented on the mangled lute. "Only brutish men break instruments," the priest remarked, shaking his head. Silas figured it was a passing comment, but to his surprise the priest kept staring at the lute, the emotion rising in his face. "Nothing short of blaspheming against Stavus justifies such an act. Music is a joy, a wonder, a gift from Stavus to his children. And I heard nothing in your song that warranted—"

"If it's a blasphemous song that you want, priest, I'll sing one for you!"

Stavus save us. Only Wyn. The priest surfaced from his thoughts, looking confused and out of sorts. "What? No! Of course I don't want to hear a blasphemous song! Whyever would—"

"Peace, Your Sunniness! I'm merely fooling with you. Can't say I've never said anything bad about ol' Stavus, but I'm gentleman enough to know better than to serenade one of his servants with a sacrilegious song."

Silas felt angry on the priest's behalf. "Apologies for my friend, Your Light. He likes to thumb his nose at everyone he comes across and then pretend it was all a jest."

The priest nodded uncertainly. "It's all right. I understand the impulse." The priest paused, chewing on a thought. "In fact, I've been wondering lately if Stavus wants me to be a little more brash. Like your friend here." He paused. "Like the two of you with that song."

Now this is unexpected. Religious men were oft known for their rigidity of thought, but the priest carried himself like a man trying to see the world anew. *Is he having a crisis of faith?*

"Lord Heron didn't like the song," Wyn remarked. "And to hear him tell it, he's now the most powerful man in all of Ragar Or. A king on the cusp. Seems a good Stavusian priest would know better than to indulge the problematic songsmanship of a handsome lutist and his better-looking fiddler friend."

The priest grinned. Spotting a chair on the near side of the room, he ambled over and took a seat, pushing the palms of his hands against the wood like a child on a too-high stool, his sandaled feet not quite touching the ground. "I've been trying to become something of a problem myself recently. It's only…I've not much practice at it, and my natural aptitude…is lacking."

"Why would a Stavusian priest wish to become a problem?" Silas asked.

The priest sighed. "It's the Lady Johanna. In my obedience to Stavus—in my fealty to Struvan lords and the Stavusian worldview—I've committed a terrible sin. I've hurt and endangered someone that I care for deeply." He shook his head with regret. "For so long, I thought that if great events ever transpired, my role would be obvious: I would help usher in a new world where the Stavusian religion reigned supreme. But now that that new world is imminent, my consciousness keeps insisting that I try and right the wrongs committed against a young lady that I admire. An Ontish lady with the dynastic name of Salk, who in all likelihood is a cursed jeyedoshi."

Silas looked on with wonder as tears began streaming down the priest's sadly laughing face. *It seems he's not faking it. Those are real emotions. Raw and honest.*

"And you would help her? If you could?"

"I would."

"Even if it meant…empowering Lady Johanna's jeyedoshi nature?"

The tone of the priest's laughter lightened. "I would, Stavus save me. I'd help her and trust that the Most Holy Deity of Light and Air would guide her hand." He shook his head. "Though it's foolish to think that such an opportunity might present itself. My power in this world has always been one of priestly influence. To ignore me is to neuter me. And now, I fear…I am an ignored old man."

"Surrendered your balls to Stavus, did you?" Wyn quipped. The fiddler mournfully shook his head in mock imitation of the priest. "A sad affliction, indeed."

The priest formed an irked line with his lips. "Give me your youth, your young man's strength… Stavus save me, give me that dagger you've got in your hand and I'll *show* you what I'd do to right my wrongs!"

Silas knew the moment had come. "What if we gave you something else instead? Like…a leaf?"

Time hung on a hook. The priest, too stunned to speak, didn't answer.

There's no going back now. Silas bent over and removed his right boot. Without looking at the priest, he reached inside and withdrew the large, orange, seven-pointed leaf rolled up and resting in the toe. Any question as to the leaf's true nature disappeared when Silas smoothed out the leaf: the mesmerizing silvery script spoke for itself.

"*The song.*" The priest's voice was trembling. "The song was a Yubriy leaf prophecy."

Silas didn't respond. Instead, following a strong compulsion, he crossed over to where the priest was sitting and handed him the Yubriy leaf. Then he recited the leaf's message from heart while the priest read along.

In the flames
of the Queen's burning heart
lies the truth that waits on a name

With a song from the one
who continues the sun
by reminding the queen of her pain
Weston

The priest's hands struck a tremor to match his voice. "You believe the message on the leaf was intended for Lady Johanna?"

"I think the message *and* the leaf were intended for *Queen* Johanna." Silas grimaced. "Look, I don't claim to understand how this all works. I saw the Dayborn king and his eldest son die in Kalandragote with my own eyes. By all rights, that makes Easton Dayborn king. But Easton Dayborn isn't here, and without him, I haven't the foggiest idea what that makes the Lady Johanna."

"Easton and Johanna bonded each other up north," the priest confided, his voice quavering. "The two of them. Alone in the woods. That's the first thing they told me."

"Wouldn't that make Johanna the queen already?" Silas felt his heart hammering in his chest.

"Yes." The priest held a thought in reserve. But not for long. "There's more. Lady Johanna is carrying Easton Dayborn's child."

Silas saw an image in his mind of the Sagekind on his deathbed. The conviction in the Sagekind's eyes even as the light departed them. His final words. 'They say she's a lesser twin. A jeyedoshi, perhaps. You must…give the leaf to her.'

The Sagekind knew. And he gave me a charge.

There's only one thing left to do.

"You must bring the leaf to the Lady Johanna. Tonight. You must instruct her to burn the leaf and inhale the smoke."

"Why?"

"If what I've been told is true, and if the Lady Johanna is indeed a jeyedoshi, she will come into possession of a great power. One that will set her free."

The priest looked as if he was going to press for specifics. But a second later he gritted his teeth and pushed away from the chair while slipping the leaf inside of his robes. "I will do it. I swear it." He looked around, and when he resumed talking it was as if he was talking to himself. "I will do this one brash thing, this one time, as penance for my part in the injustice against Lady Johanna. I will balance the scales. Whatever may come."

There was an awkward pause, and the two men shook hands. Then, quick as he had come, the priest left the room in a rush, looking the epitome of resolve.

When the priest was gone, a great wave of emotion overcame Silas. He felt emptied and naked, raw to the bone. Panic flared in him briefly, and for a moment he thought that he had made a terrible mistake. But then he realized it was simply the newness of a burden lifted. Tears gathered in his eyes.

A hand gripped his shoulder.

"It's a wonderfully terrible thing, holding a Yubriy leaf. More terrible still to let it go."

Silas's shoulders heaved, and he let the tears come. Wyn's hand stayed on his shoulder until his emotions were spent.

When it was over, Wyn gave him a couple of pats, then stepped away and drew his dagger. The sight of the gleaming steel brought Silas back into the here and now.

"What are you doing?" Silas asked with trepidation.

"My work here is done, Silas O' the Songs. So is yours. I'm getting ready to leave. If you're a wise man, you'll come with me."

"We're…leaving?"

"We'd better. I'm not sure we'd survive what's coming next."

"What's coming next?" Silas asked, though he knew the answer before the fiddler replied.

Wyn's eyes danced with flame. "A dragon, Silas O' the Songs. A dragon is what's coming next."

Johanna Salk

Philemon's voice was steady and stern. "Tell us, Lady Johanna, and tell us now. What did you make of the song? What meaning do you ascribe to the name *Weston*?"

Johanna had ignored the questions the first time Lord Dante asked them of her, during the mayhem of the song's closing moments. But now, with the room mostly cleared and Lords Dante and Philemon in her face, she had no choice but to reply.

"I assure you that I made as much of the song as you did, Lord Philemon. That was my first time hearing it, as should be obvious. As for the name Weston"—Johanna fought to keep all emotion from her face—"like the song, it may as well have fallen from the sky."

She could tell from the circumspect look on Philemon's face that he wasn't convinced. Lord Dante, however, appeared to be transitioning to a state of denial—she could see it in his pale-blue eyes. The song was powerful, an inexplicable phenomenon attempting to threaten the tenuous reality the Heron was trying to bring into existence. Rather than grapple with what the song meant, it was simpler for him to try and rewrite reality as if the song had never occurred.

"It matters not what she thinks of the song," Dante said curtly, addressing Philemon as if Johanna wasn't there. "It matters not who this fucking *Weston* is. What matters is that we put an end to this Yubriy nonsense tonight. Preferably with a knife. Send her away."

An uneasy Philemon did as he was told. Soon, Johanna's handlers were back by her side—the Heron's men and persistent Sir Whisker-Chin. Together they walked Johanna out into the street, starting in the direction of the merchant's house.

Johanna's thoughts were with the singer as she walked. *Silas O' the Songs.* She worried what would become of him. *Why did he sing the name Weston? And what did Lord Dante mean by Yubriy nonsense? Is this all connected to a prophecy?* Her dream from Hevengrow returned to her in vivid detail, especially the part where she turned at the base of the mountain and saw her son. She recalled the orange, seven-pointed leaf that flew from his mouth, joined on the wind by thousands of others, whispering his name.

Weston.

A wind kicked up all around Johanna, dancing in the dark.

Yes, she thought, addressing her jeyedoshi side. *But what I am to do? Who am I to try and save?*

The singer?

Myself?

The wind continued to dance, urging her on without providing answers.

In desperation, she corralled the wind's power. *I must try something. And what better opportunity will I have than now?* She closed her eyes and concentrated, gathering the element until it possessed the stored energy of a tremendous storm. Then, exhaling, she sent the wind barreling behind her, into the retinue of men.

She took off running as the wind-drowned shouts of the Heron's men struggled to reach her ears. Away. Away. Down the main thoroughfare, then onto a side street, too panicked for thought, her brain in blind subservience to her feet. High above, a sickle moon rocked in a bed of bright white stars, indifferent to her flight. She had no sense of the success of her attack. What thoughts she had were indictments of the flustered and foolhardy way she'd gone about things. Her feet still flying. Arguing with herself. *There were no good options, only variations of bad ones.*

She tried to attune her senses to her environs. Listened for sounds of pursuit. Severing the quiet was the yowling of a distressed cat, a man coughing in a nearby gutter, the mournful song of a nocturnal bird…and there, *listen,* there…the hastening advance of men, their gait growing ever louder. *They can hear me, same as I can hear them,* Johanna thought, but there was naught to do but flee. *No, you can fight as well.* It was difficult to divide her energies, but still she reached for the ground behind her, communicating with terra firma. She felt the slight rupturing of earth in her bones, and then she heard a grunt, and a cry. Her ears confirmed that a solitary runner remained, quickly closing the gap. *Again,* she thought, but it wasn't a simple thing; her energies were scattered. Still, she tried, reaching behind her while striding forward. She thought she could feel it, the spot where the earth needed to break. She reached for it—

A body slammed into Johanna, dragging her to the earth. When she hit the ground, the wind left her lungs and she was no jeyedoshi, only a mortal woman in considerable pain. A split second later cold steel was at her neck, the blade pressing into her skin. The smell of stinking breath. When her pursuer leaned close, she felt his whiskers on her ears.

"I'll kill you, I will, don't doubt it. Try your magic on me again and I'll gladly draw you a second smile. A red one." Content that he'd gotten across his message, Sir Whisker-Chin took a second to compose himself. Then he pulled Johanna to her feet, the blade never leaving her skin.

In the near distance, Johanna could hear men running toward them.

"Do you have her?" the men shouted at Sir Whisker-Chin.

"I do!" he shouted back.

Johanna lay on the settee in the center of the room like a corpse, her body bathed in candlelight. So many candles. The men were taking no chances. She couldn't see her captors well in the darkness, but she could hear them shifting in the loft. She knew that they were leaning over the railing, looking down on her like roosting carrion birds. Crossbows trained on her resting form. Sir Whisker-Chin had ordered her not to leave the couch. He was giving all the orders now, and everyone was listening. If the Heron had weighed in on what she had done, she wasn't aware of it.

The Heron's men were frightened of her now. That much was certain. Their fear was palpable even in the darkness. Only Sir Whisker-Chin was unafraid, or, at least, fearless enough as to make no difference. That was why he was the sole guard on the bottom floor, sitting in a chair on the opposite side of the room, cloaked in darkness. Johanna sensed that he was both willing to die and willing to kill, if it came to it.

She slept in fits and starts. Fragments of dreams, stopping as soon as they started. She dreamt of walking in the Eagle Garden and holding hands with Wulfess, sharing memories of their dead mother. She dreamt of Shayla the woods witch as a child, breathing in the smoke of a man burning at the stake. She dreamt of her father paring an apple, insisting that she swear fealty to the family. She dreamt of Easton boarding a boat, being swept out to sea. She dreamt of the spine-shaking roar of Teriquay. She dreamt again of being in the Eagle Garden with Wulfess, only this time they were discussing *Father* as if he was the one who was dead.

She awoke from the last to the sound of the door opening. Gray daylight bled through the aperture like spilled gruel. Johanna was fully awake in seconds. She sat up on the settee and saw Shupert Press standing before her, an empathetic smile on his face. But in an instant the smile melted away, and she saw the priest as she had never seen him before, looking like a warrior taking to the field.

"What are you doing here, Your Light?" Sir Whisker-Chin asked. There was no quarter in his voice.

"I would think it obvious. I'm here to pray with Lady Johanna on her bonding day."

"The bitch tried to kill us last night. Concussed a fellow and broke young Jordin's leg, all with her Corosian-cursed magic. Lord Philemon says we're to keep her here, under close guard, until we hear otherwise. Your prayers can wait."

The priest's reply was uncharacteristically sharp. "*Lord Philemon*? Is that right? Well, *Lord Dante* was the one who commanded me to come and pray with her. Now, I suppose I could go and clear Lord Dante's orders with Lord Philemon first, if you insist, but there's a fair chance someone will arrive to escort Johanna to the ceremony before I've managed it. And when that happens, I'm naming you as the reason I didn't complete my task."

Arvis glanced at Johanna, then looked back at Shupert. "This woman's a jeyedoshi. In the flesh. You understand that, don't you, priest?"

"I do," the priest responded with bite. "*You* understand that she's a Salk too, right? And that for the moment, her being a Salk is *more important* than her being a jeyedoshi? At least so far as Lord Dante is concerned?"

Sir Whisker-Chin looked suddenly uncertain of himself. They were dealing in gray matters, when he had been speaking in black and white. Arvis lifted and dropped his foot twice, like an agitated horse. "Do what you're here to do, priest. But if the bitch tries anything, I mean to kill her, consequences be damned. And don't think I won't kill you too, if you're in the way."

The priest paused. For a moment Johanna thought he intended to absorb the threat without comment. Take the conditional victory. But to Johanna's surprise, he turned and advanced on Sir Whisker-Chin, looking angry to the point of violence. "Listen to me, you malodorous dolt. I am a priest of Stavus, the Most Holy Deity of Light and Air. My order has spread the Stavusian faith in Ragar Or, the *land of the Twins,* for hundreds of years. No one is better equipped to handle a purported *jeyedoshi* than a Stavusian priest."

He drew even *closer* to Arvis and stuck out his jaw at the larger, armed man. His next words hissed like a loosed arrow. "I shouldn't be telling you this, but there is a means of curing the jeyedoshi affliction. Our order has done it before. Today, this morning…I mean to do it again. It is damned dangerous and delicate work, and involves drawing the jeyedoshi out and casting the spirit aside. If you were to interfere"—the priest balled up his fist, leading Johanna to briefly think that he was going to strike Sir Whisker-Chin—"then you had best kill me now, because otherwise either Stavus or myself or Lord Dante will strike you down once the business is concluded."

The priest's diatribe put Sir Whisker-Chin entirely on his heels. The leader of Johanna's captors tugged at the wiry barbs of hair sprouting from his face. "Forgive me, Your Light. I didn't know such a thing was even *possible*! If you want, we'll stay with crossbows trained or we'll leave you alone with her, whatever you think is best. We can even wait outside, guard the house in case anything goes awry."

"Outside is best," Shupert replied. He gave a clipped nod, then cast his gaze to the loft, including the rest of the guard in his address. "Now leave us."

Sir Whisker-Chin and the others did as they were bid. Shupert refrained from looking at Johanna as the men filed out of the merchant's house. When the last of the men was gone and the door was closed, he showed her the old genteel expression, the one she was accustomed to seeing. "My child." He closed the distance between them, a hand searching in his blue-and-white robes, his countenance turning serious. "I've been to see the singer."

The room assumed a hypnagogic quality as the priest produced a large, orange, seven-pointed leaf from the inside of his robes. Johanna found that knowing what she was seeing and believing it were two different things; it wasn't until she took the leaf from the priest and touched its vellum-like smoothness that she could accept the truth of it. Naturally, her eyes were drawn to the silvery writing that danced across the leaf's surface like an enchanted poem. Reading the words, Johanna's heart lodged in her throat.

"It can't be." Her emotions were a maelstrom. All the world was magic. "It simply…can't be."

Shupert grabbed her gently by the wrists, juxtaposing his body between hers and the windows. Kneeling, he guided her to the floor along with him.

"The singer claimed that if someone like you were to burn the leaf and inhale the smoke, you would come into possession of a great power."

"Someone like me? A jeyedoshi, you mean?"

The priest seemed to struggle with the word. "Yes. A jeyedoshi."

"What power will it give me?"

The priest shook his head. "I did not ask. I *could* not ask. I only know"—he paused, seemingly overcome with feelings and emotions that were difficult to express—"that I would rather trust you to wield that power wisely rather than stand aside while these men use and abuse you for their own ends. I think Stavus would want that as well." He paused and touched his forehead, as if fighting off a headache. "And if he doesn't, then I will gladly argue with him about it when I am dead."

Johanna nodded, too overwhelmed with emotion to even cry. Without a word, she leaned forward and kissed the priest on his cheek. Shupert accepted the kiss with all solemnity, nodding in turn, squeezing her wrists. "I have failed you time and again, my lady. This…is the least that I could do."

She shook her head slightly and started to tremble, a minor tremor that quickly spread throughout her body. The strain and stress of the preceding weeks came pouring out of her. "Possessing this power…I don't know that I'm equal to it. It's overwhelming, and it feeds fiercely on emotion. If I'm being truthful, I'm almost a slave to it. I miss Easton terribly, I'm drowning in love and fear, I want to kill and destroy everyone who has made my life a misery. If the leaf increases the quotient…I don't know what I might do."

She hadn't expected to say what she had said until she had said it. She wasn't even sure that she knew what she meant by it. She only knew that the deepest fears and truths in the center of her had come pouring out, and that Shupert Press was on the receiving end.

The priest squeezed her wrists again, and this time held them tight. He looked at her with the utmost benevolence. "Your recognition of its dangers is proof enough that the power should be yours. You will do"—he leaned closer to her—"what needs be done. When it's over, if you are in want of forgiveness, come to me, and I will grant you what forgiveness I can."

Shupert's words stilled the storm at the center of her. Her breathing slowed, and all became clear. She knew there was no time to waste. "Very well," she said. "Let's burn the leaf."

The smoke from the burning Yubriy leaf curled into silver-brown ribbons, then rose from the floor like dancing snakes. Johanna settled over the smoke and drew the serpents down into her lungs. They hissed and crackled and raced into her bloodstream once inside her, rushing, rushing, then exploding in her head, an entire universe of starlike sounds. The sounds were bright and they burned, and for a second Johanna thought she might go mad. But then there was a settling, and the brightness dulled, and Johanna could sense the language behind the sounds, a language that, if she desired, she could summon to her tongue.

The priest was coughing, stumbling away. He had inhaled a little of the smoke without meaning to. Johanna stood and went to him, offering an arm on which he could steady himself.

"Are you all right?" she asked.

Shupert smiled unconvincingly. Fought to suppress a cough. "Yes. I stood a little too close to the flame, as they say." He battled to compose himself. "More importantly, how are you, my lady?"

She was standing before the priest but she was also in Owoervyrn, the sky-black place, that place where all mankind began. Strange and terrible words sizzled in her brain like a fallen meteor. An invisible string tied her tongue to that entity which had stared at her with its left eye on Halfhead Mountain: the dragon Teriquay. The dragon was hers now, she knew, but for the asking. A word from her lips, and Teriquay would come thundering from the sky, to do as she bid.

She answered the priest as honestly as she could. "I am forever changed." She fought to find a smile. "It's what we were hoping for, right?"

The priest had a melancholic look on his face, but before he could respond, the door flew open. Lord Philemon and Richard Chesterly stood in the doorframe, with Doneg Desighart and Sir Whisker-Chin peering over their shoulders.

His Light didn't miss a beat. "I've cured her," he claimed, facing them with verve. "You may tell Lord Dante Heron that Lady Johanna Salk is no longer a jeyedoshi."

A winter-dulled green-and-yellow meadow nestled between two lolling hills on the eastern end of Tuendol, in sight of the town's Stavusian temple. Canvas tents littered the meadow, signs of a military encampment, but the Heron's men had abandoned the tents for the field, where they were standing in parallel throngs. Johanna had assumed her retinue was leading her to the temple, but now, seeing the men in the meadow, all was made clear.

"Stavus keep and bless you, Lady Salk!" a commoner cried out as the procession began the easy descent into the meadow. The town's citizens had gathered in sporadic pockets to see Johanna through the city, curious, quiet, and wary. This was the first someone had addressed her. "Beoliotius bless her Ontish children!" a different person added from farther back. Gasps followed, and Lord Doneg cursed, shouting for the commoner's head. But the procession continued apace.

Johanna kept her eyes peeled, searching for signs of the singer and his wily friend. Whether the two men were alive or dead, she didn't know.

A gleaming snow-white pavilion buttressed the meadow's end. In front of the pavilion stood a large cedarwood pergola from which flew Lord Dante's banners. Streams of white silk, artfully arranged, weaved through the pergola's planks. Pretty and picturesque, but nowhere close to befitting the extravagance customary of a bonding ceremony between two nobles. *The intention is to bond me quickly in front of a multitude of witnesses, so that the Heron may later claim my child.* But there was a halting uncertainty among Lords Yurk, Chesterly, and Desighart, who, Johanna sensed, were following the Heron's lead despite growing misgivings. *The singer's song has made them wary of me. As has Sir Whisker-Chin's reports.*

She felt the scorching heat of Dragon Tongue lighting up her tongue.

They are right to be wary of me.

The Heron's soldiers wore a motley of expressions as Johanna rode past them. Some, she could tell, hated her for being Ontish, but others were awed by her nobility, while yet others were simply drawn to the spectacle unfolding before them, the chance to see history. She found herself looking back at them, her usual guardedness in front of people who didn't know or understand giving way to the reality that these men were destined to witness whatever came next. She didn't know them, but she didn't hate them either. She hoped that their lives would be spared.

Behind her and to the right, riding on a mule, was Shupert. He couldn't stop coughing, a horrible hacking sound. He'd been laboring with the cough ever since the burning of the Yubriy leaf. *Has he given his life for me?* she wondered. She thought about *milu sfal* coursing through her blood, and how Shayla the woods witch had told her that the same flower would have killed Easton. *It's the same with the Yubriy leaf. It grants me a power beyond compare, while Shupert coughs himself to death.* And how many more would die, when she called down a dragon from the sky? Was that all there was to being a jeyedoshi? Access to a power that kills the ones you love?

She was approaching the pergola now, where Lord Dante waited. He stood sharp-chinned and thin-lipped in raiment of white, a belt of braided gold encircling his waist and a silver Heron brooch pinning the cloak at his shoulder. He glanced at Johanna with contemptuous indifference, then made a show of his importance by acting distracted, looking to-and-fro as if to suggest his own bonding ceremony was beneath him. *I'm only a tool now to an end. He wants the ceremony over with so he can move on the capital.*

Johanna and her retinue dismounted together, handing over the reins of their respective steeds to waiting hands. A cold wind rushed through the meadow, and she felt terribly alone then, shivering in the field before the Heron's thousands. Without thinking, she brought her hand to the new-growth side of her head, searching for the whorl. *I can't do this alone,* she thought. Realizing what she was doing with her hand, she returned it to her side.

If only Easton were with me.

A hand settled into the crook of her left arm. In Johanna's distraction, she hadn't seen Shupert draw alongside her. "I'm here with you, my lady," he whispered, stifling a cough. She thanked him in her thoughts, afraid to speak for fear of the language that might leap from her tongue.

They started together toward the Heron.

Johanna was wearing a beige dress with black lacings at the bust, and over it a black cloak. Her free hand went searching for the talisman that she had kept on her person since fleeing Coffyn Castle. The sennequi piece. The dragonfeeder. She felt its outline through the fabric. The two presences steadied her: the Stavusian priest and the simulacrum of Shayla the woods witch.

And me, the jeyedoshi, between the two.

The players fell quickly into their places. The lords lined up behind the Heron, with Lord Philemon standing closest. She noticed for the first time the woman standing to the left of the men, long-necked with a downcast stare. Isbel Wicker. *No. Isbel Yurk.* Playing the part of Johanna's lady-in-waiting. Isbel refused to look at Johanna, choosing instead to keep her eyes on the ground.

Johanna reached Lord Dante. Like Isbel, he would not meet her eyes. Johanna assumed that Shupert was going to lead the ceremony, but to her surprise a different priest clad in the traditional blue-and-white robes emerged from the grand pavilion. He was a stout fellow with double chins, the second of which appeared in the process of birthing a third. Taking his position before them, the priest cleared his throat and commenced with the ceremony.

"Children of the Light. Blessed are we this day to bear witness to the bonding ceremony of Lord Dante of House Heron and Lady Johanna of House Salk."

It was time.

Johanna opened her mouth to speak, and at once felt the full weight of the fearsome language gathering on her tongue. She could sense the dragon Teriquay, veiled in clouds or just beyond the horizon, drawn to her but waiting for the words. She thought of the dragonfeeder long ago, emerging from the clouds above Lake Wyglass on the back of the same dragon, burning King Reuel I and his family to a crisp.

She hesitated.

What horror am I about to unleash?

The distant sound of music interrupted her thoughts. Dreamlike and otherworldly. The surrealness of what she was hearing kept the melody at a remove. *Is that…a song?* A murmuring started up among the spectators. The noise should have drowned the music out, but instead the song won through like a ray of sunlight piercing a blanket of fog. Johanna followed the sound to the crest of the western hill. There stood Silas O' the Songs and his friend, giving a repeat performance of "The Queen's Burning Heart."

Johanna could scarce believe what she was hearing, what she was seeing.

But her eyes did not deceive her. Silas O' the Songs was alive. Singing powerfully. Bravely. Unapologetically.

They say
in the flames

of the Queen's burning heart
lies the truth that waits on a name

With a song from the one
who continues the sun
by reminding the queen of her pain
Weston

The meadow remained in a half-dazed state as the song sped to its conclusion. The sound was distant and haunting, scarcely audible, and all the more powerful for it. When it was over, the Heron stirred, red in the face. Johanna knew that he was readying the words to send soldiers after the duo, to torture and tear them apart.

But Johanna's tongue was quicker.

Noise like a peal of thunder issued from her mouth. Dragon Tongue, making the world hazy with static electricity. All eyes flew to her, befuddled by the way her words seemed to fracture reality.

From the far horizon a dragon replied, its roar cascading all the way to the meadow.

Panic swelled like a wave. No one knew where to go, where to look. Johanna's gaze flitted to the hill.

Silas O' the Songs and his friend were gone.

Dante grabbed Johanna and spun her around by the shoulder. Beside him, Philemon Yurk's eyes were wild with fear. "What have you done?" the Heron cried. But by then the panicked wave was cresting in a roar of shouts, every eye leaping to the sky.

A dragon was descending from the firmament, emerald-green and black as the bottom of a starless sea. It was beautiful the way terrifying things can sometimes be, the mere fact of its existence enough to make a mockery of mankind's guiles and games. It came on racing at a terrible speed. It reached the meadow in seconds, then reared back and began its descent, beating its gargantuan leathern wings.

All around Johanna, men were screaming and running, desperately trying to flee. The dragon, fixated on Johanna, seemed not to notice. *Teriquay.* Touching down with scaled feet, Teriquay folded her wings and settled into the soil. Then, with its great glass door of an eye, the dragon peered into Johanna's soul, the same as it had on Halfhead Mountain.

Only this time, Johanna knew what it wanted.

An answer to the question only she could hear.

Yes. I'm the jeyedoshi you've been waiting for.

The dragon inclined its head, inviting Johanna to mount her. Johanna took a step toward the snout, but the Heron, still standing behind her, again gripped her shoulder. *No, you fool,* she thought, knocking his hand away. Behind her, the colossal shadow of the dragon's head enveloped Johanna, rising to a frightful height. She sensed what was coming even as she saw it manifest in Lord Dante's expression, his pale and petrified face turning as white as his raiment. Instinctively, Johanna stepped away as the dragon's jaws came snapping down. There was an aborted shriek and then the smell of blood and smoke, and Lord Dante was no more.

Out of the corner of her eyes Johanna saw Isbel and the Struvan nobles scurrying away, eager to escape with their lives.

Teriquay swallowed the Heron's body down. Finished with its meal, the dragon bent its head to Johanna once more, indifferent to the terror it had caused. Without another thought, Johanna stepped to the beast. Boarding the dragon's snout, she walked the bridge of brilliant green scales that flashed between its eyes. All else was instinct. Turning, she poured her body onto the beast's neck, and found purchase where she could. A word of Dragon Tongue, and Teriquay's musculature rippled with power, its body and wings working together to leave the world behind.

One word resonated, mind to mind.

Fly.

Fly.

Fly.

Soon the town of Tuendol was a speck far below. Naught surrounded Johanna but the pure, clean air. Until at last the dragon roared, wanting to know where.

But when Johanna searched her Dragon Tongue, there was no word for *Easton.*

Epilogue

Four of Easton's senses had already worked out the truth, but a part of him didn't believe it until the hood was removed from his head and his eyes could confirm what his ears, skin, tongue, and nose had already told him.

The light of a threadbare moon imbued the shore with a milky shine. Waves lapped hungrily at his feet. The glassy surface of a placid sea extended far into the dark. Everything as he had surmised. The only surprise was the tall and long-limbed Thralk-Brakturian standing before him, wearing a trifold hat dancing with feathers, the tattooed tentacles of a monstrous kraken reaching up and down his sinewy arms.

The Thralk-Brakturian stood in the moonlight studying Easton, first straight-on and then with his head askance. Two shorter and less flamboyantly attired men stood to the Thralk-Brakturian's side, their lips pursed. Behind Easton, the men who had delivered him drifted away. He turned to get a look at them, but in response the Thralk-Brakturian reached out and grabbed Easton by the chin, redirecting his attention front and center.

"None of that," the Thralk-Brakturian commanded in surprisingly polished Struvan. "You belong to me now." A smile like a waxing moon spread across his face. "Prince. Easton. Dayborn."

I belong to no one but Johanna, Easton thought, though he did not say it aloud. He wanted nothing more than to find his way back to Johanna, but until he discovered the means, he wasn't about to utter her name in front of potential enemies.

He decided on a different tack. "Lady Wenavere sold me to you?" he asked. He was genuinely curious. He hadn't seen Lady Wenavere since shortly before her men took him prisoner outside the Stavusian temple in Hevengrow. He'd asked a thousand times to speak to her, hoping she might explain her rationale, but the men keeping guard of him during the journey south told him little and less. As did the men who escorted him onto the ship. As did the men who moved him from the ship to the smaller boat and brought him to this small island off the shore of the Southern Sea.

The Thralk-Brakturian laughed a dark and indecipherable laugh. "No. She did not *sell* you to me. She *gave* you to me. Though I'm sure *selling* is the story she means to tell to protect herself." The darkness of the Thralk-Brakturian's laughter distilled into a deep glower. "The Raleigh bitch is running a game. But she is tending too many flames. Idri plays along for now, but given the chance, Idri will burn her house to the ground."

Idri the Impetuous? If the fellow was speaking of himself in the third person, then Easton was standing before the most infamous pirate of the southern seas. A pirate who had managed to use the distraction of the Blackstar Rebellion to lay claim to Corkset Island. Though not without paying a price. "I've heard that the Raleighs took your eldest son hostage.

Galdren the Red. I've heard that Lady Wenavere is holding him in a dungeon beneath Goldleaf Keep."

The pirate drew a dagger from his belt and brought it flash-quick to Easton's throat. Easton, manacled, nearly fell backward, but Idri kept Easton upright with his free hand and gathered him into a violent embrace, cinnamon and *chyaweed* wafting from the pirate's breath. "That's right. She has Galdren. And I have you." Idri gritted his teeth. "One year, she says. Return you to her in one year's time, and she'll return Galdren to me. But Idri knows the game the bitch means to play. This buying of time. That's a year without my ships harrying her coastlines. A year for her to test the new political realities while keeping you in her back pocket. A year while Galdren rots away in her dungeon. And at the end, who knows? The eager way she handed you over, Idri thinks the odds are high that she knows she won't need you in a year's time, after which she'll slit my son's throat and leave me with a hostage that I may as well kill"—that nasty, gleaming smile again—"today."

Easton ignored the fear he felt from the blade at his throat. He'd be damned if he was going to die at the hands of a pirate out on the Southern Sea. He'd be damned if he wasn't going to use every last bit of strength and cunning at his disposal to make it back to the woman he loved.

"Maybe in a year's time you give me back to Lady Wenavere regardless of what she wants. Maybe by then, the two of us will find a way to extract revenge on both our behalves."

The pirate's smile changed ever so subtly, a touch of amusement working its way onto his lips.

"Maybe, Prince of Ragar Or." A pregnant pause. "Maybe."

Cast of Characters

The Dayborns

King Micah Dayborn, the first of his name, Holy Son of the Air, the Twin Ascendant, and the rightful ruler of Ragar Or

—Anjay Vint Dayborn, his bonded and the queen,

—Ajax Dayborn, his firstborn son and the crown prince,

—Greta Worrint, Ajax's common bond,

—Easton Dayborn, his second son,

—Cloudy, Easton's horse, a gray-dappled palfrey,

—Gregor Thorn, the Sagekind, purported to be the king's half brother,

—Sephery Vint, Gregor's deceased bonded, cousin to Queen Anjay,

—Deglan Whisk, a young knight loyal to Gregor Thorn,

—Black and Tan, two greyhounds loyal to Gregor, formerly belonging to Doxius Brine.

—Notable knights in Micah's service:

—Stryder, his personal guard,

—Larin Dove, Percy Moon, and Braxton Walshing,

—Hannibal Luthrow, his squire.

The Salks

Daguss Salk, Lord of High Osgood

—Lady Esme Salk, his bonded, deceased,

—Wulfess Salk, his daughter, named the Twin Ascendant by her father,

—Johanna Salk, his daughter, named the lesser twin,

—Bitterboy, her horse, a Rugarder,

—Madrig, his cousin, a giant mute,

—Jacy, Madrig's common bond,

—Rolphus, a servant,

—Thacker, a soldier in Lord Salk's service, killed by pennywolves.

The Ollspaers

Horos Ollspaer, the king of Kalandragote

—Cato Ollspaer, his son and the heir to Kalandragote,

—Onav Ollspaer, his son, deceased, killed by Cato in the twin-death rite,

—Wren Ollspaer, his sister, conspired with Horos to murder their brother Tesken,

—Tesken Ollspaer, his brother, deceased, known as the "Ten-Day King,"

—others serving Horos in Kalandragote:

—Bernsward, a Gorgostrine, or priest of the Twins,

—Gothred, the military commander of the Ascendant Few,

—Sfen, the dungeon master,

—The diviner, ordered burned at the stake,

—his vanquished foes:

—Kwelkis, defeated by Horos during a twin-death rite,

—Anis the woodkin, murdered by Horos in the dungeons below Winterworn Castle.

Struvan Lords of Note

—Dante Heron, Lord of Dagon, a.k.a. The Heron,

—Jakastor Weylcoin, Dante's sworn sword, a minor son of House Weylcoin,

—Wessel and Wenavere Raleigh, the Lord and Lady of Thistleton,

—Nicholas Raleigh, their son, deceased, formerly bonded to Johanna Salk,

—John Saylet, Lord of Oseiy, sitting regent in King Micah's absence,

—Richard Chesterly, Lord of Wellings,

—Doneg Desighart, Lord of Gray Point,
—Delton Yurk, Lord of Rathbone,
—Philemon Yurk, his estranged son,
—Arvis, a.k.a. Sir Whisker-Chin, a soldier in Philemon's service,
—Moren Arc, Lord of Greenwell,
—Anna Josephine Arc, his daughter,
—Mintor Thorn, his bastard son,
—Conway Acton, Lord of Acton,
—The Lady Ghent and her half brother, perished in the fire at the Golden Pear.

Ontish Lords of Note

—Egros Coffyn, Lord of Low Osgood,
—Darryn Coffyn, his nephew and heir,
—Grocian Mock, Lord of Dunning Harbor,
—Seydron Qorl, Lord of Qorl,
—Mactus Garstring, son of Myles Garstring, Lord of Oakenwield,
—Reginal Burntree, son of Edgar Burntree, Lord of Port Black, killed by Daguss Salk at Dunning Harbor.

The Blackstar Isles

—Trufish Boil, Lord of the Blackstar Isles, drowned,
—Axton Boil, his son, ingested poison given to him by Johanna Salk at Low Osgood.

Present at the Golden Pear on the night of the fire

—Silas Rowbry, a.k.a. Silas O' the Songs, a songwriter and lutist,
—Wyn Dunkin, a fiddler,
—Jia Brinks, a fiddler,
—Isbel Wicker, a harpist,
—Felix Fingers, a famous lutist from the Vake,
—Gay Gracie, a serving wench,
—Sawyer, her brother,

—Adolphus Morto, spokesman for the Swans, the king's performing company.

Persons of Interest (The Twin Ascendant)

—Shupert Press, a Stavusian priest, once served at the temple in Thistleton,
—The girl at the well in Hornwell,
—Her aunt, the proprietor of the Green Tree Inn,
—Mariva, a serving girl at the Green Tree Inn,
—Short Paul, a Dayborn knight,
—Tyna, the cook's daughter, Greta Worrint's friend,
—The Maybe-Smith, a citizen of Crelk,
—The kites, soldiers from Acton,
—Tern, a lady friend of Deglan Whisk,
—Marvik, her father, captain of a trading galley docked in Skithin Harbor,
—Ridgely, a.k.a. Red Ridgely, Jia Brinks's brother,
—Idri the Impetuous, a pirate from Thralk-Braktur,
—Galdren the Red, Idri's son, also a pirate.

Persons of Interest (The Prophecy of the Yubriy Tree)

—Shayla Blue Eyes, a.k.a. Hilya Mifliy, a.k.a. the dragonfeeder, a woods witch living near the base of the Edgeling Mountains,
—Merjy, a woods witch,
—Dryis, a woods witch,
—Doxius Brine, a Blackstar Islander, owner of the Three Dragons Inn, attempted to assassinate Ajax Dayborn,
—Krayton, a Wandering Tongue, Silas O' the Songs' uncle,
—Betrard, a gorgostrine, accused of stealing a Yubriy leaf, executed by Lord Daguss Salk,
—Berak, an actor in Low Osgood and an untrained jeyedoshi, killed by Gregor Thorn after attacking Ajax Dayborn,
—Rooster, a common, from Doakmont,
—The innkeep at Doakmont, said to resemble an old turkey,

—The Oseiyan, a soldier at the Yubriy Tree,
—The Five Vultures, soldiers from House Desighart that attack Silas and Wyn at the Yubriy Tree,
—Freya of the Glass Eye, proprietor of the Sea Swoon,
    —Boryl, Freya's son,
—Lumpy Head, attempted an attack on Silas O' the Songs at the Sea Swoon, killed by Boryl.

Historical Figures of Note

—Breta Barton, infamous for discovering a Yubriy leaf and predicting the death of Queen Portia Salk I. A citizen of Crelk. Condemned to die by Queen Caeress Salk I.
—Anis Salk, the eldest daughter of Daguss Salk I by way of Isa Burntree Salk. Rebelled against her father after he named his son Brogan (by way of Penelope Sparrot) the heir. Burned to death by the dragon known as White Morning.
—The dragonfeeder, the girl who rode Teriquay, the dragon that burned King Reuel Salk I and his family to death on Lake Wyglass in Low Osgood.
—Peter Scarl, a.k.a. The Gray Fog, a.k.a. the Noblekiller. Roamed the country during the reign of King Reuel Salk II, killing Ontish and Struvan nobles alike.
—Manfred Salk, second son of Reuel Salk II, dies before the War of the Three Brothers begins.
—Meg Barret, paramour to Orius Dayborn, Gregor Thorn's ostensible mother.
—Zust, a Thralk-Brakturian, served as the Sagekind to King Orius Dayborn I.
—Myleta Garstring, a.k.a. the Garstring Girl. Once pledged to be bonded to Micah Dayborn, he set her aside in favor of bonding Anjay Vint, a foreign woman from Clyesia.
—Lord Wyros Coffyn, builder of the third and present incarnation of the Three Dragons Inn.
    —Lord Kelgro Coffyn, owner of the Three Dragons Inn before Doxius Brine.
—Tiatris Qorl, bonded of King Cedric Dayborn I.

—Theron Redd, bonded of Caeress Salk I and father of Baron Salk I.
—The Dagish Prophet of Wrath, a priest of Stavus and a jeyedoshi (though refuted by Struvans who followed him), led an uprising against Twin worship in Dagon, killed by Gregor Thorn.
—Briggs Shroud, a famous Wandering Tongue.
—Philemon Grapple, a famous Wandering Tongue, devoured by the dragon known as "the Slumberer."
—Jezebel, an actress at the Three Dragons Inn, purportedly a jeyedoshi who started the fire that led to the death of Queen Portia Salk I.

The Salk Dynasty

— Daguss I the Unifier, 1–18
— Brogan I the Healer, or the Beloved; Eldest son of Daguss I and Penelope Sparrot, 18–52
— Brogan II, grandson of Brogan I, 52–52
— Reuel I, second son of Brogan I, infamously dies by dragonfire with his bonded and four children while visiting Low Osgood, 52–59
— Portia I the Wise, sister of Reul I, dies in a mysterious fire at the Three Dragons Inn, 59–90
— Caeress I, second daughter of Portia I, bonds Theron Redd, gives birth to twin boys, Baron and Daguss, 90–103
— Baron I the Redd, son of Caeress I, dies in a duel with his brother Daguss, 103–106
— Daguss II the Ascendant, twin brother of Baron I, dies without issue, 106–119
— Johanna I the Traveling Queen, firstborn daughter of Baron I, 119–154
— Portia II, eldest granddaughter of Johanna I, ascends to throne at age of seven, dies at nine, 154–156
— Reuel II, uncle of Portia II, regent during Portia's rule, second child of Johanna I, 156–170
— Brogan III, eldest son of Reuel II, king when the War of the Three Brothers begins, 170–173
— Silas I, third son of Reuel II, claims the crown after defeating his brother Brogan III in battle, 173–174

— Xeuel I, fourth son of Reuel II, last of the Salk dynasty, dies shortly after defeating Silas I in battle, 174–174

The Dayborn Dynasty

— Cedric I the Redeemer, the first Dayborn king, right-hand man of Xeuel Salk I, declared the Twin Ascendant by Xeuel before his death; descended from the line of Julet Salk, daughter of Caeress Salk I, 174–207
— Orius I, son of Cedric I, 207–217
— Micah I, son of Orius I, 217–242

Author's Note

Dear reader, I am beyond grateful that you made the decision to continue on *The Song of the Burning Heart* journey by reading *The Twin Ascendant.* I hope that you enjoyed reading it as much as I enjoyed writing it. I am already hard at work on Book Three, the final book in the trilogy.

If you haven't already done so, I hope that you will consider signing up for my newsletter over at benspencer.substack.com. It's the best way to keep up-to-date on news regarding the series. Newsletter subscribers also receive a free novelette, *Last Performance at the Three Dragons Inn,* which is set in the world of *The Song of the Burning Heart.* You can also visit my website, benspencerwrites.com, for information on the series.

As always, this book wouldn't have been possible without the steadfast love and support of my wife and daughter. Besides being my favorite people in the world, they are both wonderfully creative and absolute joys to bounce writing ideas off of. As with every book I've written, they played a major role behind the scenes.

It's hard to believe that I first began writing this series years ago. To see it grow and gain an audience in all corners of the globe has been incredibly gratifying. My goal as a fantasy writer has always been to write stylistic, character-driven works with a rich sense of history. Reading the reviews on Amazon and Goodreads has given me faith that I'm on the right path. Thank you to everyone who has played a part in supporting and promoting the series. I'm more grateful than you'll ever know.

There's one book left. It should be a little larger than its predecessors. After that, I have plans for writing a new epic fantasy series. I'm in it for the journey, not the destination. I hope you'll continue to be my traveling companion along the way.

www.ingramcontent.com/pod-product-compliance
Lightning Source LLC
LaVergne TN
LVHW041101080826
845145LV00007B/1643